WILD
COWBOY
NIGHTS

WILD
COWBOY
NIGHTS

**A FOOLPROOF
LOVE COLLECTION**

NEW YORK TIMES BESTSELLING AUTHOR
KATEE ROBERT

Wild Cowboy Nights © 2020 by Katee Robert.
Foolproof Love © 2016 by Katee Robert.
Fool Me Once © 2016 by Katee Robert.
A Fool for You © 2016 by Katee Robert.
All rights reserved, including the right to reproduce, distribute, or transmit in any form or by any means. For information regarding subsidiary rights, please contact the Publisher.

Entangled Publishing, LLC
10940 S Parker Road
Suite 327
Parker, CO 80134
Visit our website at www.entangledpublishing.com.

Amara is an imprint of Entangled Publishing, LLC.

Edited by Heather Howland
Cover design by Bree Archer
Cover art by
Photographer:
Wander Aguiar and Nigel_Wallace/GettyImages
G Allen Penton/Shutterstock
Interior design by Toni Kerr

Print ISBN 978-1-68281-477-2
ebook ISBN 978-1-68281-485-7

Manufactured in the United States of America

First Edition July 2020

ALSO BY KATEE ROBERT

Foolproof LOVE

Foolproof Love #1

KATEE ROBERT

Dear Reader,

It's been quite the journey to get this book into your hands. The Foolproof Love series was actually my first contracted category romance, way back in 2012, before *Wrong Bed, Right Guy* was ever a twinkle in my eye. It was originally supposed to be on the Indulgence line. Adam was a cold billionaire and Jules was a bartender. The book was good, but it just didn't work. In the intervening years, the story has worn many different suits, and none of them fit until I realized that my heroes simply must be cowboys.

Many things changed about this book, but Jules and Aubry's relationship never did. They are my single favorite lady relationship I've written to date. And Adam... Well, I hope you fall in love with him the same way I did. I fondly call this series my Dirty Talking Cowboys and he more than earns the title!

So settle in, clear your schedule, and let me introduce you to a little town in Texas called Devil's Falls. Our hero is a bull-rider and our heroine owns a cat café...

You're in for a treat!

Katee

To Kari. For our mutual love of growly country singers and dirty-talking cowboys.

CHAPTER ONE

"Tell me again why we're going out into the middle of nowhere for a bonfire? That's like holding up a sign *begging* some ax murder to come along and mass murder us."

Jules Rodriguez kept her eyes on the road—sad excuse that it was. Her truck rocked and shuddered as she muscled down the deep ruts. "We're not going to get mass murdered." Though her best friend, Aubry, had a point about it being in the middle of nowhere. They'd been working their way off the main road for almost twenty minutes, and there wasn't so much as a taillight in sight. She pushed down the knot of anxiety for the seventeen millionth time today.

"How do you know?"

Across the bench seat, her best friend had her knees pulled up to her chest and was staring out the side window like she expected that ax murder to come sprinting at the truck at any second. She wore her favorite pair of black jeans and one of her nerdy T-shirts with puns most people didn't understand, and she'd even picked out a pair of red tennis shoes instead of her normal boots.

Probably because she thinks she's going to have to run for her life at some point.

Aubry pointed at the passing trees. "I think I hear banjos."

"You live in Devil's Falls. I would think you'd be used to the banjos by now."

Aubry frowned, her pale face standing out against the darkness of the cab. Despite living in Texas for years, she managed to avoid anything that might resemble a tan. "I do my best to pretend they don't exist."

"Denial. It's not just a river in Egypt." She finally caught sight of light through the sparse trees. "There!"

Aubry pushed back her long, fire engine–red hair and snorted. "Who invited you to this thing again? Because if we're not going to be mass murdered—and I'm still not convinced on that note—they could be luring us in for some sacrificial killing."

"Has anyone ever told you that you have a deeply troubled obsession with murder?" Jules pulled in next to the open space at the end of a line of trucks. She recognized most of them from around town—Devil's Falls wasn't exactly a place hopping with new people. The last person to move in from out of town had been Aubry, and that was five years ago. "Besides, a sacrificial murder requires a virgin, and that ship sailed for both of us years ago."

"Good point." Aubry let loose a melodramatic sigh as she turned off the engine. "Remind me why we're doing this again?"

"Because Grant's back in town." Jules hadn't seen him since he dumped her ass on his way out of Devil's Falls after graduation—he hadn't even come back for holidays. Nine years later and his parting words were still ringing in her ears. *I don't want a life that's going to bore me into putting a gun in my mouth and pulling the trigger before I hit thirty.*

She clenched her hands around the steering wheel, counting to ten twice. It didn't do a damn thing to stop the anger eating away at her. There wasn't a single thing wrong with Devil's Falls and the life she had here. Wanting to settle down and raise a family here—eventually—while being surrounded by the people she loved was a *good thing*. It didn't make her boring.

A subject she and Grant disagreed wholeheartedly on.

"Yeah, you mentioned that jackass showing up earlier, right before you started pummeling that poor loaf of bread at the café. Personally, I'm still waiting to hear what your plan is."

She didn't have one, not that she was going to let that stop her. It never had before. "I just want a look." Maybe he'd gained the freshman fifteen—and another twenty for law school. Or something. *Something* to prove that she was better off having been dumped so unceremoniously.

"I thought we agreed that your ex is a douchecanoe."

"We did. And I'm past it." Mostly. Past *him*, definitely. Past how he'd made her feel about herself, not so much.

Aubry snorted and opened the door. "Right. You're so past it that you've dragged us out to be maybe killed, maybe sacrificed to hang out with people who are still clinging desperately to their high school glory days." She looked around, her brows drawn together. "Because, seriously, who goes to bonfires when there's a perfectly adequate bar in town? *Two*, in fact."

"The cool kids?" That was always who'd been out at bonfires when she was in school. She'd avoided the whole scene, though, despite Grant's protests. They came out here as an excuse to drink without the town

sheriff bothering them, and that had never been Jules's
thing. She barely drank the hard stuff now, let alone
when she was sixteen. And trying to navigate the roads
back to town while buzzed? No, thanks.

That may or may not have also contributed to the
whole Jules-is-boring thing.

Aubry scrunched her nose. "Ten to one, someone's
wearing a decade-old letterman's jacket and talking
about that one football game where he threw the
winning pass."

Ten to one it's Grant himself.

Jules looped her arm through her best friend's. "An
hour. After that, we can go back to town, grab a bottle
of wine, and play that horribly violent game that you
love so much."

"Deal." Aubry grinned. "And don't act so put-upon.
You love it as much as I do—you just suck at it."

"Truth." She pulled them to a stop at the edge of
the clearing. There were trucks parked in here around
the fire, too, their tailgates down and people situated
around them, chatting and drinking and a few women
even dancing. It looked like something straight out of
a country music video. She picked out a dozen people
she'd gone to high school with, the ones who'd stayed
behind and never wanted to leave, and another dozen
who had left with stars in their eyes but had filtered
back into town in the years since graduation.

"Jules? Jules Rodriguez?"

She froze. There was no mistaking Grant's deep
voice. *Too soon. I'm not ready.* But since the only other
option was dropping Aubry's arm and fleeing into the
night, she turned around with a smile pasted on her
face. And there he was, standing a few feet away, his

dark hair shorter than she remembered. No freshman fifteen there. Damn it. He looked like he'd been spending quite a bit of time in the gym, in fact.

Bet he spends the whole time he's working out checking himself out in the mirror.

The snarky thought didn't make her feel any better. There was nothing worse than being caught flat-footed by the ex who left her in the dust, only to find out that he hadn't developed some unfortunate skin problem in the intervening years.

"Grant."

He moved closer. "Damn, you're a sight for sore eyes. You look good, Jules."

"Oh, you know, Pilates," she answered breezily, already searching the crowd around them for an escape. She cleared her throat. "So, uh, how are things?"

"Great. Better than great. I just graduated from Duke. Top of my class." He gave a smile that was all teeth, like a politician. "I have a position waiting for me in my father's firm here in town."

"Imagine that." She couldn't even bring herself to pretend to be surprised. Grant always had been fond of riding his daddy's coattails. For all that he was determined to live the big life off in Anywhere but Devil's Falls, he liked being a big fish in a little pond more.

"And you? I think I heard that you opened up some sort of cat café?" He laughed. "Can't say that's surprising."

Beside her, Aubry went ramrod straight. It was only a matter of time before her friend went postal on his ass. Jules smiled, and though she wanted to holler at him something fierce, she managed to keep her tone even. She was *not* ashamed of Cups and Kittens. "It's been a real hit with the locals."

"I bet." He looked her over, head to toe and back again. His appraising gaze made her skin crawl. "I hear you're still single. You want to go get a drink sometime?"

Suddenly, Jules was a whole lot less worried about keeping Aubry back than she was about pressing her lips together to keep from laying into him. She looked around at the people circling the bonfire. A full half of them were watching this little drama play out.

Did he seriously just ask me out?

No. No, absolutely not. Nope. Never.

She had to do something, and fast. Jules wasn't a particularly violent person, but she also wasn't above hunting down Grant's truck and slitting the tires.

And maybe scrawling something witty in the paint with her keys.

No. That's not going to solve anything, and you'll just prove to him and everyone else that he can still get under your skin without even trying.

There had to be a better way to put him in his place.

Her gaze landed on her cousin across the way. Daniel stood next to a lowered tailgate next to his friend Quinn. And with them was a tall drink of water if she ever saw one. He had his back to her, but the way his shoulders filled out his T-shirt, tapering down to a lean waist and... Good lord, his pants were the very definition of painted-on jeans. Daniel said something, and he shook his head, turning so she could see his granite jawline and...

She blinked.

Holy shit, it's Adam Meyers.

He'd been around while she was growing up, always running with her cousin and their other two friends, but he'd always seemed wilder than the other boys— more restless. Even when he was standing still, there was a look in his eye like he was just waiting for the right moment to burst into motion.

Sure enough, the first chance he got, he blew out of town and up and joined the rodeo. Or that was the word on the Devil's Falls gossip grapevine.

He must be back in town to take care of his mom. Sympathy rose, blotting out her anger at Grant. Jules didn't know what was wrong with his mom, but she didn't have to be a doctor to know the woman was sick.

Knowing him, though, he won't stick around for long.

Just like that, a plan clicked into place. A stupid, reckless plan guaranteed to shut Grant down for at least a little while.

Speaking of, he was still waiting for her to say yes and fulfill his high-handed expectations, but she managed a laugh. "That's really sweet, Grant. It was great seeing you, but my *boyfriend* is waiting for me."

He frowned. "Boyfriend?"

"Oh, yeah, it's a new thing. We haven't exactly gone public with it—you know how Devil's Falls can be—so you wouldn't have heard." She gave him a pat on his arm. "It was nice seeing you. So great. Really, we'll have to catch up sometime soon." And then she stepped around him, dragging Aubry behind her.

"What are you doing?" Aubry whispered.

"Winging it." She stopped by the trio of men, all

too aware of Grant watching her. "Hi, Daniel. Quinn. Adam."

They raised their beers. Daniel looked over her shoulder with a frown. "Is that your piece-of-shit ex-boyfriend I see?"

"The very one." She disentangled her arm from Aubry's. "Speaking of, I need a favor."

"Anything for you, kid."

She tried not to roll her eyes at him calling her kid. He was a whole seven years older than her. Not exactly ancient. "Actually, it's not you I need the favor from."

Before she could talk herself out of it, she sidled up to Adam and put her arms around his neck. To his credit, he didn't shove her on her butt in the dirt, merely raising his eyebrows. Jules kept her voice low so there was no chance of Grant overhearing. "So as you've noticed, my ex is watching me really closely right now, and I might have told him a tiny white lie about me dating someone in order to avoid a devastating dose of humiliation. And since I can't date Daniel and no one would *ever* believe I'd date Quinn—"

The man in question frowned. "You really know how to hit a man where it hurts, Jules."

"—that leaves you."

Adam's face remained impassive. "I see."

There wasn't a whole lot to work with in those words, but he also had let his free hand drift down to settle on her hip, so she just kept talking. "If you could just play along and maybe kiss me like you want to do filthy things to me in the bed of your truck, I'd really appreciate it."

If anything, his eyebrows rose higher. "That guy really got under your skin, didn't he?"

"You have no idea."

Next to them, Daniel made a sound suspiciously like a growl, but neither of them looked over. Adam's hand pulsed on her hip, the heat of it shocking despite the warmth of the night. His calluses dragged over the sensitive skin bared by her T-shirt, and she shivered. *Maybe this was a terrible idea.*

She didn't have time to really reconsider, though, because he set down his beer, cupped the back of her neck, and dealt her the single most devastating kiss of her life. No, not a kiss. He took *possession* of her mouth, his tongue tracing the seam of her lips and then delving inside. He tasted of beer and something darker, something that hinted at exactly what she'd asked for—like he wanted to do filthy things to her in the bed of his truck.

She closed her eyes, giving his tongue a tentative stroke, and had to fight down a moan at the way the move made her entire body go tight.

More.

He lifted his head, breaking the kiss and slamming her back into the real world. She blinked up at him, all too aware of her body pressed against the entirety of his, of how he was hard in all the places she was soft, of how goddamn *good* he smelled. "Wow."

There went that eyebrow again. "You think it was believable?"

She'd almost forgotten she was kissing Adam Meyers because he was supposed to be her boyfriend to prove a point to her real ex-boyfriend. *Liar. You 100 percent forgot that this was pretend, and if he'd offered to drive you out into a field to get down and dirty, you wouldn't even hesitate.*

He *hadn't* offered, and this *was* pretend. Remembering that was important if she wanted to avoid compounding one potentially humiliating situation with another even more potentially humiliating situation.

She licked her lips. "Um, yes. Totally believable. Thank you."

He still didn't let her go. Instead he turned and lifted her onto the tailgate as if she weighed no more than a paper doll. "You want something to drink?"

"Uh, sure." She should get down and walk away... which she absolutely would do as soon as she got control of her shaking legs. It would have taken a stronger woman than she was to not stare at Adam's ass in those tight jeans as he ambled over to the cooler.

She turned to find Aubry doing a silent slow clap. "Don't judge me."

"Oh, I'm judging."

CHAPTER TWO

Adam Meyers had been back in Devil's Falls all of two days, and he was already going out of his mind.

He hadn't wanted to come to this goddamn bonfire. He wasn't back in Devil's Falls for a good time—he wasn't even back at all. Once he figured out what was going on with his mama, he was on the road again. Hell, it had only been a few days, and the restlessness in his blood was already snapping for a change of scenery.

Or it had been until Jules Rodriguez sidled up to him and proceeded to rock his world. That'd been a distraction he couldn't afford to pass up.

He opened the cooler and fished out a pair of beers, using the move to get his physical reaction under control. He hadn't expected to be affected like that, but she was so soft and sweet and the panic in her dark eyes had called to him.

You were doing her a favor, jackass.

Right. He glanced over his shoulder to where she was talking to the redhead. *I'd like to do her another favor. Maybe two.*

"Damn it, what are you doing?"

He'd known this was coming the second he walked away from the women. He couldn't even blame Daniel. His friend had always had been overprotective of Jules.

Adam used his boot to shut the cooler lid. "She asked me for a favor. I'd be a dick to ignore her cry for help."

"That's my baby cousin."

Cousin or not, the soft, sexy woman he'd just held in his arms was *not* a baby. Not even close. He snorted. "It's not like I'm robbing the cradle here. And it was just a kiss."

"You know damn well it was a bad idea." When Adam just stared, Daniel cursed. "Damn it, Adam. It better *stop* at just a kiss." He stalked away, snagging a beer as he did.

He didn't blame his friend for getting up in arms. Jules had always been a good girl, and Adam was many things, but good wasn't on the list. Which was most likely why she'd chosen him to act as her pretend boyfriend.

Adam turned around to find Grant standing just out of reach. He hadn't had much interaction with the guy—by the time Grant graduated seven years behind him, Adam had already blown out of town for the rodeo circuit. His mama told him stories, though. It was one of her favorite things to do on their weekly calls while he was traveling around and getting into trouble. The tidbits of Devil's Falls gossip had always grounded him. No matter how crazy his life got, or how free he felt on the back of a bull for those precious seconds before he was thrown, nothing much changed back home.

That was how he knew Grant and Jules had dated through high school and that he'd dumped her before he went off to that fancy school his daddy had paid out the nose for. It wasn't something Adam had put much thought into all those years ago, but now he had to stop and wonder what the hell Jules had seen in this guy.

Grant was too polished, too put together. Even his teeth were perfect, white and straight and screaming money. It made sense. His daddy was a big fish in Devil's Falls, and he'd never let anyone forget it. Stood to reason that his son inherited his shitty, entitled attitude.

And he was obviously chewing on something he wanted to say.

Adam stopped, aware of Quinn at his back. He doubted this preppy man was going to cause problems, but if he got a wild hair, he'd find that it was two on one. "Can I help you?"

"You're Adam Meyers."

"Guilty."

Grant shot a look over his shoulder to where Jules sat on Adam's tailgate, her long legs swinging as she chatted with her redhead friend. There was nothing over the top sexy about the way she was dressed— shorts and a plaid long-sleeved shirt that she'd rolled up to her elbows—but she drew Adam's gaze despite that. There was just something so *alive* about her.

He needed to feel alive right about now.

Adam started moving forward again, tired of the game and surprisingly eager to get back to Jules. Maybe he should kiss her again. *You know, for believability's sake.* "Excuse me."

"Wait." Grant grabbed his shoulder and smiled. There was nothing overtly wrong with the expression, but the fact he was touching him—holding him back— left Adam wanting to punch some of those too-perfect teeth out.

"I suggest removing your hand before I remove it for you."

Grant's smile didn't waver, but he *did* drop his hand. "I know the score."

What the fuck was he talking about? "Good for you."

"I mean, it's cute that you're helping Jules make me jealous, but it's not going to work."

He knew that kiss had been a desperate Hail Mary pass at saving face, but that didn't mean he was going to sell her out. It didn't hurt Adam none to play along—and, yeah, he wouldn't mind another chance to taste Jules again. She was dynamite, and he'd never been able to resist playing with matches. "Don't know what you're talking about."

"Oh, please." Grant rolled his eyes. "A few years might have passed, but that doesn't change the fact that I *know* Jules. There's no way in hell she's dating you."

"How do you figure?"

He knew where this was going. Despite his mama's best efforts, he'd been hell on wheels while he was growing up. He had too much anger, too much energy, and a chip on his shoulder a mile wide. All that combined into giving him a reputation that kept his mama up at night.

So he'd left, needing to see more of the world than this hole-in-the-wall little town. The world was too big, too full of life, to stay in one place too long. He'd hit the jackpot when he decided to try the rodeo, and that first time riding a bull had ignited something in him he couldn't resist. The second he'd picked himself up after being thrown, he'd craved another ride.

That craving hadn't disappeared over the years.

If anything, it'd only gotten stronger.

He'd put all that aside the second Lenora called him to tell him his mama was in a bad way. It hadn't been comfortable driving back into Devil's Falls—like sliding into a suit that was two sizes too small—but it didn't matter. His mama needed him, so here he was.

Grant shifted, as if just now realizing he could be getting himself into the kind of trouble that wasn't easy to get out of. "Nothing against you, of course. It's just that she's…Jules. She takes the safe road. She's a sweet girl, but she's, well, you know." He waved a hand in her direction. "A bit boring."

Adam focused on controlling the rushing in his ears. Fifteen years ago, he would have punched Grant's lights out just for saying something so goddamn stupid. He was different now.

More or less.

He moved forward, getting into the man's space. "That's my girlfriend you're talking about."

Grant went pale, his mouth opening and closing like a fish's out of water. "You're joking."

"Get out of my sight, *boy*."

Under different circumstances, it would have been funny to see how fast Grant hightailed it around the bonfire, but Adam was too busy trying to get a handle on the anger whipping through him. It was like a live thing in his chest, demanding physical action. He took a deep breath, and then another, wrestling it back under control. "I hate that guy."

"Man, chill." Quinn took one of the beers out of Adam's hand and popped the top, then repeated the process with the other. "Remember what the sheriff said about fighting—you promised to behave."

"That was when we were teenagers."

"Same rule applies. Sheriff Taylor is getting old and has high blood pressure. You don't want to be going and giving him a heart attack, now do you?"

Adam shot Quinn a look, but he took the beer back. "You're an idiot."

"Nah, I'm the smart one." He gave a lazy grin. "Though if we stand here any longer while there are two gorgeous girls waiting for us, then someone might have a legit argument about the idiot thing."

He glanced at the girls…and his cock jumped to attention. Jules was now leaning against the tailgate. The frayed edges of her shorts teased a peek of the lower curve of her ass. He was sure they'd started as something closer to modest, but they'd been washed so many times, they taunted him as she walked away, as if they'd fray just a bit more and give him the show of his life. "Those shorts should be illegal," he muttered.

"What's that?" Quinn asked.

"Nothing." Just past the girls, Adam spotted Daniel heading toward the line of trucks disappearing into the darkness. Back when they were kids, Daniel had been the straitlaced one. The one who got them out of as much trouble as Adam and John got them into. *John.* It had all changed that night on the rain-slicked road. "How's he doing? Really doing?"

"Hell, man, I don't know. It all changed when you left." There was no accusation in Quinn's voice, but Adam felt it all the same.

After John died, he should have stayed to help pick up the pieces. He knew Daniel blamed himself for the car crash, but he'd been so desperate to get out of town, he'd barely paused long enough to fill up his truck before he headed for the horizon. He hadn't even made the funeral. And he hadn't come back much in the intervening years—definitely not long enough to get past the nights of drunken partying with his buddies.

I'm back now, at least for a couple weeks, and I'm going to set shit right.

That started with the woman now watching him across the clearing with dark eyes. He had no business sniffing around Jules Rodriguez, if only because she was Daniel's cousin, and he'd failed his friend enough without adding this to the list. But Adam couldn't get the image of her desperate expression out of his head.

He couldn't hang her out to dry. Not tonight, at least.

He walked over and passed over a beer before he joined her against the tailgate. There was a respectable distance between them, but he still was acutely aware of every move she made. When she lifted the beer to sip it, Adam damn near groaned.

Jules's gaze fell to the bottle in her hands. "He didn't believe the kiss, did he?"

Adam took a long pull on his beer bottle, more to calm himself down than because he was thirsty. "He had his doubts."

"Damn." She sighed, her shoulders slumping. "Thanks for trying. A-plus for effort."

There wasn't going to be a clearer opening. That kiss had been the sole moment since he'd been back in town where he wasn't ready to climb the walls. She was *right there*, the perfect distraction all wrapped up in a package that seemed designed to make him sit up and take notice.

It would be a shitty thing to do. No.

But when he opened his mouth, different words came out. "I guess we'll just have to be more convincing."

The redhead on the other side of Jules made a choking sound. "Oh my God, you're crazier than she is."

Jules's mouth opened into a little O, and her eyes went wide. "I'm sorry, what?"

This was his chance to take it all back—all he had to do was let her down easy—but apparently Adam was too much of a selfish bastard for that. He leaned in, almost close enough to touch. "You up to giving him a little show? I can do this all night."

She bit her lip, her gaze dropping to his mouth. "That's really sweet, but I can't ask you to do that. I've already sexually assaulted you once tonight. I doubt my conscience can handle more."

"It's no trouble." Why was he pushing this? He couldn't force Jules into it, though, so he just toasted her with his beer. "Think about it."

"Oh, she's going to think about it, all right." The redhead dodged the elbow aimed her way this time. "I'm just going to, ah, mosey on over there and find myself a drink that's more of the vodka variety."

Quinn appeared at her shoulder like some kind of magician. "I got it." He presented her a red Solo cup with a flourish. "Tell me, sweet cheeks, did it hurt when you fell from heaven?"

"Nope, but I scraped my knees when I crawled up from hell." The woman rattled off her response without looking at him or sounding the least bit interested.

Quinn, on the other hand, only seemed more intrigued. "Witty. I like that. Maybe you and me should go get a drink sometime."

Jules coughed, and Adam had to use every ounce of willpower under his control to keep his grin off his face when the redhead turned to his friend, made a show of looking him up and down, and shook her head. "Sorry, cowboy, but judging from the assets you're far too proud of displaying"—she waved at his crotch area—"I've had better. Not interested."

She turned to Jules. "Can we please leave? Much more of this and I'm going to develop a sudden infatuation with my cousin."

"God forbid." Jules shifted away from the tailgate and shot a smile at Adam. "Thanks for the beer and, well, for everything else, too. You're sweet." Then she was gone, being towed by her friend through the crowd back toward the line of trucks.

Adam sipped his beer, watching her pivot her hips to avoid a drunk guy. The move made his cock perk up—again—and take notice. As if he hadn't been interested before.

He didn't look over when his friend took her place, even when Quinn said, "I love me some redheads—so snarky and full of rage."

"You're a sick, sick man."

"No doubt." He drained his beer and set it aside. "So what's your next step?"

He glanced over. "What do you mean?"

"Come on, man. I know you, and I've seen that look on your face before—usually when you're about to get me into a whole world of trouble. You're not done with that woman."

"She said she wasn't interested." His gaze tracked back to the trucks, craving another look at the way she filled out those damn shorts.

"Right." Quinn snorted. "Whatever you say."

CHAPTER THREE

Jules stepped over Mr. Winkles and made her way to the table where Mrs. Peterson was petting Cujo while she read the morning paper. "I hear that boyfriend of yours is back in town, dear."

"Ex-boyfriend." She dodged Cujo's clawed swipe and topped off the old woman's coffee.

"I also hear that his daddy is planning on grooming him to take over the family business. Very prestigious, that." She still didn't look up from her paper.

Jules gritted her teeth and made an effort to keep the smile on her face. "I really wouldn't know." *You know she's just poking for gossip. There's no malice behind it.*

It didn't make it sting any less, though.

She'd known everyone would start with the questions the second Grant got back into town. It might have been nearly a decade, but the Devil's Falls residents weren't much a fan of change. They'd liked it when Jules and Grant were Jules-and-Grant, the town's golden couple, and most would be tickled pink if the two of them picked up where they left off.

Obviously kissing Adam hasn't hit the grapevine yet.

Jules cleared her throat at the thought. "Would you like a blueberry muffin?" she asked. "They just came out of the oven."

"Oh, I really shouldn't."

They went through this same song and dance every day. Jules smiled. There was comfort in knowing what to expect, no matter what Grant believed. "If you're sure. There's banana nut, too."

Mrs. Peterson froze like a hound catching a scent. "Banana nut, you say? Well, maybe just this once."

"Be right back." She turned around, pausing to pet Loki and Rick where they were sunning themselves in a beam of light coming through the big windows in the front of the shop. They rewarded her with rumbling purrs, and Loki even managed to rouse himself to bump his head against her leg. She scratched behind his ears the way he liked.

The locals had given her grief when she bought this place and announced it was going to be a cat café, though it was the kind of indulgent grief she was used to. *Oh, that Jules Rodriguez—she's so* quirky. But when it came to the café, the proof was in the pudding, and over the course of any given week, most of them made some excuse or other to walk through the doors and cuddle one of the seven cats she kept here. It might be a little strange to some people, but this coffee shop made people happy, and that made *Jules* happy.

What was so wrong with that?

She delivered the banana nut to Mrs. Peterson and then started a new pot of coffee, her mind going back to the events of the night before as she went through the familiar motions.

Kissing Adam Meyer had been… Well, it had been a questionable plan at best. She'd wanted to create a scandal, and once news of that kiss hit town, scandal was exactly what she'd get.

She dumped the water into the machine, her body prickling with awareness she had no idea what to do with. The kiss had been pretend. She knew that rationally, but her hormones were having problems remembering it.

Especially when he'd offered to keep the charade going.

I can do this all night.

The awareness grew stronger, sparking in places it had no business being. The man was just doing her a favor, and all she could think about was how good he smelled and how sexy it had been to feel his whiskers scraping against her skin? Her imagination was all too willing to offer up ideas about where else they would feel good if she'd given him all night.

Stop it.

She slammed the pot into its place with more force than necessary. There was no reason Adam would be interested in her as anything other than a charity case, which was reason enough to thank him again for taking one for the team and then move on with her life. She didn't want charity from anyone.

She needed to stop trying to prove to Grant that she wasn't pathetic. She shouldn't even *care* what he thought—what anyone thought. She wasn't a pushover. Her life was great…minus her failed attempts in the romance department. Otherwise, she saw what she wanted, and she worked hard to get it. She'd be totally content working Cups and Kittens until she was old and gray, living in the apartment above it with Aubry, and sitting out on the balcony and waving her cane at the teenagers in the street…

"Oh my God, I'm pathetic."

"Talking to yourself is a sure sign of insanity." Aubry spoke from the corner table where she was doing something on her massive laptop—probably plotting world domination. Or gaming.

She pushed the button to start the coffee brewing, breathing in the comforting smell and doing her best to get her crazy under control. "Wrong. There are studies showing that talking to yourself is a sign of intelligence." *Thank you, Facebook.*

"Touché." Aubry glanced up and her eyes went wide. "Incoming."

Jules turned around in time to see Grant open the door to the shop. Her stomach took a nosedive. She spun back around, pretending she hadn't seen him, and busied herself with the coffeepot to buy time. She'd bet her last dollar that he was here to call her out on faking Adam being her boyfriend. Grant had never been able to let stuff like that go.

What had she seen in that guy again?

Oh, right. Popular high school football player who had turned that golden charm on her sixteen-year-old self and made her feel like something really special.

Until he crushed her under his shoe as he left her in the dust.

"Hey, Jules."

She couldn't keep pretending she didn't see him when he was trying to engage her in conversation. Jules turned. "Grant. What a surprise."

He smirked. "There's a bell over the door."

"I was talking about you showing up in the first place." She shot a look at where Mrs. Peterson had Cujo in her lap and wasn't even pretending not to eavesdrop. Jules gritted her teeth. "Can I help you with something?"

"So this is your place." He made a show of looking around. "It's…quaint."

She followed his gaze, trying to see things through his point of view. The shop was decent sized, with plenty of room for half a dozen tables and the long counter that she stood behind, as well as three elaborate cat towers. The walls were a cheery blue, and there were suns painted onto the tabletops. It was a bright and happy place and damn him to hell for trying to make her embarrassed of it.

Power through it. You can do this. "Would you like some coffee?"

"Oh, no, thanks. I'm heading to the Starbucks down the street." He smiled his million-dollar smile. "I just came by to check the place out. And because I'd hoped you reconsidered that date."

Fury temporarily stole her words. First the Starbucks comment, and now this again? He didn't get to just waltz back into town and pick her up like she was a forgotten toy. She clenched her hands, forcibly reminding herself that assaulting customers wasn't a good way to bring in business. Plus, she was *nice*. Nice girls didn't smash coffeepots over the heads of their ex-boyfriends.

But even nice girls stood their ground. She lifted her chin. "As I think I made more than clear last night, I'm seeing someone."

"Somehow, I'm not so sure about that." He tipped an imaginary hat and walked out the door, still grinning.

She should have known pretending to date Adam would backfire. Now, not only was she *quirky* for staying in a small town and owning a cat café, but she was pathetic for pretending to date someone and it being clear to Grant and everyone else that there was no way Adam Meyers would really date her. Why would he? He was exciting and wild and hot. And she was Jules Rodriguez, local good girl and budding cat lady.

"I hate that Grant makes me feel like this. Still."

Aubry opened her mouth, but whatever she was going to say was lost when she laughed. "Incoming two point oh."

"Did I do something to anger the fates? Because this is freaking ridiculous."

She braced herself for another go-round with Grant, but it wasn't his outline darkening her doorstep.

No, it was Adam's.

Her heart leaped into her throat, even as she told herself it was a completely unforgivable reaction. He'd done her a favor last night. End of story.

But that didn't stop her body from perking up and taking notice of every move he made. It wasn't how he walked in and instantly took control of the room without even doing anything. He filled the doorway, and though he wasn't as tall as Quinn, there was nothing small or short about Adam. *I wonder…*

Nope. Knock that right off.

She was nearly 100 percent sure he wasn't wearing the same jeans from last night, because these hugged his thighs, showcasing the muscles that flexed with each step, leading up to… *Oh, my.* She sent a silent little thank-you to whoever designed the jeans, because they were so fitted, it was pretty darn clear that he was perfectly in proportion *everywhere*.

She jerked her gaze to his face, but that didn't help at all, because all she could see was the square jaw, his dark eyes, and his mouth. The very same mouth she'd been kissing less than twenty-four hours ago.

Jules licked her lips. If she concentrated, she could almost taste him there.

She watched Adam carefully pick his way across the coffee shop, doing his best not to trip over Khan and Loki and Ninja Kitteh as they came to investigate the new customer. The three cats refused to take a hint, though. They rubbed on his legs, purring up a storm and making it generally impossible to take a step without trampling one of them. She bit her lip to keep from laughing at the exasperated look on his face.

He finally took a massive step over them and strode to the counter before they could catch up. "Hey, Jules."

"Hi." Did her voice sound breathy? She was pretty sure it sounded breathy. She knew Adam more by reputation than anything else, but he didn't seem so bad the few times they'd encountered each other. "Can I get you something?"

"Coffee would be great. Black, please." He frowned when Khan leaped onto the counter and put his front paws on Adam's chest, demanding to be adored. "A cat café, huh?"

The embarrassment she'd almost cured herself of after Grant left came back double-time. She focused on pouring him a cup of coffee. "What is so wrong about owning my own business? It's something a lot of people aspire to, and the fact that mine just happens to be a little *quirky* doesn't make it less of an accomplishment." She turned around to find that damned eyebrow raised again. "What?"

"Well, hell, sugar, I wasn't criticizing." He looked

around, still petting Khan. "It's a neat idea."

"Oh." She passed over the mug, feeling stupid. "Sorry. Everyone keeps hinting at Grant and me getting back together, and then Grant himself stopped by, and I guess I'm just riled up."

His mouth tightened. "That guy's an asshole. And everyone else is, too, if they expect you to fall all over him again. You deserve better, Jules."

She blinked. What was she supposed to say to that? "Er...thank you." *Lame.* She shook her head when he reached for his wallet. "It's on the house. For last night."

"Anytime." He leaned against the counter, which was too freaking close to hip height for her peace of mind, and lowered his voice. "And I do mean anytime."

There was no mistaking the invitation in his voice. Her stomach fluttered and her inner devil's advocate kicked into high gear.

It wasn't so bad pretending to be his girlfriend. You could do it again.

She told that little voice to shut up, but it wasn't listening.

Maybe this is exactly what you need to shake up the town's perception of you.

That got her attention.

What she really wanted—more than shutting down Grant—was a chance to prove that she hadn't been put on the shelf when he left her behind. She *wasn't* the early-spinster cat lady they all suspected, darn it. Maybe she could kill two birds with one stone by continuing this. Pretending to date Adam last night was all well and good, but it didn't hold up to the light of day—not unless they *made* it hold up. She drummed her fingers on the counter, watching him drink his coffee and eyeball the cat. If they kept it up for a week or two...it might work.

There's also the added benefit of more kissing.

"Adam..." She glanced over, and realized Mrs. Peterson was staring at them, once again not even trying to pretend she wasn't eavesdropping. *Crap.* "Aubry, can you watch the counter for a few?"

"Sure."

She gave Adam a bright smile. "Can I talk to you privately? You can bring Khan."

He scooped up the orange tom with one hand and his coffee with the other. "You named a cat after a *Star Trek* villain."

"Guilty." She opened the door to the back. "The others are Cujo, Loki, Rick, Dog, Ninja Kitteh, and Mr. Winkles."

He laughed. "That's a whole lot of pop culture wrapped up into tiny bundles."

"Hey, the names fit."

"I bet they do."

She stopped in the kitchen and made an effort not to wring her hands. *The worst he can say is no.* "So, uh, thanks again for doing me that favor last night."

He paced around the kitchen, seeming to take in everything as he stroked Khan's back. "It was really no problem. Kissing beautiful women isn't exactly a hardship."

He thinks I'm... She rushed on, refusing to dwell on that. He had to say something nice. He was Daniel's friend, after all. "So, it goes like this—Grant is a giant asshole."

"Agreed." He made another circuit around the

kitchen, pausing to poke at the cat-shaped cookie cutters she had out on the counter for the batch of sugar cookies she was baking later.

So far, so good. "When he dumped me and left town, he basically said the reason we couldn't be together was that he wanted to be with someone more exciting—someone who wanted more out of life than to live and die in a small town."

He turned to face her, his jaw tight. "Calling him an asshole might be too kind."

"He's hardly the only one who's ever said that to me, but that's beside the point. Everyone in this town thinks I'm destined to be a spinster. I'm not. At least, I hope I'm not. But I have no way to prove it, and I'm sick of them thinking my sole purpose in life should be to win Grant back. So, here's the thing." Time for the pitch. "If your offer still stands, I'd really, really like it if you'd keep pretending to be my boyfriend—and really give Devil's Falls something to talk about."

Adam blinked. "I'm sorry, what? I think I misheard you over the sound of this fellow's purring. I thought you just said that you want to use me to stir up the gossip mill in town."

That was the part he'd decide to focus on? "You did."

"How the hell am I supposed to do that?"

"I don't know. You're Adam Meyer—bull rider and Devil's Falls legend. You have excitement in your blood."

He stared at her, still for the first time since they walked back to the kitchen.

She sighed. "You're right. It's a dumb idea. I have a ton of them. It's a sickness."

"Wait, wait." He set the cat down and took a drink of his coffee. "You know if I'm going to be your boyfriend, we can't do it halfway."

Now *she* was sure she'd heard *him* wrong. "I'm sorry, what?"

"This is Devil's Falls. The only thing the people here love more than ranching is good gossip, which can work against you as easily as you want it to work for you. If even one person thinks we aren't serious, it'll be impossible to convince them you shouldn't crawl back to golden-boy Grant."

She was almost afraid to hope she was hearing him right. "You…you'll do it?" But then her brain caught up to everything he'd said. "Wait, what do you mean?"

His grin made her stomach leap. "We'll give them something to talk about. Something to show them you're 100 percent over that jackass."

That was what she wanted. It was just daunting when her mind was all too eager to offer up exactly *what* they could do to get the town talking and defuse the whole Jules-and-Grant fantasy. It would have to be pretty scandalous. She picked up Khan, holding him to her chest like a furry shield, though she couldn't say what she wanted protection from. "You're really agreeing to this?"

"Hell, sugar, I could never turn down a woman in need, and you fit the bill."

She could barely believe it. Crazy schemes were her and Aubry's thing, but maybe they were Adam's, too. "Thank you. Oh God, thank you so much. I owe you…" She looked around for inspiration. "Free coffee for life?"

He laughed. "I wouldn't say no to free coffee for

the duration of my time here." He lifted his mug. "This is amazing."

"Thanks." She frowned. It seemed crass to ask him straight out how his mom was doing, especially since he hadn't offered up any information to begin with. "How long are you back for?"

"Not sure yet." A shadow passed over his face, but his expression was so closed down, she didn't dare risk pissing him off by pushing for more information. It must've been worse than Jules thought.

She almost backed out right then, because if Adam was dealing with his mom being *really* sick, wasn't playing along with her scheme the last thing he needed? She hesitated. *It's not up to me to decide what he needs. He's offering me something I need right now, and this is the best opportunity I'm going to get—the* only *opportunity.* Jules stuck out her hand. "Deal?"

Adam set his coffee cup down and took her hand. "Deal."

CHAPTER FOUR

"A date? You've been back in town for two whole days. How in God's name did you manage to sweet-talk some local girl into letting you take her out?"

Adam opened the pillbox and carefully took out the half a dozen pills in varying sizes and colors and set them on the counter. "You know me, Mama. I work fast."

His mom laughed, the chuckle a whole lot weaker than her usual boisterous sound. Everything about her was weaker now. The cancer that she'd hidden for far too long had eaten away at her body, leaving her a shell of the woman he'd grown up with.

Regret bit him, hard and fast. The only reason he knew that she had cancer at all was because her lady friend, Lenora, had called him. He was still pissed the fuck off that he had to hear about it from the woman she was dating rather than his mama herself. Pissed off, but not surprised. He should have been here, making sure she was taking care of herself. He knew damn well that his mama would work herself to the bone to make everyone else around her happy. Combined with her general distrust of doctors, it was a recipe for disaster. If he'd been here, he would have known that something was wrong and insisted she go in and get checked out.

"Oh, dear. I know that look." She patted his arm. "Stop it. There's nothing you could have done."

"Mama—"

"Tell me about this girl. Is she anyone I know?"

Just like that, the discussion was over before it began. They'd have to talk about it at some point, but he wasn't willing to fight with her—not while she looked like a stiff wind might topple her over. "Jules Rodriguez."

"Danny's little cousin?" Her eyes lit up. "She's got that wonderful coffee shop with all the cats. I go in there once a week with Lenora. That Loki is a darling." She accepted the tall glass of water he'd filled for her, some censure creeping into her dark eyes. "She's a nice girl, Adam."

"I know." He braced himself for what would come next.

Sure enough, his mama said, "If I thought for a second you were going to hold still long enough to put down roots, I'd keep my thoughts to myself, but you're as footloose and fancy-free as that father of yours."

Of all the things she could have said, this one stung the most. Because it was true. He set the pills in front of her. "I'm staying long enough to get you sorted out, Mama. I promise."

"Oh, honey…" Tears filled her eyes, tears that felt like they were ripping into his very soul. There was a terrible knowledge on her face that he wasn't ready to face. Not now—maybe not ever. His mom managed a smile. "I love you."

That was it. There was nothing else he could say. "I love you, too." He waited through the torturous process of her taking her pills, and then watched her with an eagle eye while she walked back into the living room and her recliner.

She shot him a sharp look. "I've been getting

around just fine on my own before you got back, Adam Christopher. I don't need you hovering."

"In that case, I'll be going."

He hesitated by the door and looked at his mama. She used to be larger than life, a formidable woman who stood between him and the rest of the world. And here he was, leaving her again. It didn't matter that it was for a date instead of the rodeo, or that she was practically kicking him out the door. He should be here.

"Go, Adam."

As always, she knew what he was thinking without him saying it. He forced a smile. He could be positive if that's what she wanted, at least until he got some concrete answers. "Do you want me to bring anything back?"

"I'm fine. Go on your date." She waved him away.

He went, but he could feel her eyes on his back the entire time, and her words rang in his ears. The thought of settling down in one place was enough to have him breaking out in hives. It was a small part of the toxicity that had been Adam as a teenager—the desire to go anywhere but here, to get in a truck and just drive until he met the horizon. He'd failed a lot of people when he left.

Just like his father.

He shook off the thought through sheer force of will and climbed up into his truck. Jules apparently lived over that shop of hers, and so it took him ten minutes from leaving his mama's house to pulling into the parking lot. Devil's Falls was like that, though. It took fifteen minutes to drive from one end of the town limits to the other—and that was only because of the twenty-mile-an-hour speed limit and single stoplight.

He got out of his truck and looked up and down Main Street. There were the same two bars down the street, the same diner, the same hardware store, the same *everything*. Nothing had changed—not even a fresh coat of paint. The only difference between the street now and when he was eighteen was the addition of a Starbucks down by the stoplight and the café in front of him that used to be a pizza joint.

Restlessness hit him, fierce enough to have him clenching his fists. It wouldn't take much to get back in his truck and keep driving, to search out the nearest rodeo and put in his registration. Everyone in Texas knew him. They'd get him in. He could be on the back of a bull inside of two days. Then maybe he wouldn't have to think about the circles beneath his mama's eyes or the worried looks Lenora kept shooting her when she thought neither of them was watching.

No. You promised you'd stay, and that's what you're going to do.

Adam paused to take in Cups and Kittens again. It was such a random-ass idea—a coffee shop where people could come and spend time with cats—but it was obvious that it was something Jules felt passionately about. Hell, he'd spent a grand total of twenty minutes with her and he could tell that wasn't the only thing.

Judging from that kiss, she was passionate about quite a few things. Just thinking about it calmed the impulse to get the hell out of town. He could do this. The distraction Jules offered pretty much guaranteed he could do this.

It's just a matter of figuring out how far you want to take it.

Now that was a dumb thing to think. He knew exactly how far he wanted to go with Jules Rodriguez.

All the goddamn way.

Adam shook his head, damning himself to hell for the kind of thoughts that type of thing brought up. Her wrapping those long legs around his waist, her mouth on his, her making helpless little noises while he...

"Get a hold of yourself. You're not sleeping with the woman. You're taking her on a date." She was a good girl—and Daniel's cousin.

But she wants to be bad.

He ignored the voice inside him and marched around back to the door where she'd told him to meet her. He barely got his hand up to knock when it was flung open, revealing a breathless Jules. She must have run down the narrow stairs behind her, because her cheeks were flushed and her chest rose and fell hard enough that it looked like her breasts were in danger of spilling free.

Adam nearly swallowed his tongue. "What in the hell are you wearing?"

She looked panicked. "Oh, this little thing?" She pulled at the bottom of her tied-up tank top, belying her attempt at being casual. Not that he was complaining, exactly, but the shorts were several precious inches shorter than the ones she'd worn the other night—so short that the pockets peeked out in the front and he was pretty damn sure if she turned around, he'd be able to see the bottom curve of her ass.

She looked like some country-music video piece of tail.

The only thing that was the same was the well-worn boots on her feet. Jules pushed her mass of dark hair off her face and frowned. "Is something wrong? You said we were going out to burgers, so I didn't dress up and—"

Fuck, she was killing him. "It's fine." But the slice of stomach and length of her long legs and the cleavage that her low-cut tank top revealed...they were making it hard to remember that he was supposed to keep his hands to himself when they weren't in public *trying* to make a spectacle of themselves. *It's still Jules beneath the clothes—what little of them there are.* Right. He just had to remember that, and—

Adam's thoughts screeched to a halt as she turned around and bent over to pick up her purse on the bottom stair. He'd been right about the shorts playing peekaboo with her ass. He gripped the doorframe, unable to tear his gaze away from the place where her mile-long legs met the curve of her ass. The shorts didn't reveal as much as he'd expected, but somehow that only made them more erotic. He wanted to set his teeth to that curve and then lick his way around...

Stop it. For fuck's sake, if you don't, you're going to maul her right here in her doorway.

He forced himself to take a step back, and then another one. She hadn't signed on for hot and sweaty sex, and he had to remember that. This wasn't about him and his nearly unbearable desire for her—as unexpected as it was inconvenient. This was about doing her a favor.

Right. Keep telling yourself that. You wanted a distraction, now don't going complaining that you got what you asked for—in spades.

She locked the door behind her and turned with a smile. "I feel ridiculous. Do I look ridiculous?"

He had to clear his throat twice to answer. "No."

"Are you okay?" Just like that, her smile disappeared, and her face fell. "Oh God, you're lying, aren't you? I look like a two-bit hooker." She pulled on the bottom of her shorts. "I'm going to go change. This was such a bad idea. Maybe we should just call the whole thing off."

"Sugar, stop." He grabbed her wrist, changing her course so that her momentum brought her slamming into his chest. "You look great."

"You're really sweet for lying, but—"

"Jules, stop talking." He pressed his free hand to the small of her back, bringing her flush against him. Her mouth opened in a little O of surprise when she pressed against where he was rock hard. "You feel that?" As if there was any chance of her missing it with them this close. Adam waited for her to nod. "You did that to me. I see you in those little shorts and all I can think of is getting a handful of your ass as I lift you up and thrust against where you're warm and soft and wet for me."

She blinked. "Oh."

It was hard to get himself leashed, harder than it should have been, but he finally managed to take a step back and put some distance between them. "Any questions?"

"Just one." She licked her lips. "Can you teach me to do that?"

He opened the passenger door for her. "Do what?"

"Dirty talk." She hopped up into the seat, giving him another devastating flash of her ass.

He shut the door, buying some time as he walked around the front of the truck and climbed inside. Unfortunately, he hadn't gotten himself back under control by that point. "You want me to teach you to dirty talk."

"It's just…" She waved a hand at him. She'd recovered a whole hell of a lot faster than he had. Adam was almost insulted by how unaffected she seemed. Jules must have finally got her thoughts in order, because she finished, "It's really, really hot. And naughty, though I'm not sure if calling it naughty completely cancels out the hotness factor."

Hearing the word "naughty" on her lips was almost enough to have him pulling over so he could start lesson one. Instead, he gripped the steering wheel and focused on driving. "Yeah, sugar. I can teach you to talk dirty."

Though he was already starting to regret agreeing to this in the first place.

CHAPTER FIVE

Jules couldn't quite get her heartbeat under control. She'd hoped she didn't look like an idiot when she dug down to the bottom of her closet to get the not-approved-for-public-consumption clothes. She hadn't expected to watch Adam's eyes go dark or for his voice to drop a full octave when he said…those things. She shivered, staring out the passenger window.

There was no room in her world for wanting Adam Meyer. This was a business arrangement, plain and simple.

It just happened to be a business arrangement where she was having the sudden desire to see if her partner could follow through on the picture he'd painted with his words.

Teach me to dirty talk. Jules almost snorted. That was the most pathetic comeback she'd ever made, but she'd been half a second from kissing him again, and one sexual ambush was more than enough in a lifetime, let alone a week.

I want to create a scandal, but not too much of a scandal. And only when there are people to watch. Because that totally makes sense.

She realized they'd be sitting in silence for entirely too long and turned to face Adam. *Might as well own it.* "So, when's my first lesson?"

"I'll let you know."

She wilted a little but managed to get a hold of herself. Of course he wasn't going to start dirty talk lessons in the car on the way to their first fake date. There were a grand total of three restaurants in town, not counting the McDonald's that no one but teenagers and moms of little kids went to, and the Joint was where people tended to congregate on Saturday night before they wandered down the street to the bar or drove off into the boonies for a bonfire.

That was Devil's Falls, though. She liked it, no matter that people like Grant and Adam no doubt looked down on the locals—probably the only thing those two had in common. It was nice to know that on any given weekend night, she could walk down the street and find a few of her uncles or cousins playing poker at the bar, or some of the girls from her graduating class having a ladies' night out at the Joint with classy martinis and cosmos.

But…there was no way she'd be able to walk through the doors of any place in town without running into half a dozen people she knew. Something she hadn't really thought about when she'd gotten dressed. Crap.

That's the whole point of this. To prove you're not a spinster pining after Grant. You're alive and exciting and dating the town bad boy.

If that wasn't scandalous, she didn't know what was.

It sounded great—in theory. In practice, she wasn't sure she'd survive the embarrassment. "Are you sure I don't look ridiculous?" Her shorts were so short, they might be illegal. She pulled at the hem, but it didn't do a single thing to cover her more.

"You look…like a scandal waiting to happen."

She glanced at him, shocked all over again by the edge in his voice. She wasn't sure if he sounded mad or turned on. "Are you okay? If you're not feeling well, we can reschedule for another night."

"Holy fuck." Adam laughed harshly and pulled the truck onto the edge of the road. He turned to her, his shoulders filling the space between the steering wheel and the seat, suddenly seeming a whole lot closer. "Sugar, you're killing me. You're seducing me without even realizing you're doing it."

"I...am?" She realized what she'd said and lifted her chin. "I mean, I am. Good. Right?" She groaned and slouched in her seat. "I'm pretty sure you're not feeling seduced anymore."

She expected him to laugh or something, but he just reached across the bench seat and snagged her waist, dragging her toward him. She bit back a yelp when he lifted her to straddle him. "Uh, I'm pretty sure we're breaking some sort of law right now."

"Nah. We're parked and inside my vehicle. You're covered."

She twisted enough to look through the windshield. There didn't seem to be anyone around, but that didn't mean there weren't eyes on them.

Which is the freaking point. Get it together, girl.

His hands drifted over her hips, not touching so much as a sliver of bare skin, but she felt branded all the same. Was this guy hiding a forest fire beneath his skin? Adam looked at her with those too-dark eyes, his expression serious and yet somehow savage. "Are you ready to make a scene, sugar?"

She licked her lips. *Definitely not a mild-mannered nice guy—more like a lone wolf who's just as likely to cuddle you as rip your throat out.* "Yes. Public display of affection without possibility of arrest. Good thinking."

He smiled. "I'm not going to do anything you don't want me to. You say the word and I stop. Repeat that back to me."

Her heart was beating too fast, her tight clothing seeming to become even tighter with each breath. "You're not going to do anything I don't want you to."

"And?"

"I say the word and you stop." It was harder to get the last part out, mostly because she couldn't stop staring at his mouth. He'd blown her away with the rushed fake kiss the other night. How much better would it be if he was planning on actually, say, kissing her? Her body broke out in goose bumps at the thought. "Adam—"

One of his hands left her hip to frame her jaw, his thumb tracing over her bottom lip. "Rule number one to making this believable—stop overthinking and worrying about who could be watching. Just focus on me and feel."

Easier said than done. "I'm really good at over-thinking." Though it was really hard to connect her thoughts with him touching her like that, his thumb coasting back and forth, back and forth.

"I can see that." His fingers curled around the back of her neck, easing her forward. "What are you thinking about now?"

She was forced to brace her hands on his chest to avoid toppling against him, and the feel of all those muscles beneath his T-shirt made her brain short out. She kneaded her fingers, moving up to his shoulders and then down again. Belatedly, she realized he'd asked her something. "I'm sorry, what?"

"That answers that." His hand on her hip tightened.

"I'm going to kiss you now."

"Oh…okay."

"That wasn't a request, sugar."

And then he did exactly what he promised he would.

He kept it light, the slightest brushing of his lips on hers, over and over again, until she thought she might go mad with desire. She writhed against him, but he easily held her in place, taking his time, almost as if he was savoring the contact. Then, *finally*, his tongue coaxed her mouth open and he was *kissing* her.

Just like that, the spark between them went from campfire to wild blaze, flaring out of control.

One second she was wondering how in God's name one man could taste so good, and the next she was rubbing against him like he was the best kind of catnip. He groaned against her mouth, his hand on her hip moving to her behind, lining them up. The feel of his hard length against the most sensitive part of her had her going still, but only for a moment. She rolled her hips, moaning at the delicious friction.

Adam took his mouth off hers long enough to curse, long and hard, and then she was on her back on the bench seat, him moving over her, his mouth reclaiming hers. Jules wrapped her legs around his waist, arching up to meet each thrust that dragged him against the seam of her jeans. He kissed down her jaw to her breasts. "Fuck, sugar, you're one hell of an actress."

She laughed, but the sound choked off when he yanked down her tank top and sucked her nipple into his mouth. "Oh my *God*."

For some reason, that caused him to pause. He

rested his forehead against her chest. "Hold on. Give me a second."

That sounded dangerously close to him saying he wanted to stop. She grabbed his shoulders, digging her nails in. "Adam, I'm three seconds from coming. If you don't finish what you started…" She couldn't think of a threat strong enough, so she just made an incoherent sound of frustration. When he didn't immediately move, she actually whimpered. "Please, Adam. Remember what you said? I'll let you know when to stop. Well, I don't know how else to tell you to keep going. Full steam ahead. Green light. *Just make me come already.*"

His body shook, and it took her a full two seconds to realize he was laughing. "You are something else."

"As long as I'm something else that will be coming in short order." Never in her life had she been this *forward* with anything sexual, but she felt like she might burst apart at the seams if he didn't answer the beat pulsing through her body.

It was easier to demand it because this was Adam. He wasn't her boyfriend, no matter what they were pretending. He wasn't even a friend, really. He was just a seriously sexy guy doing her a favor that might nominate him for sainthood. She gasped when he grabbed her butt, sealing their bodies together. *Okay, maybe not sainthood.*

"Just this once."

She wasn't sure she could handle more than once. "Sure. Whatever you say." *As long as you don't stop.*

He hooked her leg higher and thrust against her, building up to the rhythm that had driven her so crazy. His mouth was on her neck, his words pouring over her. "I lied, sugar. I make you come once, and I don't think I'm going to be able to stop myself from doing it again. It's what a good boyfriend would do."

"Fake…boyfriend." She could barely get the words out past the pleasure spiking through her. Her orgasm rolled over her, setting her nerves aflame and making her entire body go tight and hot. "*Holy crap.*"

His laugh was almost a growl against her skin. "A fake boyfriend who gives you real orgasms." He held her for a few seconds, long enough for her to realize he was still hard as a rock. Adam didn't give her a chance to comment on it, though. He sat back and adjusted his jeans, leaving her to do the same.

Jules fixed her clothing, feeling like she was having an out-of-body experience. Had she really just dry humped her fake boyfriend in his pickup until he made her come? She had to say something, right now, otherwise they were going to devolve into what might be the most awkward situation of her life. She cleared her throat and looked around. "Oh, wow, this was a good call. I see Sheriff Taylor's police cruiser down the road. He saw something for sure, and he gossips worse than Mrs. Peterson."

There was a pause. And then finally, "Yep. That was the plan."

The words came out flat, and she twisted to look at him. "Are you okay? I'm sorry that I basically just strong-armed you into giving me an orgasm." Humiliation rolled over her despite her determination to push herself beyond her limits. "You tried to stop and I said no and, oh my God, I'm so sorry."

Adam turned to face her again. "Sugar, you couldn't have forced me if you wanted to." He grabbed her hand and pressed it to the front of his jeans, where it was still blatantly obvious that he was sporting an erection. "Don't you dare try to take that orgasm from me. It was mine."

She stared at his lap, not quite having the courage to stroke him despite the fact her palm was plastered there. "I, uh…"

"If it makes you feel better, next time I'll be the one giving the orders."

Next time. She blinked up at him. "You really weren't joking about making this as believable as possible, were you?"

His mouth flattened, but then Adam smiled and she was sure she'd misread the expression. "I never joke about fake relationships."

"Hilarious." She realized she was still palming him and yanked her hand back. "But, seriously, you have to stop me when I'm out of line. I know we were just doing it for show but—"

"Sugar, stop. Remember what I said about overthinking? You're doing it again. Sit back and relax, and let the rumor mill do its job." Before she could answer, he pulled away from the side of the road, and, two minutes later, they were in the parking lot and he shut off the engine. "Brace yourself. It's showtime."

CHAPTER SIX

Adam was having a hell of a time focusing on what Jules was saying. She was obviously really passionate about it, which was making him think of what *else* she'd be passionate about. Again. Every time she smiled, his cock jumped, reminding him that he hadn't gotten the same release she'd so obviously enjoyed back in the cab of his truck.

For fuck's sake, focus.

"…but I'm boring you. I'm so sorry."

He blinked. "What?"

"I'm prattling on and you'd obviously rather be anywhere else but here." Her self-deprecating smile tugged at him. "I don't get out much, and the stuff I talk about with Aubry isn't exactly fit for polite company, and when I get nervous, I start rambling and, seriously, just tell me to shut up right now or I'm going to keep going."

"Jules, breathe."

She took a gasping breath. "Right. Sorry again."

The woman was downright precious. He pushed his plate away and sat back. "When's the last time you were on a date?"

"Does the charity auction count?" She tugged on her tank top, which only served to make it dip dangerously. "What am I saying? Of course it doesn't count. The only reason Dave went out with me was because I donated money to the PTA, and really, he kissed like a drowning fish, so it was never going to be anything more than one dinner."

Adam took a sip of his beer, picking over what she just said. "They still do that charity auction for the high school?"

"Every year like clockwork." She made a face. "As fun as it is, I can almost tell who's going to bid on who, though there's always at least one upset every year. Last year, Mrs. Peterson bid *three hundred dollars* on Sheriff Taylor. His wife wasn't very happy about that."

Considering Mrs. Taylor was one of the scariest women he'd ever met, Mrs. Peterson had balls of steel to pull that one off. But then, he'd known that in eighth grade, when she was his English teacher. She didn't take any shit then, and apparently that hadn't changed in the years since. "So, back to your date."

"It was fine." She picked up her fork, poked at her salad, and set it down again. For once, he wasn't the twitchiest person in the room, and he was content to watch her fidget. She used her straw to stir the ice in her water, not looking at him, her head dipped so that her dark hair fell forward to hide her face.

He waited, but she didn't say anything else, and since she was managing to look everywhere but at him, he figured she wasn't going to. "Talk about damning with faint praise."

"It was for *charity*." She slumped in her chair and sighed. "It's obvious I don't get out much, isn't it? No wonder the whole town thinks I'm a lonely cat-collecting spinster."

She was so cute, it was downright painful. He just wanted to scoop her up and tell her that her adorable awkwardness was an asset—not something to be ashamed of. To hell with what the town thought. She was fresh and enthusiastic and as bracing as a dive into a mountain lake.

Adam shook his head and finished off his beer. If he was any other man, he'd tell her to forget her preoccupation with Grant. She didn't need to fake date him in order to make a point—she was doing just fine on her own.

But he wasn't any other man, and he had no intention of leaving her alone.

He held the door open for Jules and followed her out into the night. *Just get her home without mauling her again and then you can figure out what your next step is.* He couldn't call the whole thing off. Now that half the town had either seen them at dinner or likely heard about it, them "breaking up" would only add a heap of humiliation on Jules's already teetering pile, and Adam refused to contribute. She'd asked him for a favor, and it wasn't her fault that his control was slipping by the second.

She climbed into his truck, seeming preoccupied with something. That was fine. If they managed to keep silent for the whole five-minute drive, it would be all good.

But then she went and shot that plan all to hell. "I think tonight went okay."

"Yep."

"I mean, Grant wasn't there, but from the stares we got, he'll be hearing about our being seen together before too long. *Everyone* will be hearing about it." She sounded pleased, which was good. So why did it grate against him as badly now as it had back in the truck? She continued, oblivious to his inner aggravation. "What's next?"

Did she think he kept a copy of *Idiot's Guide to Being a Small-Town Scandal* stuffed in his dresser drawer? Apparently so, because she was looking at him expectantly. He turned out on Main Street. "Sugar, we already made spectacles of ourselves nearly getting busy in my truck with Sheriff Taylor half a block away, then proceeded to shock the locals just by eating dinner. Why don't we take it easy for the rest of the night?"

"I don't know." She frowned. "Shouldn't we be taking it to the next level? We don't know for sure the sheriff saw anything."

Frankly, he doubted the old man had seen anything. Adam knew for a fact Sheriff Taylor liked to nap on that very side street around that time of night, and so he wouldn't have had his glasses on. But he sure as fuck wasn't going to tell Jules that. "Are you asking me or telling me?"

She laughed. "Sorry. I haven't spent much time thinking about indulging in gossip-starting acts. The craziest I get these days is video games. I'm a halfway decent sniper."

The woman just kept surprising him. "I never would have pegged you for a first-person shooter."

"Oh, not by my own doing." She grinned. "But they're Aubry's poison of choice, so I get dragged along when she starts annihilating noobs."

Now, the redhead he could picture camped out in a dark room with a microphone on her head and a controller in her hands. She was as intense as Jules was sunny. In fact, despite being around them a grand total of an hour, he couldn't really wrap his mind around how they were friends. "How did you and Aubry meet?"

"It's a silly story."

"Humor me."

"If you insist." She turned, fully engaged. Jules seemed to spend her entire life fully engaged. "So my grandmother passed when I was a junior in college. I already knew what I wanted to do for a career—start a coffee shop with a unique draw—and she left me enough money to get off the ground, plus her blessing along with it." She smiled, her eyes going soft. "Gran was one of the few people in town—my family included—who didn't think I'd end up a lonely spinster after Grant dumped me."

Before he could comment that he thought it highly unlikely Jules would hit thirty and still be single, let alone a spinster, she continued on, "So I'd just bought and renovated the shop, and I was down at the Humane Society picking the cats that would live there. Aubry was carting her massive laptop home from the library and saw me loading what she termed 'a cat lady's starter kit' into my truck. She made some comment about cats eating you after you die, and of course I couldn't let that stand. We ended up arguing all the way back to my place and while she helped me unload the cats and get them settled. From there it's more or less history. Aubry has her quirks, same as me, and she doesn't expect me to be something I'm not."

Friends like that were worth their weight in gold. He'd had three, now two, and he'd barely seen them over the last twelve years. *I'm a leaver, just like my mama always said.* Once upon a time, those words had been a promise—Devil's Falls and its whispers and judgment wouldn't hold him back forever—but now they felt more like a curse.

He turned into the alley leading to the little carport behind Jules's shop. "And what's she think about this plan you've concocted?"

"She thinks I'm crazy." Jules laughed again. "But then, she tells me I'm crazy at least once a day, so that's nothing new."

He parked but hesitated turning off the engine. It was all too easy to step back to the last time they'd been in his truck cab and the trouble he'd let them get into. Adam gripped the steering wheel, reminding himself for the dozenth time that he sure as hell could *not* kiss Jules again.

She took the decision right out of his hands. "See you later." She dashed a quick kiss against his cheek and bounced away, opening the door and sliding out of the truck before he could respond.

Adam watched her bound to her door and let herself in, her enthusiasm infectious even over the distance. He finally shook his head and threw his truck into reverse.

Aubry was right—Jules was bat-shit crazy.

And he loved it.

Shit.

• • •

Five days passed with only a few texts from Adam, but Jules told herself she didn't care. He had his own life to attend to, just like she did. She couldn't expect him to drop everything to spend every minute of every day by her side on the off chance that Grant would wander in and see them.

Coincidentally, her ex had made a habit of waltzing

through the door at least once a day to make comments about her *boyfriend* in such a tone that she knew he still didn't believe she was with Adam.

She took the plate of sandwiches Jamie had made up special and brought them over to where Lenora and Amelia were sitting at a table by the window. Lenora smiled in thanks, but Jules couldn't help noticing that Adam's mom had lost weight. "These are on the house."

"Oh, Jules, you shouldn't have." Amelia sipped her tea, petting Rick.

Lenora sent her a look of thanks. "I know you just said you're not hungry, but you can't let this go to waste," she said to Amelia.

"Let me know if you need anything else."

She headed back to the counter, leaving the ladies in peace.

But they were apparently the only ones going to be left in peace today. As if her wishing him ill conjured him up, the bell above the door jingled and Grant strode through. "Jules!" He stopped just inside the door and examined the floor at his feet. He had this nasty habit of looking around him like he expected to step in cat shit, which made Jules grind her teeth every time she saw it.

"Grant."

"Douchecanoe," Aubry muttered from her usual place in the corner. Jules shot her a sharp look, but she appeared engrossed in whatever she was doing on her computer.

Grant came up and leaned on the counter but immediately backpedaled when Cujo hissed at him. "That thing's rabid."

"He doesn't like people." She crossed her arms over her chest. "Are you buying something today?"

"Nope. There's a double Frappuccino down the street with my name on it. I was just stopping in to see if you and your *boyfriend* were going to the swimming hole tomorrow for the Fourth?"

"For fuck's sake, you can't be serious." Aubry leaned back, stretching her arms over her head. "Going to the swimming hole is something high school kids who can't legally drink do. I'm pretty sure that'd look great on your future law résumé."

Grant's mouth tightened, his gray eyes going flinty. But then he turned back to Jules, the expression melting into a charming smile she used to believe was real. "There will be a bunch of people from our class there. You should come. Bring Adam." He jerked a thumb over his shoulder at Aubry. "You can even bring her."

"She has a name."

His smile never wavered. "Of course. I'd be delighted if you'd come and bring your boyfriend and *Aubry*." He made a show of looking around. "Unless Adam's already blown out of town? It's been over a week, and word has it that he's more tumbleweed than man."

She opened her mouth to deny it, but that would be a lie. Fake relationship or not, she couldn't pretend like Adam was staying for the long term. "Actually—"

"Hey, there, sugar."

Jules nearly jumped out of her skin when Adam walked in from the door to the kitchen, his damned eyebrow inching up.

Grant frowned. "Speak of the devil."

"Grant. Aubry." He slipped an arm around Jules's

waist. "Jules." He kissed her forehead, the innocent touch doing some very *non*innocent things to her lower stomach area.

"Hey." She turned in his arms and wrapped hers around his neck. "I've missed you."

"Not nearly much as I've missed you." He grabbed her ass, making her squeal, and turned to Grant. "What are *you* doing here? I know for a fact you get your coffee needs met at that abomination down the street."

For his part, her ex recovered remarkably fast. "I was just stopping by to invite Jules here to the swimming hole this weekend. You're welcome to come, of course."

"Wouldn't miss it." He didn't take his gaze off the other man, something dangerous glinting in his eyes. "If you're done here…"

"Yeah. Sure. I'll be going." Grant strode out of the shop at a clip almost fast enough to be called running.

"You made the puppy piddle his pants. That was mean." Aubry snickered. "I like it."

"So glad you approve." He combed a hand over Cujo's back, and Jules's mouth dropped open when the tabby arched into his hand, purring like a jet engine. His gaze traveled around the café and landed on where his mom and Lenora were watching avidly. "You ladies like the show?"

Amelia laughed. "I always thought that boy was a brat."

A brat. Well, that was one way to describe Grant.

Adam eyed the uneaten sandwiches on the plate between them. "You eat some of that, you hear? You're too skinny by half."

She arched a brow, the expression so similar to her

son's that Jules had to bite back a laugh. "I was just getting to it before you started that prize cock show."

"Mama."

"What? I'm old, but I'm not dead. I know exactly what you were up to." When he turned back to Jules, Amelia leaned over and sent her a wink.

He sure does love his mama. It made her like him even better knowing that.

Adam leaned against the counter, giving Cujo another stroke. "So Grant wants us to come to the swimming hole?"

She ignored Aubry's muttered agreement. "I get the impression Grant still doesn't believe the rumors that we're together."

"Then I guess we'll just have to kick it up a notch." His grin did funny things to her stomach, and her traitorous mind jumped back to what he'd said before their date the other night, and how good he'd felt when he made her come.

She pressed a hand to her flaming cheeks, hating that he made her blush so easily. "I guess I'm going to have to find a swimsuit."

He blinked. "You don't own a swimsuit?"

"Well, I do. But, you see—"

"What Jules is trying to say is that to describe her suit as 'matronly' would be to put it kindly."

"Aubry, shut up," she hissed, blushing even harder when Adam laughed. "You shut up, too. There's nothing wrong with wanting a suit that will keep all my goodies in place no matter how I'm moving."

His hands skated up her sides and back down to her hips. "Do you need some help picking out a suit?"

Danger! It was all too easy to imagine the kind of

trouble they could get into in a fitting room with her scantily clad in a bathing suit. "Uh, no, thanks. Aubry will help me."

She might have imagined the disappointment that flickered over his face, but it was gone too fast to be sure. "In that case, I'll pick you up at eleven tomorrow."

"How do you know what time they're going?"

"Because it's a party at the swimming hole. They always start at noon." He hesitated, almost like he thought he should kiss her good-bye or something, but then he seemed to think better of it, because he turned on his heel and marched back through the door to the kitchen.

It took Jules a few seconds to get control of her body enough to follow him. "Hey, hold up!" She caught him just inside the door out to the back parking lot. "Why'd you come in this way?" *And what are you doing here in the first place?*

"I've been working on my mama's place, so I was picking up a few things at the hardware store across the street and saw that jackass walk in here. Figured it was a good time to remind him of our fake relationship."

"Oh." She had no business feeling the disappointment that made her stomach dip. He was doing her a favor. That was it. "That's smart."

"Hang in there. He might not believe yet, but he will after by the time we leave that party." And then he was gone, disappearing through the door and leaving her to wonder if she should be looking forward to tomorrow or scared out of her godforsaken mind.

CHAPTER SEVEN

"I thought only high school kids did this shit."

Adam unhooked the last black tube and tossed it into the back of his truck. "They do. But I get the feeling Grant is trying to recapture his glory days." *And maybe Jules, too.*

Quinn snorted. "The more I hear about this guy, the more he sounds like a winner." He looked around. "Where's Daniel?"

"He's busy." Or, more likely, he didn't want to see his cousin and Adam putting on a show for a guy he hated. Adam was sorry he felt that way, but he'd seen the look on Jules's face when he walked into her shop today. Grant got under her skin in a bad way, and watching the light in her eyes dim had grated on Adam something fierce. There was enough bad shit in this world without that asshat making her feel like she was lacking.

Adam wasn't exactly a white knight, though. He was taking advantage of her with these "lessons."

Which made him no better than Grant, in the end.

Adam looked at his hands. He had calluses across his palms from rope burns, and there was the scar on his right ring finger where he'd broken it in a truly impressive way after being thrown from a bull with the name of Satan's Revenge. He'd only managed four seconds that ride, but it had been more than worth it.

What he wouldn't give to take it back and know he'd been by his mama's side when she found out about the cancer instead.

"You okay?"

He blinked. "What?"

Quinn looked distinctly uncomfortable to be shucking aside the joking demeanor he preferred. "I don't know, man. You just seem kind of lost since you got back into town. Is it your mom? I know she's sick—"

"She's fine." He wasn't ready to admit that she wouldn't even talk about the cancer with him. Not now, not like this. There would come a time when he'd have to sit her down and force it out of her, but he sure as fuck wasn't ready for it yet. Really, he should thank Jules. When they were together, he was able to forget his fear that one day he'd wake up and his mama would be gone for good.

He realized he'd spoken too sharply and sighed. "Look, it's complicated and I'm not handling it well."

"No shit." Quinn hesitated. "If you need any-thing—anything at all—I'm here. You know that, right?"

"Yeah."

"And Daniel is, too, even if he's got his own shit he's dealing with." He held up a hand before Adam could ask. "It's the same old, same old. He was never the same after John died and Hope left. The man has one foot in the grave, and it's by choice."

The car crash affected them all. Everything changed after that night, and little of it for the better. Adam wished there was something he could do for Daniel, but the truth was that he had more than enough shit to deal with on his own. *Fuck.* He swiped a beer from the cooler in the back of the truck and opened it. "What a trio we make."

"Speak for yourself. I'm the normal one."

Quinn was as normal as he could be after having walked away from his oil tycoon of a father—and his family's fortune—to be a cattle rancher. Adam shook his head. "Whatever you have to tell yourself to sleep at night."

"Like a baby." Quinn closed the tailgate. "So is that mean little redhead coming?"

"Don't know. She doesn't seem like the type to be into this sort of thing."

"You mean she's like a vampire who'll burn up in the sun and probably feasts on the blood of innocents? I totally agree."

Adam snorted. "You enjoy pushing her buttons."

"More than I should." He laughed. "I can't help it. It's too easy to get a rise out of her."

"Get your ass in the truck or we're going to be late."

Ten minutes later they pulled up in front of Jules's shop. He stopped the truck and froze when Jules and Aubry stepped through the door and onto the sidewalk. "Holy fucking shit."

"You can say that again."

"Shut up." He couldn't take his eyes off Jules. She wore a pair of cutoff shorts that might've been the same ones from the other night, but this time, there were ties peeking out the top on either side of her hips. It was like seeing the tip of a present he was dying to unwrap. Adam's cock jumped to attention as his gaze coasted up her stomach to the tiny black triangle bikini covering her breasts. There was nothing overtly revealing about the cut of the suit, but it had him fighting not to kick Quinn out of the truck and

drive her off to somewhere they wouldn't be interrupted so he could explore those scraps of cloth at
length.

"Jesus, man. If you could see the way you're
looking at her." Quinn shook his head. "Should I get
another ride?"

"What? No. It's fine." Though he wanted to tell his
friend to do exactly that. *Get a hold of yourself, idiot.*
He had to control himself—he was about to be up
close and personal with Jules, and jumping her bones
the second he saw her wasn't acceptable.

"Sure it is." Quinn hopped out of the truck, and
Adam took several deep breaths and focused on
getting his body's reaction minimized. He didn't have
long, because Jules climbed up and scooted over until
she was pressed against him from shoulder to hip,
Aubry on the other side of her.

Quinn wedged his big body into the tiny space
between the redhead and the door. "There's plenty of
room for you right here, sweet cheeks." He patted his
lap.

She shot him a look that would have sent a lesser
man bolting from the truck. "Touch me and lose the
attached body part."

Quinn just grinned. "You're all sugar and spice and
everything nice, aren't you?"

Hearing the redhead's hiss of rage was almost
enough to distract Adam from how good Jules
smelled—like coconut and suntan lotion. He smiled at
her. "You ready for this?"

"Not in the least." Her eyes were a little too wide.
"It's bringing back all sorts of memories I could do
without."

Memories of her and Grant. The thought sent a completely irrational spike of jealousy through him. That shit had gone down years ago. There was no reason for him to want to wring the man's neck for knowing that he'd once gotten to touch Jules whenever he wanted, or that he'd held her heart close enough to break it.

Or, hell, that he still affected her strongly enough nine years later that she was willing to get up close and personal with a near stranger to prove a point.

Adam turned back to the road, clenching his jaw to keep words inside that he had no right to. He didn't have *any* rights when it came to Jules, and it'd do him good to remember that.

The rest of the trip up was done in painful silence. He was almost grateful for the fact that Aubry had taken an instant dislike to Quinn's poking at her, because her icy one-word answers to him made conversation between Adam and Jules damn near impossible. He parked next to two other trucks. Of the two, he pegged the shiny pavement queen to be Grant's—the red Ford must have had all of ten miles on the engine. His ten-year-old Dodge looked battered and beaten by comparison.

He'd be an idiot not to see the similarities between the trucks and their owners.

It was enough to give a lesser man a complex.

Adam got out of the cab before anyone could say something to tip him over the edge and strode around to the back to start unpacking the tubes.

"Is everything okay?"

He didn't look over at Jules. "I could live the rest of my life happy knowing I wouldn't hear that question again from another damn person."

If he expected her to rabbit away from his snarled words, he was sadly mistaken. "You don't have to do this. We can just say something came up and skip it."

Even if he was willing to do that—and piss-poor mood or not, he couldn't let Jules down so spectacularly—the chance to bolt disappeared when Grant came around the back of the truck and waved. "I'm glad you made it." He did a double take when he saw Jules. "I can't believe your mama let you out of the door dressed like that."

She narrowed her eyes. "Funny thing—I have my own place, and I'm not sixteen anymore."

"I can see that." And then he proceeded to rake her with his gaze in a way that had Adam seeing red. He stalked over to slip an arm around her waist, telling himself all the while that he was playing a part.

It sure as fuck didn't *feel* like a part. It felt like he was half a second from beating that smug piece of shit's face in. Adam put every ounce of that desire onto his face when he clenched his teeth in a way that only a fool would call a grin. "Didn't your daddy ever teach you that it's not nice to eye-fuck another man's woman, let alone when he's standing not two feet away?"

Grant took a step back and seemed to catch himself because he straightened, his shoulders going back. "You know as well as I do that she's not the kind of—"

"Boy, I suggest you rethink the words that are about to come out of your idiot mouth."

Grant's teeth clicked together when he snapped his mouth shut. He glared. "Hurry up. The party's already started." Then he strode away, yanking his shirt off and pausing to shove it into his truck before he disappeared down the path leading to the swimming hole.

"Well, that was…" Jules let out a shuddering breath. "I'm sorry I got you into this."

"I offered to keep this thing going, remember? You didn't get me into anything I didn't want to do." He forced the tension out of his body. He'd wanted to do this because Jules offered a one-of-a-kind distraction from the shit his mom was going through, but that didn't do a damn thing if he didn't *let* her distract him. "I'm just in a piss-poor mood, and it has nothing to do with you."

"Okay." She didn't sound sure, though. But she brightened immediately. "I'll grab the beer."

He was quickly learning that Jules covered up nearly any uncomfortable emotion with cheer. It should have been annoying as fuck, but it was strangely endearing. Then she shimmied out of her shorts and he forgot about everything but the fact her heart-shaped ass was barely covered by her bikini bottom.

He rubbed a hand over his face, his chances of making it through the day without killing Grant Thomas—or fucking Jules senseless—disappearing before his eyes.

CHAPTER EIGHT

Jules could feel Adam's eyes on her, and it was driving her crazy. She tried to focus on where Aubry floated next to her, her friend's giant hat shielding her face and chest, and her equally giant sunglasses masking any expression of judgment that she was sure to be leveling at Jules right about now. "Sorry."

"You keep saying that. I keep not believing you. In fact, I don't think that word means what you think it means." She held her hand out, and Jules passed her another beer from the cooler strung between Jules and Adam's tubes. Aubry took a long drink and sank lower into the hole in the middle of her tube. "But it could be worse."

"Dear God, was that an actual admission of you having fun doing something outside surrounded by *nature*?"

Aubry laughed. "Let's not get ahead of ourselves. It's entirely possible that some undiscovered-until-now alligator will appear to pick us off one by one." She seemed to consider. "But if that bastard starts with Grant, I might be okay with my inevitable fate."

She looked over to where Grant floated near them, surrounded by Kelly, Kelli, and Jessica. They were all former cheerleaders, and all were conveniently single and looking to sink their claws into an up-and-coming lawyer.

That's not fair. You were panting after Grant for years.

As if he could read her mind, Grant shot her a look over his shoulder and grinned. "Hope you're having as great a time as I am, Jules."

She gritted out a smile. "Of course. This is just peachy."

"Sugar, you're lying through your teeth." Adam snagged the line between their tubes and towed her closer to him until they squeaked as they rubbed together.

"Only totally." She lowered her voice. "The water's freezing, I'm mostly naked, and now Aubry's got me thinking about mutant alligators. I used to love this, but for the life of me, I can't remember why."

"Is it because of that trio?"

"No." She let her head drop back to rest on her tube. "Yes. Maybe. I don't know. I don't want anything to do with him, but *seeing* him makes me crazy."

It was probably karma kicking her in the lady bits for thinking she could stick it to Grant by doing the same damn thing. She should have taken a page from his book and let him think she had a harem of men stashed away, all ready to drop everything and see to her needs. She laughed at the thought.

"What's so funny?"

She debated not telling him for half as second, but it was too much. Besides, the brisk breeze had eased them just out of earshot of the rest of their group. "Just picturing if Grant's and my positions were reversed and I had three gorgeous men hanging on bated breath for my attention. The imaginary look on his face is very satisfying, if you were wondering."

"I wasn't." Adam put his hand on her knee, the contact shockingly warm. "I'm hurt, sugar. You think one of me isn't man enough for you?"

Jules was suddenly very aware that she was wearing a sad excuse for a swimsuit and that it wouldn't take but a second to divest her of it if Adam was interested. She went very still, torn between wanting to laugh the whole thing off and wanting to take his hand and slide it higher up her thigh. Her skin felt too tight, her nipples pebbling in a way that had nothing to do with temperature. "Oh, no. You're great. I mean, uh, yeah." *You can do better than this.* "So, about that dirty-talking lesson…"

His hand tightened almost imperceptibly. "You want that lesson *now*?"

"No time like the present." It was such a bad idea, but dragging Adam into some of the trees lining the swimming hole was an even worse idea. "How do I start?" She cleared her throat. "Adam, I'd very much like you to stick your bits into my bits."

Adam laughed, the sound deep and carrying. "Holy shit, sugar."

"That's not exactly the reaction I was going for." She frowned and tried again. "I want your c-co… Dang it, I can't say it. Why can't I say it? It's a freaking male chicken."

He tilted his sunglasses down so he could shoot her a look over the top of them. "There isn't a damn thing in common with a male chicken and my cock."

The way he said it, as if it was just another word, inexplicably made her stomach tighten. And his hand was still on her knee. "Fine. I already said I suck at this. Teach me, Master Adam."

"Patience, young padawan." He kneaded the sensitive skin above her knee. "You want to know the trick to dirty talking? It's to say everything with confidence. You don't give the other person enough time or space to stop and think and feel awkward about what they're hearing." His hand inched higher. "Like right now, I want nothing more than to untie one side of that tiny bikini and touch that pretty pussy of yours, spreading you where only I can see you. I'd tease you, sugar, dragging you closer and closer to orgasm. And them?" He jerked his chin at the rest of their party. "They wouldn't have a fucking clue."

Her body felt too hot and too cold, all at the same time. She shifted, pressing her legs together, trapping his hand between them. *This is a lesson. He's not really going to do that…no matter how good of an idea it suddenly sounds like.* She could be student to his teacher without begging him to follow through on his example. Really, she could. "Oh." She took a breath and tried again. "I thought the whole point was that they knew what we were up to."

"Right now, we're focusing on the dirty talking. Now, your turn." His voice deepened. "What would you do to me, sugar?"

I can do this. It was too much to look at him, though, so she leaned back and closed her eyes, the words barely more than a whisper. "After you…make me come…" Her face felt like it was on fire. "It wouldn't be enough. I'd want to return the favor." He made an indecipherable sound, but she kept going because if she stopped now, she wasn't going to start up again. "I'd kiss you. I very much like kissing you, Adam." She licked her lips, almost able to taste him. "And while I was kissing you, I'd, ah, stroke you." *Maybe this isn't so bad.* His hand made rhythmic circles on her skin, relaxing her further. "I'd slip my hand into your shorts and touch you there." She could almost imagine doing exactly this, his hard length filling her hand. "I want to see you go wild and know it's because of me."

"Sugar—"

But she was on a roll. "I think I'd like to give you head."

The only warning she got was him standing and his grip tightening and then suddenly her world flipped upside down. Jules shrieked, her face barely an inch from the water, her ass in the air. "Adam!"

He didn't answer her as he dragged their tubes to the shore and looped the rope around a half-downed tree. He didn't stop there, though. Adam marched into the trees, not stopping until she could barely hear the faint sounds of their friends talking. Only then did he set her on her feet. She glared. "What the hell?"

"You wanted everyone to know what we're up to? Now's the time." He grabbed her hand and pressed it to the front of his swim trunks.

"That's not..." Her words failed her at the feel of him in her hand, hot and hard through the wet fabric. It felt better than she'd imagined. *Take your hand away. This is supposed to be pretend. Take it away right this second.* But she didn't. Instead, she stroked him lightly. "What are we doing?"

His eyes had gone dark again, turning almost black as he backed her against a tree. "I don't know." And then his mouth was on hers.

She met him halfway, looping one arm around his neck, the other pinned between their bodies. This wasn't pretend. This wasn't even on the same planet as pretend. *This is a mistake.* But the thought was swept away on a tide of desire unlike any she'd ever experienced before. He untied her top and jerked the fabric down, baring her breasts. He kissed his way down to her chest, sucking on first one nipple and then the other, lashing their sensitive tips with his tongue. "Fuck, sugar, I knew I was in trouble the second I saw you in this goddamn excuse for a bikini. So fucking sexy." His hands were gripping her hips so tightly, it was as if he thought she'd float away if he let go. "And then you go and start talking filthy at me…I'm not a goddamn saint. You want a scandal? We're about to create one."

She tangled her fingers into his hair, holding him against her. "If this is what being scandalized feels like, I've been missing out."

"Damn straight." He chuckled against her skin. "I'm going to undo your bottoms right now, sugar. The same rules from the other night apply."

As if she was going to do a single thing to keep him from making her come again. If he could nearly make the top of her head explode while they were both wearing all their clothes, how much better would it be with them naked?

She lifted her hips, a silent invitation he seemed only too happy to accept. Adam met her gaze as he pulled the string loose, letting the fabric slide down her other leg. And then she might as well have been naked. Before reason could reassert why this was a terrible idea, his hand was there between her thighs, a light touch that was more about exploring than domination. He watched her face the entire time as he pushed a single finger into her. The position was almost unbearably intimate, so she closed her eyes, concentrating on the sensations building.

"You like this, don't you, sugar? You like knowing that you drove me so fucking crazy that I carted you out here like a wild man. Every single one of them knows what I'm doing to you, and I don't fucking care. All I can think about is sinking into your wet heat and hearing you come for me again." He pumped his finger in and out of her, slowly, as if savoring every second of it. "I'm going to taste you here, sugar."

She barely had time to process that, and then he was on his knees, lifting her and spreading her thighs, pinning her between his mouth and the tree behind her. He kissed her center the same way he kissed her mouth—as if he owned every part of her. Maybe she'd be worried about that later. Right now all she could do was hang on and try to keep her cries from echoing through the trees around them.

CHAPTER NINE

Adam was totally and completely out of control, and he didn't give two fucks. He was consumed with driving Jules out of her goddamn mind. He should have known that things would end up this way the second he picked her up. He was so tired of fighting his attraction to her. She obviously wanted him as much as he wanted her.

It's just sex. We can stop anytime we want to.

He'd worry about the fallout later. Right now he had more important things on his mind—Jules's orgasm. He licked and teased and did his damnedest to drive her as crazy as she'd been driving him since he agreed to this devil's bargain. Her whimpers and whispered pleas were music to his ears, and he didn't stop, didn't slow down, didn't so much as change his pace until she gave a muffled cry and her entire body went tight. He gave her one last long lick and then gently set her back onto the ground. "That's how crazy you drive me, sugar."

She blinked down at him. "That's pretty crazy."

"Tell me about it." He climbed to his feet and set about putting her to rights, tying her bikini bottom back into place and reaching for the top.

Jules grabbed his hands. "Wait, what about you?"

"What about me?"

She gave his swim trunks a significant look. "This is the second time you've taken care of me and not gotten your own release."

He knew that. Hell, he could feel every beat of his heart in his cock, and it was as distracting as the fact she was standing here having this conversation with her breasts bared. "Now's not the time." He wasn't sure there ever *would* be a time when it was right, because he didn't trust himself to keep his head on straight, not if he was already reacting this way and he hadn't even been inside her.

"Bullshit."

He frowned at her. "I don't think I've ever heard you swear before."

"There's a time and place. This is both." She swung around, pushing him against the tree with more strength than he would have anticipated. "Now don't even try arguing with me, Adam." Her sunny grin made something in his chest lurch. "I'm about to have my wicked way with you."

"Jules—"

But it was too late. She was on her knees and working off his wet trunks with efficient motions.

You're full of shit. It's not too late. All you have to do is walk away to put a stop to this.

He didn't. He didn't so much as utter a word as she freed his cock, her hum of approval the sexiest thing he'd ever heard. She shot him a look from beneath her lashes. "Now, if you're still having second thoughts, just close your eyes and think of England."

"I'm good." He wanted every second of this memory etched in his brain. Adam laced his fingers through her long dark hair, pulling it away from her face so he could see everything.

"Suit yourself." She took his cock into her mouth, a slow, savoring motion, licking him like he was her favorite kind of ice cream. "Holy wow, Adam—you're packing some serious heat."

There was no appropriate response to that because she took him deeper this time, working him like she had all the time in the world. Watching his cock disappear between her lips did a number on him, the pleasure so intense it was an active fight to keep his eyes open and his body still.

There was no chance of holding his words in. "That's it, sugar. Take me deep. You're making me feel so fucking good I can barely stand it." That earned him a particularly hard suck, and he temporarily lost the ability to breathe. "*Shit.* You're so goddamn lucky I don't have a condom on me, or I'd be on you in half a second, spreading those sweet thighs and sinking into your wet heat. You want that, sugar, don't you?"

She made a sound of agreement, her eyes flashing open to pin him in place.

"Yeah, I thought so. But you deserve better than to be fucked out in the woods like we're horny teenagers. I'm going to take you in a bed, where I can have you in every position imaginable."

She let go of his cock with a wet sound. "Are you taking requests?"

How she could joke in this moment when it felt like he was going to burn to ash on the spot was anyone's guess. He tightened his grip on her hair, not guiding her, just letting her know how close he was to losing it. "I'll consider it."

"I want to be on top."

It was a good thing the tree was holding him up, or his knees would have given out. Adam could perfectly picture what it would be like, her tight little body riding him, her breasts bouncing with each stroke, her dark hair everywhere, her eyes giving him the exact same look she was giving him now—the one that said she was having the time of her life and loving every second of it. "I think we can make that happen."

"Perfect." And then she was back, sucking him deep, working him until he had to let go of her hair with one hand and reach above his head to cling to the nearest tree branch.

"Sugar, if you don't stop what you're doing, I'm going to lose it."

"Good." The word was full of feminine satisfaction. She cupped his balls with one hand, her fingers digging into his hip with the other.

And he was lost. Adam couldn't keep his eyes open, no matter how hard he tried. He came violently, pumping into her mouth with a curse, and she swallowed down every drop. They were silent for several minutes afterward, Jules resting her head on his thigh and him staring up into the treetops and wondering what the fuck he was going to do.

Once again, she recovered faster than he did. Jules patted his thigh. "That was most excellent. They definitely know we were up to no good, and if Kelli can keep it to herself, I'll eat my shoe." She hopped to her feet and fixed her top. "Do you need a minute?"

"Ah...no. I'm good." He'd have to be. Adam pulled his trunks back on, wincing at the feeling of wet fabric against his skin.

"Cool. We better get back. I'm sure by this point, Aubry's decided that we've been murdered by an alligator or a serial killer or something to do with banjos."

How the hell could she be so bouncy when it felt like his entire world had been rocked to the core? Irritation rose at how keen she was to have everyone know exactly what they were just doing, even though he knew he had no right to it. This was what she'd wanted to begin with—scandal.

Well, oral sex in the woods with a party fifty feet away is pretty fucking scandalous.

Sheer pride kept him moving as he followed her back to the river. He searched for something to say. "Your friend is an odd one."

"We all like what we like. Aubry just likes her space and her computer and weird B horror movies and theories about how the world is going to end in a zombie apocalypse."

"Noted." That sounded weird as fuck to him, but who was he to judge? There were plenty of people that thought climbing on the back of a pissed-off bull was a study in insanity, and he'd done it more times than he could count. The truth was he never felt more alive than that second before the gate snapped open and the animal burst into motion.

Except for maybe when he was with Jules.

Damn it.

He held her tube so she could hop into it and then pushed them both out into the swimming hole. He wasn't sure what else there was to say. He'd just lost his mind and dragged her into the woods like a crazy person, and then she'd given him the single most devastating blowjob of his life. It wasn't even the technique—though that had been beyond reproach. It was the fact she seemed to be having such *fun* while she was doing it. Sex had been a lot of things for him in the past—intense, distracting, toxic—but never fun. He wasn't sure what to do with fun.

They paddled around the bend and there was the rest of their party, standing and bullshitting on the minuscule beach. Aubry stood away from the rest of them, her hand shielding the sun from her eyes as she searched—obviously for them. "Jules!"

"Shit," Jules muttered. They barely got within reach of the beach when she jumped out of the tube with a splash. "I'm fine. I didn't get eaten."

Quinn crossed over to them and gave Adam a long look. "Are you sure about that?"

The choked sound Jules made had Aubry zeroing in on her. "Oh, we're going to have words, and soon."

"Great."

And then there came Grant, the pinched look around his mouth doing nothing to make Adam feel less like punching his face in. "Took you two long enough. We thought one of your tubes might have popped."

Jules's grin was bright enough to blind. "Nope. Nothing like that."

"I…see." Grant took her in with one long look and then turned the same expression on Adam. "You work fast, don't you?"

It didn't matter that Adam had been feeling kind of shitty about how things just played out. He wasn't about to have *this* asshole adding on the guilt. "None of your business."

"Oh, I think it is. I'm concerned for Jules."

The woman in question inserted herself between them, though Adam couldn't begin to say which of them she was planning on saving. "*Jules* is standing right here and can hear you both. Why don't we get moving? I'm working the second shift and I don't want to be late." She didn't give them a chance to argue, moving back to the tubes, Aubry on her heels. The redhead took Adam's tube, shooting him a sharp look over her shoulder. A look he fucking deserved.

Grant and his three chicks headed for the fire pit, leaving Adam and Quinn standing on the beach. Quinn crossed his arms over his chest. "Daniel's going to kill you."

"I don't know what you're talking about."

"You're not even bothering to lie well when you say that shit." He shook his head. "I'd get my story straight, and fast, because he's going to hear about this sooner rather than later. You know how this town works."

Yeah, he knew. Nothing stayed secret for long in Devil's Falls—which had been exactly the point. But if Adam had half a brain in his head, he'd track Jules down tonight and explain nicely to her he couldn't do this anymore and that he was sorry for taking advantage of her in her obviously unstable emotional state.

That was the problem, though.

He wasn't sorry, and he didn't want to stop.

CHAPTER TEN

"I thought Adam was your *fake* boyfriend."

Jules had known this was coming the second she got out of Adam's truck. Frankly, she was surprised Aubry had waited until they were alone to pounce. She moved around the now-closed café, wiping down tables. Her cousin Jamie had already closed the till and taken off for some hot date, so it was just Jules and Aubry and the cats left. "We are."

"So you were having *fake* sex out in nature like horndog apes?"

She rolled her eyes. "We didn't have sex." Because *he* put on the brakes. She'd been so out of her mind with pleasure, she wasn't sure she would have been smart enough to call the whole thing off just because there wasn't a condom handy. And *that* was downright unforgivable. She wanted to be scandalous—not stupid. And having unprotected sex with a fake boyfriend, no matter how safe Adam made her feel, was stupid beyond belief.

"But you *wanted* to have sex."

Yes. She did. A lot. More than a lot. Jules scrubbed at a coffee stain in the center of one table, pausing to nudge Ninja Kitteh out of the way when the striped cat came to snoop. "We're two consenting adults. I don't see how it matters."

"Totally not my point." Aubry double-checked the lock on the front door and headed for her table.

"Then, pray tell, what *is* your point?"

Her friend frowned. "I'm not judging—not really. That's not what we do. I just don't want to see you get hurt because your heart gets involved. That guy might be cool as hell—and he is—but he's spent a grand total of like a month in Devil's Falls in the last however many years. A guy like that doesn't have roots, and your roots are deeper than deep. You're not leaving this place and he's not staying."

"Don't project your relationship issues on me." As soon as the words were out of her mouth, she regretted them. "Oh my God, I'm a horrible friend for saying that. I'm sorry. I'm just so on edge with Grant and Adam and...there's no excuse. Forgive me?"

"Always." Aubry zipped the laptop case closed. "And you're right. I'm even more of a hot mess than you are when it comes to men. I'm just a Ford tough mama bear who's feeling protective. If he breaks your heart, I'm liable to set his truck on fire."

The scary part was that Jules wasn't exactly sure if her friend was joking or not. It was a step of crazy that Aubry would never take for herself—if she had, then her asshole ex would definitely have seen the results— but for Jules...yeah, she'd do that and worse. She walked over and hugged her friend. "I love you."

"I know. I love you, too. Just...be careful."

"I will. I promise." Even as she said the words, she knew they weren't the full truth. When it came to Adam, she was on a roller coaster and the safety brakes were gone. There was only one possible outcome, but she couldn't bring herself to care. It would be one heck of a ride before she crashed and burned.

"No, you won't, but that's okay." Aubry stepped

back. "Do you have a hot date tonight, too, or can we *please* shoot some people? I have so much pent-up aggression after spending the afternoon trapped on that horrid body of water with the biggest asshat in town."

Jules laughed. "Grant's bad, but I don't know that he's *that* bad."

"One, yes, he is. Two, I wasn't talking about him."

Jules turned off the main lights in the café, leaving the one over the counter on. Even though she knew the cats didn't care, she didn't like leaving them in complete darkness. She checked the lock on the front door one last time and then followed Aubry through the kitchen and up the back stairs to their apartment. "Quinn isn't a bad guy. I think he's funny."

"Funny for a performing bear."

There was no arguing with her friend when she got like this. When it came to new people, Aubry was judge, jury, and executioner—nine times out of ten, she hated them on sight. Apparently she'd already passed judgment on Adam and Daniel's friend. To be fair, he seemed to really like getting a rise out of her. "If you say so."

"This is why we get along so well. You don't expect me to like people."

She unlocked the door at the top of the stairs and held it open. "You like me."

"You aren't *people*. You're *my* people. Totally different thing." Aubry dropped her laptop on the tiny dining room table and plopped down on the overstuffed couch taking up the majority of the equally tiny living room. "Let's do this."

"I don't suppose you want something like food

before we start?"

"Food is for the weak."

Jules laughed. She should have known that would be the answer. "All the same, I'm going to order pizza. There's nothing in the fridge."

"I wish this place had more options for delivery. Little Johnny Jacob has started giving me judgmental looks when he brings me food."

"That's because you prefer to just order pizza instead of going down the street to one of our restaurants and interacting with real-life people."

Aubry turned on the Xbox and propped her feet on the table. "I believe we just covered this—people are not my favorite."

"Noted." Jules picked up her phone and froze when there was a knock on her door. "Okay, I know Johnny Jacob is good, but no one is *that* good." She walked over and opened the door and then stared. "What are you doing here?"

Adam stood on the top stair, looking all sorts of delicious with his worn jeans and black T-shirt. He held up hands laden with beer and a pizza box sending out the most amazing smells. "I brought pizza and beer."

"Let him in," Aubry yelled from behind her. "I'm liable to waste away from starvation if I don't eat soon. They'll find me on the couch, and there will be whispers of, 'If only Jules had let her fake boyfriend inside in time. Such a tragedy.'"

"I thought you said food was for the weak." She stepped back, holding the door open for Adam. "You're an awful drama queen—and inconsistent to boot."

"Noted," Aubry sang a second before the sound of video game gunshots filled the room.

Jules led Adam over to the small kitchen and grabbed three of the bright plastic plates that made her mother cringe every time she saw them. She opened the pizza box and put two slices on each plate while Adam popped the tops off three beers. They deposited the food and beer in front of Aubry, but she shook her head. "You two need to talk. Git."

"Did you just say 'git'?" There went Adam's eyebrow.

"Don't you, like, ride bulls or something? You're a cowboy. I'm speaking your language." She tore her gaze away from the screen for half a second. "Seriously, though—what kind of death wish do you have that you'd climb onto the back of a pissed-off bull? Did your daddy not tell you he loves you enough?"

Jules saw the tightening in Adam's jaw and the way his shoulders braced ever so slightly. She shifted her grip on the plates and touched his arm. "Let's go into my room." When he turned toward her door, she shot a glare at Aubry and hissed, "Stop being rude." Jules didn't give her friend time to respond before she nudged Adam fully into her room and shut the door.

Looking around, she realized this was the dumbest plan ever. They had to step over her dirty clothes pile to get to the bed, which was covered in her *clean* clothes pile. *Probably should have found time to fold laundry in the last week.* She couldn't let him sit there while she scrambled to put away her clothes and unmentionables. It didn't matter if he'd had his mouth on the same parts of her that those unmentionables covered. It was just *weird*.

She skirted the edge of the bed and moved to the window. "Sorry about the mess."

"It's fine." But he was looking at everything like he was committing it to memory. With her luck, that was exactly what he was doing. She set the plates down long enough to muscle open the window. *That* got Adam's attention. "What are you doing?"

"Come on." She slipped out the window and reached back in to grab the plates. A few seconds later, Adam joined her on the roof. "I like to come out here and think sometimes."

He peered over the edge to where they could see the majority of the main street. "And spy on the poor people of Devil's Falls. No wonder there's so much gossip."

She started to argue but then laughed. "Maybe a little spying. People stumble out from the bar"—that didn't actually have a name beyond "the bar"—"and they forget that sound travels." Jules took a sip of her beer. "Plus, no one ever sees me up here."

"Fair enough." He went after his pizza with the single-minded focus of someone who didn't know when their next meal would be—or who wanted to avoid conversation.

The problem was that avoiding conversations wasn't something Jules was particularly good at. She would rather burst through the awkwardness like the Kool-Aid Man came through the wall—all at once, just to get it over with. It wasn't subtle, but subtlety wasn't really in her skill set. "So, I don't know what to think of what happened earlier."

He chewed his bite and swallowed, not looking at

her. "You mean when you came against my mouth and then sucked me off."

Her body flushed hot. *Guess he's not great at being subtle, either.* "Yeah, that." He didn't immediately jump in with something reassuring, so she just kept talking. "It was good. It was really, really good. I just, ah—"

"I'm not staying."

The words came out so harshly she had to take a moment to fight back her instinctive response. Finally, she said, "I never asked you to."

"Right." He set the plate down and stretched out his legs. "So, now that we've gotten that out of the way—"

Is he serious? "Adam, we have to talk about this. I mean, obviously we're not dating for real, and I don't exactly go hook up with almost strangers on the fly under normal circumstances. I just…" God, she didn't even know what she was trying to say.

"Sugar, breathe." He took her hand, the contact steadying her. "It's okay. We don't have to go there. I lost control. I'll make sure it doesn't happen again."

That was *not* what she wanted. Jules bit her lip, searching his face. In the fading light of the day, his eyes were too dark as he stared at her mouth. He wanted her. He wouldn't have lost control in the first place if he didn't. So why was he trying to give her an out?

For such a supposed bad boy, he's sure got a lot of honor.

The realization struck a chord in her chest. She finished off her beer and set it carefully aside. "I don't want you to have control." Before he could do anything but frown at her, she crawled over and straddled him. "Look, I know this isn't real. I obviously have no experience in this sort of thing or I wouldn't need to scandalize the town in the first place." She took his hands and set them on her hips. "Why don't we just enjoy ourselves while you're helping me out?"

His lips twitched, but his grip tightened on her hips a little. "Sugar, we don't have to do this. We can keep the gossip mill churning without taking things beyond where we went earlier."

Yeah, there really is *an honorable man in there.* "I know, but I want to." She could feel him growing hard between her thighs, and she settled against him with a little sigh. Jules leaned forward until her breasts were pressed against his chest. She felt a little silly trying to proposition him, but he wasn't tossing her on her butt, so she must not be doing too badly. She held her breath and kissed the spot on his neck right below his jaw. "Adam, I would very much like to have sex with you."

CHAPTER ELEVEN

Adam could hardly believe this shit was happening. If he was a better man, he'd set her aside and explain why this would only end in tears for her. Jules wasn't the type of woman to be able to get to a certain level of physical intimacy without her heart becoming involved. He liked her. He didn't want to hurt her.

But he wasn't a better man.

She's a grown-ass woman. She knows her own mind.

It was an excuse and a weak one at that. He didn't care. For all his words, he didn't want to stop this any more than she did. But he still held back. He wrapped his fist in her hair, using the leverage to guide her back so she had to meet his gaze. "You're sure about this?"

"I wouldn't say it if I wasn't."

He didn't quite believe her, but he allowed himself to be persuaded. "Come here, sugar." He wrapped an arm around her waist and scooted them away from the edge of the roof until his back hit the side of the house. From here, no one on the street below could see them.

Scandal be damned, I'm not about giving them a peep show.

He coasted his hands up her sides, lifting her shirt as he did. He checked her expression when he hit the same level as her breasts, but there was nothing but eagerness there. So he pulled her shirt over her head and dropped it next to them.

She gave a little cry when he took off her bra, at once eager and needy, and that nearly undid him on the spot. He knew this wasn't supposed to be real. Except it sure as hell *felt* real when he helped her wiggle out of her jeans and resume her position straddling him.

It felt all too real. He ran his hand down the center of her body, between her breasts, over her stomach, to cup her pussy. Adam groaned when he found her hot and wet. "You drive me to distraction."

"Sorry."

"Don't be." This being a distraction was supposed to be the point. He pumped first one finger and then two into her. "I enjoy the hell out of it. Wear a dress next time we go out, sugar, and I'll do this to you while I drive us around."

Her eyes had drifted half shut, her hands gripping his shoulders. "I think that qualifies as distracted driving."

"Nah, I'll take care of you." He shifted his movements, exploring until he found the exact motion that made her body jerk taut. "Like that."

"Oh God." Her hips rolled, trying to take him deeper, but he'd found the sweet spot and he wasn't about to let go of her until he was ready. "I've been thinking about licking that sweet little pussy of yours against that tree."

"Adam!"

He grinned, amazed that she could sound so shocked while obviously enjoying their current circumstances. "Lesson two in dirty talking—learn to say 'pussy' and 'cock.'"

"C-c—" She made a face. "Cock. See! I can say it."

Hearing the word on her lips was like she'd reached down and squeezed that part of him. He kept finger fucking her, fighting to get the words out through clenched teeth. "Unzip me, sugar. I want to feel you stroking me when you say it again."

Her eyes went wide, but she obeyed, carefully unzipping his jeans and sliding them down far enough to free him. Her first stroke was almost tentative, but he kept her too distracted with what he was doing between her legs to be self-conscious. "Say it again."

"Cock." This time there was no hesitation or stuttering.

"Mmm. And whose cock are you stroking right now?"

"Y-yours."

He pulled her closer, the move dislodging both their hands, and guided his cock between her legs, the position too tight for him to enter her. He lined them up so he rubbed against her clit and grabbed a hold of her hips, rocking her against him.

Watching the pleasure on her face was almost reward enough. Almost. "Tell me what you want, sugar. Explicitly."

She bit her lip. "I want you—your cock—inside me."

He had to hold still for a second to fight back the need to give her exactly that right that second. "And how do you want it?"

"I...don't know."

It struck him that it might be the fucking truth. How in God's name had a hot little thing like Jules Rodriguez made it to twenty-six without knowing what she liked? He kept moving her against him, driving them both crazy. "You have one of those buzzy toys?"

It was hard to tell in the shadows, but she looked like she might be blushing furiously. "I have several."

At least she wasn't shy about meeting her needs while solo. He kissed her neck. "And how do you like using them?"

"I…" Her breath hitched. "God, that feels good."

"I'm not going to stop. Answer the question."

She shivered. "I tease myself. Until I can barely stand it. Then I…"

He gently bit her earlobe. "Keep going."

"Then I stroke myself as hard as I can."

Adam groaned. He could perfectly picture her like that, naked in her bed alone, stroking herself with some toy until she came apart. "I'm going to make it good for you, sugar."

"Then *hurry*."

He dug into his pocket for the condom he'd thought he was an idiot for bringing tonight. It was a study in frustration to let her go long enough to rip open the wrapper and roll it on, but he managed.

She started to sink onto him, but he stopped her. "Last chance."

"And for the last time, I want this. I want *you*."

He knew she only meant it in this moment, but it still struck a chord deep inside him. When had he last felt wanted by a woman—him as a man, not as a conduit of pleasure? Had he ever? He let go of her, and she sank onto his cock, inch by inch, until they were sealed as closely as two people could be. "Fuck, sugar, you feel so good. Better than I could have dreamed."

"Yes." She lifted up and slammed back onto him, but their position made it difficult to get a good momentum going.

He rolled them, laying her down on her clothes, and thrust into her. "You want it hard?"

"*Yes.*" The word was barely more than a moan on her lips. "Like that."

He fucked her with everything he had in him, slamming into her until he had to muffle her cries with his hand. She consumed him, her summer scent wrapping around him, her muffled cries in his ear, the taste of her on his tongue. He couldn't get enough, couldn't stop, couldn't slow down. He needed her orgasm more than he needed his next breath.

"Adam, oh my God, Adam, don't stop." Her nails dug into his ass, urging him on. As if he was in any danger of stopping.

"I won't, sugar." He kissed her again, holding her as tightly as he could, until her entire body went tight and she came, her pussy milking him and dragging him over the edge. Desire consumed him, leaving nothing but ashes in its wake.

• • •

Jules was pretty sure she heard baby angels singing and that the heavens opened up to shine on her.

Or maybe that had just been a truly outstanding orgasm.

She lifted her head and looked at Adam, who seemed just as floored as she felt. Maybe that was wishful thinking on her part, but he kissed her before she could overthink things too much. "How are you doing?"

"Well and truly satisfied."

His grin made things low in her stomach clench, which made his jaw go tight, which made her hot all over again. Adam stroked a hand up her side, idly cupping her breast and circling her nipple. "You have anywhere to be in the next hour?"

Hour? She shifted. The fact they were having this conversation while he was still inside her wasn't in her realm of social niceties. "Uh, no?"

"Perfect." He kissed her again, his tongue sliding along hers. "Because I'm nowhere near done with you."

Sweet baby Jesus. She just stared as he got to his knees and pulled his pants back up. "You're not?"

"Sugar, I know it might be shocking, but I'd like to have sex with you while we're both naked and have full range of motion." His grin made her toes curl. "Not that I'm even remotely complaining about how things just went down."

She should have known that letting go of her previous expectations was important when it came to this man, but obviously she hadn't managed it, because he kept surprising her. "Okay." She licked her lips and peered down at the street below them. "Do you think someone heard us?"

"Sugar, focus." He pulled her to her feet, and she didn't miss the fact that he stood between her and the edge of the roof, blocking the sight of anyone who bothered to look up. She almost pointed out that someone catching a glimpse of her up here with him in an obvious state of undress would surely get tongues wagging, but the look on his face stopped her.

Stop overthinking. Just enjoy this. You got an orgasm for the record books.

And he wants an hour to do it again.

She stifled a giggle and ducked back into her room, pausing long enough to make sure she could still hear the gunshot sounds and music from Aubry's game. Satisfied that her friend wasn't going to come barging in to save her or something, she turned to face Adam. "You want me focused? I'm focused."

"Perfect." He scooped her up and dropped her on the bed, scattering her laundry and surprising a laugh out of her.

She propped herself up on her elbows and watched him strip. His eyebrows rose. "When you look at me like that, I feel like a piece of meat."

"Not just any meat—grade-A prime rib."

If anything, his eyebrows rose higher. "You're something else."

"Something awesome." It had to be the orgasm going to her head, because she felt positively punch-drunk. "Now get over here and lay one on me."

He crawled onto the bed, his muscles flexing beneath golden skin. "Oh, sugar, I'm about to lay something on you all right."

She barely waited for him to kiss her before she pushed on his shoulders. "Wait, wait, wait. You promised I'd get to be on top. It's most definitely my turn now."

"I'm not going to argue with that." He flopped onto his back, pulling her with him so that she sprawled over his chest. Adam's eyebrow cocked up, a grin pulling at the edges of his lips. "Well, you have me at your mercy. What are you going to do with me?"

Everything. With all his skin laid out for her enjoyment, she didn't know where to start. She sat up so she could see more of him and trailed her hands down his chest, watching the way his muscles jumped beneath her touch. He had the body of a man who *worked*, his muscles clearly defined without being over-the-top. "I'm going to have some fun." More fun than should be legal.

Adam's gaze traveled over her breasts, making her nipples pebble and her skin tingle. "You have a very limited time before I toss you down and have my way with you."

"I thought I was in charge here."

He rested his hands on her sides, his thumb tracing her hipbones. "You're enough to tempt a saint to sin, sugar. And I'm nowhere near a saint." He stroked up her sides to cup her breasts. "Though I like the view too much to stop—you're right on that note. The sight of you sliding up and down my cock... Yeah, I'm willing to take a backseat for that."

Funny, but it didn't feel like he was in the backseat while coaxing little shivers from her body by kneading her breasts. Jules arched her back, pressing herself more fully into his palms. "Don't stop."

"I won't." But he paused. "I don't suppose you have condoms in this place?"

Her cheeks heated, but she wasted no time scrambling for the top drawer of her nightstand. When she got there, though, she paused. For all her optimism of getting laid sometime this decade, she hadn't even bothered to take the cellophane off the box. Jules shot Adam a look, but there was no way she could unwrap it without him hearing and/or seeing.

But the alternative was to not have sex with Adam again, so...

Jules decided right then and there that she could afford a little dose of humiliation with *that* carrot dangling in front of her.

She ripped into the wrapper, tearing it off like a kid with a Christmas present. "I am only 75 percent prepared. Don't judge me. They didn't cover this in Girl Scouts."

His laugh rolled through the room, foreplay all on its own. "Never a dull moment."

"Wouldn't dream of it." She finally freed the box and yanked out a condom. Or, rather, she yanked out a string of a dozen condoms. Jules held it up, feeling sheepish. "How are we looking for an hour's worth of time?"

Just like that, the amusement was gone from Adam's face, replaced by desire. "Why don't you get that sweet ass of yours over here and find out?"

Lord, but she was more than happy to do exactly that.

CHAPTER TWELVE

"You're going out with the Rodriguez girl again, aren't you?"

Adam paused in the middle of shoving a bottle of wine into a backpack. There was absolutely no reason to feel guilty. Jules knew this was temporary. Hell, if anyone should feel hurt, it was him, because it seemed like every time he turned around, she was going on about making a scene and creating a scandal. *That* was her focus, not falling head over heels for him. But none of that stopped the slow turn of his stomach when he straightened to face his mama. "Yeah."

She searched his face, her brown eyes somehow seeming faded, like a part of her had already given up. "Good."

He blinked. "What?"

"You've got two ears in your head, son. You heard me just fine." She turned around and wobbled to the recliner. "Jules is a good girl."

He followed, still half sure he'd heard her wrong. "Which is exactly the reason you told me to stay the hell away from her before this point."

"Maybe things have changed."

"Nothing's changed." He helped her sit down. There had been another doctor's appointment this morning, and, like all the others, she wouldn't let him come with her. He tried really hard not to resent his mama's decision, but it was a chicken bone stuck in his throat. It wasn't like he didn't know exactly how bad things were. Hearing it from the doctor firsthand wouldn't change anything.

Except maybe it would. Maybe it would make everything a whole hell of a lot more real. Maybe I'd lose my shit.

Or maybe there'd be some avenue to pursue that my mama refuses to try.

He looked at the backpack he'd been stuffing with things for his date with Jules, suddenly feeling like the lowest piece of shit in existence. "I don't have to go."

"Adam—"

"You're right. I shouldn't. I'll go get us some dinner and we'll watch that chick flick you've been tittering about with Lenora—the one with that guy who writes letters to his girlfriend while he's away at war." It sounded boring as hell, but it wasn't about what he wanted.

Her hand on his arm stopped him, her grip surprisingly strong. "No."

"But, Mama—"

"*No.*" She shook her head. "I love you, my boy, but you can't stop living just because I'm sick. You're here for me and that's all that matters. Go take your girl out, show her a good time, get into a little trouble. *Live.*"

He looked down at her, recognizing the stubborn set of her mouth. It was the same one he saw in the mirror when he'd made a decision he wouldn't be swayed from. She wanted him out of the house tonight and going to spend time with Jules. He might not get her reasons, but he wasn't going to be able to change her mind. "If you're sure."

"I am. Lenora is coming over. We want to cuddle

and critique the movie alone." Her expression softened into a small smile. "It would be a dreadfully boring night for you."

"Time spent with you is anything but boring."

Her eyes shone a little. "Baby, you're the best son a woman could ask for."

"Yeah, well, I had the best mama a boy could dream of." And if he didn't get the fuck out of here, the barbed ball of emotion in his chest might actually break free. He'd done a damn good job of keeping it locked down since he found out she was sick, and he had no intention of letting it out anytime soon. He covered her hand with his and squeezed. "You call me if you need anything."

"I will."

There was nothing left to do but leave. Adam zipped up the backpack and walked out the front door without looking back. He'd learned a long time ago that a final glance over his shoulder was a great way to have regrets dogging his heels every step of the way.

• • •

Jules was finishing up her shift when Adam pulled up to the curb. There was something really sexy about that man in an obviously well-loved truck that had seen him through the years. Had it been the only thing he'd kept with him all that time? Her heart gave a funny lurch at the thought, and she turned back to lock the front door to cover the reaction.

It's just because we had sex. I've always been awful at keeping emotions out of it...probably because I never thought to try.

"Looks like your boyfriend is here!" Jamie sang from her place by the register. She grinned from ear to ear when Jules shushed her. "What? This is the most exciting thing to happen to you in your entire life. I know everyone loves Grant, but you traded up, girl!"

She shushed her cousin again, trying to ignore the buoyancy Jamie's words brought and turned back to find Adam within reachable distance. Jules tugged at the bottom of her sundress, not sure what to do with her hands. Was she supposed to kiss him? Wave? A freaking handshake?

Adam took the decision away from her, hooking the small of her back and pulling her against him. "Hey."

"Hey." She frowned. "Are you okay? You look like you haven't been sleeping." She'd been having a hell of a time getting shut-eye, but that was all self-induced. Every time she closed her eyes, she was assaulted with memories of their time together. Her trusty friend B.O.B. had been getting a solid workout as a result.

But Adam didn't look like he'd spent far too much time wanking it. He looked…haunted.

His mouth tightened. "I thought we covered the fact that I hate that question."

They had. But a silly part of her thought that maybe things would have changed because of last night. She forced a smile. "My mistake." It hurt, though. It didn't matter that she had no right to the emotion—it still burrowed deep, twining through her and squeezing hard enough that she could barely draw a breath for one eternal second. "So what's on the agenda tonight?"

He held up a backpack. "Moonlight picnic."

Jules blinked. "That sounds…" Romantic. Which it most certainly couldn't be, because he'd been very clear about what this thing was. The hurt still lingering from him shutting her down had her mouth getting away from her, "Explain to me how that's going to get Grant off my back?"

"Sugar, it's going to be a good time."

That wasn't an answer. And she had no doubt it *would* be a good time—too good a time. They'd had sex a grand total of twenty-four hours ago, and she was already having trouble keeping her emotions inside that cute little boundary fence she'd constructed. No, the very last thing Jules needed was a romantic picnic with Adam. She straightened her shoulders and started down the street. "Okay, then." She headed to the door. "Call me if you need anything, Jamie."

"I won't!"

She pushed out into the early summer heat, driven by the messy emotions turning her insides into a maze of confusion.

"Where are you going?"

She didn't know, but her gaze landed on the bar and inspiration struck. "I'm going to go take some shots."

"What?" He caught up with her, matching her pace. "What's gotten into you?"

Just that you're sending mixed messages like whoa, and I can't deal with it. I also can't tell you that you're sending mixed messages, because you flat-out told me that this couldn't be anything, and I'm an idiot for looking too much into a theoretical moonlit picnic because it's all about the plan.

But she couldn't say that aloud. It sounded crazy in

her head, and giving it voice would just confirm that she was a basket case. "I'm giving people something to talk about. If you want to go on a romantic picnic afterward, fine." She crossed the street and pushed through the front door.

Jules didn't spend much time in the bar because Aubry was kind of a shut-in and preferred to drink in her comfort zone. Plus...why would she walk down the street and pay double for alcohol she could just buy at the store? Especially when the bar's wine selection left something to be desired.

She eyed the scattering of people. There were Kelli and Kelly over by the jukebox, dancing all slow and sexy with each other. *Maybe I was wrong and they* like *like each other.* But then they shifted and Jules nearly cursed. Grant. Because *of course* Grant would be there. As she was trying to figure out the best course of action, he lifted his head and met her gaze.

Crap. There was nothing for it. If she turned around and bolted, he'd know he was the reason. She felt Adam's presence at her back, as comforting as it was aggravating. *When in doubt, rush ahead as quickly as possible.* Good, sound advice that had gotten her into more awkward situations than she cared to count.

She looked around the room a second time, searching for salvation. A group of old-timers huddled around the bar, and she recognized her uncle Rodger, Daniel's dad. *Perfect.* "Uncle Rodger!" Jules sailed over and gave him a hug. He was a giant bear of a man who, with his long hair, craggy face, and beard, would look at home in some illicit motorcycle club. And he made the best cupcakes this side of the Mississippi. "What are you doing here?"

"Poker night." He lifted her off her feet and squeezed. "You've lost weight, Julie Q."

"Guess you better make me a dozen of those red velvet cupcakes. Better yet, make it two dozen."

He gave a great laugh. "I'll do that." The smile fell away from his face as he set her down and looked over her shoulder. "I heard a rumor you were dating that Meyer boy, but I didn't believe it. Tell your uncle Rodger it isn't so."

The only way they could get Grant to believe it was to get the entire town to believe it. Jules didn't like lying to her family, but it was only a tiny, white lie. "What can I say? He's swept me off my feet."

"I bet." One of the men behind Rodger snickered, but the sound died quickly when her uncle leveled a glare over his shoulder.

He sighed. "I suppose you're too old to have me threatening him with my shotgun? Your daddy and I were dying to do that song and dance back when you were in high school, but that Thomas boy didn't seem like that much of a threat." His brows slanted down over his eyes. "But then he went and broke your heart."

Jules had never wanted lightning to strike her on the spot so badly as she did in that moment. "That's so great that you're going to trot out my past humiliations for everyone's amusement, but that's ancient history— and no, you don't get to play big badass uncle and try to scare Adam away. I like him." *Possibly too much.*

"That's what I'm afraid of. You know it's my job to look out for you while your parents are off living the big-city life."

"They only moved six hours away, and we see them

once a month."

"Too far, if you ask me."

If they'd asked her, it was, too, but it hadn't been her decision. She missed her parents like whoa, but her mom always entertained her with stories about new restaurants they were trying and how she'd talked her dad into taking a salsa class, and Jules couldn't help but be happy for them. They were happy.

Adam's arm settled around her waist, and her entire body sparked to life. God, she was in so much trouble. This close, she got a whiff of his spicy cologne, and it smelled like something a cowboy in a commercial would wear—manly and rough and…what the heck was she thinking?

Jules started to move away, but he tightened his hold on her. "Rodger."

"Adam." Her uncle eyed the arm around her waist, almost like he was considering whether to make an issue of it or not. Apparently he decided Jules was a grown woman and could make her own decisions—or, more likely, he was going to go straight to the nearest phone to tattle on her to her parents. "Y'all have a good night."

"We will." She grinned so hard that her cheeks hurt. "And on that note…shots!"

"Sugar—"

She ignored Adam and slipped out of his hold. The bartender winked at her. "Hey, darlin'. I haven't seen much of you these days."

It took Jules a whole second to place him. "Stuart! I thought you up and moved to San Antonio."

"I did." He grinned, his teeth bright against his dark skin. "I went, I saw, now I'm back. Devil's Falls is a siren call that I couldn't ignore." He gave her a long, slow look. "You're looking good."

"She's also looking taken."

Jules rolled her eyes. "Stuart, this is Adam. We're dating." *Sort of.* "Adam, this is Stuart. We went to high school together."

"Holy shit. I heard you were taking a walk on the wild side, but seeing is believing." He leaned across the bar and lowered his voice until she could barely hear him. "I have to say, I thought for sure you were going to marry Grant and pop out a couple kids."

Yeah, she knew. That's what everyone had thought after graduation, and probably again now that he was back in town.

Not. Interested.

This was exactly why she'd come up with this insane plan to begin with. The only problem was that she had a feeling proving them all wrong was going to come back to bite her in her butt, because Adam was a wildfire that would burn her up if she wasn't careful.

And a tiny part of her wanted to douse herself in gasoline and welcome the flames.

CHAPTER THIRTEEN

Adam wasn't sure when the night had taken a turn for the what-the-fuck, but Jules seemed determined to throw herself into getting shit-housed drunk to be *scandalous*. She was three shots down and weaving on her feet. He recognized that look in her eye, though. There would be no backing down, and if he tried to derail her, it would backfire.

Whoever put it into the woman's head that she was on the shelf was a goddamn fool.

"How about—"

"You're right. Stuart, another purple nurple!"

Stuart shot him a wide-eyed look but started pouring Jules another of the sickeningly sweet shots. Adam wasn't sure why she couldn't just shoot whiskey. It was a classic. He leaned against the bar. It was time to distract her before he had to carry her out of here over his shoulder. "So you're planning on showing Grant up by, what, getting blackout drunk and passing out facedown in a pile of your own puke?"

"Ew, gross. No." She made a face and then had to catch herself on the bar when she swayed too much to one side. "Don't be silly. I'm stunning him with my amazing drinking abilities."

"Amazing is one way to put it." At least her uncle had left ten minutes ago. The man had been staring at him intently enough that Adam was half sure he'd walk out the door and find Rodger and his friends waiting for him. "Why don't we head back to your place?"

She shook her head. Well, she shook her entire body. "Not yet. I want to play darts. Or maybe start a bar fight. That's a thing people do in bars, isn't it?" She frowned. "I don't get out much, and Aubry is the one who starts fights, so I never get to drink too much and let go. Let's let go tonight!"

A fight was not on the books, and letting her drunk ass anywhere near pointy objects was the worst idea he'd ever heard. Adam looked around the bar, searching for inspiration. He'd never realized how many potential weapons there were just sitting around until he had a drunk good girl wanting to get into some trouble. "Bar fights are overrated."

"*God.*" She grabbed the shot Stuart set on the bar and downed it before Adam could blink. "Of course you've been in a bar fight. I bet you've been in a ton."

More than he cared to remember, all for reasons he *couldn't* remember. He didn't drink much these days, but in his early twenties, he'd been angry and felt like he had something to prove. Trouble had been his middle name, and he'd gone looking for it every chance he had.

Hell, that was why he'd started riding bulls to begin with. That moment before the gates slammed open, he wasn't thinking about how tight his skin got when he stayed in one place too long or the sad look in his mama's eyes when she realized he was itching to leave Devil's Falls again. There was just Adam and the bull and the next few seconds of freedom and adrenaline.

When had his life gotten so empty?

He worked to keep the smile on his face. "It's overrated."

"I wouldn't know." Her expression was so woeful,

he almost laughed. She instantly brightened. "I love this song!"

He hadn't even been aware of the song changing, and then she was off, shooting around him and veering to the dance floor where she started... He stared. Only someone being really, *really* nice would call that dancing. She looked like a marionette whose strings were cut, all jarring motions and jerking limbs.

It might have been the cutest thing he'd ever seen. Awkward. Horribly awkward. But cute.

Adam sighed. "I need a beer."

Almost instantly, one appeared at his elbow. Stuart didn't immediately move away. "She's a good girl."

"So I keep hearing." Along with the part no one but his mama seemed to be able to say. He *wasn't* good. Oh, he wasn't bad. But he wasn't anywhere near Jules's level. She practically shone with goodness. Hell, she owned a business whose sole purpose was to make people happy—and she'd managed to rescue half a dozen cats in the process. She was so sweet, it should make his teeth ache.

But then he thought about her sunny smile that only seemed to appear when he was inside her.

Adam's body kicked into high gear, and it was everything he could do to keep his reaction from physically manifesting. He turned away from the bar, beer in hand, to find Grant on the edge of the dance floor. Whatever the man said had Jules's back going straight and her shoulders going back in a stance he recognized. *Shit.*

He strode across the bar, arriving at her side in time to hear Grant say, "Jesus, Jules, it was a joke. Obviously I wasn't being serious."

There were tears shining in her eyes, and the sight of them snapped something inside Adam. He moved between her and her ex. "You know what, I'm getting really tired of your brand of shit."

Grant took a step back before he seemed to catch himself. "It's not my fault Jules is drunk and took it wrong."

"You offered to *let* me give you a BJ in the bathroom!"

Just like that, any good intentions Adam had went up in smoke—and there hadn't been many to begin with. "You think you're a big-time operator because you played ball, then went off to a fancy school and got yourself a law degree. Guess what? You're still back in Devil's Falls, the same as everyone in this bar. You're no better than anyone else. In fact, you're a whole hell of a lot worse."

"And what have *you* done? Thirty-three and a washed-up bull rider." Grant sneered. "I'm sure there's an opening at the Gas 'N' Go for the night shift."

"Oh, no, you didn't!"

Adam made a grab for Jules, but she slipped through his hands like water. And then she was in Grant's face, poking him in the chest. "Damn you to hell and back, Grant Thomas. I know for a fact your mama raised you not to talk to your betters like that."

He shook his head. "If you're not going to put that mouth to good use, then go home, Jules. You're making a spectacle of yourself." And then he was gone, walking out of the bar like he hadn't a care in the world.

Adam started after him but stopped, his need to make sure Jules didn't take a nosedive superseding his desire to beat that jackass's face in. He turned to find her pointing at the two blondes seated at the table Grant had occupied before all this got started. "You can't seriously think that's sexy."

The one on the right shrugged. "He's hot."

"He's an idiot." The other one laughed. "But he buys us all the alcohol we can drink."

"Good lord, that's a low bar to set." Jules threw up her hands. "I don't even know why I bother."

The first one cocked her head to the side. "Because you're nice?"

"I need another shot."

Adam snagged her around the waist. "Hold your horses, sugar. You drink any more tonight and you're going to have to scrape yourself off the floor in the morning."

"Don't care."

"You might not right now, but you will when you wake up hugging a toilet." He hauled her to the bar and dug out the cash to pay for their tab. "We're getting out of here." Hopefully the fresh air would sober her up a little.

They hit the street, and he kept his arm around her in case the world decided to start spinning on her. Jules marched ahead, though, practically dragging him behind her, keeping up an ongoing rant about Grant. "I can't believe him. It's like he came back into town solely to rain on my parade. I *like* my life. I'm happy. I have a plan that I'm totally on track with. Why does he have to show up and make me feel like I'm failing?"

"Why do you care so much?" That's the thing that really bugged him. The town was one thing, but she *really* cared what Grant thought of her. The guy made a few dickhead comments and here she was, creating a fake relationship and doing all sorts of crazy shit to prove him wrong.

Was she holding a flame for the guy?

Adam's stomach turned at the thought. People didn't jump through the sheer number of hoops that Jules had unless there were lingering feelings. There was no damn good reason for the knowledge to burn him up inside, but he felt like he'd swallowed a dozen hot coals.

While he was aggravated as all get-out, she stopped and leaned back against his chest. "I don't want to go home."

He couldn't take her back to his mom's house, and he didn't have a place of his own. He walked them to his truck and opened the driver's side door to double-check under the seat. Sure enough, there were two thick blankets under there. Most of the time, he forked over the money for a hotel room, but there were the nights when he chose the solitude of his truck over dealing with that bullshit. "You want to go for a ride?"

"A ride, huh?" She turned in his arms and waggled her eyebrows at him. Or she tried to.

Adam shook his head and lifted her into the truck. "Not like that, sugar. You're drunk as a skunk."

"Which means it's the perfect time for some nooky."

Maybe under different circumstances. But she was too drunk for a yes to really be a yes, and, fake girlfriend or not, he wasn't the kind of man who was into that sort of thing. Tonight she didn't need sex. She needed someone to take care of her. "Scoot over." He followed her up into the cab and shut the door.

Five minutes later, they left the town limits of Devil's Falls in the rearview mirror. He took them out to one of the spots that had been his favorite as a teenager. He and his friends had spent more nights than he could count out on the edge of this field, drinking and bullshitting and passing out in the beds of their trucks. He shut off the engine and stared at the stars while the engine ticked. "He's not worth it."

"Hmm?" She scooted over and burrowed under his arm to lean against his side.

"Grant. He's not worth it. You're so far out of his league, it's not even funny." *Out of both our leagues.*

A soft snore was his only response. Despite everything, he smiled. She really was something else. He'd never put much thought into the kind of woman he'd eventually settle down with—or into settling down in general. But he could almost picture it with Jules. Life would never be boring, that was for damn sure.

As if on cue, the restlessness in his blood kicked up a notch, like an itch he could never quite scratch, reminding him that he'd been in the same place for two weeks, longer than he'd spent in one town in twelve years. If his mom…

No, it's time to face the truth. It's not an if. It's a when. If the cancer doesn't take her, old age will at some point.

When his mom died…

Adam pulled Jules more tightly against him and rested his chin on the top of her head. He could barely stand to think the thought. How the hell would he be able to spend time in Devil's Falls when every time he turned around, he'd be assaulted with memories of her and have to experience the loss all over again? It had been unbearable after John died. With his mom it would be so much worse.

Even if she lived to the ripe old age of a hundred, the open road was too tempting a siren call for him to ignore for long. He needed the horizon stretching out before him, the thrill of the next bull ride promising an adrenaline rush like no other.

The closest he'd come to it outside the rodeo was the woman in his arms, and hell if that didn't make him a dick for using her to quell his thrill-seeking nature. It couldn't last, though. Nothing had kept him in one place for long before, and he didn't imagine anything would in the future.

No, he wasn't staying. He couldn't.

CHAPTER FOURTEEN

Jules woke up wonderfully warm…and certain that some small animal had crawled into her mouth and died. She shifted, not quite willing to leave the safe circle of Adam's arms—because she'd know that spicy scent anywhere.

"Morning."

She looked up, finding him far too close to risk opening her mouth. There was no help for it. She slithered out of his hold and to the other side of the bench seat. Eyeing the distance between them, she decided caution was the better part of valor and held her hand in front of her mouth. "Morning."

His eyebrows crept up. "What are you doing?"

Being an idiot, apparently. Considering what she remembered of the night before, he shouldn't be surprised. "Morning breath."

If anything, he looked even more amused. "Here." He opened the glove compartment and pulled out a bottle of water, a tiny toothbrush, and a travel-size tube of toothpaste.

She was so shocked, she dropped her hand. "You carry around a toothbrush setup in your truck?"

"As you said…morning breath. It's always good to have a backup ready if I'm not in a hotel room for whatever reason." He passed them over and waited while she considered. "If you're one of those people who are weird about toothbrushes—"

"No, it's fine." Considering where both their

mouths had been on each other in the last week, sharing a toothbrush shouldn't be a big deal. It just felt kind of…domestic. Intimate.

Or maybe she was so hungover, she was thinking crazy thoughts.

Jules climbed out of the truck and went to work, brushing away until her mouth felt minty clean and there wasn't a trace of morning breath left. Then she waited while Adam did the same. It gave her the opportunity to really remember how much of a hot mess she'd been the night before. Regret soured her stomach—or maybe that was the purple nurples. "I think I'm dying."

He spit. "Nah, you're just feeling the effects of too much alcohol in too little time." He gave her some serious side eye. "Not going to lie—you were in rare form last night."

"Sorry." She should have just gone with the moonlight picnic. There was probably good food involved, and there *definitely* had to have been sex on the books. Instead she'd gotten drunk and made a fool of herself in front of half the town. *Talk about making a scene. I'm surprised I haven't already gotten a call from Jamie—or worse, Mom.* She didn't even want to look at her phone in case she was wrong.

Wait. Jules patted her pockets. Oh, crap. Her *phone.* She didn't have it. Aubry must have been going crazy imagining all the ways Jules might have been killed when she didn't come home. Hopefully she'd assume she spent the night with Adam.

She was *definitely* going to hear about this when she got back to the apartment.

He held the door open for her. "Happens to the best of us."

Maybe. But it never happened with her—mostly because even if she got particularly drunk, her bed was only a handful of steps away. *I'm never drinking in public again.* Her stomach made a truly embarrassing sound and she glared at it. "Shut up."

"You want to get some breakfast?" He started the truck, heading back toward the main road. "You'll feel better if you eat."

That was debatable. Right now, all she wanted was to crawl into a hole and never surface again. "Are you sure you want to be seen with me?"

He laughed. "Aw, sugar. You might have been a little bit of a shit show last night, but trust me—I've seen worse. I've *been* worse."

That was strangely comforting. "I should know better. I'm not twenty-one. Four shots in half an hour is more than enough to make me act a fool." She crossed her arms over her chest and slumped down. "I hate that he makes me so crazy. That they *all* make me so crazy. Everyone thinks that I've accomplished all I'm going to in life—that I had my chance at greatness and Grant and blew it—and they've written me off as a result." She should be past it by now, shouldn't she? But Grant showing back up in town was like rubbing salt in her wound. Every time she turned around, someone was giving her considering looks like they should be asking her if she was *really* okay. She'd walk to hell and back before her pinnacle in life was dating *that* man.

That said, the whole situation wasn't *all* bad.

There had been Adam, after all. Fake boyfriend or

not, spending time with him wasn't exactly a hardship. *Assuming he's not going to drop me off on my front doorstep and hightail it out of town as far and fast as this rig can take him.* "I don't suppose you still want to have sex with me?"

"Sugar, come here."

She slid across the seat and yelped when he grabbed her hand and pressed it against the front of his jeans. His length met her touch, hard enough to make her bite her lip. Adam's eyes were dark as he looked into hers. "I'm always ready for you. If you think for a second getting a little drunk and trying to fight your ex is enough to make me change my mind about wanting you, you've got another think coming."

"Oh."

"All the words in the world and that's the one you respond with."

She could do better. Really, she could. Jules swallowed hard. "I'm glad. I like having sex with you."

Adam threw back his head and let loose a laugh that resonated with something in her chest. "Damn, sugar. You're something else — and before you go overthinking things, I mean that as a compliment."

Considering every other time someone had said something of that nature, they hadn't meant it as anything positive, she wasn't used to being complimented. "You are a strange, strange man, Adam Meyer."

"It's been said before." He turned onto the highway, heading away from Devil's Falls. There were a grand total of four towns within easy drivable distance, and the only one in this direction was Pecos, so they had a good thirty minutes before they got to wherever he was headed.

She settled against him. "I know this is like two weeks late, but you really aren't what I expected."

"Oh, yeah?"

She ignored the tight way he spoke. "You're such a...well, a good guy. From the way some of the locals talk about the legendary Adam Meyer, I expected a hell-raiser." People still talked about the time he started a brawl after the Devils' rivals beat them in the division championships. Yeah, he'd been all of seventeen at the time, but he'd gone on to be a freaking *bull* rider. Every rodeo cowboy she'd met over the years was a hard-core adrenaline junkie. Adam just seemed so...well, not chill exactly, but not like a junkie jonesing for his next hit. He was intense and sometimes he moved around a room like the walls were closing in, but he wasn't anything like she'd imagined.

And that wasn't even getting into the sex and how out-of-this-world good it'd been.

He still didn't say anything, so she just kept talking. "Do you like bull riding?"

"I love it." His hands tightened on the steering wheel. "Those few seconds are the only time everything around me becomes crystal clear and quiet. I feel fucking invincible."

"Before you're thrown butt over teakettle and have to run away because the bull is angry and looking for someone to take it out on."

He smiled. "Yeah, before then."

It felt almost like he was opening up to her, so she pushed her luck a little. "I hear you're something of a rodeo star."

"That's not why I do it."

She traced the veins in his forearm as he drove.

"You must have a whole lot of stories that would scare years off your friends' lives."

"A few." There was that smile again, the one she was seriously starting to crave. "Down in San Antonio a few years back, there was this big, mean old brute by the name of Sue."

Jules blinked. "Sue. As in the song?"

"The very one." He chuckled softly. "Well, he has a nasty history of putting his riders in the hospital, to the point where the odds of hitting eight seconds is so far against them, a man can make a pretty penny if he manages."

There was no mistaking the self-satisfied tone of his voice. "You did it."

"I did it. I went eight point one seconds." His eyes went a little distant. "It was one hell of a ride, sugar. There hasn't been any quite like it since." He glanced down at her, his smile fading. "I never told anyone back home about it. Mama would worry, and I don't like the boys to think I'm bragging."

There was something almost sad about that. He'd done some incredible things, and to not be able to share it with anyone… Jules snuggled closer to him, wishing she could soothe the faint ache she heard behind the surface happiness of his words. "How did you even get started on that? Was it something you were determined to do as a kid, with the added bonus of giving your mother gray hair?"

A terrible, hopeless expression passed over his face, but he was answering her before she could ask what had put it there. "It was never on my list. I actually had started working with your cousin on your uncle's farm before I graduated high school, and I liked it a lot."

If she thought picturing Adam on a bull was hotter than hot, picturing him on a horse and herding cattle was downright devastating. There was something so attractive about a man, rugged and a little dirty, working the land and animals. She looked away, trying to get a handle on her hormones. "Why'd you stop if you liked it so much?"

"Something just clicked inside me at graduation. It was like a whole new world of possibilities opened up, and I couldn't wait to get the hell out of Dodge." He hesitated. "Not going to lie, I considered coming back right around the time I hit twenty-one. Your uncle Rodger offered me a job, and the other guys were running things at the ranch. I came back to help out over the holidays, but…"

That was when John died.

She knew the story. Everyone in town did. How Adam, Quinn, Daniel, John, and John's little sister were on their way back into town when a truck swerved and hit them. John had been killed on impact, and his little sister had her leg horribly mangled.

Jules swallowed hard. "Losing him must have been awful." She knew her cousin had never quite recovered.

"It was." He was silent for a beat. "I lasted until his funeral, but then I started getting restless again. Since then, I haven't stayed in one place more than a week or two."

And they were topping out two right now.

Jules couldn't imagine it. She loved her family, loved her friends, just plain loved Devil's Falls. It was her home and it might be a pain occasionally, but the good far outweighed the bad. She understood needing a break, but Adam had started driving and never come back. "I bet you've seen some cool stuff in all your traveling, though."

"Yeah. There are places where you can drive for miles and miles without seeing another person. Sometimes I camp out in the truck under the open sky and just…am. And the rodeo is something else. The energy is off the charts, amping up the people, which amps up the animals. It's a show unlike any other."

She'd only been a few times, and the last time, she'd seen one of the bull riders get trampled. He'd fallen after a great ride and while everyone was cheering, he hadn't gotten up fast enough and the bull had done a number on him. He lived, but he'd never ride again.

The thought of that happening to Adam…

Jules did her best to think of *anything* else. "But you're back in town for your mom—because she's sick."

"Yeah."

Even after the short time they'd known each other, she recognized his tone of voice. He was shutting her out. Again. It shouldn't hurt. She had no right to the information. She wasn't *really* his girlfriend.

And he's not staying.

She *had* to remember that, to keep it in the forefront of her mind. To do anything else was emotional suicide.

CHAPTER FIFTEEN

Jules shut the door softly behind her and turned the lock. She inched backward, skirting the floorboard that creaked...and screamed.

"Where were you?" Aubry sat on the couch, wrapped up in a blanket like a burrito, only her face and hands showing. She peered at Jules through blood-shot amber eyes. "You left your phone here."

"I know. I'm sorry. I didn't plan to be out this long." She plopped down on the couch next to her. "Have you been up all night?"

Aubry shrugged. "There was a new map pack on my game. And then you didn't come home, so I figured I'd just keep playing."

Her friend had always loved gaming, but this was a lot, even for her. *I'm a horrible person. She was worried about me and I was getting drunk and passing out.* She should have borrowed Adam's phone and called. "You want to go get some breakfast?"

"Already on it. Johnny Jacob is bringing me the breakfast special from the Finer Diner."

She blinked. "I didn't realize Finer Diner delivered." Probably because they *didn't* in the twenty-six years she'd lived in this town. "Is that a new thing?"

"Not officially." Aubry leaned back with a sigh and set her controller aside. "I didn't feel like dealing with people, and cooking is for savages."

"You just think that because you could burn water."

"Details, details." She waved that away. "I'm tipping him twenty bucks, but it's worth it to avoid going down to the diner." She shuddered. "People see me sitting alone and think that it's sad and I look lonely, and they sit down and talk and, worse, they expect me to talk back."

"You poor thing." She patted her head. There was a knock on the door, and she hopped up to get it. There was a wad of cash in the frog mug by the door and she grabbed that on her way. Johnny Jacob smiled when she opened the door. "Hey, Jules!"

"Johnny." She passed over the cash. "You're up early."

He was starting to come out of that awful stage of puberty where the body seemed determined to go through as many awkward changes as possible in a seriously short amount of time. He was still breaking out and gangly to the point where she wanted to feed him a cheeseburger or twelve, but now there were hints of the man he'd be. *Where the heck did the time go?*

He grinned. "I picked up a second job for the rest of the summer. I've got my eye on that sweet little Ford for sale down on Upriver Drive."

"Good for you." She took the plastic bags from him. "You have a nice day now."

"You, too." He stopped at the top of the stairs. "Hey. Is it true that you're dating Adam Meyer?"

Apparently the plan was working. She didn't know if she found that comforting or just exhausting, especially after this morning. "Yep."

His face lit up. "That's so *cool*. Did you know he rides bulls? He's held the record down at San Antonio for seven years." There was a fair amount of hero worship on his face, and she couldn't blame him. Adam really was larger than life. There was a lot he'd done that was insanely cool, whether to a teenage boy or a twenty-six-year-old cat café owner.

I like him. Crap.

"He's pretty great."

"He's *the best*. If I wasn't going to college, I'd totally be a bull rider. I bet he gets mad chicks." He flushed beet red. "Er, sorry, Jules. I didn't mean anything by it. I just—"

"It's okay. I'll see you around." She eased the door shut, her good mood slipping away. Because Johnny Jacob was right—Adam Meyer was like catnip to women. He might not have put that power to use since he'd been back in Devil's Falls—probably because *she'd* jumped him the first time he was out and about—but that didn't change the fact that he'd probably left a string of broken hearts behind him.

She set the food down in front of Aubry on the coffee table and resumed her seat. "Why does it bother me that Adam may have banged his way through half of Texas?"

"Because you like him." Aubry took out the foam containers and set them in a neat little row. "But you know you're not really dating and that this thing is ending at some point, so you don't have the security of being able to discount his past."

That was it exactly. Jules sighed. "Pretending to date him was a mistake." Especially when it had become clear that they couldn't keep their hands off each other.

"Then we don't you date him for real?"

She frowned as Aubry nudged a container over to her. "For me?" She opened it. "Holy crap, you got me French toast with blueberry syrup. How'd you know I'd be back in time?" It didn't matter that she'd just eaten with Adam. There was always room for French toast with blueberry syrup.

"I had a feeling." Aubry smiled her Cheshire cat smile. "Now, back to your clusterfuck of a love life…"

"I love you, but you kind of suck at pep talks." She cut up the French toast and doused it in the syrup. "I can't date him for real. That's not what he agreed to, and if I suddenly pull something like that, he's going to freak out. Aubry, I can't even ask him if he's okay without him shutting me down. The man has more issues than *Vogue*."

Aubry made a sound suspiciously like a moan at her first bite of omelet. "I'd think you're used to it after dealing with me all these years. You're an old pro at people with issues."

It was true that her friend had some…triggers. And hated people. And would hole up in their apartment for weeks on end if left to her own devices. She chewed, closing her eyes in pure bliss. "That's different."

"Not really. I don't know if you've noticed, but Adam has a ring of space around him wherever he goes." She took another bite. "I wish he'd teach me how to do that. I go out and randos come up and tell me that they'll pray for me or to keep my chin up because it can't be *that* bad. This?" She pointed at herself. "This is my face. This is the way it looks."

Jules had never really thought about it, but Adam *did* kind of have a don't-screw-with-me vibe. "He's just gone through a lot."

"We all have. There's no reason not to date him for real if he's making you all twitterpated."

She ate half her French toast before she responded. "What if he says he doesn't want to date me? He's not staying in Devil's Falls. He's made *that* abundantly clear."

"Look, Jules, I'm going to be honest with you." Aubry set her food aside and rotated to face her, her expression solemn. "There's only room in this relationship for one paranoid, antisocial, budding agoraphobic. That's me. You're the bright and sunny one that makes people smile just by walking into the room. You're my better half. Maybe you could be his better half, too."

Jules leaned back and stared at the ceiling. "When did you get so smart?"

"I'm really good at diagnosing other people's problems. Mine? Not so much." Aubry went back to eating. "Now, finish your food and go shower. You smell like a bar."

CHAPTER SIXTEEN

It had been too long since Adam was on the back of a horse. So when Daniel mentioned that he needed some extra help around the ranch, he'd jumped at the opportunity. He'd been driving himself, his mama, *and* Lenora crazy being cooped up in the house, and she'd practically shoved him through the door the second his friend called.

He just hadn't expected Daniel to saddle him up a stallion named Hellbeast. He stared at the giant animal. The horse was gorgeous, standing at seventeen hands and perfectly shaped. He was a glossy chestnut with white stockings, looking more suited to the show ring than cattle herding. "Hellbeast."

"You heard right." Daniel finished cinching the saddle on his bay. "He's not as bad as he seems."

Adam took a step closer and stopped when Hellbeast snorted. "Really?"

"Yep." His friend grinned. "He's worse."

"This wouldn't be you getting me back for fake dating your cousin, would it?" He took the reins and moved forward. The best path with any foul-tempered animal was to show no hesitation. He had a feeling the second Hellbeast scented fear, he'd take off for the horizon, whether he kept his rider on his back or not.

"Would I do that?"

He swung up into the saddle, holding the horn when Hellbeast sidled sideways. "Yes."

"He likes to try to jump the south fence, so watch

out for that."

Adam shot him a look. "I know you're pissed, but murder seems like an overreaction."

"Murder?" Daniel shook his head. "You're Adam Meyer, famous bull rider. If anyone can handle little ole Pumpernickel, it's you."

"I thought you said his name was Hellbeast."

They started away from the barn. The stallion kept a tight trot, his stride liquid and absolutely perfect. Daniel adjusted his cowboy hat. "That's just what I call him, though don't do it in Jules's hearing. She's got a soft spot for the beast."

Of course she did. He'd bet *Pumpernickel* adored her, too. She was the kind of woman who could sing the birds from the trees and charm everyone she came across. Except maybe Grant. The thought soured his mood. The more he thought about her with that jackass, the more it bothered him. What the hell had she been thinking, dating a guy like that? He was human waste.

And maybe Adam was fucking jealous.

They rode south along the fence line. The job today was mending fence posts. It was tedious work, but by lunchtime, he'd worked hard enough that his muscles burned pleasantly and his thoughts were clear for the first time in what felt like forever. He stretched, his back popping.

"You know there's a place here if you decide to stay."

He didn't look at Daniel. His friend, of all people, should know why he couldn't stay. The fact that he'd stuck around long enough to see graduation was a small miracle. As his mama often reminded him, he was a leaver, same as his daddy.

"I get wanting to leave this place in your rearview. Believe me, I do. But…" Daniel trailed off. "I don't know why I'm trying to convince you. I have half a mind to take a page from your book and move away for good."

Before he could ask what his friend meant, the sound of hoofbeats had them both turning. A figure raced across the open field, crouched over the back of a dark horse. She pulled up with a few short feet to spare, grinning down at them from beneath her wide-brimmed hat. "Howdy, fellas."

Adam couldn't stop staring. He'd spared a thought to what Jules might look like on the back of a horse, but seeing her in a faded black tank top and jeans whose fit could only be described a lovingly clingy made his brain short-circuit. She handled herself like she'd been born in the saddle—something he should have considered with Daniel being her cousin and all. "Jules."

"I brought you guys lunch." She shrugged out of a backpack he hadn't seen before then. "Hope you like ham and cheese, Adam. It's Daniel's favorite, and Aunt Lori is feeling generous."

"Probably buttering me up to set me up with a daughter of some friend of hers," Daniel grumbled, taking the bag from her.

Adam didn't miss the worry that clouded her expression. Everyone seemed to be worried about Daniel. He turned to look at his friend. The man seemed moodier than he had been twelve years ago, and he couldn't help thinking about what Quinn had said at the bonfire about John's death changing Daniel fundamentally. Crippling guilt would do that to a person.

The man in question grabbed a plastic container from the backpack. "Thanks, kid. I'm going to go check the posts farther down." He untethered his bay and swung up into the saddle. And then he was gone, cantering away.

Jules's feet hit the ground, and she walked her horse over to loop the reins around the fence. "You boys sure do have the market cornered on brooding, don't you?"

"Don't know what you're talking about."

She scooped up the backpack. "Of course you don't. You're just a little ray of sunshine."

"Yep." They sat next to the fence, and he accepted the sandwich and baggie full of chips. In the winter, lunch would be a sandwich and a canteen of soup— probably chicken noodle or tomato. He unwrapped his ham and cheese and took a bite, hit by a wave of homesickness that threatened to take him out at the knees. It didn't make sense. He *was* home.

But not for good.

Will I even be *here in the winter?*

He set the sandwich down and leaned back against the post he'd fixed earlier, his appetite gone. Some days he'd go through an entire day without having to face that fact that his mama was fading away before his eyes. And then it'd hit like a lightning strike, charring him to the bone. "She's got cancer, you know."

Jules froze. "I'm sorry."

It said something that she didn't ask whom he was talking about. She knew his mom was sick. Fuck, everyone in this godforsaken town knew his mom was sick—and probably had known before he did. He'd failed her in so many ways. Even knowing there wasn't a damn thing he could do about her cancer, he couldn't shake the feeling that he was failing her now, too. "I should have been here." He didn't know why he was saying this shit aloud, let alone to Jules. She'd signed on for the fun side of the girlfriend experience, not the baggage that came with it.

"I don't know if it'll make you feel better or worse to know it, but she hid it for a very long time, even from her lady friend, Lenora. They come into my shop every week, and I knew she looked a little peaky, but she just said she wasn't sleeping well. Even if you'd been here, I doubt she would have told you until she was forced to."

She was probably right, but that didn't make it any easier to bear. "But I would have *been* here."

"You're here now."

"Yeah, I guess I am." He forced himself to pick his sandwich back up and take another bite. He'd need the calories to finish out the day, whether he was hungry or not. "So, what are you doing out here?"

"Oh, me? I usually help out on my days off when there isn't something that I need to be doing for Cups and Kittens." She took a long drink of water. "And I might have known you were out here, so I volunteered to bring you guys lunch."

He smiled. "Now the truth comes out."

"Guilty." She twisted a strand of her dark hair around her finger. "I wanted to talk to you about something, but in the light of everything, I think it was a horrible Aubry-induced idea."

Color him crazy, but any idea that came from that

redhead made him curious. "Tell me."

"I'd really rather not." She huffed out a breath when he leveled a look at her. "Okay, fine. Do you want to be my boyfriend for real?"

He'd anticipated all sorts of words to come out of her mouth…but not that. "You want to date me."

"I know we're already sort of dating, but it's fake dating. I want to real date." She scrunched up her nose when she frowned. "Though, to be honest, I don't really know what would be different. Maybe more sex? Or you tell me what's wrong when I ask if you're okay?"

"Sugar—"

"You're not staying. I know." Her smile was all sorts of tentative. "But you haven't left yet. I like you, Adam. And I think you like me, too."

Hell, yes, he did. Too much. Jules wasn't the leaving kind. She was the type of woman that had a man thinking all sorts of insane thoughts about settling down and kids and coming in from work to find the windows lit and dinner on the stove. The kind of woman who had "home" written all over her.

You'll break her heart if you say yes. Maybe not today, maybe not tomorrow, but it's coming.

But not today.

He pulled her into his lap. "Well, fuck, sugar, you make one hell of an argument."

Her hands landed on his shoulders. "Is that a no?"

"Nope." He ran his hands up her thighs. "These jeans should be fucking illegal."

"What? These are work jeans." She frowned. "You didn't really answer my question."

"Sure I did. Yes, sugar, be my girlfriend." *Until I*

leave Devil's Falls in my rearview once and for all. He dipped his thumbs beneath her waistband. "Now let me get you out of these jeans."

She laughed and slapped his hands. "Daniel's going to be back any time, and as much as I want to jump your bones, I'd rather not have to pay for the therapy he'd inevitably need if he saw us bumping uglies."

"Jump my bones? Bumping uglies? I don't think my dirty-talking lessons have had their desired effect. We'll need a repeat."

She leaned forward until her lips brushed his ear. "Come by when you get off work. I'll be waiting for you with nothing but a sheet on."

"Lose the sheet and you've got yourself a deal."

Jules laughed, though the sound turned into a moan when he used his grip on her hips to slide her against the hard ridge of his cock. "Maybe I'll be wearing panties and cowgirl boots. Or these jeans and nothing else. You'll have to show up to find out."

He cursed low and hard. "I'm going to be in hell for the rest of the day. I hope you're happy."

She pressed a quick kiss to his lips and wriggled free. "I am."

And hell if she didn't sound it.

CHAPTER SEVENTEEN

Jules paced from one side of her apartment to the other. *This was such a dumb idea. What if he doesn't show up. Worse, what if he* does? She looked down at her getup—boots and panties and a long-sleeved flannel shirt that she'd left unbuttoned. When she got dressed, she'd had that look on Adam's face fixated in her mind. He would have had her right then and there in the field without a second thought.

But that was the problem. He'd had the entire afternoon for second thoughts. It didn't matter if he'd said he was coming over and that he'd be her boyfriend for real—he could have changed his mind.

She eyed the closed door to Aubry's room. Her friend had taken one look at her, shaken her head, and gone off to hide. Not that Jules could blame her—she felt a whole lot like hiding right now, too.

A knock on the door had her considering diving for the thick, knitted throw blanket on the back of the couch. What had she been thinking, dressing like this? She looked like one of those cowgirl wannabes in a music video. It didn't help that her boots, having seen better days, probably ruined the effect. They were the boots of a woman who *worked*.

She started to kick them off, but whoever it was at the door knocked again. Jules hurried over and peered through the peephole. *Adam.* There was no way he didn't know she was here—especially since *she'd* been the one to tell him she would be. She rested her forehead against the door. "Get it together, Jules."

"Sugar, if you're going to talk to yourself, you might as well let me in so you can talk to me instead."

Her eyes flew open. "Sorry, but I think I'm going to die of embarrassment."

"Let me in." His voice turned coaxing. "Do you know how I spent the rest of my day?"

It was strange having this conversation through the door, but she didn't immediately move. "How?"

"Hard as a rock and aching for you. Let me in, and I'll tell you all about it."

She opened the door to find him grinning. "Said the big bad wolf to the little pig."

The expression melted away as he took her in. Adam's eyes went dark, and he rubbed a hand across his mouth. "Fuck, sugar, I changed my mind. I'm not going to tell you a damn thing. I'm going to show you." He cleared the doorway in a single step, backing her into the apartment and kicking the door shut behind him. "The redhead?"

"She has a name." Jules took several steps back, her heart beating too hard.

"I know." He shadowed her movements, following her as she backed around the kitchen table and toward her bedroom.

"She's in her room."

He passed the doorway into her room and kicked it shut behind him, too. "Then you better be quiet or we're going to traumatize the hell out of her."

"Keep—" She shrieked when he burst around the corner of the bed and scooped her into his arms. Jules braced herself, but he didn't throw her onto the bed this time. Instead he laid her down and sat back, looking at her like… She didn't have words to describe how he was looking at her.

He smoothed his hands up her legs, spreading them as he reached her thighs. "Fuck, sugar." His thumb played down and stroked over her panties. "Wet, just like I knew you'd be."

"I guess I like being chased."

His expression was nearly pained. "That's good. I like the fuck out of chasing you." He hooked the sides of her panties and dragged them down her legs. "One of these days, I'm going to set you loose in a field in nothing but these boots. And then I'm going to chase you down and fuck you right there in the grass."

It was suddenly a whole lot harder to draw a full breath. She could picture it perfectly, that hungry look on his face as he stalked after her, the wheat whipping at her legs, her body exposed to the breeze.

"You like that. Good." He got her panties past her boots and tossed them to the side. "Spread your legs, sugar. Show me how much you want me."

She did what he said, feeling a little foolish, but that feeling faded as he started talking. "Did your little tease act this afternoon leave you as worked up as it did me?"

"Yes."

"Mmm." He gripped her thighs, spreading her wider yet. "And did you come home and get one of those little buzzy toys out?"

How did he know?

He must have read something on her face. "You're far too relaxed to have spent the last few hours like I did."

A blush spread across her cheeks. "I've come three

times since I got home."

He froze, his eyes narrowed. "Three."

"Yes…"

"Three fucking orgasms you denied me." He yanked her to the edge of the bed as he went to his knees beside it. "Three orgasms that should have been mine."

"Well—" She had to slap a hand over her mouth when he licked up her center, zeroing in on her clit. She was already sensitive from all the orgasms earlier, and the pleasure was so acute, it was almost painful as he sucked her clit into his mouth. "*Adam.*"

"I'm taking what's mine, sugar. With interest."

He went at her like a starving man. There was no stopping, no passing Go, no collecting two hundred dollars. There was just an Adam-induced orgasm hurtling down on her. She grabbed her comforter and screamed her pleasure into it, writhing against his mouth.

But he wasn't done. He was nowhere near done.

The aftershocks had barely faded when he flipped her onto her stomach. "That's one."

Surely he didn't really mean to…

His hand cupped her, sliding through her wetness, two fingers spearing her and then withdrawing to slide over her oversensitive clit. Over and over again. With her butt in the air and her face pressed against her mattress, she should have felt horribly exposed, but there was no room for feeling anything but what he was doing to her. An impossible pressure built in her, spiraling higher and higher with each stroke. "Adam, please."

"Did you think of me when you were rubbing that

vibrator all over your clit? I think you did. I think you knew exactly how hard I was for you, and that only got you off harder knowing that I was riding around with a cockstand to end all cockstands."

It *had* felt naughty to be pleasuring herself while she knew he wasn't able to. She moaned, trying to thrust back onto his fingers, but he slapped her butt hard enough to sting. "Hold still, sugar. This is my rodeo, and you've got to pay your dues."

"You're so mean."

"You have no idea." He pinched her clit, the shock of the pain sending her hurtling into another orgasm. Jules collapsed onto her bed, her legs shaking and her breath coming so hard, she sounded like she'd just run a marathon.

He rolled her onto her back. "Breathe, sugar."

"I'm...breathing." Sort of.

Adam licked between her legs again, but the earlier fury driving him seemed to be at least partially abated because he took his time as if savoring the taste of her. She lay there, half sure she was having an out-of-body experience. It was the only explanation for her wanting to grab his hair and grind herself against his face even after two orgasms in entirely too little time.

She stretched her arms over her head, arching her back. "You make me crazy."

"Believe me, the feeling is fucking mutual." He spread her folds, fucking her with his tongue the same way he'd fucked her with his fingers. It made her feel sexy and wanton and like someone else entirely.

"Adam."

"That's right, sugar. Me. Not your fucking buzzy toy." He lifted his head, something dangerous flickering over his face. "Where is it?"

She pointed to her nightstand before common sense caught up with her. "Wait—" But it was too late. He'd yanked open the drawer and brought out B.O.B.

Adam eyed the bright pink Lelo vibrator. "Interesting taste." He turned it on, a wicked grin spreading over his face. "On second thought, I think your buzzy toy and I would make a fucking amazing tag team." He slid the vibrator into her, adjusting the setting until she had to fist the comforter over her head.

"Oh my God."

"One more orgasm, and I'll let you come on my cock." He fucked her slowly with the vibrator. The sensation of his hands on her body, combined with the toy between her legs, made the pleasure almost impossible to bear. "That's it, sugar. Let go. I've got you."

He lined it up with her clit, squeezing her thigh with his free hand. "You look so fucking beautiful when you come. Knowing I'm the cause of it... Yeah, I can't get enough of that. I'm going to fuck that tight pussy of yours, sugar, until you're begging me to never stop."

Considering how close she was to doing just that, she believed him with every fiber of her being. She shuddered, her orgasm looming.

Which was when he took away her vibrator. She barely had time to protest when he was there, covering her, his cock replacing the buzzy toy. The feeling of him filling her sent her over the edge. Jules buried her face against his neck and sobbed as she came, his hands on her and his cock inside her the only solid thing in her world in that moment.

He slipped one arm beneath the small of her back and the other hand cupped the back of her head as he thrust into her, his mouth on hers, his tongue fucking her as thoroughly as his cock. The sensation was too much, forcing her orgasm to crest again. This time, he followed her over, his strokes becoming less smooth and his body going tight on top of her as he groaned her name.

She lay there, staring at her ceiling, wondering if this was all a dream. Surely the single sexiest man she'd ever known hadn't just made her come three times in short order. That was just too good to be true.

And then Adam had to go and make it even better. He turned his head and kissed her neck. "Sugar, I'm going to take you on a real date."

CHAPTER EIGHTEEN

Adam scrubbed his truck down, wondering what the hell he'd been thinking yesterday with Jules. *I'm going to take you on a real date. I'll be your boyfriend.* He was setting himself up for failure. "I'm *not staying*, goddamn it."

"Are you talking to yourself?"

He glanced over to find Quinn standing at the bottom of his mom's driveway. "What are you doing here?"

"So damn rude." His friend shook his head. "But I know what you really meant to say." He grinned and waved, his voice ticking up an octave. "'Hey, man, nice to see you. It's been a hell of a week and your gorgeous face is exactly what I needed.'"

Adam shook his head. "No, pretty sure that's not what I meant at all. And I don't sound like that."

"Sure you do." He settled into the rocking chair on the porch, absolutely dwarfing the thin wood with his large body. "You still doing that thing with Daniel's cousin? Because rumor has it that you were seen making out like high school kids on her front doorstep yesterday in the early hours of the morning."

"Rumor has it, huh? This town never changes."

Growing up, more often than not, it'd been his name uttered as the hell-raiser who couldn't keep himself out of the back of the town's lone police cruiser. It wasn't anything personal—there just wasn't a whole hell of a lot to talk about other than football, ranching, and who was getting into trouble this week.

"Sure, it changes. Just ask my old man." Quinn deepened his voice and screwed up his face in a scowl. "'Back in my day, we respected our country and didn't act like damn fools.'"

"You are seriously god-awful at impressions." Adam chuckled. "How's Sir Charles, anyways? He made his peace with you working with Daniel instead of heading up his oil empire yet?"

"Hardly." Quinn stretched his legs out and laced his fingers behind his head. "If anything, he's getting more desperate to bring me back into the fold. At the obligatory family dinner last month, he invited *two* blondes with tits the size of melons and dollar signs in their eyes. Mother was thrilled. Naturally."

"Naturally." He crouched down and went to work on his wheels. When he was a teenager, he'd envied the fact that Quinn's dad was determined to have him follow in his footsteps. Once he hit his early twenties, though, he recognized it for the ball and chain it was. Charles Baldwyn cared less about his son's happiness than he did about continuing his family traditions. Adam still wasn't sure if an overbearing ass of a dad was better than no dad at all, but he'd stopped envying his friend. "How long did he manage to go without offering one of them up in marriage?"

"A whole hour." Quinn sighed. "You'd think they'd be bothered by him dangling them in front of me like a piece of meat, but they didn't so much as blink."

"Money makes people stupid."

"Isn't that the truth?" He crossed his feet at his ankles. "That was a nice subject change—very subtle. But you still didn't answer my question about little

Jules Rodriguez."

He didn't want to get into it. He could fool himself into thinking this wasn't going to end in a complete train wreck—mostly—but Quinn would have no problem calling him out. "I don't want to talk about it."

Quinn dropped his hands and sat up straight. "What the hell is going on with you and that girl?"

"She's only seven years younger than us. It's not like I'm robbing the fucking cradle."

If anything, his friend just looked *more* interested. "See, that's the thing. I thought you guys were playing a game—you do her a favor and make that asshole ex of hers jealous, and she occupies you so you don't drive your mom insane pacing around the house. But that's not what it sounds like when you say stuff like that. Are you actually interested in her?"

Yes. He pushed to his feet and grabbed the hose, spraying down the truck. "It's not like that."

"Are you sure?"

Adam didn't say anything until he'd finished washing off the truck and disposed of the soapy water in the bucket. "You know she's just using me to create a scandal."

"And?"

He sighed and turned to face his friend. "And that's a temporary thing no matter which way you look at it. She doesn't want to settle down with the hell-raiser who gets the gossip mill raging. She wants the slow and steady guy who's going to be there with her every night and making her coffee and shit in the morning and…" He rubbed a hand over his face. "It's not me. That's never going to be me."

"Yeah, you keep saying that. Maybe you just

haven't found a good enough reason to put down roots and be that guy—until now."

That's what he was afraid of. Not that he'd put down roots, but that he'd start to and then the restlessness in his blood would start up again. He'd turn back into a tumbleweed before a gale-force wind, yanked right out of whatever life he thought he could have here.

And, really, what did he have to offer Jules? He was a few years out of being a washed-up bull rider who'd been lucky enough not to be permanently injured but who didn't exactly have any applicable skills otherwise. The thought tightened his throat. Rationally, he knew he couldn't ride bulls forever, but he didn't have any long-term plans beyond working the rodeo in whatever capacity he could. Which was pathetic when he really sat down to think about it.

And his mama…

"I'm not that man." He said it more firmly, as if that could quell the growing thing in his chest that was determined to take on a life of its own. It was all twisted up with his dread about what might happen to his mama, a weird mix of fear and hope and something else that he had no name for. He tried to smile. "You know me—I am what I am."

"Sure—before. But you've been back in town almost three weeks now, and you're not going insane or fleeing at the first chance you get." He motioned at the truck. "Hell, you're downright respectable these days."

His gave his front door a long look. "I have my reasons. They aren't permanent."

"Sounds like you have more than one these days." Quinn held up his hands when Adam glared. "Sorry,

sorry. Can't help that I miss you when you're off living life like a country song."

"For fuck's sake." Adam ducked into the garage and grabbed two beers. He walked back, dropped into the chair next to his friend, and passed one over. "You're ridiculous."

"It should be my middle name." Quinn took a long drink of his beer. "So why are you getting your ride all shined up?"

He didn't want to admit it, but his friend would pester him if he tried to avoid the topic. "I'm taking Jules out on a real date."

Quinn threw back his head and let loose a booming laugh. "Oh God, that's the funniest shit I've heard all day. Sounds like you're doing a hell of a job of keeping things in perspective with her."

"Something like that." He was doing such a good job, he'd gone from pretending to date her to actually dating her. He took a deep breath and turned the conversation, grateful when Quinn allowed it this time. They chatted about cattle and Adam told a few of his wild rodeo stories, and before he knew it, it was time to go pick up Jules.

His friend stopped by the driver's door and Adam rolled down the window. The joking expression on Quinn's face dropped for the first time since he'd shown up. "Daniel's cousin is a good girl."

"Are you fucking kidding me?" He expected this from his mom and the townsfolk in general—it even made sense for Daniel to be warning him off since Jules was *his* cousin. To have Quinn doing it, too…it stung. A lot. "I'm not stringing her along. I've been honest with her from the beginning, and she's been with me every step of the way. Jules is a grown-ass woman, and I doubt she'd take kindly to everyone and their dog being so sure that I'm going to break her heart."

Quinn raised his eyebrows. "Touched on a sore spot, didn't I?"

"I get tired of everyone thinking I'm a piece of shit." Even if he agreed with them most days.

"Nobody thinks that—or at least no one worth mentioning." He shook his head. "All I was going to say, jackass, is that I think she might be good for you." He turned around and walked off without another word, leaving Adam staring after him.

He'd done a *spectacular* job of proving to his friend that he was managing to keep calm and rational about this situation. He headed for Jules's place, kicking himself again for letting what everyone else thought of him get under his skin. She knew the score. Fuck, *she* was the one with a future that didn't fit him in the least. She'd be a fool to let her heart get involved.

Except she asked you to be her boyfriend. And you said yes.

It didn't mean anything—not really. Even if they were dating for real—which wasn't that different from them pretending to date—she knew he was leaving. He knew he was leaving. The entire fucking town knew he was leaving. It'd be fun while it lasted, but it *couldn't* last.

He stopped in front of her café, shut off the engine, and headed inside, still arguing with himself. He wasn't some monster, taking advantage of little innocent Jules Rodriguez. *She'd* come to *him*. *She* was the one who wanted sex. Yeah, he'd taken them all the way up to that point, but she'd pushed them over the edge.

If anything, people should be worried about how *he* was going to take the goddamn breakup. He'd never been with a woman like this before—someone who seemed to bring joy into any room she stepped into, someone who always had a new and wacky perspective on life, someone who was *happy*. Grant might have set her on her heels temporarily, but that wouldn't last. Jules was the type who bounced back, better than ever, and she would this time, too.

Just like she would after he left.

It was *Adam* who wasn't sure how the hell he was going to go back to life on the road after he'd known what it was like to hold her in his arms.

CHAPTER NINETEEN

Jules walked out of the kitchen to find Adam standing in the doorway of her café, glaring down at the trio of cats twining around his feet. She eyed them—Cujo, Rick, and Dog—wondering if they'd done something to deserve the look. With those three, there was no telling. They got into more trouble than the rest of the cats combined. But Adam didn't seem to be bleeding and there were no suspicious wet spots on his pant legs—talking down Mr. Lee the last time *that* had happened had taken all of her not inconsiderable persuasive skills—so she was almost afraid to ask what was wrong.

Oh, right, I shouldn't even do it anyways, because he gets so freaking snarly about it.

So she pasted a smile on her face. "Hey, there."

He looked up, and the scowl disappeared. Jules actually rocked back on her heels. *Good lord, being smiled at by Adam Meyer is as good as one of those purple nurple shots. Better, even.* Adam carefully stepped over the cats and stalked toward her. "Hey, sugar."

She barely had a chance to process his intent before he pulled her into his arms and kissed her. His lips brushed hers, which should have been PG, but one of his hands was at the small of her back, pressing her fully against the front of his *very* aroused body, and the other was in her hair, tugging hard enough that she knew exactly who was in charge of this encounter. Her toes curled in her boots, and she went all soft and melty. When he lifted his head, all she could do was blink up at him. "Hi."

His grin was so self-satisfied that her toes curled all over again. "You said that already."

"Did I? I think I'm in danger of saying it a third time." She clamped her mouth shut before she could do just that.

He leaned back a little. "You ready for our date?"

"Yes...don't I look ready?" She glanced down at herself. She'd chosen a dress from Aubry's closet that was a mash-up of pinup and country girl—in that it was plaid, which was as country girl as Aubry got. Jules had picked it because it was fancier than anything she owned, and it seemed like she should get fancy for a *real* date with Adam.

"You look good enough to eat."

"I hope you mean that in a non–Hannibal Lecter way, or I'm going to have to call the police," Aubry called out.

They both looked over to where Aubry sat in her usual corner seat with Mr. Winkles in her lap, a cup of coffee in her hands despite the fact that it was well after five in the evening. She speared Adam with a glare over the top of her glasses that would have had a lesser man hightailing it for the door.

Adam just grinned. "I mean it in a flirting way that has nothing to do with cannibalism."

She glared even harder. "I'm onto you, country boy. Treat my friend right."

Some of the humor fled his face, but his smile didn't waver. "Sure thing." He turned back to Jules and offered his elbow. "Do you need to do anything else before we go?"

She was as prepared as she was going to be. Aunt Lori was watching the café until her cousin Jamie showed up to finish off the shift and close. She crouched down carefully to give each of the cats at Adam's feet a scratch, though Cujo dodged her reach and leaped onto the counter to get closer to his face. *Thanks a lot, you silly thing.* She pushed to her feet and looked around. There were half a dozen other things she could find to occupy herself before they left, but anything else she would be stalling. "I think I'm good."

"Then let's get out of here."

They headed out onto the street, and she stopped short at the sight of his truck. It shone brightly in the evening sun, free of any dirt or dust or mud. "You cleaned your truck."

"My mama taught me that you don't pick up a lady in a filthy truck." He opened the door for her, looking as out of place as she suddenly felt.

Jules climbed up, wondering at the awkward feeling coursing through her body and making her want to fidget. This was a date. A *real* date. It shouldn't be any different than any of their other dates. She'd never had a problem speaking her mind with Adam, so why was she just staring at him mutely as he started his truck and headed down the road?

The minutes ticked by, the silence only getting stranger as time went on. They hit the town limits, and Jules was ready to scream. "Why is this so weird? We've been naked and in more compromising positions than I care to count and suddenly I feel like I'm sixteen and on my first date and don't know what to do with my hands."

Adam's hands flexed on the steering wheel. "I don't know."

She waited, but he didn't say anything else. There had to be some way to fix this, because the thought that she'd ruined them by changing things made her sick to her stomach. It was bad enough that he was leaving town at some unknown date in the future and that she'd likely never see him again—for this to end *before* he left? No. Absolutely not. She craved him like her favorite blanket and wine and B.O.B. all rolled into one. Except he could hold down a conversation and he really listened to her. Usually.

She had to do something, and she had to do it now.

Holding her breath, Jules slid across the bench seat until she was pressed against Adam from shoulder to knee. He took the hint and lifted his arm to rest it on the back of the seat. It wasn't putting his arm around her, but it'd have to do for now.

You can do this. You're in charge of your own destiny. You're bold and fearless and oh my God, I can't believe I'm doing this.

Before she could talk herself out of it, she went for his zipper.

Adam tensed. "Sugar, what do you think you're doing?"

"I'm being scandalous." She unbuttoned the top of his jeans and dragged his zipper down. "Stop talking before I chicken out."

"Chicken out from— *Holy shit.*"

She took him in her hand, almost breathing a sigh of relief when he grew hard. This, at least, hadn't changed. "I liked how things were between us. I don't want them to change."

"Do you think now is really the time for this conversation?"

Yes, because it was easier to put herself out there when she knew she had him at a slight disadvantage. She stroked him, using the motion she knew he liked. "I think it's the perfect time. I like you, Adam. I know that's silly, and I know you're leaving, and I know I can't ever ask you if you're okay, but I don't care. I want to enjoy the time we have, and we can't do that if we're sitting here not talking."

Adam pulled onto the shoulder and put the truck in park. "You have my full attention."

"Oh, well, good." She kept touching him, suddenly not sure where she wanted to take this. *Liar. You knew exactly what you wanted from the moment you decided to go for it.* With that little voice in her head driving her on, she kissed him.

Adam took control of the kiss immediately, gripping the back of her neck with one hand and angling his body so she could keep stroking him. "You are something else, sugar."

"You keep saying that. I keep taking it as a compliment."

"Good."

He reached down and hooked her knee, bringing her up and over to straddle him. It happened so smoothly, she didn't lose her grip and was left staring at him. "Tell the truth—do you practice that move? Because no one should be that good naturally."

He laughed, the deep sound rumbling between them. "I'll never tell."

Which was as good as admitting that he had. She waited for that splinter of jealousy to dig deeper, but there was nothing there. Who cared about his past—or his future, for that matter? Right now, in this moment, he was hers and hers alone. She kissed him again, wriggling closer, which hiked up her dress. He took the hint, running his hands up her legs to cup her butt and bring her down to line up the hard ridge of him against her clit.

She pulled away enough to say, "I want you inside me."

"You're reading my mind." He slid over to the middle of the seat and kept an arm around her waist as he fumbled in the glove compartment, coming up with a condom.

She eyed it. "How long has that been in there?" Weren't there some rules about keeping those things in a cool, dry place or risking them breaking? A glove compartment in Texas might be dry, but it sure wasn't cool.

"I put it in there this morning." He gave her a panty-melting smile. "Just call me optimistic."

"You're a scoundrel." She grabbed the condom from his hand. "I like it." It was quick work to rip the wrapper and roll the condom onto him. This was good. This, they knew how to do. The rest of it would fall into place once they had a chance to reset the clock.

Adam pulled her panties to the side, and she wasted no time sinking onto him. Jules closed her eyes, the feeling of fullness nearly overwhelming. She moved, taking him deeper. "This feels too good to be real."

"You took the words right out of my mouth." He unbuttoned the front of her dress and pushed it off her shoulders, taking her bra with it and baring her breasts.

"Fuck, sugar, your body is a work of art." He let go of her hips to palm her breasts as she rode him. "You're so goddamn sexy, it makes me crazy. How the hell am I supposed to focus on anything else when every time I think about you, I can practically feel that tight little pussy of yours squeezing my cock?"

She gripped his shoulders and rolled her body, making him hit a spot inside her that had her moaning. "Sounds like a...personal problem."

"You have no fucking idea." He squeezed her breasts and then released them, the imprint of his hands burning itself into her memory. "And this?" He fisted the fabric of her dress, lifting it above her hips. "You sliding down my cock is a sight I could spend the rest of my life watching and never get tired of. Whoever made you feel like you were somehow less is a fucking idiot. You're perfect. You're better than perfect."

His words warmed her, even as her body sparked with the beginning of an orgasm. "Adam—"

"Need a little something to get you over the edge, don't you, sugar?" He grabbed her hip with one hand and slid his other down to stroke her clit. His grip guided her pace, taking the control from her even as his fingers took her exactly where she needed to go. Jules buried her face in his neck as she came, her shudders racking her entire body.

Adam laid her down on the seat, the position allowing him deeper. "Feeling you come around me, knowing that I'm the cause of it—there isn't another thing in this world like it." His voice went hoarse. "I've never had someone make me lose control like you do."

She clung to him as his strokes became more

uneven, his hold on her tightening as he followed her over the edge, knowing that she was the cause of it making her entire body spark with pleasure all over again. "Adam, you're more addicting that nicotine."

"Oh, yeah?" His laugh rumbled through her. "I can't say I don't like hearing that."

She smiled, though the truth settled in her stomach. Nicotine might feel good in the moment, just like being with him did, but it was ultimately a toxic substance that only left pain in its wake.

Kind of like her relationship with Adam.

CHAPTER TWENTY

Adam stared at his drink, feeling like a jackass. Jules had been right—things went weird as soon as they got into his truck. He'd known it, and he hadn't done a damn thing to stop it, not with Quinn's words still ringing in his ears, joining the chorus of everyone else who'd warned him away from her. Instead of making her comfortable, he'd let the silence draw on, punishing them both for thinking they could do this.

And then Jules had taken matters—and him—into her own hands. She was right—if there was one thing they knew how to do, it was have sex. They'd been doing just fine before becoming official and there was no reason anything had to change.

"You're thinking awfully hard over there."

He looked up to find Jules crossing her eyes at him. Adam laughed. "Life is never boring when you're around, is it?"

"On the contrary, most people think my life is incredibly boring. Or at least proceeding as expected." Her smile dimmed, but she seemed to make an effort to reclaim it. "But it's mine, and that's all anyone can really ask for, right? I like Cups and Kittens and I like my best friend, even if she's a bit on the antisocial side, and I maybe I don't have a ton on the horizon when it comes to my love life, but I'm only twenty-six. I'm hardly a spinster that should just swear off the whole thing now—especially since we've been running around causing a ruckus. That's sure to open up some new avenues for me."

He started to point out that they were, in fact, on a date right now, but the truth slammed into his chest all over again. *I'm not what she wants.* He'd known it before—it was a truth he hadn't been able to escape from the very beginning—but somehow hearing her talk about potential prospects while sitting across the table from him made him sick to his stomach. He didn't want to think about her going out with another guy, or her sharing her goofy smiles with some other dude, or, fuck, her letting someone else between those sweet thighs.

"Adam?"

He realized he was clutching his cloth napkin in a white-knuckled grip. "Yeah, sorry." He had to get it together. He didn't have a goddamn right to be jealous of some future guy. He was here with her now, but he wouldn't be forever. That was *his* choice.

He just had to remember that.

"Why a cat café?"

She pressed her lips together but seemed to decide it wasn't worth asking him what the hell was going on in his head. Which was good, because he didn't fucking know. Jules took a sip of her water. "There have been quite a few studies done that show having a pet—any pet—is enough to combat everything from poor physical health to depression to plain old loneliness. Animals never ask for anything but love, and that's a gift that a lot of people don't have in their lives. But not everyone can have a pet of their own for various reasons—which is where I come in."

It was so…Jules. Loving and thoughtful and kind. "You get a lot of traffic in there."

"Yep." She smiled. "Just being able to stop by, have a cup of coffee, and spend some time with a cat curled up in your lap is all some people need to restart their day. The cats love the attention. The people love the cats. And I love making people happy, so it's win-win across the board." She frowned. "Or win-win-win. Whatever. You know what I mean."

"I do." He'd always wanted a pet—though he was more inclined to dogs than cats—but his life made it hard to have one. There were other guys on the circuit who managed it, but to Adam, dogs represented stability. It wouldn't be right to have one without a yard or property to let him run free on. Being cooped up in the truck for hours on end, or tied to a fence while he rode…it would just be wrong.

"See. This is nice. We can hold down a conversation."

He chuckled. "And if the topics stall out, you can always slide on over here and offer up another solution."

Her face flamed red. "Shh, someone will hear you."

"I thought that was the whole point." He couldn't quite keep the irritation the thought brought out of his voice.

If anything, her blush got deeper. "That's was before. That's not what I want now."

Well, hell, he liked the sound of that. He looked around. El Pollo Delicioso was hardly five stars, but it had cloth napkins and more on the menu than tacos, so they were on a real honest-to-God date. That didn't mean he was going to stop giving her grief, though. "Come on, sugar. I'll make you feel good—again."

"You're out of control." She bit her lip. "I like it."

He *felt* out of control, like one wrong step would send him hurtling into something that was completely out of his realm of experience. The jealousy from earlier hadn't abated. If anything, it was getting worse with each passing heartbeat, because he *knew* this couldn't last forever. The longer it went on, the more the loss bloomed in the back of his mind. He was going to lose her, and he was only just realizing how much he *wanted* her.

He didn't want this to end.

Adam stared across the table at her, the realization a weight in his chest threatening to drown him. He couldn't tell if it was a good thing or a bad thing. All he knew was that his life would be a sad specter without Jules in it. He opened his mouth to tell her that, but a shadow fell over their table.

"If it isn't the cute couple."

For fuck's sake. Adam sat back and crossed his arms over his chest. "Grant. You know, you and Jules aren't together anymore—haven't been for years. Why the hell do you keep showing up every time I turn around? Stalking is frowned upon in these parts—not to mention illegal."

Grant narrowed his eyes. "Jules and I are friends, aren't we, Jules?"

"Actually—"

"I just came over to say congratulations. You've convinced me."

"Great." Adam rolled his eyes. "Of what?"

Grant looked from him to Jules and back again. "That you're dating. A friend of mine saw you in, shall we say, a compromising position not more than an hour ago on the side of the road like a common—"

Adam felt like the top of his head was going to explode. "Boy, I suggest you don't finish whatever you were about to say. I'm taking my lady out to a nice dinner, and you're over here, fucking that shit up. Leave."

"Yeah, well, I was just going." Grant turned to leave, muttering, "I could never get her to fuck me in *my* truck."

Adam didn't make a decision to move. One second he was staring at the little pissant's back, and the next he was on his feet and grabbing Grant's collar. "Let's take a walk."

"Adam!"

He ignored Jules, walking Grant out of the restaurant by his throat and giving him a shake for good measure. "In what world would you think I'm the kind of man to let you talk about my woman like that?" Another shake. "Here's a hint—I'm not."

Jules burst through the door. "Adam, stop! Adam, he's turning purple."

He tightened his grip on Grant's neck. "This is the last time I'm going to say this, so I suggest you keep from passing out long enough to hear it. Stay the fuck away from Jules. If you haven't noticed, she doesn't like you. She's too good of a person to say that, but I'm not. You do or say something to hurt her feelings again, and I'll put you in the fucking hospital."

He let go. Grant dropped to his knees, clutching his throat.

"What the hell is wrong with you?"

He already knew, before he turned to her, that she wasn't talking to Grant. Adam growled. "We're leaving." He didn't give her a chance to argue, hooking an arm around her waist and practically carrying her away from her wheezing ex.

They were in the truck when she spoke next. "We just walked out on our bill."

"I'll go by tomorrow and take care of it." There was no way he trusted himself to be within punching distance of Grant. Adam pulled out of the parking lot so fast, the momentum threw Jules against him. He knew he needed to slow down, to *calm* down, but he couldn't get himself under control.

It felt like the entire night had been one giant avalanche to this point. He'd known it was coming, but he hadn't been able to escape it. Jules was too damn good for him, and if she didn't know it after that clusterfuck, then he was luckier than he deserved.

"Do you trust me?"

She huffed out a breath. "What kind of question is that? Of course I do, even when you're acting like an idiot."

"Good." He turned off the highway, taking a little dirt road that hadn't gotten much use in high school and didn't appear to get much now. The truck bumped and shook over the potholes, but eventually spit them out in a field with nothing around for miles. "Come on." He got out, grabbed the two blankets from beneath his seat, and walked around to lower the tailgate. Jules followed, but she didn't look too happy with him. He laid the blankets out in the bed of his truck and turned to her. "I'm sorry. I was out of line."

"You think?" She frowned up at him. "What *was* that? I know Grant's an awful person, but he's not worth getting brought up on assault charges."

He let go of the steering wheel and realized his hands were shaking. "He shouldn't have said that about you."

"You're right. He shouldn't. But they're just words."

Except he'd seen her face the moment she registered what Grant had said. If there'd just been anger present, maybe Adam could have let it go—*maybe*—but there had been shame there, too. He reached for her, slowly, giving her time to decide if she'd let him touch her.

Jules didn't move, allowing him to cup her face. He stroked her cheekbones with his thumbs. "I don't want you to regret what we've done. There's no shame in any of it."

"Guess I can't be scandalous without seeing some negative effects, huh?"

He shook his head. "Take everyone else out of the equation. Do *you* regret what we've done?"

"I…" She sighed. "No. I've managed to become a town scandal, at least temporarily. It's going to change the way people look at me, and that's something. These last couple of weeks with you…I'll always look back on them fondly." Her smile was a little bittersweet. "Though I think I'll keep most of this out of the stories I'll tell my grandbabies one day. They're not exactly appropriate for tiny ears."

There it was again—the ever-present reminder that this thing between them wouldn't last forever. The knowledge that there would be another man Jules would fall in love with, a man who'd put a ring on her finger and who'd be there in the delivery room with her when she delivered their children. A man who'd get to spend the rest of his life by her side.

And it wouldn't be Adam.

His chest clenched so tightly, he couldn't draw a full breath. So he did the only thing he could think of.

He kissed her.

CHAPTER TWENTY-ONE

There were so many things left to say, but Jules let Adam sweep them both away. She couldn't ignore what he'd done to Grant, just like she couldn't ignore the fact that when he touched her, her entire body lit up. And then he looked at her with those dark eyes and actually *cared* about the things she found important.

God, he cared more than he'd ever let anyone see.

Let me in. Please, just let me past those walls you've built so thickly around yourself.

She couldn't let the words out. They were the keeping kind of things, and he'd told her time and time again that he wasn't staying. Expecting him to suddenly fall for her and change his mind wasn't fair to both of them. *She* was the one messing with the rules after she'd assured him she'd be fine with the boundaries he set.

This was never meant to be more than a crazy footnote in my life.

Except it didn't *feel* like a footnote.

It felt world ending.

So she let him kiss her and she wrapped her arms around his neck, needing to be as close as they could be to settle the fears rising in the back of her mind.

Fears that, when he walked away, he'd take a bloody piece of her heart with him.

He lifted her onto the tailgate. "Let me make love to you, sugar. Just this once."

Her heart leaped into her throat, blocking the words she had no business so much as thinking. Jules nodded, because there was nothing else left to say that wouldn't ruin it. She felt absurdly like crying as he pulled off her boots and lifted her dress over her head. "Adam—"

"There's time for that tomorrow."

He was right. They had tonight, and everything could wait for sunrise. She nodded. "Okay."

"Good." He stripped quickly and set both their clothes in the bed of the truck. Then he kissed her again, backing her up and laying her flat on the blankets. "Never lose *you*, sugar." His lips brushed the sensitive spot behind her ear. "There isn't anyone like you out there—I've been around the block enough times to know—and the world would be a dimmer place if you compromised any part of yourself to appease someone else." He eased her bra off, his lips moving over her skin, saying words she never knew she wanted to hear. "You're better than a goddamn eight-second ride, Jules Rodriguez, and I'll never meet your like again."

She started to say…God, she didn't even know what…but he moved down her body, slipping off her panties and spreading her thighs. "And tonight, you're mine." And then his mouth was there against the most intimate part of her, touching her just as his words had a moment before.

Jules gave herself over to him, letting go of her worries for tomorrow and her irritation over how Adam handled things back at the restaurant. He was like a wild thing, barely tamed. Just like the bulls he loved to ride or the stallions on the ranch. He'd let her cuddle up to him, but one wrong move and someone was going to lose an arm.

Not her. She'd spent enough time with him to be sure of that—he'd never hurt her. But that didn't mean a single thing when it came to the people around her.

"You're thinking too hard."

"I can't help it." Her life would be so much easier if she knew how to turn off her stampeding thoughts.

Adam sighed, his breath on her sensitive skin making her squirm. "Let me help." Then he pushed two fingers into her and sucked her clit into his mouth, setting his teeth against her. The sensation was so intense, it was just this side of pain. Jules's mind went blank, and her body went tight.

"Holy good gracious."

He pumped his fingers slowly, dragging them over that spot inside her. She pressed her heels against the bed of the truck, trying to take him deeper, but he laughed softly and used his free hand to pin her hips. "Not yet, sugar."

"Adam, *please*."

He gave her one long lick. "Are you still thinking too hard?"

"I... What?" She squirmed, but he had full control—just like always. She'd always considered herself an independent woman, but there was something about being at Adam's mercy that flat-out did it for her. She tried lifting her hips again. "More."

"All right, sugar. I'll give you more."

She cried out when he removed his hand, but the unmistakable crinkle of a condom wrapper had her shutting right up. This was good. This was even better. He crawled up her body and settled between her thighs. She wrapped her legs around his waist, arching against him. "Kiss me."

"Bossy." He cupped the back of her head and took her mouth even as his cock slid home.

Something inside her that had been rattled and uncertain settled in that moment of perfection. *We have the now. Stop asking for more than he's willing to give. He said I'm his for tonight, and that'll have to be enough.*

But she needed more. Jules dragged her nails down his back. "You make me so hot and crazy and *gah*."

"Tell me more." He began to move, the slightest strokes that drove her to distraction but nowhere near enough to send her over the edge.

"I was *okay*." She dug her fingers into his ass, pulling him deeper. "Mostly okay. Somewhat okay."

"Mmm." He nibbled on her neck, keeping up that infuriating movement.

She couldn't catch her breath. "One look, Adam. That's all it takes. You give me that look and I'm ready to drag you into the nearest enclosed space and drop my panties."

"Good." He picked up his strokes, withdrawing almost all the way out before pushing back into her. "Because I feel the same fucking way, sugar. Every time I stop moving for more than five seconds, all I can think about is the feel of you beneath me, taste you on my tongue, and smell your coconut shampoo. It drives me fucking insane."

"I'm sorry," she gasped.

"I'm not. I fucking love it." He hitched her leg higher on his waist, driving deeper yet. "And the thought of you sharing your future with another man makes it feel like I have fifteen-hundred-pound bull trampling all over my chest." He lowered his voice, so soft that she could barely hear him over the sounds of her breathing. "I want that future. I want it so bad, I can barely stand it."

She started to say…something…but he was already moving, flipping her over and drawing her up onto her hands and knees. "But tonight is mine, sugar. And I'm going to make sure you never forget me."

Forget him? *Impossible.*

He slammed into her, driving a cry from her lips. And then there was no more time for talking. She clutched the blankets, shoving back against him even as he gripped her hips tighter, the sound of flesh meeting flesh joining the cricket sounds in the field around them. "Touch yourself, sugar. I want to feel you come around my cock."

She obeyed without thought, sliding her hand between her legs and stroking her clit. Combined with him filling her, it didn't take long for the first spasms to start. "*Adam.*"

"That's right. Take it all." He slammed into her again and again, driving her out of her mind with pleasure, until she was sure she couldn't take it anymore. Only then did his strokes become irregular, and he let himself go with a curse.

He collapsed next to her, pulling her back against his chest. She stared up at the sky, a blanket of stars that somehow made this even more intimate.

Too soon, her mind kicked back into gear, replaying every single word he'd said since they left the restaurant. She fought to keep her body relaxed, but his sigh proved just how sucky she was at it.

"Relax, sugar. We'll talk in the morning."

Maybe. Or maybe that would give him time to reconsider whatever he'd meant when he said he wanted a future with her. She bit her lip so hard it was a wonder she didn't draw blood, barely able to wrap her mind around it.

A future with Adam Meyer.

It was the one thing she hadn't allowed herself to consider. And why would she? He wasn't staying in Devil's Falls.

But what if he did?

Jules liked him—a lot. She liked that he didn't seem to think she was boring or "good ole Jules" or feel the need to patronize her and tell her how he knew better. In fact, he'd done nothing but empower her.

She liked the way he obviously loved his mom. He might not have spent much time back home over the last decade, but he still cared a whole lot. And Amelia loved her son more than anything else in the world. Jules knew that because she was a shameless eavesdropper when it came to her customers. Amelia was always telling Lenora about Adam's latest escapades with the same tone of voice Jules's mom used to brag about her good grades. It was really sweet.

And there was the sex. Good lord, the sex. It really wasn't fair how out-of-this-world good it was.

He was kind of prickly, but he had a dry sense of humor that she adored. And Aubry didn't scare him. That alone was a big point in his favor. Not to mention, since her best friend hadn't hacked into his cell phone or something else insane, she'd pretty much given her seal of approval. That mattered.

Adam brushed her hair to the side and kissed the back of her neck. "You're doing it again."

"I'm sure I have no idea what you're talking about."

"I'm just as sure that you do." He grabbed the blanket on the other side of her and covered them both with it, settling down again at her back. "It'll all still be there in the morning, sugar. Obsessing about it now isn't going to change a damn thing, except you'll lose sleep."

Easier said than done. She turned in his arms to face him. "Can you do that? Just turn it off?"

His face was little more than a shadow in the darkness. "Some days I'm better at it than others." There was a world of…something…in his voice. Something she didn't have a name for.

She couldn't ask if he was staying. It wasn't the right time, and if he said no, it would just hurt her. So she went with an equally dangerous topic—but one that had nothing to do with her. "You never mention your dad."

"Not much to mention." He sighed. "He was a leaver, as my mama likes to say. He managed to stick around for four years after I was born, but it killed a part of him to be stuck inside these town limits. He rolled back through a couple times as I was growing up, but Mama was never all that happy to see him, knowing she'd see the back of him again before too long. I'm just like him."

He didn't say any of it with anger, more with a quiet fatality she didn't know what to do with. "Adam, there's no such thing as fate. You make your own future."

"You don't understand. I have this…I don't even

know what to call it—restlessness, for lack of a better word. It starts in my chest and builds and builds until I feel like I'm coming out of my skin. It's been there ever since I was a kid, and the second I was old enough to get out, it eased the feeling. The only thing that takes it away completely is being on the back of a bull."

How could she compete with that? She'd heard stories about rodeo widows, women who loved a man who loved the rodeo. How could a flesh-and-blood person stand against the roar of the crowd and the adrenaline rush of trying to stay on a rage-filled animal's back for eight seconds? It didn't sound all that wonderful to Jules, but she was unforgivably biased.

Adam leaned against the tailgate. "And now with my mom sick… I just don't know how it's going to end up."

Meaning the cancer could take her.

If it did, not only would Devil's Falls lose one of its favorite ladies, but Adam would lose the last anchor drawing him back to this place. She didn't fool herself for a second into thinking Quinn and Daniel were enough to bring him home, not when he'd be faced with memory after memory of his mother.

And, no matter how she was starting to feel about Adam, *she* would never be enough for him. That was startlingly clear.

"It's okay, Adam. It will be okay."

But the sinking feeling in her chest wouldn't go away. The only thing that had kept him in place for more than two weeks was his mom. If she lost her battle with cancer, he would run as far and fast as he could and not look back.

CHAPTER TWENTY-TWO

Adam woke up with a naked Jules in his arms, and hell if that wasn't a way to start the day. He blinked at the bright sunlight and shielded his eyes. She lifted her head. "What time is it?"

"I don't know." He eyed the sky. "Still early. Maybe seven."

"Crap, I have to get going." She sat up, giving him the view of a lifetime, and grabbed her dress. "I open the café today."

As much as he wanted to pull her back down and lose himself in her for a few hours, she was right. Responsibilities waited. His mama had a doctor's appointment today, and he was determined to bully her into letting him go with her. He sat up and stretched. "Let's get you back to town, then."

Jules pulled on her dress and sent him a grin he felt right through his chest. "Last night was something else."

"Yeah, it was."

Her smile dimmed. "But we *do* have to talk about Grant at some point. He was a jackass last night, but you can't just go around manhandling him because he said something…ill-advised."

Ill-advised about summed it up. "Sure I can." When she frowned, he relented. "Sugar, I'll mind my p's and q's, but I'm not civilized enough to sit back and let him insult you. If that's what you're looking for, I'm not your man."

She yanked on her boots. "Just try not to get arrested, okay? Sheriff Taylor is getting close to retiring, and having to haul you in will do a number on his blood pressure."

He finished buttoning his jeans and pulled her into his arms. "You know, Quinn said the same damn thing to me back at the bonfire. Clearly I have a reputation if you all are so worried I'm going to give the good old sheriff a heart attack."

"Well, if he caught sight of what kind of trouble we've been getting into in your truck, I think that's a very real risk."

Adam laughed. "You spend an awful lot of your time taking care of other people."

"Some people don't have anyone to take care of them." She ducked out of his hold when he went for a kiss. "Morning breath!"

"I think we've already established I have a solution for that."

"Good point." She bounded around the side of his truck, reappearing a few seconds later with the fresh bottle of water he'd put in there yesterday, toothbrush, and toothpaste. "You know, I'm not really a fan of camping out, but this has been fun." She shot a look at the bed of his truck, covered with rumpled blankets. "Or maybe I've been listening to too many country songs."

"No such thing." He waited for her to brush her teeth and then followed suit. "Everything worth knowing can be found in a country song."

"I thought the saying was that 'everything I need to know in life, I learned in kindergarten'?"

He grinned. "That, too."

The drive back into Devil's Falls passed in comfortable silence, Jules cuddled up against him. The words he'd said—and hadn't said—last night were a jumbled mess in his chest. He would lose her if he didn't find a way to say what needed to be said—then actually put those words into action—and he didn't want to lose her. He pulled up behind her shop and put the truck into park. "Sugar, I have something to say."

She went still against him. "I'm listening."

"I don't know what the future will hold—"

"No one does."

He waited, and she ducked her head.

"Whoops. You're saying your thing and I'm interrupting."

"I know it hasn't been that long, but I can't imagine my life without you." He opened his mouth to tell her that he wouldn't leave, that he'd do his damnedest to be the man she wanted, but he couldn't force the words out. Despite everything, they still felt like a lie. Instead, he said, "I don't know what's going to happen, and I can only take things one day at a time, but I want you, sugar. Just you."

When she looked up at him, her eyes were shining with unshed tears, her expression looking almost… worried. "Oh, Adam." She kissed him, a quick brushing of her lips against his, and then she was gone, slipping out of his truck and practically running inside.

He stared at the door for a long time. "That went… well." She hadn't told him to fuck off, but she hadn't exactly seemed happy, either. He glanced at the clock. Dealing with Jules's weird reaction would have to wait—he had to leave now if he wanted to be on time for his mom's appointment. Thank God Devil's Falls was so small or he *would* be late.

The doctor's office was a tiny little building off Main Street, and Dr. Jenkins had been practicing long enough that he'd treated Adam's mom when she was a kid. The man was ninety if he was a day, but Mama wouldn't hear of going to someone else. There *was* no one else in town, and she didn't like the thought of going into Odessa more than strictly necessary.

He walked through the door and froze, feeling like he'd just come through a portal into the past. The same faded posters hung on the walls—all cute baby animals with affirming statements—and the same faded blue fabric covered the uncomfortable seats. The receptionist had changed, though. It used to be John's mom that worked here, but the whole family had moved away after his death.

Not that Adam blamed them. Sometimes it was easier to leave the past behind than to face it, day in and day out, while the walls slowly closed in and suffocated any chance of happiness a person had.

The woman behind the desk smiled brightly. "What can I do to help you?"

"I'm looking for Amelia Meyer."

"I'm sorry, sir, I can't give out that information." But the slight shift in her posture told him all he needed to know. His mom had beat him here. Hell, she'd probably moved up the appointment, hoping that he'd miss it altogether.

He eyed the door leading back to the appointment rooms. If he remembered correctly, there were two total. He was so goddamn tired of getting information secondhand from his mama, especially since she tended to sugarcoat everything to the point where it was damn near a lie. He wasn't sure if she was trying to protect him or herself, but he needed to hear what was going on straight from the medical source.

"Excuse me." He turned and strode through the door.

"You can't go back there!"

Too late. He was already past the first open exam room and walking into the second one. His mom and Dr. Jenkins jumped, the former looking as guilty as a sinner in church. Adam shut the door on the squawking receptionist. "Mama."

"Son." She crossed her arms over her chest and lifted her chin. "You're early."

"And yet somehow I was almost late." He ambled over and sat in the spare chair, pinning the doctor with a look. "Bring me up-to-date."

Dr. Jenkins was a nice man who specialized in pediatrics. He hadn't known what to do with Adam as a kid, and he didn't know what to do with him now. He adjusted his glasses, what was left of his white hair standing out against his dark skin. "Now, Adam, you know I can't do that without Amelia's permission."

Her sigh was defeated enough to give Adam a twinge. His mom stood and straightened her dress. "You go ahead and tell him what he needs to know, Matthew. Though you'll have to excuse me. I don't need to hear this again." She walked out of the room with the dignity of a queen, which only made Adam feel even more like an asshole.

He turned to Dr. Jenkins. "I'm sorry for barging in, but she won't give me a straight answer."

"Yes, I'm well acquainted with Amelia's stubbornness." He gave Adam a look over the top of his glasses.

"It's a family trait, if I remember correctly." Dr. Jenkins sat back and rubbed a hand over his face. "I won't mince words with you, Adam. It's bad. It took her a long time to admit that what she was feeling wasn't just age, and by that time the cancer had been at work for God alone knows how long."

Adam had to force the words out. "How bad?"

"She's got stage-four lung cancer." Dr. Jenkins's entire being came across as sympathetic. "She's refused chemotherapy, and I don't know that I'd recommend it considering her age and overall health. Unfortunately, the cure for cancer is sometimes worse than the cancer itself, and I believe that would be the case with your mother."

He heard the words, but he couldn't process them. He'd known it was bad. Of course he'd known it was bad. But bad and fatal were two different things. He swallowed, the motion doing nothing to help his dry throat. "If she'd come in earlier, would it have made a difference?"

"There's no way to tell."

Which wasn't a no. His chest was so tight, he couldn't draw a breath. *My fault. If I'd been home, I would have known something was wrong. I would have made her come to the doctor. It would have made a difference.*

"It's not your fault."

Dr. Jenkins had always seen too much of Adam. As a teenager, he hadn't wanted the man's sympathy. As an adult, he didn't deserve it. He pushed to his feet, weaving a little. "Thanks for telling me."

"Adam—"

"I'll see you around, Doc." He sidestepped the

older man and walked out of the room. His mama wasn't there waiting, but he didn't expect her to be. She was pissed he'd barged in, probably pissed that he'd shone the hard light of day onto her situation and forced her to face it. His mama had always been great at self-denial. She denied that his dad leaving had hurt her, just went on without a hitch in her step. But when he was seventeen he'd caught her holding a faded photograph and crying like her heart was breaking. This wasn't any different.

Except heartbreak wouldn't kill her.

Cancer would.

He hit the door to the outside and started walking, bypassing his truck. He wasn't in a good place to be getting behind the wheel right now, and walking might help him get his head on straight—doubtful, but anything was better than standing still right now. He didn't have a destination in mind, but he wasn't particularly surprised to find himself standing in the doorway to Cups and Kittens. Jules was busy with a few other customers, so he took a seat in the corner— the same one Aubry always seemed to be camped out in. Almost immediately, one cat jumped up onto the table in front of him, and a second made itself at home in his lap. Adam stared down at the long-haired orange cat and gave it a tentative pet. When he was rewarded with a purr loud enough to be a jet engine, he did it again. The monstrous feeling inside him didn't uncoil, but he managed to draw his first full breath since hearing the news.

His thoughts tumbled over themselves as he tried to come up with a solution—any solution—to this impossible situation. This wasn't something he could just power his way through until the world rearranged itself to suit him. This was his mother's health. Even if she was willing to do the treatment, Dr. Jenkins hadn't seemed optimistic that it would be worth the cost.

Which meant there was little they could do.

"Adam?"

He didn't look up. If he did, she'd see the pain he couldn't manage to mask on his face, and then she'd ask him if he was okay, and he'd lose it. "I've got to go."

He carefully set the orange cat on the table and walked away.

CHAPTER TWENTY-THREE

Jules waited all of a heartbeat before she followed Adam out onto the street. He wasn't exactly a sharer, but she'd have to be blind not to see the pain written over every line of his body. "Adam, wait!"

He stopped, but he didn't turn to face her. "Now's not a good time, sugar."

Her realization last night settled in her chest, feeling like it'd cemented her heart into place. There was no reason to be surprised he was shutting her out. Hadn't he done it every single time she'd asked him what was wrong? But she took a deep breath, shored up her courage, and said, "You can talk to me."

He still didn't turn around. "Talking never did anybody a damn bit of good."

"You won't know until you try." She touched his arm, trying to quell the panic rising with each breath. *Please don't shut me out. Please just talk to me. Please show me that we weren't doomed before we started.*

Adam jerked his arm out of her grasp. "Talking is all anyone in this shitty little town likes to do—except when it counts. Then everyone shuts the fuck up. So, no, sugar, I'm not going to pour my heart out to you to make you feel better about yourself."

She stumbled back a step, her heart dropping to her stomach. "That's not why I offered to talk."

"Isn't it? You want to fix me, and you want reassurance that I fit into the plans you have for your future. Well, I can't give you either." He started to turn away.

"And I'm never going to be the man who will settle down with you."

The woman she was a month ago would have let him walk away. She would have mourned the end of things, but she wouldn't have had the fire burning in the pit of her stomach driving her to chase him down the sidewalk. "No one can fix you, Adam Meyer. Not until you're ready to hold still long enough to realize that your inability to stay in one place has nothing to do with your dad and everything to do with *you*. You're a self-fulfilling prophecy, and you could change if you wanted to."

He glared, his hands clenched at his sides. "Really, Jules? Changing my entire life around to suit your needs isn't as easy as coming up with some quirky plan to scandalize a small town before you move on with your life."

"That's not fair."

But he wasn't listening. "Here's a piece of advice— being the town scandal comes with more strings attached than you want to deal with. It's better to leave the whole damn thing behind."

"There you go again, running the second it looks like you're in danger of putting down roots. Brave, Adam. Really brave."

He shook his head. "This was a mistake. I should have seen it earlier."

This is it. He's not even waiting to leave town to walk away from me. She stared at his back as he moved away from her. "Fine. Walk away from me. It's what you're good at." His step hitched, and for one endless moment, she thought he might turn around, might come back and actually *talk* to her.

But then the moment passed and Adam kept walking.

Jules's breath whooshed out, and it took everything she had not to crumple into a ball on the street and start crying. When the heck had she started to care about that man so much? She was an idiot, and quite possibly insane. She turned, feeling like she was walking through molasses, and looked straight into Grant's gray eyes. *And I thought today couldn't get any worse.*

He smiled. "Trouble in paradise?"

Did he think she cared about what he thought when her heart was walking away from her, the pain cutting deeper with each step he took? She'd thought herself in love with Grant back in the day, but it hadn't been a drop in the ocean compared to what she felt for Adam. So Jules lifted her chin and stared down her nose at her ex. "Here's a tip, Grant—fuck off." She marched into her café and shut the door behind her.

It was clear from the expressions on the handful of customers around that they'd seen and/or heard everything. She tried for a smile. "Does anyone need a coffee refill?"

Mrs. Peterson walked over and took her hands. "I'm so sorry, honey. But after Grant, you really should have known better."

The walls around her seemed to be moving closer. She carefully extracted her hand. "Adam is nothing like that…that…*douchecanoe*. How dare you even compare them? He's stubborn to the point of idiocy and proud and in pain, but that's no reason to put him in the same box." In a distant part of her mind, she knew she was ranting, but she couldn't seem to stop. "And for God's sake, I'm twenty-six. Just because I've been dumped unceremoniously twice in my life doesn't mean I'm doomed to be alone, and I'll thank you—and everyone else in this town—kindly to remember that. At the very least I should have three shots to get it right before you regulate me to the shelf!"

She strode across the room and through the door into the back, not looking at anyone for fear of seeing more pitying looks. Jamie jumped about ten feet when she barged in, but Jules ignored her cousin and just kept walking, up the stairs and into her apartment. Aubry jumped nearly a foot in the air when she walked through the door, but her surly expression disappeared the instant she saw Jules. "What happened?"

It took two tries to get the words out. "Adam and I are over."

Aubry straightened, her amber eyes narrowing. "You were fine three hours ago. What did he do? Do I have to get out my body-burying kit?"

She was only half sure Aubry was joking. It didn't make her feel any better that her friend was willing to go to such lengths for her. "If you go to jail, I won't have anyone."

"That's not true. Your parents love you very much, even if they live a million miles away, and your extended family is as meddling as they are numerous." She huffed. "Though I guess they're pretty cool, too."

"Aubry…" She stumbled over and sank onto the couch. "Something happened—something bad. I knew he was leaving—I couldn't escape that fact—but I thought we had more time. Maybe I'm asking too much. I just want him to let me in, but it feels like he shuts me out of anything that isn't the good parts of him. What kind of relationship is that?"

"I'm not going to pretend I know a damn thing about relationships, but even I know that wanting the whole of someone isn't a bad thing." She glared out the window as if he was standing right there. "He's an idiot. A big-headed, knuckle-dragging, troublemaking idiot. He doesn't deserve you."

That was the problem. She wasn't sure it was the truth. She took a deep breath. "I should have known better. It shouldn't matter so much what the town thinks of me. Instead of coming up with some crazy plan with my fake boyfriend, I should have done what every normal single woman in her twenties does and joined an internet dating site. There's a world outside Devil's Falls, and I'm sure I could find someone who isn't a troll or a serial killer to love me."

"Jules—"

She stood. "I don't want to hear it."

"Too goddamn bad." Aubry grabbed her elbow and yanked her back down onto the couch. "Life is about risk—don't you look at me like that, I know I don't follow that rule—and you took one. And for the last fucking time, you're not boring. A boring woman would have married Grant and been his little wife with no identity of her own. You don't have to be a wild child or fuel for the gossip mill to be unique and amazing, and I'm stopping now before we both start to cry."

She shook her head. "But everybody—"

"I know for a fact that the only person who thinks less of you for the choices you've made is Grant. That's why you get your back up when anyone else says anything remotely close to you being a cat lady or on the shelf or whatever other hot-button terms you don't like."

Aubry had a point. She *knew* Aubry had a point, but it was so hard to agree with her with Adam's words ringing in her ears. Stability. That's what she'd always sought for herself. She'd known Adam wasn't the most stable guy around, but… "He just walked away. He wouldn't even talk to me."

If there was one thing she learned from her parents' twenty-five-year marriage, it was that people had to be able to fight in a relationship and still have the security to know it wasn't the end of things. She didn't have that with Adam. She wasn't sure she ever would, even if their fight hadn't happened today.

"Adam's a broken individual. Trust me, it takes one to know one." Aubry hugged her. "And, just like me, you can't fix him through sheer force of will. The world would be a better place if your sunshine could drown out other people's rainstorms—it just doesn't work like that."

But she didn't want to change him. Not really. She liked all of Adam's hidden depths and a thousand other little things about him. The only thing she wanted was for him to let her in, to let her help him shoulder the burden. If his mom really was terminal, then he'd need someone to lean on. He couldn't do it alone, not without breaking, not when he obviously loved Amelia so much.

But he wouldn't take help from her. She suspected he wouldn't take help from *anyone*.

Or maybe he would…

Jules straightened. "I have to make a call." She

disentangled herself from Aubry and pulled her phone out of her pocket. It took all of a second to find Daniel's number and call it.

He answered almost immediately. "Yep?"

"Adam needs you." Her voice broke, but she charged on. "He won't talk to me, but something happened, and he needs to talk to someone."

"Does he know you're calling?"

"No."

Daniel was quiet for a long ten seconds. "We don't talk about some things, Jules. It's just the way it is."

What was it with the men in her life who couldn't deal with emotion? She took a deep breath and tried to keep the strain from her voice. "I know you have unresolved issues—all of you do—but if you let him shoulder this alone, it's going to kill something inside him. Please, Daniel. Please at least try to talk to him."

Her cousin sighed. "I'll try. That's all I can do."

It would have to be good enough. "Thank you." She hung up and turned to find Aubry staring at her. "What?"

"You really fell hard for this guy, didn't you?"

Too hard, too fast, too much all around. She slumped back into the couch. "I really did."

"I think this calls for a tea party." Aubry stood. "And by tea party, I mean we're going to drink vodka out of teacups and eat our weight in ice cream while we bitch about the men who've done us wrong."

"I don't deserve you."

"Aw, Jules, that's where you're wrong. You're better than all of us—you're just too good of a person to see it." She disappeared into her room and came back with two fine china teacups on saucers. "Now, do you want to shoot some noobs, or is this the kind of hurting that requires a sappy romance movie?"

Jules's eyes burned. "You're the best friend anyone could ever ask for."

"Just don't go around telling people that."

"Your secret is safe with me."

CHAPTER TWENTY-FOUR

Adam didn't have a place in mind when he started driving after grabbing a six-pack from the market, but he ended up in the cemetery, winding through the narrow paths until he stood in front of his friend's headstone. He opened a beer and finally made himself read it.

John Moore
Beloved son and brother
December 16, 1981—December 16, 2002
It's been too long.

And somehow not nearly long enough.

He opened a second beer and, after a self-conscious look around, upended it on the grass covering his friend's grave.

Adam sighed. His mama wasn't talking to him, and Lenora had practically ripped out his throat when he tried to push the subject. As much as he hated to admit it, she was right—they both needed time to cool off. The problem was the truth wasn't going anywhere, no matter how many laps he drove around town.

She's really going to be gone for good, long before I'm ready to let her go. I don't know that I'll ever *be ready to let her go.*

His mama was the closest thing to roots he had in this life. What was he going to do without that? It didn't matter that he didn't see her all that often normally—knowing she was carrying on life in Devil's Falls had always steadied him, just a bit.

"So what's brought you out here looking for answers?"

He took a long pull of his beer and turned to where Daniel approached. He wasn't ready to talk about it. He didn't know if he'd ever be ready to say it aloud. So he went with something easier to bear. "You know, John was one of my best friends, and I've never come out here to visit him."

"He's gone. Visiting his grave doesn't make him any less gone."

The words didn't sit well with him. There was nothing more final than a gravestone, and the thought that in too short a time he might be standing in front of a different gravestone made his throat burn. "Have you been out here?"

"Yeah." Daniel tipped back his head and closed his eyes. "I share a six-pack with him once a month."

It was becoming startlingly clear that Adam had well and truly fucked up when he left town—and he'd been fucking up ever since. "I should have come back sooner. I should have been here for you and Quinn."

And for Mama.

"We were all fighting our own demons in our own way. You did the best you could."

But that wasn't the truth. He could have done better. Oh, he'd spent the last decade telling himself that no one expected any different from him. He was just like his old man. The bad egg. The hell-raiser. So when he blew out of town, restlessness driving him like a leaf before a hurricane, it was only the last in a long list of things adding up to him being the piece-of-shit leaver he'd always known he was.

He'd never once considered that he could change.

"My mama's dying. Cancer."

Daniel finally looked at him. "Shit, I'm sorry. I didn't know."

"No one did. The only reason *I* know is that I bullied my way into her doctor's appointment." And suddenly the words were there where there hadn't been any before. "I should have been here. All this time, I should have been here."

"You had your reasons for leaving."

Adam suddenly hated that everyone was so goddamn willing to give him a pass. "What could possibly be more important than being here? All these years wasted, chasing some adrenaline high while I was missing the shit that really mattered back home."

"Fuck, Adam, what do you want me to say? Was it shitty that you left right after graduation? Yeah, it was. And, yeah, it would have been nice to have you here instead of passing through town like a fucking tumbleweed. But you made the decision that you made. I wasn't willing to lose another friend over it."

Especially not after they'd lost John.

"I'm sorry." He felt like he'd been saying that too fucking much lately. What did sorry really mean if he didn't do a damn thing to keep this shit from happening again?

"There's nothing to be sorry for. We all did stupid shit when we were eighteen and full of more come than common sense. If you keep beating yourself up about it, you're never going to get past it." He looked at Adam. "But you're not eighteen anymore. So what are you going to do?"

About his mama.

About Jules.

About his goddamn life in general.

He rubbed a hand over his face. That was the problem—like Daniel said, they weren't eighteen anymore. He'd spent so long running from the idea of settling down, he wasn't sure what it'd be like to stand and fight. But he already knew that chasing down his favorite adrenaline rush was only a temporary solution. "I don't know."

"Here's a hint—apologize. Your mama loves you as much as you love her." Daniel pushed to his feet and finished off his beer. "And, Adam, none of us knew she was sick—not like you're saying. If no one in Devil's Falls could tell, how the hell would you be able to? Do you have some sort of X-ray vision that you've neglected to tell me about?"

"No."

"Yeah, I didn't think so." He awkwardly squeezed Adam's shoulder. "Just be there for her. That's all she wants."

That seemed to be all anyone wanted from him. Except Jules. Jules fully expected him to leave at some point and had plans to eventually settle down with some future guy.

Something must have showed on his face, because Daniel hesitated. "I hate to even ask, but what the hell happened with Jules? One second you're making googly eyes at her, and the next she's calling me upset and telling me to track your stupid ass down."

Of course she'd been the one to call Daniel. It didn't matter that he'd said some awful shit to her— she was still trying to take care of him. "It never would have worked. I don't deserve her."

But he wanted to.

Daniel leveled a long look at him. "Yeah, well, not with you being own self-fulfilling prophecy. You're not your old man. You never were, though you've been determined to prove otherwise since you were a kid." He set the empty bottle back into the six-pack. "Let me know if there's anything I can do to help with your mom." And then he was gone, striding across the cemetery to where his truck was parked at the entrance.

The possibility that he wasn't his father 2.0 had never really occurred to Adam. Oh, he'd fantasized about making different choices when he was too young to know better, but when push came to shove, his instincts were always to walk away. To pursue the next adrenaline rush. Adam glared at the horizon, waiting to feel the pull for the next ride, the next highway to nowhere.

For once in his life, it didn't have the same siren call as what was behind him—Devil's Falls, his mama, and Jules.

"Better late than never." He headed for his truck. He wasn't sure where to start, but he owed his mama an apology. He'd mishandled things, and having the best of intentions didn't change the fact that he'd pissed her off something fierce.

The drive back to her place passed in a blur, and then he was striding into the kitchen, where his mama and Lenora were puttering over of pot of what smelled like chicken noodle soup. Lenora took one look at his face and said, "I'll be in the living room if you need me."

He wanted to tell her that his mama didn't need her for a conversation with her son, but it was right that Lenora stood with her against the world—even him. His mama had stood alone for far too long, and he was honestly glad that she'd found happiness in the midst of everything. "Mama."

She braced her frail shoulders like she was going to war and turned to face him. "Son."

He didn't want to fight. Fuck, he was so tired of fighting. "I wish you would have told me."

"That was my choice to make."

"Mama—"

"I don't know if it helps or makes it worse, but I haven't known nearly as long as you seem to think." She shot a look at the doorway Lenora had disappeared through. "She wouldn't take no for an answer when it came to contacting you."

He exhaled. She hadn't hid it from him. Not really. That was just his knee-jerk reaction upon hearing that she had stage-four cancer. It had never occurred to him that it had surprised her as much as him. *Great job being sympathetic, ass.* "I've made a mess of things."

"You're overprotective." She smiled. "There are worse things, especially when I can't blame your bull-headedness on your father."

He managed a smile, though it felt brittle. "I don't know how to do this. I don't know how to be there for you without stepping on toes and trying to *fix* things."

"Oh, baby." She crossed the tiny kitchen and took his hands. "Some things you can't fix, no matter how hard you try. I was never going to make it out of this life alive. None of us are." She hugged him. "Give me the benefit of choosing how I'm going out. I don't want the chemo. The cancer is doing enough to me, and I can't bear the thought of my body wasting away any faster than it already is."

Stubborn to the very end.

Just like me.

It struck him that he'd been so focused on his old man that he'd never really considered what he'd inherited from his mama. If his father was a leaf on the wind, his mama was as steady as the sunrise. *I could have learned a thing or two from her if I'd just held still long enough to realize that.* He didn't know how to prove to her that he was determined to change, but there was only one place to start. "I'm going to buy a house."

His mama's eyes went wide. "What?"

"It's time. If you don't want chemo, I'm not going to push you. It's your decision. But I'm going to be here every step of the way and I'm going to help how I can."

Her grip tightened on his hands. "And after?"

That was the question, wasn't it? Daniel's words echoed through his mind.

You're not eighteen anymore.

It's time to stop acting like a scared kid.

"I hear the Rodriguez ranch needs help. Daniel would be more than happy to put me to work."

A shake passed through her body. "Truly?"

How had he never seen how much his leaving hurt his mama? *Selfish to the core.* Adam hugged her, holding her as tightly as he dared. "I'm not leaving again." If he could give his mom something, he'd give her this. He pressed a quick kiss to the top of her head. "What I think we both like to forget is that I had two parents. I'm tired of following in the footsteps of that piece of shit."

"Language."

"Sorry, Mama. My point is that maybe I could learn

a thing or two from the better half of the equation."

Her smile was a reward all its own. "You're a good man, baby."

It was the first time she'd ever said that to him, and if he didn't quite believe her, not yet, he was determined to make it the truth. He let go of her and stood back, his mind already turning to how he'd make a real life for himself here. He had a ton of money saved up because he'd stopped blowing through it after the first year of bull riding and had lived pretty low-key in the meantime—more than enough for a down payment.

"Baby?"

"Yeah, Mama?"

"What are you going to do about the Rodriguez girl?" Some censure had leaked back into her tone. "I was by Cups and Kittens earlier today, and she looks like she got hit by a truck." There was no doubt in her mind that he was the cause, and he couldn't even get pissed because it was the damn truth.

He'd well and truly fucked up.

"I'm going to make it right." He didn't know how, and he'd more than deserve it if Jules told him to take a hike while she moved on with her life. Adam didn't give a fuck. He'd fallen for her, and he'd do whatever it took to fix things and prove to her that he was the perfect man for her. He just had to figure out how.

His mama patted him on the arm. "You better. She's a good girl. I think she'd make an excellent daughter-in-law."

He laughed. "Yeah, well, let's take things one day at a time."

"That's the only way you can take them, baby." She kissed him on the cheek. "Now, go get your woman."

CHAPTER TWENTY-FIVE

Jules spent the week after breaking up with Adam in a strange haze. She did everything she could think of to snap out of it, but nothing worked. Not riding, not playing bloodthirsty video games with Aubry, not cuddling her cats. Nothing. She caught herself thinking about Adam half a dozen times a day, wondering if he was okay or if the pressure had gotten to be too much and he'd left town.

It hurt to think of never seeing him again.

It hurt worse to think of running into him randomly on his visits back in town.

Everything hurt.

She'd tried to comfort herself by promising herself that she'd find someone else, that she'd finally take the leap and sign up for internet dating, but the words were just that—words. They didn't comfort her in the least. She'd sat for an hour and just stared at the registration page before closing the browser completely. What did some guy on the other side of a screen have that made jumping through the required hoops worth it?

Would he give her dirty-talking lessons or, even better, would he hold her close and whisper things that made her hot and twisty without laying a finger on her? Would he get Aubry's stamp of approval and seem to actually enjoy going toe-to-toe with her? Would he make love to Jules in the bed of his truck beneath a summer sky?

And if he managed to achieve that herculean feat…would she be picturing Adam the entire time?

The more she thought about it, the more she had to face the facts—Adam Meyer had well and truly ruined her for anyone else.

She checked the clock, breathing a sigh of relief that she could finally close. There hadn't been anyone in for over an hour, but she didn't like to keep changeable hours. People depended on her being open the hours that were posted, and doing otherwise just didn't sit right with her, whether there were customers or not. She stepped over where Ninja Kitteh was lounging in the middle of the floor and walked to the door to lock it.

And froze.

Adam stood on the other side of the glass, looking even better than she remembered. Her heart leaped into her throat, and she had to clench her hands to keep from opening the door and throwing herself into his arms. *He walked away. Just because he didn't actually leave town in the last week doesn't change a single thing.* She had to remember that, though it was hard to with him looking at her like he'd been in the desert for weeks and she was an oasis.

"Can I come in?"

She didn't have to be able to hear him to know what words his lips formed. Numb, she nodded and opened the door. *Stupid. So freaking stupid.* But she'd proven time and again that she didn't have a lick of common sense when it came to this man. "Hi."

"Hi." He looked down as Khan came and rubbed himself on Adam's legs, purring furiously. "How are things?"

Awful. Terrible. No good. "Great."

"Good." He gave in to the cat's demanding and picked him up. Khan looked at Jules, smug as all get-out. As well he should be—he was in Adam's arms and she was standing just out of reach.

She was in the lowest of low places if she was jealous of a *cat*. "Great."

"You said that." A small smile quirked the edges of his lips, and she wasn't sure if she wanted to kiss him or smack him for walking back in here and making her heart break all over again.

She crossed her arms over her chest. "What do you want, Adam? Because I think you made your position pretty freaking clear the other day."

"Come for a drive with me."

"What?" She'd braced herself for him to say a lot of things, but that hadn't even been on the list. Adam was a lot of things, but cruel wasn't one of them. "Absolutely not."

"Please, sugar. I want to show you something."

"Is it a hole in the ground where you're going to stuff my dead body?"

He shot her a reproachful look. "It's funny—your mouth is moving, but I'm hearing the redhead talking."

Probably because Aubry was a hell of a lot smarter than Jules. She had things down. She stayed inside and interacted with people solely on her own terms—with the safety net of a computer between them. *She* wouldn't be standing here, seriously considering going somewhere with a man who'd broken her heart. "Adam, I can't do this. I'm barely getting through as things stand, and taking a drive with you is only going to make it worse. I don't think

I can survive another go-round."

Instantly the smile was gone from his face. "I'm sorry for that, sugar. I really am. Let me make it up to you."

I can't. It would be a mistake of epic proportions. "No."

"You're really putting a wrench in my grand gesture, you know that?" He sighed. "I guess we'll have to do this a different way."

She blinked. "Uh, what?"

"Come here." He pulled out his phone and started typing.

What the heck is going on? She slowly crossed the distance between them, feeling like she was approaching a rabid animal. He'd either run or attack, and she wasn't sure which would be preferable at this point.

"Here." He hooked her waist and pulled her into the circle of his arms, turning her so her back met his chest. She was so distracted by the sheer presence of him and the longing the feeling of him touching her awoke that she almost didn't realize he was trying to show her his phone screen. Jules frowned at it. "That's one of those house-finding apps." She liked to search them when she was bored, though she had no reason to move from the comfy little apartment above the café.

His chuckle made her shiver. "Look at the house."

It was a cute little thing. Two bedrooms, one and a half baths. Just outside town on twenty acres. It needed some love and probably a few months' worth of renovations, but it had promise. Her chest ached, something like hope sprouting there. "Why am I looking at a house?"

"I bought it yesterday." His breath ghosted over her ear. "Or at least I started the process of buying it. That shit takes forever. But the earnest money is in place, and assuming all the paperwork goes through, it'll be mine just inside of thirty days."

The screen started to blur before her eyes. "You're buying a house."

"I'm buying a house." He turned her in his arms, his hands on her hips. "I'm staying, sugar. I've been running for my entire life, and I finally found a reason to stop."

"Your mom."

His eyes were intense on hers. "She plays into it, I'm not going to lie. But you're the one who made me stand still long enough to realize what I'd be missing if I left again. Devil's Falls isn't perfect, but it's got one point in its favor that no other town I've ever been to has."

"What's that?"

"You." His hands flexed on her hips like he wanted to pull her closer. "When I said I'd never met anyone else like you, I was telling the truth. You make this world a better place, and you make me want to be a better man."

They were words she'd wanted to hear so badly, she almost convinced herself that he hadn't actually said them. "But…" She could barely process this 180. She'd been halfway prepared to spend the rest of her life wasting away into spinsterhood, holding close the memories of the last few weeks to keep her warm at night, and now here he was, saying things she never would have dreamed he'd say. So she focused on the—slightly—easier thing. "You bought a house."

"I bought a house." He inched her closer. "And I'm

going to be honest with you—someday I want you living there with me. We can take it slow, but if you'll give me a second chance to do this right, that's it for me. You're the one I want, and I fully intend on there being a ring and a couple of babies in the plans."

A ring. Babies. A house. Her heart leaped into her throat, making it hard to get words out. "You don't do anything halfway, do you?"

He grinned. "What's the point?"

Truer words were never spoken. She put her hands on his chest, resisting the last little space between them. "What happened the other day?"

This was it. If he shut her out again, she'd know that his words were just that. She could compromise on a lot of things, but this wasn't one of them.

He rested his forehead against hers. "My mama has stage-four lung cancer. That's why I was losing my shit, and that's what I wouldn't tell you because I could barely stand to think it."

Oh, Adam. "I'm so sorry."

"Me, too."

She took a deep breath, forcing herself to ask the question she really needed answered. "Are you sure you're not just reeling from the news and reacting?"

"Yes, that shit sent me for a loop, but I've found my feet. My mama and I have talked, and I'm working to be as at peace with her decisions as I can be, but that's what they are—her decisions. I'm going to support her and be here for her." He framed her face. "And I'm going to court you good and proper, Jules Rodriguez."

She licked her lips. "Court me?"

"Yep. I've gone and fallen for you, and there's only one right way to go about these things."

She felt like she'd stepped into an alternate dimension—one she wanted so desperately, she could almost taste it. "I'm not dreaming, am I?"

"I sure as fuck hope not."

He was really here. He was really saying these things. He was really willing to fight for her.

Jules hugged him close, putting everything she had into it. "I can't say anything to make the situation with your mom right, but I'll be here for you to lean on when you need it." And she'd do whatever it took to help him cope with the inevitable pain. She didn't want to say the words that rose inside her, but she couldn't leave a single stone unturned when it came to Adam. "Are you sure this isn't all to make her happy now, and that you'll leave after she's…"

"Gone?" He held her close, propping his chin on the top of her head. Strangely enough, it felt more intimate than anything they'd done up to this point. "I know nothing I say will convince you of this—that I'll have to show you to prove it to you—but I'm not leaving, sugar. If you want to keep your distance until you believe me, that's fine. I'm willing to wait."

It dawned on her that he really would. He'd wait for as long as it took to convince her that this was real and he was earnest. She leaned back. "So, marriage and babies, huh?"

"Eventually." His eyebrows rose. "Though I'm willing to negotiate on the number of rug rats."

"How noble of you."

"Not in the least." He smiled. "I mean to keep you forever, sugar. And when we're old and gray, we can scandalize the folk in Devil's Falls just for the hell of it."

EPILOGUE

Adam supported his mama's arm as they walked down the aisle to her seat in the front row. She couldn't get around as well these days, but she was determined not to use her chair today. It broke his heart a little bit, but she'd surpassed all the doctor's estimates and was still holding on to her joy of life in the bargain. He couldn't ask for more. "Here we are."

"I'm so proud of you, baby. I don't say that enough."

He helped her into her chair and crouched in front of her so they were almost eye to eye. "It means the world to me every time you do."

Her eyes shone. "I was wrong all those years ago to compare you to that man. I can't help wondering if…"

"No, Mama. I don't have any regrets. If things had been different, maybe I wouldn't be marrying the woman of my dreams today."

She nodded, her mouth trembling up into a smile. "I love you, baby."

"I love you, too. Now sit here and get comfortable—I think we're about to start." He smiled at Lenora as she took her seat next to his mom. "You ladies have your handkerchiefs?"

Lenora laughed and waved him away. "Don't you worry your pretty head about it. I've got us covered."

"Good." He looked at his mama. "You just wait here after the ceremony. I'll be back to walk you to the cars."

"We've got it taken care of." Quinn and Daniel appeared next to him, both dressed to the nines in suits that matched his—black and gray. Daniel pulled him to his feet, and Quinn smiled down at the women. "I'll be your escort to the reception. Be kind—my ego is so delicate."

His mama and Lenora tittered. "You're a good boy, Quinn."

"Nah, I'm just really good at faking it." He turned to Adam. "Get to the altar, man. It's time."

Time. The moment he'd been waiting for since Jules agreed to take him back. He knew she'd been unsure about it at first, but he never wavered. He wanted her. He wanted to be here. Nothing was going to change that—not now, not ever. And things slowly settled down. He got a job working with Daniel on the Rodriguez farm and started renovating his house. Jules moved in after six months, and here they were, a year later, about to make this thing truly official.

He'd never thought he could be so happy.

The music started, the groomsmen and bridesmaids walking down the aisle. There was Quinn walking with Aubry, who looked like she'd rather chew off her own arm than touch him. And Daniel with their other cousin Jamie.

And then the music changed, and there she was. His entire world narrowed down to where Jules stepped out into the aisle, her gaze going directly to him and staying there, her big, beautiful smile striking straight to the heart of him.

Quinn nudged him. "Breathe, man."

Adam inhaled, not realizing he'd been holding his breath. "Thanks."

"No problem."

Jules made her way to him, her dress—a princess dress was what she called it—trailing behind her. She looked like something out of a dream, but she could have been wearing a potato sack for all he cared. She handed her bouquet off to Aubry and took his hands. "Hi."

"Hey."

The pastor started speaking, but it might as well have been Latin. Nothing else mattered but the woman standing before him and the vows they repeated. Vows promising forever, through thick and thin. Vows making it official—he was hers and she was his. He'd heard of idiots getting cold feet at making a promise like that, but Adam had never been more sure of anything in his life.

"You may kiss the bride."

He swept her into his arms and dipped her down into a kiss while their family and friends cheered. He set her back on her feet. "Hello, Mrs. Rodriguez-Meyer."

"Hello, Mr. Meyer." She grinned. "Shall we do this thing?"

"We shall." He offered his elbow to her and they walked back down the aisle, husband and wife. From there it was another blur to the limo until the door shut between them and everyone else.

She stretched her feet out. "Whew, that was crazy. Are you going to think less of me if I kick off my heels and take to the dance floor during the reception? These things are killing my feet."

"I wouldn't dream of it." He pulled her into his lap. "I love you so much, it just blows my mind."

"Good." She kissed him. "Because I love you more."

"Bullshit." He dipped his head and captured her earlobe between his teeth, biting gently. "And you're going to pay for saying so."

"Oh, yeah? How do you plan on doing that?"

His hand was already on the back of her dress, seeking out her zipper. "I have a few ideas."

"Adam! We can't."

"Sugar, I already told the driver to take the long way around."

Her laugh warmed him to the very bottom of his soul. "You dog."

"You better get used to it." He slid her dress down, freeing her breasts. "Because you're not getting rid of me."

"I love you." She gasped when he leaned her back, careful of her perfectly done-up hair. "I love you so much."

"I know, sugar. I love you, too. I'm about to show you just how much."

ACKNOWLEDGMENTS

To God: Another year, another book, another set of challenges and rewards I never could have dreamed of. Thank you.

To Heather Howland: It's hard to believe this was the first category series you contracted from me—and the evolution this story has gone through since then. Thank you so much for helping me bring it to life and make it the best story it could be.

To Kari Olson: For always being down for some awesome country music recommendations. My wallet is still weeping, but Adam wouldn't be quite as hot without some serious inspiration behind him. My playlist is killer for this series because of you!

To the Rabble: For being Adam's first cheerleaders and for being so enthusiastic about this series! I hope he rocked your world like he rocked mine!

And to Tim: Yeah, yeah, you knew this was coming. Thank you for being my rock in the storm and for sharing the sleep deprivation so I wasn't a total zombie while working. Love you like whoa!

Fool ME ONCE

FOOLPROOF LOVE #2

KATEE ROBERT

Dear Reader,

I have a penchant for "unlikeable" heroines. You know the ones—the heroines who make some people crazy while reading, who some readers feel should stop being so difficult and see what an amazing guy the hero is. Aubry falls into this category. She's snarly and stand-offish and she simply doesn't have the time or desire to let the hero cozy up to her. The woman is, quite frankly, a bundle of issues. We got to see some of that in *Foolproof Love*, but getting to really delve into her headspace was a treat for me. She's a gem, and I hope she wins you over the same way she wins Quinn over.

And Quinn? Well, that man is hotter than he has right to be. He's got an easy going surface, but beneath that, he's just as intense as Aubry. They make quite the pair!

Katee

To Hilary, the Jules to my Aubry.

CHAPTER ONE

A wedding? Might as well be a goddamn funeral for all I'm going to enjoy it.

Quinn Baldwyn grabbed three beers out of his fridge, very carefully not looking at the invitation he'd stuck to the front of it. It was a constant reminder of the sword hanging over his neck—one he couldn't avoid indefinitely.

His sister's wedding. He hated running the gauntlet that was his ambitious family during the monthly dinners required to keep them off his back. Having to face the firing squad *and* all the bells and whistles at this wedding? Even worse. He didn't have to see the elegant invitation to know that Jenny—and their mother—had pulled out all the stops in the wedding planning or that he'd be expected to put on his monkey suit and play the doting son.

It made him so fucking exhausted just thinking about it.

He'd stopped playing the political games his father demanded of him over a decade ago, and he wasn't about to be drawn back into that world. Not now. Not ever. He much preferred the quieter life he'd chosen, working on the Rodriguez ranch, leaving the damn oil business to his family. The *only* reason he hadn't cut out his old man completely was because of his little sister, Jenny. She lived in that world, and attending the dinners—and the wedding—was a small price to pay to make her happy.

A small price, though one that grated.

"You're taking your sweet time in there, Baldwyn."

He took a deep breath and tried to let the tension out of his shoulders. If there was anyone who'd pick up on it, it would be Adam and Daniel, and then he'd never hear the end of it. As far as they were concerned, Quinn's father could take a flying leap and be done with it. They didn't understand that it was easier for Quinn to do the bare minimum to keep his little sister from being torn in her loyalties. If he told his old man where to stick it, he'd be banished in truth, and Jenny would have to openly defy their parents to see him. He wouldn't put her in that position. He refused to.

The only problem was that the older he got, the more his father started asking probing questions about his plans to settle down and create some more Baldwyns. With Jenny's wedding right around the corner, there was no one else to focus on pairing off, and as the only son, as far as his father was concerned, it was Quinn's responsibility to continue the family name.

"Quinn?"

He turned, forcing a smile onto his face. "Hey, pretty lady."

Jules stood in the doorway, a bright smile on her face. The expression dimmed when she took him in. "Is everything okay?"

Not in the least. But he held up the beers. "Just getting my barmaid on."

Instead of being appeased, she frowned harder. That was the problem with women—they saw too much. Oh, his buddies knew that something was chewing at him, but they were more than happy to let him stew over it until he was ready to talk. If he was never ready to talk? Hell, that was okay, too. But now that Adam was married to Jules, she was around a lot more often, and the woman was incapable of seeing a person in need without wanting to meddle. She meant well, but there was no fixing his situation. "Jules—"

"It's okay if you don't want to talk about it. Adam's not really a sharer, either." She took two of the beers from him. "I'm used to it."

She wasn't trying to guilt him, but guilt rose all the same. Quinn sighed. Telling Jules Meyer-Rodriguez "no" was like kicking a puppy—it just wasn't done. And, damn her, she knew it. "Look, it's complicated."

"Okay." She set the beers aside and hopped onto the kitchen counter, swinging her legs like a little kid. "I can do complicated. Hit me with it."

What could it hurt to get some of his frustrations off his chest? He leaned over to look out into the living room, but for all intents and purposes, Adam and Daniel seemed engrossed in the Cowboys game going on. *I bet that ass sent her in here on purpose.* He popped the cap off his beer and took a swig. "If I tell you, you'll leave it alone?"

"No promises." She'd said it cheerfully. Everything about the woman was cheerful. It'd be aggravating as fuck if she wasn't so genuinely nice. How she'd become such a good friend with that vicious little redhead, Aubry Kaiser, was beyond him.

He took another drink. "My sister is getting married."

"Oh, how exciting!" She pressed her lips together. "Unless you don't like her fiancé? Because that's not exciting at all. That's horrible." She brightened. "Are we going to break up their wedding?"

"Hold your horses." He held up a hand, rocking back on his heels. "That little scheme you had going with Adam last year has gone to your brain and made you power mad. And Brad is just fine. A little on the boring side, but fine." As far as he could tell, anyways. The guy loved Jenny and wasn't scared of their old man. More importantly, Jenny loved him to distraction and he made her happy. Quinn couldn't ask for much more.

"Okay, then what's the problem?"

Here it was. He almost backed out, made his excuses, and took off. But if he'd learned one thing about Jules, it was that she was more than capable of chasing his ass down and pestering him until he told her what she wanted to know. Frankly, he was surprised it had taken this long for her to turn her fixing eye on him and his problems. "My old man has decided he's a matchmaker, and he's getting more pointed with the women he's trotting out in front of me like prize dogs."

Jules made a face. "Charming."

"You have no idea." The last woman had been named Barbie. She was perfectly nice, but her breast size was larger than her IQ and all she'd done through the entire dinner was talk about all the things her new diet wouldn't allow her to eat. Call him crazy, but if he'd been looking for a woman — and he most definitely wasn't — it would be someone he could hold down more than a five-minute conversation with.

"Well, there's an easy solution." She grinned. "Just take a date. She'll run off any prospective women your family is looking to hook you up with, and if you can convince your dad that you're serious about her, maybe that will get him off your back in a more long-term way."

He opened his mouth to tell her that was an insane idea but closed it without the words escaping. It was crazy—committable, even—but she had a point. The only problem with that plan was that he didn't know a woman he could take to a wedding without her getting it into her head that he was looking for something more serious. He dated casually, and he liked keeping it that way. Hell, he liked his life the way it was. He didn't want or need the oil money his old man kept wafting in front of him, and he definitely didn't need a woman intent on him putting a ring on her finger. "You know of anyone?" He straightened. "Hey, you want to go to a wedding with me?"

"Hands off my woman, Baldwyn." Adam appeared in the doorway and shot them both a look. "Whatever you're planning, sugar, I'm putting my foot down. One zany scheme a decade is more than enough."

She propped her hands on her hips. "How can you say that? My zany scheme got me you, didn't it?"

Adam raised his eyebrows. "I didn't say it was a bad plan."

"Oh, stop. You two are going to give me cavities." Quinn shook his head. "Forget I asked. I don't need any help with this." He'd figure something out—and fast. The wedding was two weeks away.

More than enough time to find a woman to attend a wedding and pretend we're serious enough to keep my old man off my back without her getting any funny ideas.

"I think you're wrong, Quinn. Luckily, I'm here to help!"

She grinned, a light in her eyes that he couldn't

ignore. Whatever he and Adam had said to dissuade her, the wheels were turning in that pretty head of hers, and he was damn sure he wasn't going to like what came of it.

• • •

Aubry Kaiser glared at her computer. Even Ninja Kitteh curled up in her lap, purring like a jet engine, wasn't enough to distract her. No matter how much she focused her not-inconsiderable willpower, the words on the screen didn't change.

She took a deep breath and looked around Cups and Kittens, the cat café owned by her best friend, Jules. Life went on, the cats in their usual places, lounging around the tables and in convenient sunbeams, the sole other human occupant reading a magazine and ignoring her completely. Just the way she liked it.

But the problem with nothing being abnormal was that she ran out of things to look at thirty seconds into her perusal.

She gave Ninja Kitteh another stroke and looked back to her computer.

A few years ago, the email sitting in her inbox would have made her elated enough to dance on the ceiling, but that was a few years ago. Right now it just represented all the things that were wrong with her life. She reread it for the twelfth time.

You've done it! You're cordially invited to a closed alpha test of the new Deathmatch in San Diego on June 3rd.

She knew for a fact these invites only went out to a handful of people, and part of her was screaming with sheer, unadulterated joy as a result. The Xbox game, Deathmatch... Well, she wouldn't be completely dramatic if she said that it saved her life when she was a teenager. She'd lived in that little hellhole of a trailer with her shitty mother and her mother's equally shitty string of boyfriends, and there hadn't been a single person in her school whom she'd connected with. She'd been adrift and depressed, and then she'd picked up the game on a whim.

And found her tribe.

Her playing—her interacting with people who shared at least one fandom with her—had given her the strength to pursue her interests, to get the hell *out* and never look back. When she was sixteen, she would have done bodily damage to someone to secure an invite like the one sitting in her inbox. The intervening years hadn't done anything but deepen her love of the game and the community.

To say she was a fan was a serious understatement.

And this wasn't even a demo like the ones they'd hosted for large groups at the con in the past—this was a chance to be one of the first sets of eyes on the new game. Ten people were allowed in. *Ten*. It blew her mind that she'd been invited at all.

But accepting this invite came with such serious drawbacks, she could barely draw a full breath even thinking about it. She'd have to leave the little town of Devil's Falls, Texas and drive to California. If that wasn't bad enough, alpha test or not, she'd still have to go to Deathmatch's annual convention, DeathCon. Last year, there'd been five thousand people there, all crammed into one convention center.

Black spots danced across her vision, and she

struggled to inhale. So many people, all outside her comfort zone. Even knowing how unbearable it'd be, she wanted to go. Good God, she wanted to go. It was more than getting the opportunity to play the alpha version of the newest Deathmatch. It was for bragging rights and prestige and a public recognition of how freaking amazing she was at this game.

It was the chance of a lifetime.

And she was going to have to turn it down.

Ninja Kitteh gave a meow, a sure sign that her best friend Jules—and probably Adam—were back from their football-watching venture. They'd invited her like they always did, but as much as she disliked organized sports, she disliked Quinn Baldwyn more.

He was a big brute of a cowboy, and he liked to poke at her just to get a reaction. She *knew* that's what he was doing, but that didn't stop her from practically hissing every time she saw him. It was bad enough that she had to share Jules now—though she was legitimately happy for her best friend of six years—but to have to share her time with *him* was nearly unforgivable.

"Honey, I'm home." Jules sailed through the back door and smiled. "How are things?"

Jules's cousin, Jamie, shrugged. "The usual, though Loki is in as foul of a mood as this one." She jerked her thumb at Aubry.

"Hey!"

Jules pinned her with a searching look. "It must be the day for it."

"I can hear you." Aubry crossed her arms over her chest, doing her damnedest not to slouch down and glare harder. She knew she was the cranky one, the snarly one, the one everyone in Devil's Falls gave a wide berth.

Except that asshat Quinn.

Jamie took off like a little coward, leaving Jules standing there watching Aubry with a contemplative expression that she did *not* like.

"What?"

"Just thinking."

Aubry grimaced. "No, I know your thinking face. That's not your thinking face. That's your hatching plans face. Don't try to talk to me like I don't know the difference."

Jules dropped into the seat across from her. "I wouldn't dream of it."

"What are you planning?" Aubry asked. Ninja Kitteh rearranged himself, and she held still so he could get comfortable before she started petting him again. "You might as well just tell me so we can get this over with."

"What's got you so upset?"

Aubry hesitated and then decided to let the subject change go. Jules could be as stubborn as a mule when she wanted to be, and she obviously wasn't willing to talk about whatever was wheeling around in that head of hers yet. When she was ready, Aubry would hear about it, whether she wanted to or not. She sighed. "I got an invite to DeathCon to play the new Death-match."

"I thought that didn't come out until next November."

"It doesn't. And that's Deathmatch IX. This is Deathmatch: Redemption." Even saying it was down-right painful. "It won't be out until *next* November."

Jules frowned. "I think I'm confused. Shouldn't you be dancing around and doing your booty shaking victory wiggle?"

"I don't have a booty shaking victory wiggle. That's you." She normally settled for sitting there and looking smug. But there was no room for smugness in her current situation.

"Right. I forgot. All the same—spill."

It was like saying it aloud made her even more pathetic. She didn't want to admit how weak she was, even to Jules, who wouldn't judge her in the least—though she might give Aubry a well-deserved kick in the ass. "There're going to be thousands and thousands of people there—people I don't know—all packed in like people-shaped sardines." She shuddered. "If I believed in hell, this would be my version of it."

"Aubry, of course you believe in hell. You were just talking about how you'll own a nice little piece of property there when you die." Jules rolled her eyes. "But I'm getting off topic."

"Yes, you are, and I don't like you pointing out how I'm going to burn my way through the afterlife." Though the bantering *was* making her feel a little bit better.

"The point is that I still don't see why the glum face and lack of victory lap. This is a big deal, right?"

"The biggest deal." She clutched Ninja Kitteh closer, earning a warning growl. "It's a once-in-a-lifetime opportunity. Out of the millions of people who play this game, I'm one of *ten* they picked to test the alpha version."

Jules sat back. "I know you don't like people, but shouldn't you make an exception for this kind of thing? Just this once."

She wanted to. God, she wanted to so much she could barely stand it. "Would you go with me?" Maybe if she had a shield between her and the crowds, she'd be able to survive the encounter.

"I would…"

Aubry cursed. "Sorry, I forgot. You have that trip planned with Adam and Lenora for his mom. I'm a horrible fucking friend for forgetting that." Adam's mom had passed away a month ago, and her dying wish had been to have her ashes scattered in the Gulf where she and Lenora had their honeymoon. They were leaving next week to drive down there and spend a few days doing a memorial of sorts. Right in the middle of DeathCon.

"It's okay."

"It's not. How's Adam holding up?"

Jules sighed. "As well as can be expected, but he's talking to me about it, so we're working through it. This kind of loss isn't an easy bounce-back, no matter how long he had to come to terms with it."

She knew. And she even liked Adam enough to be genuinely sorry he was going through this. He was a good man, and he made her best friend so deliriously happy it was a wonder Jules didn't spend her days walking around on little clouds and singing at the top of her lungs. "I'm sorry."

"I know. I am, too." She shook her head and started typing something on her phone. "But we are, once again, getting off topic. Back to DeathCon—what if there was an alternative?"

"Alternative?" Aubry stopped panicking enough to send her best friend a suspicious look. "How can there be an alternative? I don't like this alternative you speak of."

"Hmm?" Jules looked up from her phone. "We'll figure something out. I know how you feel about people, especially people in crowds, but you can't miss this opportunity. No matter how much you kind of hate everyone."

She did, but it didn't stop that comment from stinging, just a little. "I don't hate *you*."

"That's because we're lady soul mates." Jules glanced at the door, making the small hairs on the back of Aubry's neck stand up. She was *definitely* up to something.

Aubry narrowed her eyes. "Maybe we should talk about that alternate option now." She did *not* like the way her friend seemed so calm.

"In a minute."

She straightened but was temporarily distracted by the front door of the café opening. Adam walked through, sending Jules a downright devastating smile as soon as he saw her. He always did that. It didn't matter if he'd been gone an hour or a full day, he always looked at Jules like she was the best thing he'd ever seen.

Aubry was not jealous of her best friend for having that kind of relationship. She most definitely *was not*.

Then Adam stepped aside and *he* walked in. Quinn. She froze, almost overwhelmed by the sheer size of him, even across the room. He was well over six feet tall and had a physique that would have been seriously attractive if not attached to his particular personality. She knew the second he noticed her, because his brows slanted down for half a moment before his face relaxed into a grin. He never snapped at her, never snarled, but he said the most unforgivable crap.

"Hey there, sweet cheeks. Looking good."

Like *that*. Sweet cheeks. What the hell was wrong with him? She hunched down into her seat and stared at her computer, but the screen just served to remind her of the opportunity her issues were forcing her to miss. If she was a normal, well-adjusted woman, she'd have no problem shooting back an email accepting the honor that the invitation signaled. For fuck's sake, they were going to comp her a room. That wasn't something they did for just anyone.

Too many people. Not enough space.

The feeling of claustrophobia was only accented by Quinn ambling across the room to the table and looming over her. "Stop hovering," she snapped.

"Now, don't be mean. I know for a fact I don't stink."

No, he didn't. He smelled of some kind of cologne that made her think *man*. The kind that would have advertising with a guy who looked like Quinn up on the back of a horse, cowboy hat firmly in place, probably a lasso in his hands and a determined looked on his face.

He dropped into the seat next to her, draping his arm over the back of her chair. He didn't touch her, though. For all the casual intimacy he showed with everyone else, he never touched *her*.

Probably because I threatened to rip off his arm and beat him to death with it last time he did.

She shut her computer, all too aware of the heat she could feel emanating from his body. He was like a human-sized forge. She realized she was staring at his chiseled jaw line and jerked her gaze away…right to Jules's considering face.

Heat spread across her face and she realized, to her horror, she was blushing. *Oh my God, what's wrong with me?*

Jules didn't give her a chance to recover, either. She leaned forward. "I think you two can help each other."

It took a second for her words to penetrate, but Aubry was already shaking her head. "No, absolutely *not*."

While, next to her, Quinn said, "Jules, I think you're swell, but you need to be committed if you think for a second I'm going anywhere with this crazy woman."

She spun to face him, forgetting her rule about touching, and poked him in the chest. "Me? No one's crazy enough to go anywhere with *you*."

"Tell that to all my lady friends." He gave her a grin that was just this side of vicious. "Though, if you're looking for *that* kind of company, I might be willing to make an exception."

Aubry went ramrod straight. He did *not* just offer her a pity fuck. "Over my dead body—but, who knows, you could be into that sort of thing."

"Hardly." He made a face. "I like my women warm and willing. But on that note, you're right. You don't fit either bill."

A gasp of outrage slipped free. "Watch your step, cowboy. I know plenty of places to hide a dead body."

"Sweet cheeks, in my current mood, I almost hope you try."

A delicate throat clearing had Aubry ripping her gaze away from the smug look on his face to her best friend. "Jules, you're out of your godforsaken mind if you think for a second we'd last an hour without killing each other." No matter how good he smelled.

"Actually, that's why I think it'll work perfectly." She grinned. "Quinn needs a date to his sister's wedding to keep his family's matchmaking efforts in check, and you need someone to be a walking barrier between you and everyone else at this convention thing." She motioned to Quinn. "He'd make a great barrier."

"Only because he's abnormally large." A man his size could block out the entire room, which would be perfect if she could guarantee he wouldn't open his equally large mouth.

"Aw, sweet cheeks, I didn't think you noticed."

Jules snapped her fingers at him like she did at her cats when they misbehaved. "Stop poking at her or she might actually *try* to bury you in the desert." She sat forward, practically vibrating. "And Quinn, you have to admit that Aubry is very good at repelling everyone in her vicinity—no offense, Aubry."

"None taken." She'd worked hard to perfect her resting bitch face so people would leave her alone in public. Of course, in a town like Devil's Falls, it was just as likely to draw in people who wanted to help. They meant well, and she managed not to hold it against them. Mostly.

"Plus, if you're worried about one of your lady friends getting the wrong idea, that's not something you have to deal with if you take Aubry."

She glanced at him, sure that he was going to shoot Jules down the same way she had, but he had a strange look on his face—almost like he was actually contemplating it. Shaking her head, she said to Jules, "No. How many ways can I say it? No. *Nyet. Non. Nein. No.*"

It was tempting to get up and storm out, but her computer was here and Quinn was blocking her exit from the table. She turned to him again. "This is insanity, and you're crazier than I am if you're even considering it."

"You don't know my family, sweet cheeks."

"*Stop calling me that.*"

"Yeah, yeah." He rubbed a hand over his mouth. "What's this convention thing Jules is talking about?"

She didn't want to even entertain this idea long enough to explain it, but she could see Jules wiggling in her seat across the table, so it was only a matter of time before she shared the information anyways. Aubry sighed. "DeathCon. I have an invite to attend and test the upcoming Deathmatch: Redemption."

"Damn." He sat back, a look of almost respect flitting across his face. It disappeared as quickly as it'd come, replaced by his grin that seemed to charm everyone else—except Aubry. She didn't trust that grin any more than she trusted the strange pull she felt when he was around. There were no two ways about it—Quinn Baldwyn didn't fit in any of her neat little boxes she shoved people into.

She didn't like that. She didn't like it at all.

She liked it even less when his grin widened. "This plan of Jules's is starting to grow on me."

CHAPTER TWO

Quinn couldn't believe he was actually contemplating this, but Jules had a point. A fake date would fit all his needs, and Aubry Kaiser, as vicious as she was dangerously attractive, fit the bill.

He skated a glance over Aubry. She was a little alternative for his tastes, with her tattoos and bright red hair, looking like some kind of exotic bird that had wandered into the legions of cowgirls and down-home belles that were Devil's Falls born and raised. Pretty in a pixie sort of way, but with a mouth more likely to cause pain than pleasure.

Yeah, she was exactly the kind of girl who could hold her own against his family's barbs. The woman had skin thicker than an armadillo and a don't-give-two-fucks attitude that impressed him, despite himself.

She didn't look convinced, though.

He couldn't blame her, but the reward might be worth spending more time with her—that and the added bonus of getting a chance to see if he could get beneath her skin.

It wasn't a good idea—he damn well knew that. He had enough complications in his life without throwing a woman like Aubry into the mix. But Jules was right. He needed a date, and this woman would do nicely.

If he could convince her to agree.

He met Jules's gaze over the top of the table and nodded once. She jumped up so fast she almost knocked Adam out of his chair. "I think I left the stove on."

"Sugar—"

"Come on." She grabbed his hand and towed him out of the room without a second glance.

This was Quinn's one chance. If he missed this pitch, he would have to find a different solution. He removed his arm from the back of Aubry's chair and did his damnedest to adopt a sincere expression. "I know you don't like me much."

"That's the biggest understatement in the history of understatements."

Yeah, he kind of thought so, too. He took a deep breath and tried again. "You want to go to this convention and play this game—don't bother to lie and say you don't."

Her mouth set in an unforgiving line. "I wasn't planning on it. Yes, I want to go, though 'want' doesn't even begin to cover it. Obviously you've been too busy lifting rocks or wrestling bulls or whatever you cowboy types do to notice, but Deathmatch is kind of my life."

He'd noticed. She might be as cute as a pit bull about to take a bite out of the mailman, but even he'd noticed that Aubry cared about exactly three things: Jules, whatever work it was that she did on that laptop she always seemed to be carting around, and Deathmatch. He'd only seen her play it a few times in the past year, but the sheer joy that suffused her face when she was murdering people on that damn game was pretty fucking sexy. Not that he'd ever admit as much. But that was the only time he'd allowed himself to think about what it'd be like if he got her out of those tight jeans and T-shirts with a variety of nerd sayings on them. He'd spent one buzzed night imagining exactly how far down her tattoo descended past her collarbone and, fuck, it had been hot as hell.

But the long and short of it was that he just plain didn't like her any more than she liked him. And Quinn didn't sleep with women he didn't like. It was in poor taste, and ultimately unsatisfying.

He tapped his fingers on the table, disturbed by the turn of his thoughts. In an effort to focus, he said, "What do you need in order to actually go to this thing?"

Her long-suffering sigh made him grit his teeth. He knew she thought he was some kind of knuckle-dragging Neanderthal and, to be perfectly honest, he hadn't done much to disabuse her of the notion, but it got old sometimes.

Aubry started shutting down her computer. "I don't like people."

"*That* I did notice."

She dropped her gaze, something almost vulnerable in those amber eyes. "No, I mean like I have near-crippling social anxiety. Put me in the middle of a crowd and you'll find me curled up into a ball trying to remember that I'm not suffocating to death."

Quinn blinked. He had a hard time envisioning a situation where she wouldn't be in full control and delivering barbed commentary, but he knew something about panic attacks. His littler sister had them from time to time.

But there weren't two women more different than Jenny and the woman sitting next to him.

His sister needed a quiet space and calm words to talk her through an anxiety attack, but when he'd read up on it all those years ago, it seemed like each person was different. Some needed a physical link to hold it together, some complete silence, some needed something else altogether. It was purely personal.

In order for him to deal with Aubry's potential attacks, he needed to know what was required to bring her down. "So, again, what do you need to do this?"

"Nothing you can give me."

"And what about work? This is kind of last minute to request time off."

"All I need to keep up on my clients' websites is right here." She closed the laptop. "But that's irrelevant for a number of reasons. The first being that I don't like you and you don't like me, and that's fine. It's better than fine. But it means I don't trust you and you can't do shit for me when it comes to my anxiety if I don't trust you."

She had a point, but he couldn't let it go. When she stood, he stood with her. "Aubry—"

"I'm sorry that your sister's wedding is presenting you such an awful conundrum, but I'd be even less helpful at a wedding surrounded by strangers than I would be at DeathCon—and that's with me *wanting* to go to DeathCon. I sure as hell don't have any desire to go to this girl's wedding. Why don't you ask one of your lady friends?"

That was the problem. He might have *lady friends*, but he didn't have much in the way of friends who were ladies. To be honest, Jules pretty much summed it up. There was no one he…well, "trusted" was a good word. There was no one he trusted to take with him who wouldn't look too much into the invitation, which would only make a bad situation worse.

"Jules said I would make a good wall, and she's right. Have you ever seen me walk through a crowded room?"

Aubry hesitated. "Only at Jules's wedding."

"Then you know for a fact I can clear a space in front of me. When I walk, people get out of the way."

Another hesitation. She was cracking. "Only because you're so gigantic, they're probably afraid you're going to trample them to death."

Yep. He definitely had her interest. He could see it. She must *really* want to go to this convention if she was actually considering going with *him*. He took a step back and spread his arms. "So then let me be your wall—both at the convention and at the wedding. What have you got to lose, except missing out on a once-in-a-lifetime opportunity?"

• • •

Deathmatch had driven Aubry out of her goddamn mind. That was the only explanation for her actually toying with the idea of saying yes. Either that, or Jules had rubbed off on her more than she ever could have guessed. Aubry might talk a good game, but the truth was when it came to pulling off plans, her friend was the one who threw herself into motion and made it happen. It's how she ended up owning her very own cat café before she turned thirty, and it was how she'd ended up with Adam Meyer, town bad boy. *She* was the force of nature. Aubry was the one who sat in her safe little corner and kept up an ongoing commentary.

What if I took the risk? Just this once.

Sure, last time she'd gone out on a limb, her asshole family had chopped the damn tree down, but this wasn't the same situation. Quinn might be an ass, but he was hardly going to throw her under the bus just for the sake of doing it.

She hoped.

She put her laptop into her bag and faced him. "If I think about doing this—*if*—I require clear terms."

"Tit for tat." His face gave nothing away. "We'll share a room—both at the convention hotel and at the wedding itself. Don't look at me like that. You know damn well DeathCon's hotel has likely been sold out for months, and I'm not going to do you a damn bit of good if I'm staying somewhere else. At the wedding, we'll share because my family knows me too well to believe I'd wait for marriage to have sex." Aubry snorted, but he kept going. "You have to sell this. You can snarl and do that adorable snarky comment thing you do, but you can't look at me like I'm dog shit on the bottom of your shoe."

He thought she was adorable. She hated the faint heat she could feel in her cheeks at that realization. "I think you're asking the impossible."

"Do you? I think you're just a bit disappointed that you don't get to experience all I have to offer." He leaned forward, giving her another whiff of that tantalizing cologne. "I think the lady doth protest too much when it comes to wanting me."

Aubry burst out laughing. "Oh my God, does that line actually work with women?" She tried to keep her tone light, but she knew she was blushing. Worse, she knew Quinn could see it.

Sure enough, his blue eyes tracked over her cheeks, and his grin made her stomach do a slow turn. "I think it just did." Before she could screech at him, he continued. "But it's not meant to this time. This arrangement is purely business."

As much as she wanted to tell him to take a hike, Aubry would never forgive herself if she passed up this chance. She straightened, took a deep breath, and held out her hand. "Okay, I'll see what I can do. Deal?"

"Deal." He ignored her hand and took a step closer, towering over her even though she was wearing thick-soled boots. "And, sweet cheeks, if you're going to pretend to be my girlfriend, you should know damn well that we seal this with a kiss."

"What are you, a demon from *Supernatural*? That's not how people seal bargains."

"It is when it's like ours."

Before she could do more than sputter, he hooked the back of her neck and kissed her.

Aubry hadn't been kissed in a truly embarrassing amount of time, which was why she froze and didn't immediately shove his larger-than-life ass away from her. Or that was what she told herself as her hands came to rest on his chest—his very nicely muscled chest. His hand was hot on her neck, his grip tight enough that she was fully aware of who was in control of this situation, but his mouth was light on hers.

She still hadn't figured out if she wanted to bite him or kiss him back when he lifted his head and said, "I knew you weren't all piss and vinegar."

The almost surprised expression on his face slammed her back into reality. She'd just stood there like a bump on a log and let *Quinn* kiss her. What the fuck was wrong with her? She shoved him.

Or she tried.

When she pushed on him, he didn't move, but she hopped back a full foot. "You are insufferable!"

"You say the sweetest things." He turned and

started for the door. "Tell Adam and Jules I'll see them later."

She watched him go, wondering if she'd just made a horrible mistake. Oh, who was she kidding? She *knew* she had. Going to DeathCon with Quinn was a no-brainer. She would be so busy fighting not to have a panic attack and excited about Deathmatch she'd be able to ignore his towering presence. At least in theory.

But the other half of the bargain? How was she supposed to pretend they were in a relationship when she could barely stand to be in the same room with him? And that was ignoring the fact that she didn't know what the hell an actual relationship looked like. She certainly hadn't seen one between her mother and the men she paraded through their doublewide when she was growing up. Or from the boys who'd tried to talk their way into her pants, starting around the time she hit puberty.

Hell, the only healthy relationship she'd ever held down was with Jules, and that hardly counted because she liked Jules just fine but had no desire to roll around naked with her.

Not that she had a desire to roll around naked with Quinn. Because she definitely did *not*. Besides, this wasn't about whether she theoretically did or did not find the idea of sex with Quinn attractive. This was about *pretending* she did. His parents or whoever he was trying to fool wouldn't be convinced if she just stood next to him. She'd have to, like, touch him. Or hold hands. Or kiss. Or…

What do people in relationships even do—besides bang a lot?

Aubry dropped into her chair and laid her head on

her folded arms. She couldn't even model her behavior after Jules and Adam because her friend was such a foreign creature in so many ways. She was so *sunny*. Aubry couldn't fake that. She didn't want to try.

She was just…herself. Cranky and kind of twisted and maybe old beyond her years.

It wasn't too late to back out. All she had to do was give up DeathCon and there was nothing holding her to that damn wedding. Quinn might not be the most awful person in existence, but she wasn't inclined to do him this type of favor out of the goodness of her heart. She wasn't sure she had a goodness of her heart.

But she didn't want to give up DeathCon.

Now that there was a real chance she could play that demo, she didn't want to give it up.

Even if it meant playing girlfriend to Quinn at some hoity-toity wedding. Aubry lifted her head. How hard could it really be? There would probably be alcohol there, so that was something. An open bar was too much to ask for, but if she was supposed to be Quinn's girlfriend, there was no reason he couldn't foot her tab. It was only fair.

She sat up, feeling significantly better about the whole thing.

"This is doable. It's only a few days. Really, what's the worst that could happen?"

There were so many ways to answer that question she didn't even want to start.

CHAPTER THREE

"What do you mean, you don't fly?" Five days out from their trip, and she was just *now* springing this on him? Quinn could barely credit the words coming out of the crazy woman's mouth.

Aubry crossed her arms over her chest and some-how managed to glare down her nose at him, despite the fact that she barely came up to his shoulder. "Do you know how horrible death would be in a plane crash?"

"Sorry, no. I don't spend much time thinking about how different ways to die would feel." He'd noticed she seemed to see serial killers under every rock, but he hadn't actually thought she'd have a problem with one of the most common modes of transportation. Silly him. He put his phone down, already regretting having shown up at her place to negotiate this.

But he'd thought it'd be a simple cut and dried thing—he'd book the flights and she'd get the rental car from San Diego to Napa Valley. He was fine with footing the larger bill… Or he had been until she threw this totally unnecessary wrench into his perfect plans. He glared. "You do realize that more people die in car crashes every year than in planes going down— as in, exponentially more."

"I'm aware."

Of course she was. It seemed like the type of fucked up little fact she'd keep tucked into her back pocket. "Then what's the problem?"

"Don't you start with logic and that nonsense." Aubry paced around the tiny kitchen counter. Hell, everything in the apartment she used to share with Jules was tiny. The few times he'd been here, he'd felt just as uncomfortable as he did now, as if one wrong step would send him crashing through some breakable item. It made him feel big and clumsy, and he hated it.

"You would seriously rather spend several *days* in closed quarters with me than risk a tiny chance that our plane might fall out of the sky in a ball of fire?"

She went paler, if that were even possible. "That's not funny."

"No, what's funny is that your fear has no fucking basis in reality and it's going to cost us days of travel for no reason. Except, no, it's not funny. At all."

"I knew this was a mistake." She turned and plopped down onto her well-worn spot on the couch. It was practically a little nest, with a blanket curled around her body and a set of Xbox controllers in front of her on the coffee table. Hell, even her cell phone was already sitting on the cushion next to her.

She spends a shitload of time here, all playing that damn game.

She'll be crushed if she isn't able to play that stupid demo.

He looked away, uncomfortable with the sudden desire he had to make sure she got her chance. He appreciated her passion, even if he didn't always understand it. She wasn't the type of girl he usually hung out with. She obviously didn't like the outdoors or getting any kind of dirty, and he'd bet his left nut she'd never been on the back of a horse.

But she loved that damn game. If it was Jenny, he'd

want someone to step in and help her out so she could do something she loved without her anxiety getting in the way.

The only reason you're doing this is because she reminds you of your sister, whom she's nothing like at all...Yeah. Sure.

He forced himself to unclench his hands and release as much tension as possible. "If we do this, we do it on my terms."

"I'm not trying to negotiate with you here. I'm flat out telling you that I won't fly."

It was really difficult to have any kind of empathy for the woman when she was willing to bite any hand he offered her off at the wrist. "If we're driving, we need to leave on Monday instead of Wednesday."

"What? Why the hell do we need two days to drive to California? It's only fifteen hours."

Only fifteen hours. She was killing him. "I'm aware, sweet cheeks." He enjoyed the way her face turned red and her eyes blazed when he used that particular nickname. "But after that amount of driving, you're going to need some extra time to settle in."

"The hotel is only for Wednesday and Thursday."

She was just determined to make the whole thing more difficult than it had to be. "Yeah, I got that part, too. We'll just get a hotel for one more night in town." She looked so outraged he couldn't help another little dig. "It'll give you that much more time to perfect pretending you worship the ground I walk on."

Aubry snorted. "Let's not get carried away. I said I'd try to pretend I can stand you. And besides, I wouldn't worship the ground *anyone* walked on, let alone a boyfriend."

Her phrasing was so strange he started to ask her if she'd ever had a boyfriend to try it out on, but then he stopped. He might enjoy poking at her and watching her blood pressure rise, but if he was going to be cooped up in the car with her for days on end, pissing her off before they even got started would be a lesson in insanity. He might not be the smartest man in existence, but even he had some sense of self-preservation.

Besides, no way she'd never had a boyfriend, prickly or not. Most of Aubry could be termed sexy. Her curves made his mouth water when he was able to forget the attitude they were attached to. There had to be some guys out there who liked contrary women. He just wasn't one of them. Quinn preferred his women to be the agreeable sort—agreeable and sexy as hell.

But then, maybe she was more agreeable than he thought. He was honestly kind of surprised she'd let him get away with that kiss the other day. Though it *had* been sexy as fuck to have her lips go soft against his. And the way her fingers had kneaded his chest had made him think more kitten than the tigress he was used to.

He shook his head. What the fuck was he even thinking? There was no woman more off-limits than Aubry, especially now that she'd agreed to act as his date for the wedding. He couldn't afford to let something like sex muddle the waters between them. They didn't like each other, and he was more than fine with that.

The longer he stood here, the more likely he was to say something they'd both regret, so he pushed off the wall and headed for the door. "Whatever. Just be ready bright and early Monday morning."

"I don't do bright and early."

He opened the door and glanced over his shoulder. "You will on Monday. Be ready or I'll climb into bed with you, and we both know how *that* would end."

Her screech of fury was music to his ears, and he broke out into a little whistled tune as he jogged down the stairs and out the door.

• • •

Aubry hauled her suitcase down the stairs, cursing Quinn with every insult she knew under her breath. It was seven in the goddamn morning and she hadn't had her coffee yet.

As if her thinking it had summoned said coffee, Jules appeared in the doorway that led to the café, a travel mug in her hands. "It'll be okay."

"I'm supposed to be the one saying that to you. You're going to scatter your mother-in-law's ashes." Aubry had been so wrapped up in her fury at Quinn she hadn't been focused enough on what Jules was going through. Yes, Jules had Adam, but that didn't mean she and Aubry weren't friends anymore. She sighed. "I've been a bad best friend."

"You've been fine." Jules passed over the coffee and squeezed her arm. "And both Adam and I will be fine, too." She looked chagrined. "Honestly, I feel like I should be apologizing for pushing you into this trip with Quinn. It seemed like a good idea at the time, but now I'm wondering if it isn't going to be a horrible mistake."

"Oh, I can save you from wondering that—it's

already a horrible mistake." The stricken look on her friend's face instantly made her feel like an ass. "No, it's fine. I'm joking." Mostly.

It wasn't being around him for the next few days she was worried about. It was that, when he'd threatened to climb into bed with her, she'd actually caught herself considering it for half a second. That was utterly unforgivable. She didn't hook up. For fuck's sake, she didn't even *date*. To break both those rules with a man she could barely stand?

No. Absolutely not. Aubry might be kind of crazy, and she might be anti-social enough to worry her therapist, but she wasn't *that* nuts. Even contemplating that level of crazy was asking for the kind of trouble she wasn't sure she could deal with.

It didn't stop her from wondering what it would be like if he really kissed her.

"What's got that look on your face?"

Aubry jumped, trying to stomp down on the guilt weeding its way outward from her stomach. She had nothing to feel guilty for. "Nothing."

"Aubry—"

The back door opened and Quinn stepped through, filling the door frame. He took them both in. "Guess I'm not crawling into bed with you, sweet cheeks. You missed the time of your life, and you don't even know it."

There went her blush again, flaming across her cheeks and making her want to snarl. The way Jules's mouth dropped open did nothing to help Aubry's mood. She grabbed her suitcase handle and started for the door. "Call me when you get settled in your hotel," Aubry said.

"I, uh, okay."

And then she was through the door and out into the sticky June heat. If there was one thing she missed about Ohio, it was the summers that were just shy of blistering. The milder winters down in Texas almost made up for the melting summers, but it was hard to remember that when she'd been out of air conditioning for a grand total of five seconds and was already starting to sweat.

She caught sight of the truck idling at the curb and stopped short. "Are you on crack?"

The truck looked like it had been alive longer than she had, and it wasn't one of those pristine rebuilt oldie trucks, either. This thing had been lived in since it came off the production line or however the hell trucks were made.

"Not last time I checked." Quinn scooped up her overnight suitcase and tossed it into the bed of the truck. He eyed the bag in her hands, which only made her clutch it to her chest. No way in hell was she letting him toss her computer around like he just had her clothes.

Satisfied her equipment was safe, she focused on the problem at hand—mainly, the sad excuse for trans-portation in front of her. "That is *not* going to get us to San Diego. I'm not even sure that will get us past the town limits."

"Don't listen to her, Betsy." He patted the hood.

As if I needed another sign that this is a horrible mistake I'm going to regret.

She was *already* starting to regret it. "Why can't we just rent a car?" At least then there'd be some sort of contingency in place and the vehicle would be somewhat reliable.

"No."

She blinked. "What do you mean, no?"

"I'm speaking English, sweet cheeks." He waltzed around and opened the passenger door. "Now get that hot little ass up in here and let's get this show on the road."

Knowing she'd created this situation of her own free will only made it more annoying. She set her computer case onto the bench seat and climbed up after it, having to grab the "oh shit" handle to haul herself into the truck. Quinn didn't give her a chance to get settled before he slammed the door behind her and strode around to climb up into the driver's seat.

It was only when they pulled away from the curb that his words penetrated. She turned to glare at him. "What is your obsession with my ass?"

"Have you seen it?"

Is he joking? She glared harder. "I don't like you."

"Well, hell, I don't like you, either. But I'm not blind, and I happen to be an ass man." He sent her one of his grins that she hated so much and slipped a pair of Aviators on. "And yours, sweet cheeks, is perfection."

Her stomach gave a funny lurch, and warmth that had nothing to do with the disgusting heat outside curled through her. It was so dumb that a compliment from *this* man was enough to make her feel a little squishy, but apparently she was more starved for attention than she ever could have guessed. "Just don't be getting any ideas."

"I have all the ideas in the world. Do you want me to describe them to you?"

"You wouldn't." *He totally would.* Before he could follow through on his—hopefully empty—threat, she rushed on. "I don't know if that kiss curdled your brain or what, but I have no interest in flirting with you, let alone going further. I'd rather seduce a snake."

"More like a python."

He's insinuating… Her damn cheeks heated and she put a few seconds into seriously debating just throwing herself from the moving vehicle.

She slid her sunglasses into place, using the shield to glance at his lap. *Python, my ass. He's probably got a micro peen that's inversely proportionate to how huge he is everywhere else.* She'd seen the term on a show once and looked it up, and…there were some things a woman just couldn't un-see. It made her perversely happy to picture Quinn with one of those little anteaters.

Aubry checked the time. She'd been in the truck with him a grand total of three minutes. This didn't bode well for the next fourteen hours and fifty-seven minutes. *What am I going to do?*

In any other situation, she'd just whip out her computer, stick in some headphones, and ignore everyone around her, but that wasn't an option with her motion sickness. *I am a bundle of issues.*

Quinn whistled a few bars of a popular country song. "Besides, that wasn't a kiss."

"Pretty sure I was there. Your lips touching mine equals a kiss."

"If that's your idea of a kiss, you've been missing out. Now, why don't you come over here and cozy on up? We should start practicing for the wedding."

Practicing pretending they were dating.

I can't take any more of this conversation.

"Maybe later." She dug around in her bag and came up with her headphones. She plugged them into her phone and pulled up the audiobook she'd downloaded for just this occasion. She glanced at Quinn, wondering if the book would be enough to block out his overwhelming presence just a few feet away. It was the latest in an erotic thriller series, which shouldn't have worked as a genre, but the author was phenomenal. Hot sex scenes and scary serial killers should be more than enough to keep her distracted.

She didn't like her chances, though.

CHAPTER FOUR

At first, Quinn was kind of glad when the vicious little redhead popped on her headphones and turned to stare out the window. Despite all his bluster, he wasn't interested in spending the next fifteen hours trading barbs. But somewhere around hour three, the music on the radio stopped being enough to occupy him and his mind started wandering.

Wandering right to the woman curled up on the seat next to him.

He hadn't been lying about her ass being phenomenal. She must be doing squats while she played that damn game or something, because every time he caught sight of her in jeans, he wanted to take a bite out of those sweet cheeks. Her ass was the kind that he'd lovingly term "grabbable." The kind of ass that would fit his palms perfectly, that he could use to hoist her higher onto his body until she wrapped those equally sexy legs around his waist and…

He watched her out of the corner of his eye. Hell, her mouth was pretty sexy, too. Her lips were just as full as the rest of her, and it was all too easy to imagine what they'd look like wrapped around his cock.

Quinn froze.

What the fuck am I doing?

Admiring her ass was one thing. Actively fantasizing about her—especially when she was *right there*—was something else entirely. It was the kind of thing that'd get him into trouble if he wasn't careful.

One more thought down that road and he'd be hard as a rock, and *that* would make for an uncomfortable situation.

What if…

Knock that shit off. Right now.

He forced himself to focus on something—any-thing—other than her. There wasn't much else to think about. Things at the Rodriguez ranch had been going smoothly through the expansion. They'd brought in forty head of cattle and hired new guys to cover the increased workload. There had been a few hiccups, but nothing he and Adam and Jules's cousin, Daniel, couldn't handle.

The three of them had been best friends when they were growing up, and it'd been good to have them all back together again, now that Adam was in Devil's Falls permanently, but that didn't change the bitter-sweet feeling that came over him sometimes when he thought about the fact they should have been *four* in-stead of three. Their other best friend, John, had died thirteen years ago, but that didn't make his absence any less noticeable. It was like a missing tooth—it didn't hurt most of the time, but he was almost always aware of the empty space.

John's death was the reason he'd told his old man to take a hike and gone into the cattle business. Life was too short. If one of the best people he'd ever known could have it taken from him in a split second, what the hell was he doing, going into an industry that he hated? All the politics and lobbying and ma-nipulating to get ahead, and for what? More money that he didn't need.

So he left, hell-bent on doing his own thing.

Quinn never felt more alive than when he was working himself to exhaustion, with the clear Texas sky over him and the earth beneath his boots. He wouldn't give that up for all the money in the world.

He glanced at the clock. Four hours down, which meant they weren't even halfway. *Damn*. It was going to be a long-ass trip if Aubry ignored him the entire time. It was his fault for throwing around sexual innuendos, but the look on her face had been priceless.

I'm paying for it now, aren't I? Can't get the damn pictures out of my head.

"Stop staring at me."

He didn't jump, but it was a near thing. Quinn stretched one arm out over the back of the seat and curled her bright red hair around his finger. "Can't help myself."

"Is that flirting?" She slapped his hand. "I really can't tell because you're so clumsy at it. Just like everything else you do."

If that wasn't a gauntlet thrown at his feet, he didn't know what was. Quinn wasn't normally this pushy with women—he didn't have to be—but with her sitting there, looking all smug behind her bright green sunglasses, he wanted to... Fuck, he didn't know. Shock her a little. "You know, I've been thinking—"

"Good God, don't strain yourself."

"—and I'm thinking that I need a better nickname for you. Sweet cheeks might be accurate, but no one in my family is going to believe I'd call the woman I'm in a relationship with something that...lowbrow."

She tilted her sunglasses down to stare at him over the top of them. It made her amber eyes stand out all the more. "How about you call me nothing at all?

Because that sounds ideal from where I'm sitting."

"Nah. I've always been a fan of pet names."

"One—I can tell. Two—save your pet names for your actual animals."

She'd left that one wide open, but he chose to ignore it. Just this once. He twined her hair around his finger again. "I was thinking bunny."

"You can call me bunny if you want to provoke me to actual physical violence."

Yeah, it didn't fit, either. He relaxed back into his seat, starting to enjoy the idea of this. "Cherry."

"Hard pass."

"Cookie."

"No way."

He wondered when she'd noticed that he was still stroking her hair. He hadn't been lying when he said they would have to put on a good show for his family. That meant he had to get her used to him touching her, at least in these innocent ways. Or that was what he told himself as he kept playing with the ends of her hair.

And touching in the not-*innocent ways?*

To distract himself, he said, "Peaches. No, don't look at me like that. You got to pass on three—that's your limit. And you smell like peaches." He leaned a little closer, keeping one eye on the road, and adopted his best Nicholas Cage voice, "I love peaches. I could eat peaches for hours."

"Ew, *gross*."

He sat back and laughed. "You have a problem with a man worshiping you that way?"

"I have a problem with *Nicholas Cage* comparing my lady bits to a fruit and, frankly, the image of him down there is enough to kill any desire the act would cause."

She sounded so horrified that he laughed again. Or he started to. The problem with teasing her like this was he was now picturing *himself* between her thighs. Quinn shifted, trying to get his instant physical reaction under control. His cock wasn't in a cooperative mood, though, and his brain kept serving up images of Aubry's back arching, her fingers digging into his forearms, her head thrown back in ecstasy he was giving her.

Jesus Christ.

He let go of her hair like it burned him and straightened. He had to get out of this truck, and fast, before he forgot just how bad of an idea hooking up with the woman was. There was a sign up ahead advertising gas in two miles, which might as well have been a signal from God that he was walking a thin line.

• • •

Aubry was almost pathetically grateful when Quinn announced they were stopping for snacks and to top off the fuel tank. She didn't know what to do with a flirting Quinn, even if he was doing it solely to make her uncomfortable. She kept wondering what it would be like to be kissed by him—*really* kissed—and if he actually had a micro penis or if he was in proportion and *gah*.

She barely waited for him to put the truck in park before throwing open the door and jumping down to the ground. She was so distracted she made it all the way into the gas station before she realized it was a prime place for some *The Hills Have Eyes* action. There was a thick layer of dust over everything, and she was pretty sure most of the food had seen its expiration date come and go some twenty-odd years ago. She peered at the clerk out of the corner of her eye, but he was just a pimply teenager like the million pimply teenagers manning gas stations across the country. She made a beeline for the bathroom, all the while berating herself for even walking through the door.

What was Quinn thinking, stopping here? There had to be some place closer to actual civilization where they would be less likely to get killed by a family of cannibal mutants.

Once she was done, she stared at herself in the smudged mirror. *You can do this. Just remember that you don't like Quinn. The only reason you're even thinking these kinds of thoughts is because your hormones are out of control. It could be anyone causing it. The only reason it's* him *is because he's here and he's healthy and he's got all his teeth. It doesn't mean anything.*

The pep talk did nothing to help. Less than nothing, because now she was *really* thinking of what it would be like to go there with him. The universe had created a cruel joke when it formed Aubry. Her sex drive had always been out of control—a direct parallel to how much she hated people. She'd never had a problem keeping the edge off with her variety of sex toys, mostly because the thought of getting naked and sweaty with anyone in Devil's Falls didn't appeal to her in the least.

Or so she would have thought before she'd

voluntarily locked herself in a truck cab with Quinn Baldwyn.

A banging on the door had her jumping halfway out of her skin. "Come on, peaches. We need to get back on the road."

She cursed long and hard, flipping off the door for good measure. None of it cleansed her mind, like she'd hoped. It was official—she might not be able to stand the man, but her hormones didn't hold the same dislike for him. *This is so bad.*

Aubry washed her hands again for good measure and used a paper towel to open the door. Quinn stood there, his arms braced on either side of the doorway, a shit-eating grin on his face. "Were you touching yourself and fantasizing about me?"

She'd never tell him. His ego might inflate enough to fill the tiny room and suffocate her. She nudged the door open farther with her foot. It was impossible not to notice how he filled up the doorway—or the way his position pulled his T-shirt tightly against his chest. The man was *cut*. "Don't flatter yourself."

"I don't have to. I know the truth, no matter how much you try to deny it." He leaned down and stage-whispered. "You want me. That's why you hate me so much—you can't stand the fact that you'd lose your fucking mind the second you were in my arms."

Her face went red hot, and she cursed the German heritage that made every emotion flare across her pale skin. "Nope."

"Not a missionary girl? I can get down with that." His voice dropped an octave, making her toes curl. "Maybe you're down with some oral worshipping, if it's not done by old Nick Cage."

She broke out in goose bumps at the thought of sitting on Quinn's face. *No, no, no.* She started to push him out of the way, but her hands got stuck somewhere around his pecs and she just ended up staring at him from an inch away. As much as she wanted to claim otherwise, all he'd have to do was lean down and kiss her, and she'd lose it. Her entire body hummed so hard it was a wonder she wasn't vibrating. It wouldn't take much. She wasn't sure if she was ashamed of that or grateful for it. All he'd have to do was slip a hand into her jeans, one stroke, and she'd be there. She knew the signs well enough to know that.

But then he took one large step back, a strange look on his face. "You done in there?"

"What?" She shook her head, trying to clear it. "Uh, yeah."

What was *wrong* with her? Quinn had been aggravating her like this since they met. Yes, it was a little more pointed since they'd gotten into his truck, but the truth was that he hadn't changed the rules of the game. She was the one in danger of doing that. No wonder he'd stepped back and looked at her like she was crazy. She went from being ready to cut him to putting serious consideration into what a Quinn-spawned orgasm would feel like.

He doesn't actually want to go there with me. He's just being a dick and trying to make me uncomfortable—like he always does.

She had to remember that. If she threw herself at him in some mistaken conclusion she'd drawn, the humiliation might just kill her. She obviously needed some sexy alone time, because this was ridiculous. She marched down the gas station aisle, decided that a pack of gum probably wouldn't poison her, and paid for it.

By the time Quinn reappeared and got back in the driver's seat, she had control of herself. Mostly. Part of her wanted to apologize for making things weird back in the bathroom, but if she acknowledged it, he'd just make fun of her for thinking he might actually be serious about wanting her. Of course he didn't want her. Quinn didn't even like her.

For the first time, that thought actually bothered her a little.

CHAPTER FIVE

Quinn climbed back into his truck with one thought driving him—he had to get them to San Diego so he could get the fuck away from Aubry long enough to clear his headspace. It had to be the heat, or the stress of the upcoming wedding, or maybe the faint sheen on her exposed skin that made him think filthy thoughts. *Something*. He'd known the woman for over a year now, and he'd spent more time that day imagining her naked than the previous three hundred and sixty-five days plus. He was out of control.

He checked the clock. Five hours and thirty minutes. That was how long it had taken her to get under his skin. It didn't help that she'd stepped into him and given him *that* look. The one that said if he just made a move, she'd be a sure thing. In his wildest imagination, he never would have guessed he'd ever get the green light from Aubry Kaiser.

And he'd been half a breath from backing her into that filthy bathroom and bending her over the sink.

He started the truck without looking at her, but he couldn't let the strange silence extend between them. It was too full of things that might be his imagination, and he had to put a stop to that shit right this second. "Look, about back there… When I make these jokes, I'm—"

"Not serious. Got it."

He looked over, but she was staring out the passenger window, her entire body turned away from him, her arms wrapped around herself. As if he'd hurt her.

Guilt tried to worm through him, but he smothered it with everything he had. He'd made no promises to Aubry, and he hadn't been particularly mean since they started this trip. It wasn't his fault she was looking into shit.

Except I'm *looking into it.*

He ignored that. "Things are—"

"For fuck's sake, Quinn, stop. I don't want you. My common sense was temporarily high-jacked by my hormones. It won't happen again."

He should be glad to hear that—it was what he wanted when he brought up the uncomfortable conversation to begin with—but the easy way she dismissed the attraction between them was like a splinter, poking and prodding at him. There *was* chemistry there. Maybe they were too smart to do anything about it, but it existed.

Quinn turned up the radio. It didn't help. He could practically feel Aubry sitting there, and the fact she seemed to be engrossed in whatever she was listening to again only made it worse. She'd dismissed him completely and, though it should make him happy that things weren't going to be any more weird than they already were, it aggravated the fuck out of him knowing she could turn off the attraction as easily as flipping a light switch.

He wanted his mouth between her legs. He wanted her on top of him. Fuck, he wanted her in every way he could possibly think of. It didn't make sense.

"What're you listening to?"

"You know, generally when someone has headphones on, it means they don't want to talk."

He knew, which was why he was provoking her—to

get them back onto familiar territory. "And here I thought it was because you were anti-social and avoiding human contact in any way possible."

She didn't look over. "Ding, ding, ding, we have a winner. If only you could take a hint."

"Aw, peaches, I can take a whole lot more than that." *Fuck*. He hadn't meant to say that aloud. Quinn tightened his grip on the steering wheel and gritted his teeth.

"I'm sorry, what?" Aubry moved one side of her headphones off her ear and appeared to give him her full attention. "Did you just allude to the fact that you like to be the catcher?"

"What? No."

"That's exactly what you did. 'I can take a whole lot more than that' were your exact words." Her mouth curving up into a downright sweet smile. "I never pegged you for a bottom. Do you frequent truck stops and utilize glory holes, too?"

He growled under his breath. "Even if I was comfortable enough in my masculinity to be down for taking anything a lady can give me, that doesn't make me a bottom, peaches. Far from it. And glory holes are fucking disgusting." He forced himself to relax his hands and take a deep breath. "Though if you have a hole you'd like me to glorify—"

"Gross. So much gross."

There they were—on solid ground once more. As tempting as it was to go back to silently stewing, that way lay madness. He had to keep her talking so he could remember that this was *Aubry*, red as the devil and mean as a snake. She might have a hot little body that he'd kill to get his hands on, but it wasn't worth the price he'd have to pay when it came to *her*. Forgetting that was inexcusable. "So what'd you have to do to get a fancy invite to play this game?"

"Be better than everyone else." She'd said it without a trace of ego. It was just her truth.

A truth he had a hard time believing. "I know you spend a terrifying amount of time holed up in that apartment of yours, with only the online game for company, but there are a few million other people around the world who do the same thing."

"And I'm better than all of them."

"Who decides that?"

She sighed. "What makes it so hard for you to wrap your puny brain around my being one of the best out there? The fact that I'm a woman? Or is it that you're standing in the face of greatness and it makes you feel less like a man?"

That startled a laugh out of him. "Neither. I'm talking the odds, plain and simple."

"Well, take your odds and shove them. There were exactly ten invites that went out for this alpha test, and I'm one of them. That speaks for itself."

Yeah, he guessed it did. It was still weird to think about. "So someone ran the numbers and decided that, what, you've killed enough people in this game that you deserve a medal?"

"You can phrase the question as many ways as you want to and it's not going to change the outcome. The short answer is yes. I'm very, very good at murdering people. Within the game, of course."

"Of course." He drummed his fingers across the steering wheel. "I guess I better watch my back around you, huh?"

• • •

Aubry didn't know what Quinn was trying to pull, but she was over this conversation. All she wanted to do was bury herself in her book until the humiliation passed. Add in the fact that he felt the need to point out he didn't actually *want* her and, yeah, she wasn't getting over that anytime soon. Since she couldn't physically walk away from him, mentally doing it would have been good enough.

Except he seemed to want to talk, even if it was to tell her how unbelievable it was that she had actually gotten an invite in the first place.

She put her headphones on again, but froze when the engine made a weird clanking sound that she could hear even over the country music he insisted on playing. "What was that?"

Quinn was too busy cursing to answer her, and the truck gave a death knell as he guided it to the side of the road. Aubry just sat there for a minute, trying to process the reality that they were, in fact, broken down on the side of the highway in Texas in the middle of June. She closed her eyes, counted to ten, and then opened them again, but nothing changed. "Please tell me this isn't happening."

"Oh, it's happening." He threw open the door, letting in a blast of heat that threatened to melt her on the spot, and moved around the truck to open the hood. She watched a cloud of white smoke escape and groaned. What were the odds of this happening to her right when she was the most desperate to be anywhere but in the same vehicle as Quinn?

Oh, right. They were in the junker he'd insisted was reliable. The odds were fantastic.

She waited a minute, and then five, but when Quinn didn't come back around with an update, she climbed out of the truck. It shouldn't have been possible to be hotter outside than it was in the truck, but it was just this side of searing. She shoved her hair out of her eyes and marched over to where he was talking into his cell. "What's going on?"

He held up a finger. "Yeah, on Highway 10 just east of Clint. Yeah, that works. Thanks." He hung up and turned to face her. "The tow truck will be here in ten.'"

"Tow truck." She looked around. There was nothing as far as the eye could see. "If we'd taken a rental, this wouldn't have happened."

"Now's not the time for 'I told you so.'"

"On the contrary, there was never a better time. You said this thing was reliable." She marched over and kicked the wheel, and then cursed when her foot screamed in pain. "I hate you, and I hate your truck, and I wish I'd never agreed to this stupid plan." She made a beeline for the passenger door. "In fact, I'm going to call Jules and tell her what a shitty plan this is, and that I fully expect pie to make me feel better when I get back into town."

"Whoa, hold on."

"There will be no holding onto anything." She batted at him when his arm came around her waist, bringing her up short. "Get your paws off me."

"You can't call Jules."

"I can and I will." She tried to take a step but ended up just scraping off what felt like half her flip-flop on the asphalt. "Let go."

"She's with Adam on a plane right about now."

Just like that, all the fight went out of her. He was right. She couldn't call Jules, not when her friend was going to be focused on Adam and grieving. *I am possibly the worst friend ever.* She pinched the bridge of her nose. "If I say you're right, am I ever going to live it down?"

He didn't answer, and she opened her eyes. Their reflection was slightly distorted in the passenger window, but even she could see he had a seriously tense look on his face. She belatedly realized that they were pressed together, her back to his front, and that he was...

Oh my God. She couldn't resist leaning back into him, just a little. *Yep, that's* not *a micro penis.* A shiver worked its way through her, leaving goose bumps in its wake, and her nipples perked right up, showing through the thin fabric of her T-shirt. There was no way he didn't feel her reaction, not with his arm creating a band across her ribs, his forearm against the underside of her breasts.

Even as she noticed, he started to release her, his hand sliding over her stomach, but he stopped when he hit her hip, his pinkie finger dipping below the waistband of her shorts, just a little. It wasn't anywhere near anything vital, but that little intrusion made her moan all the same.

"*Fuck.*" The word was barely audible, but she *felt* it in the way his body tensed behind her.

She shivered again, torn between telling him to back off and getting the top button of her jeans all undone for him. If she didn't make a decision—and fast—he was going to back off again. It was written all over the tension she could feel emanating from his body.

Aubry started to reach for his hand, still undecided on whether she wanted to encourage or threaten him, but he moved, bending down to brace one hand on the truck in front of them, the other still on her hip. The move brought his mouth against her ear, and his harsh exhale made her shake.

She arched against him. She couldn't help it. Her body took over, a primal part of her knowing he could give her all the pleasure she could handle, and was only too happy to extend an invitation by rubbing her ass against his hard length.

His grip on her hip tightened, but he didn't try to stop her. "You're playing a dangerous game."

She knew. They had to stop for so many reasons, the least of which was that they were on the side of a freaking highway and it was only a matter of time before a car drove past.

But she didn't want to stop.

Apparently Quinn didn't, either, because he moved his hand, sliding beneath her shirt to splay across her lower stomach, his fingers still just inside her shorts. They weren't anywhere close to where she *wanted* them, but it felt unbearably intimate all the same. He exerted the slightest pressure, guiding her back against him, silently urging her to roll her hips again. So she did.

He rewarded her by sliding his hand a little further into her shorts, his fingertips just beneath her panties. "Undo the top button."

She obeyed with shaking hands, half sure she was dreaming this whole thing. But no, this was Quinn, his big body wrapped around hers, his hand dangerously close to pushing her over the edge and he hadn't even done anything yet.

He nipped the back of her neck as his hand slid the rest of the way into her panties, every nerve she had tightening as he leisurely stroked her once, twice…

So close.

The sound of tires on the asphalt snapped her back to herself. They were on the side of the *highway*. She looked over to see the tow truck approaching, the driver's face clear enough to see his wide eyes as he took in the scene they made. *Oh. My. God*.

Aubry shoved away from him. She did her best to ignore the way her body shook from denied pleasure. She couldn't believe she'd been so stupid as to give him a clear invitation *again*—let alone undo her button *for* him—and it was that same stupidity making her want to tell the tow truck driver to get lost.

Clearly the heat had boiled her brain.

For his part, Quinn recovered faster than she did. He met the driver halfway between vehicles, and they walked over to stare at the no-longer-smoking engine. She had half a thought that neither of them knew anything about engines at all and they didn't want to admit it, but it was entirely possible she was acting as uncharitable as her mother always accused her of being.

She grabbed her computer out of the truck as the men seemed to come to the conclusion that they'd actually have to tow the vehicle into the nearest actual town—which she learned was El Paso. It was a good twenty miles away, which would make for a truly delightful ride since she could smell the tow driver from five feet away, and he seemed to be missing half his teeth.

This is why I go out of my way to rarely leave the apartment. Shit always goes sideways at the first available opportunity.

She stewed the entire way into the mechanic's, and the *only* saving grace of the driver's stink was the fact that it kept her distracted from the fact that she and Quinn were forced to press together from shoulder to knees. Or the fact that every time she looked at his hands, she could feel them sliding into her shorts…and lower. And it sure as hell didn't distract her from the fact that she wanted his hand back between her thighs, coaxing her into an orgasm.

Or that she didn't want it to stop with his hands.

CHAPTER SIX

"What the fuck do you mean it's going to be in the shop overnight?"

The mechanic, an old, grizzled man that was about half Quinn's size, shrugged. "I've got to order in a part, and even if those dipshits over there manage to get me the right one today, I'm not paid enough to stay open late for the likes of you."

"How much?"

The guy—Larry, from his name tag—laughed. "More than you can pay, sonny." He leaned in and lowered his voice, shooting a glance to where Aubry stalked around the front of the shop, glaring at everything. "Here's a tip that I won't charge extra for—there's a nice little B&B round the way. Take your lady and put some effort into loving away that foul mood she's got going."

He'd be lying if he said the thought of sex chilling Aubry out hadn't occurred to him—especially when Jules had accidentally let it slip six months ago that Aubry didn't date and hadn't had that particular itch scratched in what might be *years*—but he wasn't the man who'd be able to manage that herculean feat.

Except, after how things had gone down next to his truck, he kind of wanted to. Quinn shook his head, trying to focus on the man in front of him rather than the woman pacing in front of the dingy window like a caged animal. "Pretty sure that's just her personality."

"In that case, my condolences." The man patted him on his shoulder. "And there's a bar next door to the B&B that has half-priced margaritas from now to closing."

That was going to be a necessity if they weren't getting out of here tonight. Quinn scrubbed a hand over his face. "You're sure you can't get my truck fixed up before closing?"

"I'll call Sue over at the B&B and let her know you're coming."

Guess that was that. Now all that was left to do was let Aubry know about the delay. He headed to the front of the shop and planted himself in front of her, forcing her to stop her pacing. "I have bad news and I have good news."

"What's the bad news?"

"Why am I not surprised you don't want to start with the sweet?"

"Because you're not as dumb as you look." She snapped her fingers, looking all the world like a queen deeming to notice an ant beneath her boot. "Now—the bad news?"

"They can't get my truck fixed up before morning."

"Are you *kidding* me?"

"It's fine." He glanced down and blinked. "You're looking a little pale."

"I can't…" She pressed a hand to her chest. "Give me a second."

His forced amusement vanished. Holy shit, she was having a panic attack. He recognized all the signs. "Come on, peaches." He half carried her to a faded plastic chair and guided her head between her knees. There was no telling what would ground her, because she hadn't told him when he'd asked, but he'd try what worked for Jenny and adapt as needed. "Breathe, yeah, just like that, in, hold it for one, two, three. Now exhale. Good girl."

Ten breaths later, she lifted her head. "Sorry."

It was on the tip of his tongue to make a smart-ass comment about the fact she'd never once apologized to him before now, but he bit it back at the last second. She might be a pain sometimes, but she still looked pretty shaky. He'd known a panic attack could bring down the strongest person, but there was something about seeing *Aubry* so shaken that made him want to yank her into his arms and hold her until she was herself again.

No wonder she didn't want to go to that damn convention by herself. If one unexpected delay was enough to set her back on her heels, what would being around a couple thousand people do? He realized he was still covering her hands with his and forced himself to let go of her. "You ready for the good news?"

"Sure." She managed a smile, though it wasn't anywhere close to convincing.

"There are half-priced margaritas."

"Well, damn, Quinn. You should have led with that."

He helped her to her feet, telling himself that he was just worried she'd take a nosedive, but the truth was that he kind of liked touching her. She smelled good despite the hellish day they'd had, like citrus and the warm summer sun. She must have noticed him watching her, because she took two large steps away, putting herself out of reach. "I'm fine."

"Didn't say you weren't."

"No, but you're looking at me like I'm about to

take a concrete nap." She shoved her hair out of her face. "Did you find us a place to stay? Equally important—can we walk there?"

"Yes to both." He led the way outside and down the block in the direction the mechanic had instructed. Aubry kept pace, but she was still looking a little peaked around the edges, so he walked slower than he normally would have. It wasn't being nice. It was making sure he didn't have to carry her ass in this heat.

Sure it is.

The B&B was a cute little thing tucked back from the street and was charmingly decorated in bright colors. It was manned by a cute little old lady with an accent thick enough he was glad for his sort-of-fluency in Spanish. Once she realized he could converse in that way, she switched over with a grin. "What's brought this handsome man through my door?"

"I'm looking for Sue. Larry said he'd call and let her know we were heading this way." Quinn grinned right back. She kind of reminded him of Daniel's aunty. She was as gently forceful as she was short, and she usually wore the same amused look that this woman did.

"Ah, yes, overnight stay for the happy couple." She accepted his card and passed over an honest-to-God key with the number four attached to it. A few signatures later and they were headed upstairs.

Aubry opened the door and stopped, halfway in the hall and halfway in the room. "You've got to be kidding me."

"You keep saying that." He nudged her the rest of the way into the room...and broke out laughing when he saw how it'd been decorated. There was a heart-shaped bed he was almost disappointed to find didn't seem to vibrate, and everything was done up in ways that suggested love and romance — from the heart-shaped candles scattered about to the curtains with their little hearts printed on the fabric. It was truly impressive.

He walked over to look in the bathroom and whistled. "Check out that tub." It was big enough to fit Aubry *and* him.

He turned around before that thought could take root, but it was too late. All he could picture was her straddling him, bubbles sliding over her skin, her red hair wet, and her eyes with that same expression she'd had by the truck before they'd been interrupted.

Back when he'd almost taken them off the deep end.

Quinn spun on his heels and nearly ran over Aubry. "I'm going for those margaritas." He didn't wait for a response. He just grabbed the second key and walked out of the room, closing the door softly behind him.

It didn't help. He could still smell her on his skin, which shouldn't have been possible, and it seemed like his control had splintered the second he got into the damn truck cab with her. Now he couldn't get the damn images out of his head, and with her showing interest there wasn't a whole lot standing in the way of burying himself in her until he could feel her coming around him.

Nothing but the fact that they weren't dating, weren't friends, and could barely stand each other.

• • •

Aubry stared at the door and then looked around. Quinn hadn't *acted* like he thought she was more of a freak than he normally did, but maybe her practically shoving his hand down her pants, followed by a panic attack, had been the last straw. She couldn't help losing it. She'd been so focused on just surviving the trip that hearing the trip was actually going to take two days instead of one sent her into a tailspin.

No, that wasn't completely accurate. She'd been strung so tightly from getting *so close* to orgasm and denied, and then having to sit next to Quinn while they rode into town, and *then* realizing she was going to spend an extra day in close quarters with a man who didn't know if he wanted her or didn't want her—and whom *she* couldn't decide if she wanted to jump his bones or shove him out of the truck and take off…

She'd lost it.

Quinn had handled her panic attack, though. He hadn't touched her other than to help her sit, and there had been no taunting or jokes, just his smooth voice anchoring her, walking her through it. If she'd had any doubts that he'd be able to stand as a wall between her and the strangers at the convention, they were gone now. He'd do what needed to be done to keep her from freaking out.

It made her feel weird to know that, so she refused to focus on it. And she sure as hell wasn't going to think about the fact they were sharing a room tonight—and every night from here on out, until this godforsaken trip was over.

Instead, Aubry walked around the room one more time. It was exactly what it seemed at first glance—a lovers' nest. Her gaze fell to Quinn's phone sitting on the dresser and she shook her head. There was no way she would go searching for him if she needed him, half-priced margaritas or no. Not that she'd need him. She wouldn't. What she *needed* was to get her head on straight.

She grabbed a set of clean clothes and headed for the shower. It would help center her and wash away all the insanity of the day. Or that was the theory, at least. As long as she tried not to be too weirded out by the fact there was no actual *door* in between the bathroom and the rest of the room.

The reality was that as soon as she got beneath the hot spray, her over-sensitized skin went into overdrive. All the pent-up feelings she'd wrestled down after they were interrupted rose to the surface, and she closed her eyes and braced her hands on the wall. She didn't make a habit of touching herself when she was on the go—probably because she was never on the go—but maybe she could make an exception…just this once. She glanced at the doorway to the bedroom, but she was just as alone now as she'd been two seconds ago.

She closed her eyes, tilted her head back, and slipped her hand between her legs. Her body was already primed from all the near-miss with Quinn, so it was the easiest thing in the world to imagine him on his knees in front of her, hiking one of her legs over his massive shoulder, *that* look in his blue eyes as he lowered his mouth to press a kiss to her inner thigh. A moan slipped free as she stroked herself, following the imaginary path his mouth would take. She reached her clit and circled it with her middle finger just like he'd done. She was so close. So freaking close.

A low curse had her eyes flying open. She froze, a

deer in headlights, when she focused on Quinn standing in the doorway to the bedroom. One breath passed, and then another, with them staring at each other across the steam-covered bathroom. She'd almost convinced herself that this was a desire-fueled hallucination until he took a step forward. "Tell me something."

It was too late to cover herself—not that she was particularly inclined to be bashful anyways. He'd had her on edge for *hours*. It was only fair that she returned the favor in whatever way she could. From the look on his face, she was doing a damn good job of it. She licked her lips. "What?"

"What are you thinking about right now while you've got your hand between your legs? What almost happened on the side of the road? Or about delivering some particularly violent finishing move in that game of yours?"

Maybe it was lust curdling her brain, but she didn't even hesitate. "You." When he cursed again, she kept going, enjoying the intense expression on his face. "On your knees, your mouth driving me to orgasm." It was perversity that had her adding, "Though, to be honest, I think it's better in fantasy than it could ever be in real life."

His brows slanted down, a forbidding look coming into his eyes that made her nipples tighten. "How do you figure?"

"Oh, you know." Her voice was breathy, but she was too distracted to be annoyed by how intensely he affected her. "I know my body better than anyone else ever could. So I'd just be setting myself up for disappointment."

He'd closed the distance between them without her noticing, until he stood just in front of the shower door, his big frame taking up entirely too much space. "Want to bet?"

"You can't be serious." He just looked at her, and she laughed. "You want to bet that, what, you're better in reality than whatever I can dream up? Does that line ever actually work on a woman?"

"You tell me."

Damn it, he had a point. She wanted to say yes. God, she wanted it so much, she was practically shaking. *That's just one more denied orgasm.* Aubry trailed a hand down her sternum, her heart picking up at how intently he followed the movement. "I don't like you."

"Doesn't matter."

No, she supposed it didn't. She'd never done anything like this before—casual sex wasn't in the cards for someone like her—but there was a first time for everything. And if she didn't come soon, she might go insane. Aubry stepped back into the spray of the water, opening the door as she did. "Just this once."

"Peaches, I'll make you a deal." He pulled his shirt over his head and tossed it on the ground. His chest was just as cut as it had been last year when she'd seen him at the swimming hole, but this time she was allowed to touch him. It shouldn't be possible, but that made him *more* attractive. Quinn laughed darkly. "Are you listening?"

Nope. I'm too busy checking you out. She took a deep breath. "I'm listening."

"This is going to be as good as your fantasy—better than your fantasy. And when it is, you're going to be in my bed and on my cock for the duration of our trip."

Her jaw dropped. "Did you not hear what I just said?"

"I heard, and I'm telling you that you'll change your mind the second I get my hands on you."

The scary part was that she wasn't sure he was full of it. He had such a magnetic confidence that she was tempted to believe he was actually capable of what he was promising. "And if you're wrong?"

"I'm not wrong." He unbuckled his pants and let them drop to the floor, revealing that Quinn apparently walked around commando.

Oh my God, I'm never going to be able to get that knowledge out of my head. That, or the fact he did *not* have a micro penis. She stared at his cock, deciding right then and there that there was no way *that* thing was going inside her. It was a study in impossibility. "We're not having sex."

"I'll promise you something else." He stepped into the shower stall and slid the glass door closed behind him, and suddenly there wasn't enough room and she didn't know where to look because she was having a seriously hard time lifting her gaze from his waistline.

Aubry took a shuddering breath. "What's that?"

"We won't have sex until you beg for my cock."

She went ramrod straight. "That's never—"

Quinn kissed her. It was *nothing* like before. There was nothing polite or soft about this kiss. It was hard and dominant and every bone in her body went liquid at the feeling of his tongue sliding into her mouth. One of his hands skated up her spine, bringing her body flush against his as he explored her mouth. Because that's exactly what he was doing, testing her, teasing out different responses.

I am in so much trouble.

He moved down her jaw line to set his teeth against her shoulder. "Tell me how I gave it to you in your fantasy."

"That's…" She gasped at the feeling of his cock against her stomach. "That's cheating."

"No, peaches. It's really not." He went down to his knees, perfectly replicating how she'd imagined it, right down to the look in his eyes. He ran his hands up the insides of her legs, spreading her as he did, and lifted her to pin her against the shower wall. The cold tile against her back was a direct counterpoint to the hot water peppering her sensitive breasts, and the equally hot man crouched between her thighs.

She had the sudden thought that he hadn't been wrong—not about making it better than her fantasy, and not about her begging for his cock before he was done with her.

CHAPTER SEVEN

Quinn hadn't had any plans when he came back to the room after he realized he'd left his phone on the dresser, but hearing Aubry's moan from the bathroom had drawn him like a moth to the flame. It had broken something in him seeing her in the shower with her hand between her thighs like the best kind of wet dream.

And now here he was, between those very thighs, about to get a little taste of heaven. He looked up the line of her body, taking in the tattoos covering her entire torso, creating a frame around her breasts that made them look like they were just begging for his attention. First, though, he had something to prove.

Or maybe he just couldn't stand the thought of going another second without tasting her.

He nipped her inner thigh, making her wait for what she wanted, loving the way her entire body quivered at the contact. She wanted it as much as he did. "Tell me."

"You're doing just fine on your own."

Hell, he knew that, but he still wanted to hear her husky voice whispering her dirtiest fantasies. "All the same."

"Fine." She tried to roll her hips, but he easily held her in place. "Your mouth, my clit, tonguing and licking and sucking and driving me out of my goddamn mind until I come, screaming your name."

He'd thought he couldn't possibly get any harder.

He was so fucking wrong. Quinn rested his forehead on her lower stomach, trying to get control. *You said she'd beg for your cock, and you meant it.* But he wanted to throw all that out the damn window and take her now. Christ, he wanted to so much he could barely breathe past the desire pounding through his blood.

He nuzzled her between her legs, gauging her reaction as he gave her a long lick. She cried out, the sound so unexpectedly sweet that he couldn't stop himself from doing it again. He'd had every intention of teasing her until she begged, but he couldn't stop. He licked her again. Aubry's moan was music to his ears, and her hands coming down to cup the back of his head, holding him in place, was the hottest fucking thing. As if he was going anywhere.

"My clit. Quinn, please."

There was nothing sexier than a woman who knew what she wanted, and Aubry's breathless voice telling him how to please her was exactly that. He moved up to her clit, doing exactly as she'd described earlier, sucking and licking and tonguing her. Her hands tensed on the back of his head, and that was the only warning he got before she cried out his name and came against his mouth.

He froze, breathing as hard as she was, belatedly realizing the water had gone lukewarm at some point. Now was when things would go sideways. He'd let her off the wall and she'd make some snarky comment, and then they'd go back to the uncomfortable would-they-or-wouldn't-they standoff that they'd had going all day.

Not fucking likely.

He shifted his grip on her and stood, without ever letting her feet touch the ground. She wrapped her legs around his waist, still looking a little dazed. "What are you doing?"

Fuck, he didn't know. He just knew he wasn't ready for this moment to end. "I'm not done with you yet, peaches."

She blinked. "But...I came."

"Yeah, you did." He turned off the shower and opened the glass door. "Once." He carried her into the bedroom and laid her down on the bed, settling between her thighs. There was a lot going on behind those amber eyes as the after-effects of her orgasm started wearing off, but he wasn't about to let a little thing like common sense stop him now that he'd had a taste of her.

Quinn kissed her, long and slow, taking his time and exploring her mouth as he thrust against her, his cock sliding against the wetness between her legs. It was a struggle to keep his strokes short so there was no chance he'd get anywhere near her entrance. He had every intention of keeping his earlier promise to make her beg. He broke away enough to say, "You've thought about me before."

She shook her head. "Nope."

"Liar." He palmed her breast, loving the way she filled his hand, the challenge in her eyes even as she arched against him. She could take anything he could give and keep coming back for more. "I've thought about you. Enough times that I drove myself crazy."

"You—You have?" It might have been the first time he'd heard her less than one hundred percent sure of herself.

"Seeing you last summer in that old-school one-piece? Yeah, I thought about it. I thought about pulling it down so I could see your rosy nipples." He moved down her body to suck first one nipple and then the other into his mouth, flicking each tip with his tongue. "I thought about that wicked mouth of yours wrapped around my cock."

"You just wanted to shut me up." She gave a breathless laugh that turned into a moan when he pushed a finger into her. She was tight, so tight he had to work to get a second finger into her. He stroked her slowly, waiting until she lifted her hips every time his fingers entered her, urging him to pick up the pace.

"Maybe." He kissed her hipbone and then worked his way over her stomach, still fucking her with his fingers. "I've thought about you riding my cock, feeling you go tight around me just before you come."

"Oh, just that." She ran her hands up her sides to cup her breasts.

"Yeah, just that." He ducked down and licked her clit in the same way that had driven her crazy before. "I've thought about this, too. About licking you until you come, and then sucking on your sweet little clit until you can't decide if you want to beg me to stop or beg for another orgasm."

Aubry lifted her head, her familiar glare in place, though the affect was kind of lost by the glazed look in her eyes. "Your fantasies seem to feature me begging a lot."

"Yep." He gave her another long lick. "Though if you want to give stern instructions, I'll take that into consideration."

She laughed, the sound choked off when he pushed

a third finger into her. "Oh. My. God."

"Tell me what you want, peaches. I'll even consider giving it to you."

"That's…you're…" Her back arched, her eyes shutting and his name on her lips. "*Quinn*."

Holy shit. He could get addicted to the sight of her coming and knowing he was the cause of it. When they were like this, it didn't matter that they could barely stand the sight of each other under normal circumstances. He liked driving her crazy. He thought she might like returning the favor if given half a chance.

He fully intended to give her that chance.

• • •

Aubry didn't know when her life had taken a hard left turn, but she couldn't find it in herself to question it too much, with an orgasm rippling through her. She gasped and cursed and fought against the pleas crowding the inside of her lips. Because now, having a taste of what being in bed with Quinn would be like, she wanted the whole nine yards. It didn't matter that it was the most awful idea in a long history of awful ideas, or that the second they had sex, it would be the beginning of the end.

The end of what? You don't even like the guy half the time.

More than half the time.

But for the first time in longer than she cared to remember, she felt alive and free and there wasn't a single worry plaguing her. There was only this room and this man and the way he made her feel. He shifted to lie next to her, his hand still idly stroking her between her legs. It wasn't enough to do more than draw a little moan from her, but it was clear he wasn't done yet.

Good.

She stretched, the move pushing his fingers deeper into her. Two orgasms in and the size of his cock was looking more like an enticement than a challenge. All she had to do was open her mouth and say those damning words.

If you do that, it means he wins. It means you'll never hear the end of it.

Something must have shown on her face, because he kissed her, deep and probing, before lifting his head and saying, "The rules have changed, just for this week."

"Oh yeah?" She tried to smother the hope flickering to life in her chest, but it was nearly impossible. If there was a way to have her cake and eat it, too, then for once in her life she was going to jump and worry about the potential consequences later.

"We're supposed to be dating." He circled her clit with his thumb. "So think of this as some really intensive practice."

"Practice." It was absurd, but the word actually made her feel better.

"We have to be convincing." He kissed down her neck. "And you're not thinking about slapping me right now and I've had my hands all over you."

"True." She knew she was grabbing onto the flimsy excuse with both hands, but she didn't care. "I don't feel much like punching you in the throat right now."

"That's good." His laugh vibrated against her skin, but then his voice deepened. "You want my cock, peaches. Let me give it to you."

She pressed her lips together, trying and failing to see the pitfalls in front of her. It was impossible. All she could focus on was how empty she felt, even with his fingers still stroking her. She wanted more, and she wanted it now. Aubry ran her hand over his arm, silently marveling at the strength she could feel there. "Just this week. Then we go back to normal."

"Deal." He urged her to spread her legs a little wider. "We'll be back to sniping at each other, and we'll never speak of this again."

She lifted her head and kissed him. "In that case, Quinn, you better have a condom secreted away somewhere, because I think I might die if I don't have your cock right now."

He slid off the bed and strode to the dresser. Behind the giant bouquet of fake flowers, there was a bowl she hadn't noticed—a bowl filled to the brim with pink and red condom wrappers.

She propped herself up on her elbows and watched him rip a wrapper open and roll it onto his length. "I think you might have to give that mechanic a gigantic tip."

"I'm inclined to think you're right." He stopped at the edge of the bed. "How do you want it, peaches?"

It was official. She was still in the shower and fantasizing this entire thing.

Emboldened by the thought, she grabbed his hand and pulled him onto the bed, guiding him onto his back. *No matter which way I spin it, this isn't real. That means I can do whatever the hell I want.* "I like the picture you painted before." She straddled his hips, bracing herself on his big chest. "I'll make you a deal."

He raised his eyebrows. "Since our last deal worked out so well, I'm in."

"You don't even want to hear it?"

"Sure I do." He cupped her breasts, squeezing gently until she hissed out a breath. "Though if it involves watching you ride my cock, I'm going to tell you right now that we're both coming out the winners in this."

"I'd settle for us both coming."

"Peaches, you read my mind."

She rose and reached between them to stroke his cock. *So big.* She wanted it. She wanted it all. Aubry positioned him at her entrance and sank down an inch. Quinn gripped her hips, slowing her descent. "Easy."

"I don't want it easy. I want it hard and hot and rough."

Something changed on his face, and she realized that he'd held onto the slightest bit of control until this point. It was gone now. He pulled her down and his hips rose, sheathing his cock in her to the hilt. Her breath escaped her in a sharp cry that had nothing to do with pain. She tried to move, to shift, to do something to relieve the growing pressure inside her, but Quinn kept their hips pinned together. "That's it, peaches. Feel every single fucking inch of me."

"I...can't." She shook her head, still trying and failing to move. "I need more."

"I've got more for you." He lifted her and slammed her down onto him. She moaned, wanting to help him, but he had full control despite her being on top. Quinn half sat up and used one hand to grasp the back of her neck, pulling her down against his chest. He kissed her, still fucking her, the contrast between his grip and what his cock was doing between her legs nearly making her eyes roll back in her head. He broke away enough to say, "This is what you wanted."

"Yes." There was no point in playing coy. She gripped his shoulders, hanging on for dear life. There was nothing soft or sweet or gentle about what he was doing to her. It was hard and gritty and sexy beyond belief.

And she loved every second of it.

Her orgasm hit her like a freight train, bowing her back and ripping a desperate little cry from her lips that she'd deny she made until her dying day. Quinn's hands spasmed on her hips, his face twisting into a grimace and her groaned name slipping from his lips.

He said my name as he came. It didn't mean a damn thing. She'd done the same. It was hormones and desire-fueled insanity at its finest.

It was still the sexiest thing she'd ever heard.

That, more than anything, got her moving. She slid off him—or she tried to. His arms went tense around her. "Where do you think you're going?"

Trying to find some space so my head can stop spinning. She couldn't say that to him. They might have called a temporary truce, but it wouldn't last if he sensed weakness. That was just how they worked. So she snarled at him. "I'm going to wash you off me."

"Nope." He rolled them, settling between her legs and pinning her in place, though he kept most of his weight off her.

"What the hell do you mean 'nope'?" She shifted, trying to wiggle out from beneath him, but her traitorous body zinged in response.

"Do you remember what I said in the shower?"

She did, but she was trying very hard not to look

into it. "You just wanted to talk your way into my pants."

"Peaches, you weren't wearing pants." He thrust a little, his cock still half hard inside her. "I said when you begged for my cock, you'd have it for the duration of the trip."

"And if I don't want it?"

He idly ran a hand up her side to cup her breast. "Do you?"

Yes. The sheer force of the thought surprised her. It was just pent-up hormones clamoring for getting their needs met. It didn't *mean* anything. If she could remember that, she might just get through the week. "I—"

"Truth."

She stared at a spot on the ceiling and gritted her teeth against the urge to tell him she'd happily spend from now until kingdom come on his cock. Once she had a little control over herself, she said, "Fine."

"You can play coy, peaches, but I know the truth." He feathered his fingers across her nipple, making her squirm. "You can't hide it when I'm inside you."

That's what she was afraid of.

CHAPTER EIGHT

Quinn let Aubry have her space the next morning when they collected the truck. To be honest, he needed some space, too. He'd had her countless times through the night, her body an addiction he hadn't known he possessed until he felt that first orgasm. But once would never have been enough. Hell, he'd lost count and that *still* wasn't enough.

He turned to watch her put her bag into the cab of the truck. Today she wore a red plaid dress that should have looked ridiculous, but on her it worked. His body went tight imagining what she might be wearing—or *not* wearing—underneath it.

There's no reason I can't find out.

No reason except all of them. He never should have crossed the line with her, but he'd done more than step over it. He'd nosedived right into oblivion. There was no going back now, not until they finished this trip and got back to Devil's Falls. With the familiar town around them, they'd fall back into the way things used to be. Maybe. Even now, he couldn't quite imagine trading edged insults with her like they used to. Not when he knew how she tasted.

He paid Larry and grabbed his keys. By the time he made it to the truck, Aubry was already in the cab and looking everywhere but at him. He decided to let her stew a little and they headed out of El Paso without a word. Thirty minutes later, the tension left her shoulders and she reached for her headphones.

That was when he pounced. Keeping his eyes on the road, Quinn unfastened her seatbelt, hooked an arm around her waist, and towed her over to sit against him. She gave a seriously impressive snarl. "Are you trying to get me killed?"

"Nah, I just had a little entertainment in mind."

"If you think I'm going to sit here without a seat-belt—Oh." She accepted the half of the belt he offered her and dug into the crease in the seat for the second half. Once it was clicked around her waist, she gave an audible sigh of relief. "Okay, what were you saying?"

"You have a serious set of neuroses."

"Not wanting to die in a car crash isn't being neurotic. And I'm following the law."

"Car crash, plane crash, serial killer. What else are you afraid is going to kill you in imaginative ways?" He ran his hand from her knee up the inside of her thigh as he spoke, edging the hem of her dress up until he caught sight of a pair of Wonder Woman briefs. Her nerd credit was off the charts, and he was really digging it.

Not that he'd say as much to her.

"Uh, well." Her breath hissed out when he cupped her through the cotton fabric. "There's always the off chance that a mutant breed of alligator is going to show up and start picking off people."

"Texas has been in a drought for years."

"Don't muddy my fears with logic."

He kept stroking her, not putting enough pressure behind it to do anything but drive her to distraction. "I seem to remember something about mutant cannibals, too. What do you have against mutants?"

"Nothing if they're students of Professor X."

He huffed out a laugh. "I understand that reference."

She turned so fast, she almost toppled over. "Did you just make a nerd joke at me? I'm pretty sure you just made a nerd joke at me."

"Did I?" He knew damn well he did, but her reaction was pretty fucking priceless. Before she could get too distracted, he slipped his hand into her panties. "What else?"

"What else what?" She spread her legs a little, giving him better access, her eyes half closed. He liked Aubry like this, soft and hot and wet for him.

He pushed a single finger into her. "What else are you afraid is going murder you in cold blood?"

"Werewolves, vampires of the non-sparkling variety, pretty much every stranger I meet, guys who think stalking is a compliment."

Her voice changed on the last one, and he went still. "You have much experience with that?"

"I don't have to. I've been on this nifty little thing called the Internet."

Her other fears ranged from insane to pure nonsense, but that one grated on him. He didn't play games online, but Daniel and his cousins did, and Quinn had seen firsthand how some of the little dickweeds they played against responded to Daniel's lady cousins. How much more abuse did Aubry field because she was better than ninety-nine percent of the other players—mostly dudes?

Her hand closed around his wrist. "Maybe we should just—"

"Peaches, look at me." He waited for her to do it before he spoke again. "I won't pry. I'm just going to make you feel good for a little bit. Okay?"

She looked vulnerable for the first time since he'd met her, but the expression quickly passed, replaced by the Ice Queen mask she liked to wear. "If you insist."

"Lose the Wonder Woman briefs."

"What do you have against Wonder Woman?" But she was already lifting her hips and sliding them off.

He reclaimed his hand's place between her thighs as soon as they were gone. "She's standing between me and what I want."

"Oh."

"Tell me something."

"You're chatty today."

Yeah, he was, but apparently the best way for them to hold down a conversation was with his hand between her legs, so he wasn't going to let the opportunity slip past. "You spend all of your time in front of one screen or another."

"Mmm." She pressed her lips together. "I didn't hear a question in there."

"How the hell do you have such a rocking body? Because I'm really digging the muscle tone you have going on in your legs."

Aubry laughed, the sound low and amused. "DDR."

It took him a few seconds to compute—or maybe he was just distracted by sliding a second finger into her. "Dance Dance Revolution? You're shitting me."

"It's great cardio. Now, as fun as this has been, you promised me some entertainment."

She could play like she was humoring him all she wanted. She was the one who draped her left leg over his lap, leaving herself completely open to him. Aubry gave a smug smile. "How long do you think you can last before you pull this ancient beast over to the side of the road and have your wicked way with me?"

"Aw, was that a challenge?" He pumped his fingers into her, her body welcoming him in a way he was already starting to crave.

"And wave the red flag in front of your bull?" She hissed out a breath. "God forbid."

He leaned over, still keeping his eyes on the road. He circled her clit and then palmed her again, liking the way she felt against his hand. "I'm going to fuck you until you can't walk right—when we get to San Diego. Until then, you'll have to deal with the poor substitute of my fingers."

• • •

Time lost all meaning for Aubry. There was only the cab of Quinn's truck, his hand between her legs, and his voice in her ear. Her dress was bunched up around her hips, her lower body bared for anyone that drove past them, but she didn't care. All that mattered was the orgasm he kept looming until she started begging. Only then did he let her come…and start the whole process over again.

They took a few breaks, but they happened in a blur. She went through the motions as quickly as possible so she could get back into the truck and the man who was so damn skilled at assuaging the ache in her core that beat in time with her heart.

It was somewhere outside Phoenix that she lost it. Aubry knocked his hand away and went for the button of his jeans. He started to stay something, but she snarled, "Shut up." She freed his cock and slid down the seat so she could take him into her mouth. Her seatbelt pulled at her hips, but she was so beyond caring at this point. It was still buckled. That was enough to keep her fear in check.

Quinn's curse was music to her ears. One hand threaded through her hair, cupping the back of her head as she swallowed him down, down, until she couldn't take any more. She wasn't about to let that deter her, though. She fisted a hand around the base of him, stroking as she sucked. There was nothing but the need to drive him as crazy as he'd driven her.

"That's it, peaches. Suck me hard." His voice was downright guttural, and *she* was the cause of it. Aubry moaned, stroking him faster. His hand on the back of her head went tense. "I'm close."

A warning. A promise.

She sucked harder, keeping up the motion that made his thigh clench. His cock swelled in her mouth, his curse in her ears, and then he was coming. She kept sucking, swallowing him down, a purely feminine part of her satisfied in a way she'd never experienced before. She looked up at him, his blue eyes dark, his breathing coming as hard as hers, and knew that she could make him lose control again now whenever she felt like it. Yes, he could do the same to her, but that power was downright intoxicating. She gave him one last stroke before she sat up. "Damn, Quinn. Just… damn."

He recovered enough to give her a cocky grin. "Pretending to be my girlfriend isn't so bad, is it?"

"Sure." His words tried to douse her feel-good mood, but she fought off the feeling. This wasn't real.

She knew that. He knew that. Anyone who mattered knew that. Yes, they'd had sex and were going to keep having sex until it reached its natural conclusion. But that was all there was. She'd be a fool and a half to forget that.

Aubry couldn't quite make herself move away from him, though. And then he took the decision away from her and draped his arm across her shoulders, tucking her against his side. "Get some sleep. We have a few hours yet, and I know you didn't get much last night."

He was right, but he hadn't, either. She frowned. "Are you going to be okay to drive?"

"I'm bright-eyed and bushy-tailed. If I start getting sleepy, I'll start playing with you again." His grin widened. "That's sure to wake me right up."

She shivered at the thought of waking up to that. The man was insatiable—and she liked it. She yawned. "If you're sure."

"I'm sure." He guided her head to his shoulder. "Now close your eyes, because I'm telling you right now, you're not going to get a wink of sleep once we check into that fancy hotel they have you set up in."

She was sure there was no way she'd manage to pass out, but the next thing she was doing was opening her eyes as they exited the highway into the outskirts of San Diego. It was late enough that they'd missed rush hour, so Quinn was able to navigate to the hotel the convention had booked for her without too much trouble. She expected a normal room, but she followed the instructions the lady had given her at check-in to a freaking suite.

Aubry walked into the room and spun a slow circle,

whistling under her breath. "Toto, we aren't in Kansas anymore."

"Thank God. Kansas is a terrible place." Quinn strode over to look out the floor-to-ceiling windows that afforded a view of downtown. "Damn, peaches, just how good at this game are you?"

"I told you. The best." She hesitated. "Well, one of the best." There were still players out there better than her. She pinched herself, hardly daring believe this was real. She walked into the bathroom and whistled again. There was a walk-in shower and a tub that made the one at the B&B look like a bucket in someone's backyard. *This is insane. There has to have been a mistake.* There wasn't. She knew there wasn't. The whole situation was almost too surreal to be possible. Who would have thought she'd make it *here* when she started playing Deathmatch in that shitty little trailer all those years ago? Not her. Not anyone from where she'd grown up, either.

"What time is your thing tomorrow?"

"Noon." Most hardcore gamers she knew were night owls by necessity. Even if they worked in web design like she did, most people had to hold down some sort of day job with normal hours and play in their time off. So the developers were giving a nod to that by starting in the afternoon.

"Give me a few to take a shower and then we can go get some grub before we settle in for the night." He reached into the shower and turned on the water. "I'm starving."

She took a slow breath, doing her damnedest to convince herself that the walls weren't really closing in. "If it's all the same to you, I'd rather order in."

"Peaches." He waited until she looked at him to continue. "You have me at this shindig to ground you, correct?"

"More like to put your mass to use as a walking wall between me and the rest of the world."

The edges of his mouth quirked up, but his blue eyes stayed serious. "Consider dinner a trial run. I'll protect you from any mutants that might show up—of both the cannibal and reptile variety."

"Zombies."

He frowned. "What?"

"In big cities, it's zombies." When he just stared, she felt compelled to explain, no matter how stupid he would no doubt find it. "If the zombie outbreak were to happen in Devil's Falls, I have a pretty decent chance of surviving, despite having next to no applicable skills outside of the internet. Y'all like your guns as much as you dislike outsiders, and so the chances of the town battening down the hatches until it all blows over, without so much as one casualty, is highly probable. Here in San Diego? We wouldn't stand a chance."

For a second, she was sure he'd rip her argument to shreds, but he finally just shook his head. "As crazy as that is, it kind of makes sense."

"It's not crazy. And having a zombie plan is just good business. The CDC even went so far as to put out ads about how to survive a zombie apocalypse a few years ago." She made a face. "Though they technically did it so people would actually pay attention to their advice, it still holds."

"In that case, I won't let any of the walking dead near you if you'll share a meal with me in an actual restaurant." He looked so damn serious, not like he was making fun of her at all.

She bit her lip. "But there are so many…people…in restaurants."

Quinn leaned in close enough for her to catch a whiff of his cologne. Her toes curled and her body went tight in anticipation. But he just whispered. "If you make it through dinner without bolting, we can come back here and I'll fuck you on every single surface this hotel room has to offer."

Her breath stalled in her lungs. "I thought you were already going to do that."

"Nah, I was already going to fuck you until you couldn't walk right. This is something else altogether."

She wasn't sure she followed the logic, but Quinn had already more than proven he was capable of driving her out of her mind with pleasure. She'd be an idiot not to take him up on what he was offering. Besides, he had a point. They needed some kind of trial run before the demo tomorrow. This would do as well as anything.

He'd be her anchor. She tried and failed to ignore the fluttering in her chest at the thought.

CHAPTER NINE

Quinn held the door open for Aubry, taking a deep breath of the frigid air conditioning that El Diablo had to offer. The restaurant wasn't particularly fancy, though it came highly recommended by the bellman at the hotel. From the smells filling the dining area, he had the right of it. Quinn kept his hand on Aubry's back, as much to gauge her tension level as for the sheer enjoyment of touching her. And, yeah, she was about ready to flee for the hills from the way her eyes were darting around the room.

He caught the hostess's eye. "Two, please."

"This way."

They followed her through the tables filled with people, Aubry's shoulders hunching more with each step. Luckily their table was against a wall, nearly in the corner. He positioned her with her back to the wall, putting himself between her and the rest of the room. She didn't notice, because she was too busy staring at her plate. In the last thirty seconds, her pale coloring had taken on a sickly hue and he could hear her breathing coming faster from across the table. "Peaches, look at me."

She reluctantly lifted her gaze. "Why couldn't we have ordered in?"

"Look at me," he repeated. "Focus on me." He gave her a cocky grin. "I'm the only one in this room who matters anyways."

Like he'd suspected, that snapped her out of it, at

least partially. "Narcissistic much?"

"Nah, I just call it like I see it." And if she was focusing on him, she wasn't worrying about all the other bodies in the room. He had to keep her talking, though, because the second she paused, that scarily impressive brain of hers would kick into high gear and then they'd have to start from scratch. "You know, Jules never told me what you do for a living."

"You've been probing Jules for information about me?" Her tone gave nothing away, but some of the panic in her eyes retreated. "That's stalkerish in the extreme."

"I prefer the term self-preservation. I needed all the ammunition I could use to defend myself against your witty barbs."

She rolled her eyes. "Now you're just being ridiculous."

On purpose. "Back to the topic at hand…"

"I design websites and graphics." She shrugged. "It's not exactly my great passion, but it pays the bills and I can do it from Devil's Falls, so it meets my needs."

She was a study in contradictions. He'd never met a crazier woman when it came to some of her neuroses, but she was obviously passionate both in bed and when it came to that damn game of hers. Everything about her was extreme—either she hated or she loved, but she never toed the line. Except, apparently, when it came to her job. He smiled at the waitress when she delivered water to their table and took their order, and then turned his attention back to Aubry. "So what would you do if you were going to follow your great passion?"

She shrugged. "I don't know."

"Peaches, you've delivered insults harsh enough to strip flesh from bone, but you've never lied to me — until now." He leaned forward, propping his elbows on the table. "Tell me. I promise not to laugh at you."

"No, you don't." She took a sip of her water. "And, anyways, that's not what I'm afraid of — not that I'm afraid of anything about this conversation, exactly. It's just that some things aren't talked about."

He blinked. "I don't know where you get some of your ideas."

"Oh, God, *fine*." She hunched down in her seat. "I want to design video games."

"Cool."

Aubry fiddled with her silverware. "In theory, sure. But the reality isn't cool at all. Even if I had the balls to submit my game to a company for consideration, the chances of it getting picked up are less than one percent, and if I went the indie route, there's a whole host of other hurdles I'd have to get over. That's not even bringing up what it's like being a woman in the gaming industry — "

"Aubry."

She sat back and finally looked at him. "What?"

He mentally revisited everything she'd just said. He wasn't sure she'd taken a breath the entire time. "You have a game done?"

"It's not *done*-done. It's playable and there are a few levels put together, but that's it."

"That's amazing." He didn't have a creative bone in his body, and while he could enjoy a video game here and there, he'd never really put much thought into what it took to actually create one. "You have to send it in."

"Nope." She shook her head. "Did you miss everything I just said?"

"I got it loud and clear. But let me ask you something—what's the worst they could do?"

"Death threats come to mind."

Quinn took a drink of his water, considering how to approach this. "But what if they said yes?"

"Back to the less than zero chance that they would."

"There's no such thing as less than zero."

"Sure there is—"

"In algebra. Not in reality." Hell, the woman was like a dog with a bone. He held up his hands as the waitress deposited chips and salsa onto the table. "I'm not saying you have to do it right now. I'm just saying it'd be a damn shame if you took away even the slightest chance of seeing your game sold in stores because you were scared of a little rejection."

She picked up her fork and poked at her salad. "You don't understand."

"Enlighten me."

She rolled a grape tomato around her plate. "You and Jules, and even Adam, walk around like you own the entire world. Not in a bad way, you're just so crazy confident, it would never occur to you to quit something just because someone told you it was impossible. I'm pretty sure Jules would see that as a personal challenge. I'm not like that."

"You're a little bit of a basket case, I'll grant you." He waited for her half-hearted smile. "But, hell, I didn't think you cared what anyone thought."

"I don't. It's not that. It's…" She finally stopped

playing with her food and speared the tomato. "I'm already half convinced the game is shit. I don't need someone else to tell me so and confirm it."

If that wasn't the most depressing outlook he could think of, he didn't know what was. Quinn opened his mouth to argue further, but decided there had to be a better way to come at the subject. He'd think about it later and bring it up when she didn't have all her walls firmly in place.

Like when he was inside her.

He grinned at the thought, which had her brows slanting down. She pointed her fork at him. "I am highly suspicious of that look on your face right now."

"As well you should be." He dipped a chip into the salsa and popped it into his mouth, chewing slowly, enjoying the way she squirmed. The best part of this entire conversation was the fact that she hadn't once noticed the restaurant fill up around them. He had no doubt the second she stopped focusing on him there'd be a potential panic attack on the horizon, and he wasn't about to let her go through that again if there was any other option.

So he kept talking. "I always wanted to be a cowboy when I was a kid."

"And look at you, a cowboy. Will wonders never cease?"

He shot her a look. "Careful there. Your claws are out. What do you know about my family?"

"Other than the fact they use one of the most destructive 'resources' to fuel their ambition—and your truck—and they had a spill in the Gulf Coast a few years back that killed off a truly terrifying amount of wildlife? Not much."

That was what most people knew about his family, and he'd never been particularly interested in getting into the nitty gritty of it. "My great-granddaddy struck it rich back in the day and Baldwyns have been in the oil industry ever since—until me."

"How does that even happen? An oil industry heir turned cowboy? Aren't you like filthy rich or something?"

"My family is." He wondered if that would make her think differently of him, like others did. He'd learned to hate the calculating look that sometimes came into their eyes—those people never lasted much longer with him after that moment. He didn't want anything to do with the oil industry, and he didn't want to spend his time with someone who was going to push him toward that end.

He didn't like the thought that Aubry might number among them.

• • •

Aubry took a bite of her salad and chewed while she contemplated Quinn. He was tense and looked edgy, like he expected her to whip out a machete and start swinging. She wasn't sure what she was supposed to say to take that look off his face, but she figured the truth was the best way to go. "Guess we can't choose our family." Hadn't she learned that time and again the hard way? Yeah, her family was a far cry from some several generations of oil-rich craziness, but the same rule applied. "So why a cowboy? I know we're in Texas and all, but did you watch too many John Wayne movies or something?"

Some of the tension around his eyes disappeared. "Maybe." He took a bite of his burger. "More likely it was spending so much time on the Rodriguez farm when I was growing up. I saw how happy Rodger and Lori were, and I wanted that."

She couldn't blame him for that. Jules's aunt and uncle were something else. She'd never seen anything like the casual way they loved each other, like a pair of well-broken-in jeans. They just *fit*.

Aubry kind of doubted Quinn was talking about that, though.

His blue eyes saw too much. "That was a pretty skilled change of subject. We were talking about your game."

"And now we're not." She turned the conversation to things less close to her heart. As nice as it was that he hadn't told her how crazy her dream of designing video games was, she'd rather not deal with him trying to spare her feelings. She played so many games, and hers was like a child with a crayon compared to a Renaissance master. Laughable. And his false confidence in her just made her feel weird. That wasn't what they were to each other. She had a cheerleader in Jules—or she would if she ever admitted to her best friend what she wanted—so she didn't need one in Quinn. Especially when his quiet confidence almost made her think maybe she had a shot.

By the time the waitress brought the check, Aubry was weaving in her seat a little. She yawned and tried to cover it up. He laughed, dropped a stack of cash on the table, and stood. "Let's get you back to the hotel."

It was only then she realized she'd sat in a full room of people for who-knew-how-long and hadn't freaked out. Aubry started to look around, but he was there, a wall between her and the rest of the room. "Come on, peaches." He held out his hand.

Surely having so many people in this room is against some kind of fire code?

The ever-present band around her chest started to close and she made a grab for Quinn's hand. The touch of his skin against hers steadied her, just a little. He nodded once and led the way out of the building. She could breathe a little easier on the street. "I'm sorry I'm such a basket case."

"You have nothing to apologize for."

She knew that. Really, she did. But this wasn't like things were with Jules. Her best friend took Aubry as she was, massive list of flaws and all. It would be madness to expect Quinn to do the same.

You're not keeping him.

Right. Naturally. She hadn't forgotten that. It was just hard to remember in this moment, with his hand in hers and their walking back to a hotel after what could be termed a date.

She gritted her teeth as a woman on a cell phone bumped into her. *Not a date. The only reason he's here at all is because he needs a fire-breathing dragon for his sister's wedding and you fit the bill.*

It didn't matter that they'd had some seriously hot sex. It certainly didn't matter that she kind of admired the fact he'd left the riches his family offered behind him and run off to be a cowboy. And it sure as hell couldn't affect the way she saw him, that he was seriously good at anchoring her when her neuroses got out of control.

It's the sex making me all crazy. I haven't had sex

in… She silently did the math. *Six years. So I guess I'm due a little insanity of the male variety.* At least she could be assured that Quinn wasn't going to go batshit crazy on her like every single one of the guys online she'd contemplated meeting had.

And those were the ones that had passed her background checks.

But knowing that wasn't going to save Aubry from her hormones betraying her. She breathed a sigh of relief when they walked into the hotel and made a beeline for the elevator. The only problem was that being out of the crowds only brought home the *other* issues she was experiencing.

Like the fact she was in danger of having… feelings…for Quinn.

Non-hate feelings.

She had to call the whole thing off. Or at least the sex part. They'd proven she could fake—yeah, fake—liking him. That was good enough. It *had* to be good enough.

CHAPTER TEN

Quinn could tell there was a difference in Aubry as soon as he closed the hotel room between them and the rest of the world, but he couldn't quite put his finger on what it was. She wrapped her arms around herself and wandered farther into the room, stopping in front of the big windows opposite the door. "We need to talk."

"Well, hell, no good ever came of a conversation that started like that."

She ignored his attempt to make light of the whole thing. "I can't do…this."

No. He clamped hard against the word, stopping the word before he voiced it. *Damn it*. He should have seen this shit coming. Things between them had never been anything but complicated, and there was no reason sex would fix that. He should have known it would only make it worse.

He *had* known. He just hadn't cared. He'd wanted Aubry, and she'd wanted him, and so he'd thrown caution to the wind and crossed that line. The problem was Quinn wasn't ready to take a step back into familiar territory. Not yet.

"What's changed?" He moved closer, but kept an arm's length between them. Aubry wouldn't respond well to him crowding her. She might even go for his throat. While there was a time and place to provoke that type of response, it wasn't now.

"If you hadn't noticed, it's been a while for me."

He'd noticed. He would have had to be exception-
ally dense not to have noticed.

She still wouldn't turn to look at him. "Besides, I
thought you had a rule that you didn't sleep with
women you don't like. We've broken it enough times
already."

"I don't think it's up to you to decide if we've
broken *my* rules." He didn't know why he was fighting
this so hard. She was right. He might not despise her
like he had in the past, but that was still a long way off
from deciding they were going to be best friends or
hang out for any length of time after his sister's
wedding. They wouldn't. He ignored the pit in his
stomach that opened at that thought. "You like fucking
me."

"It's acceptable."

He laughed. "I lost count of how many times I've
made you come in the last twenty-four hours.
Acceptable doesn't begin to cover it."

She shot him a look over her shoulder. "On top of
all that, I think I've more than proven I can act like I
like you the way a girlfriend would. So we don't have
to go there again."

He might—*might*—have let it go if she'd said she
wasn't interested. But that wasn't what she was saying.
Hell, Aubry was throwing every excuse at him to prove
she didn't want him, each one flimsier than the last.
This final excuse was the one he couldn't let stand,
though. Quinn took a step toward her, the light of the
room creating a mirror in the window in front of her.
He searched her face, not liking how unsure she
looked. She'd been fine during dinner—skittish, sure,
but *fine*.

Which meant somewhere along the way, she'd started overthinking things.

"Acting." He ran his hands up her arms to settle on her shoulders, massaging the tense muscles at the bottom of her neck lightly with his thumbs. "Acting is just another way to say lying."

"That's your problem if you choose to see it that way." Her head fell forward, giving him better access to her neck.

Got you. He kept massaging her shoulders. "I don't think it's a problem at all. I'll tell you a secret." He moved closer until he was almost pressed against her and leaned down to whisper in her ear. "I kind of like you, too."

"Kind of like me? God, Quinn, how the hell does your neck hold up that big head of yours?"

"Lots of muscles."

She snorted, but then lifted her head. "I just…" A deep breath. "I don't do the whole sex without attachments thing. It's not my jam."

He wanted to ask for more information, but doing so ran the risk of him spooking her, and that was the last thing he wanted to do. "Then let's be friends with benefits."

"We aren't friends."

"We could be." He could actually *feel* her gearing up to argue with him, so he took a step back and grabbed her hand. "Come on."

"I will not be coming on anything."

Quinn laughed. "That remains to be seen, but that's not on the books right now." He towed her into the bathroom and guided her to sit on the edge of the tub. "We could be friends."

"You keep saying that. I keep not believing you."

Hell, he wasn't sure he believed it himself, but the thought of never going there with Aubry again wasn't one he was willing to accept. Not now. Not when they had so much left to explore between them. The thought of never touching her again… Yeah, he wasn't ready to give that up. So he started the hot water and blocked the drain. "Then I guess I'll just have to prove it to you."

"How? By drowning me in the bathtub?"

He shot her a look. "Has anyone ever told you that you are paranoid to an excessive degree?"

"If they have, I've ignored them because they're obviously plotting my demise." She gave a small smile. "But can you blame me? There are a lot of scary things out there in the world."

"Peaches, there are a lot of scary things in your head."

"It's called an overactive imagination, combined with a lovely dose of anxiety that I was born with." She shrugged. "But even so, just because you're paranoid doesn't mean the world isn't out to get you."

"If you say so." He tested the water temperature and, satisfied, pointed at her. "Strip."

"Strip?" She blinked. "I thought this was some kind of seduction. Aren't you going to run me a bath and slowly remove my clothes while whispering sweet nothings in my ear and then wash my hair while I bliss out?"

"What the hell kind of books have you been reading?"

"Fiction, obviously." She grumbled under her breath, stood, and took off her clothes. He wanted to ask her about her tattoos, but that could wait, too. This wasn't about that. While she was divesting herself of her panties, he strode into the room and rummaged through her bag to find her headphones and cell phone. This wasn't going to solve all their issues, but it would at least ensure she wasn't calling the whole thing off because of a knee-jerk reaction.

He refused to examine too closely why he wasn't willing to just let it end.

Quinn made it back into the bathroom in time to see her slip into the water. The sight of all her skin wet made his mouth go dry and his body go hard. He almost—*almost*—threw his good intentions out the window right then and there. But it would mean short-term gain and he'd lose her again in the morning—for good this time. "We'll talk tomorrow." He set her stuff on the edge of the tub and walked out of the bathroom, closing the door softly behind him.

• • •

Despite Aubry's best intentions, they didn't talk that night. She took her time in the bath and when she walked out of the bathroom, Quinn bundled her up into bed, turned out the lights, and, for all intents and purposes, seemed to fall fast asleep with her in his arms. She lay staring at the ceiling for what felt like the entire night, wondering when her life had gotten so *weird*.

Between one blink and the next, dawn came. Or that's what it felt like. In reality, it was entirely possible the sound of Quinn's steady breathing had lulled her into a false sense of security and she passed out cold. She'd never admit it, though.

Aubry sat up and shoved her hair away from her eyes. A quick check of the clock had her panic flying into full throttle. "Oh my God, wake up." She shoved Quinn's shoulder and scrambled out of bed. They only had an hour before the demo, and it would take at least half that to find the room and get signed in and… "We have to go. Right now."

"What?" Quinn sat up, looking so deliciously rumpled that she might have reconsidered her decision not to jump back into bed with him if they weren't already so *late*.

She rushed to her suitcase and dug through it. Nothing was right. It didn't matter that she'd played with some of these guys in the past—this was a first impression kind of situation. *I am awful at first impressions.* This was why she didn't meet people face-to-face. She could fake her way through interactions online because she had the comfort of either her apartment or Cups and Kittens. She was in her safe places. There was nothing safe about DeathCon. There would be so many *people* and some of them would even want to, like, hold down a conversation with her. "I can't do this."

Quinn's hands settled on her shoulders. "Breathe." He reached past her and grabbed a pair of her favorite jeans and a black T-shirt that said *Dear Nasa, your mom thought I was big enough. Love, Pluto*. Then he guided her to her feet and practically shoved her into the bathroom. "Shower. You have ten minutes."

That got her moving again. "Thanks." She slammed the door in his face and rushed to shower and washed her hair. After she was dry and dressed, she pulled her still-wet hair up into a ponytail and threw on some shimmery black eyeliner and mascara. It wasn't too crazy, but between that and the slicked back hair, it gave a certain *don't fuck with me* vibe that she hoped would actually keep people away from her.

Aubry opened the door to find Quinn taking up the entire doorway. *My vibe and the giant by my side.* "Did I take too long?"

"That's a trap question and I'm not about to answer it." He nudged her into the bedroom and shut the door between them. A few seconds later the shower started.

She stared at the door, her fears taken a temporary backseat to the image of Quinn in the shower, the water coursing over his big body. His big cock. She shivered. They hadn't actually had shower sex yesterday, but he'd more than proven he could toss her around like a sexy rag doll. It would be nothing for him to lift her and pin her against the tile wall and slam home. She'd be helpless to do anything but cling to him as he pounded them both to orgasm. *Maybe...*

"Peaches?"

She jumped. While she'd been fantasizing about him, he'd managed to shower and get dressed. He looked... He looked downright edible. *Down, girl.* She grabbed her purse. "Let's go."

"Hold your horses."

"I know you might have a hard time reading a clock with your cowboy education, but right now it says that we are in serious danger of being late and I can't be late and walk in there and have everyone stare at me." She slapped a hand over her mouth. "That was mean. Actually, that was worse than mean. I don't think you're stupid. Aggravating as fuck, yes.

Stupid, no."

He crossed his arms over his chest. "Are you done yet?"

She paused, considered, and then nodded. "Yes."

"Good." He pointed at her feet. "You might want some shoes before you walk out the door."

She looked down, cringing at the sight of her Marceline socks peeking out the hem of her jeans. "Shoes. Right." Aubry yanked on her combat boots, the motions of lacing them up calming her down, just a little. "Have I mentioned how nervous I am?"

"You don't have to, being as how I'm not an idiot."

She winced. "Sorry about that."

"No, you aren't. And that's okay." He motioned between them. "This is what we are—we snap and snarl and insult each other. The fact that we also fuck like nobody's business doesn't change that."

She didn't see how it *couldn't* change that, but if she tried to argue, they'd *definitely* be late. So Aubry pushed to her feet and kept her mouth shut on that subject. "You ready?"

"I was born ready."

She snorted and headed for the door. "Yeah, yeah."

It wasn't until they hit the lobby—and the masses there—that she remembered she'd been anxious in the first place. Aubry rocked back on her heels, her breathing picking up, but Quinn was there, his hand on the small of her back, his voice in her ear. "It will be okay. Take my hand."

She obeyed before she had a chance to decide if she wanted to hold his hand. He moved in front of her, their connection a tether he used to tow her through the crowd. As he promised, people got the hell out of his way, leaving a nice little path for her to walk in. She tried not to notice that, though. Instead, Aubry focused on the spot between his shoulder blades. His back was broad enough that she couldn't see past it without trying, and she had absolutely no interest in trying.

It occurred to her that Quinn might not know where they were going, but she would have to yell at him or pull him to a stop to ask, and right now the only way she was getting through this was to keep moving. The room changed, the walls much closer together, but there were just as many people. They pressed in on all sides, just beyond the barrier of Quinn's shoulders, and she huddled closer to him, until she was almost stepping on the back of his heels.

He walked into a room and instantly the noise level halved. She waited one breath, two, three, and finally gathered the courage to look around. The space was dominated by six big-screen televisions, each with a pair of chairs in front of it. There were probably a dozen dudes there, and they all turned to look at her with interest, some of them more polite about it than others.

A harried-looking kid who couldn't be more than eighteen hurried over. "Aubry Kaiser?"

"Yes." Her voice was barely audible, so she cleared her throat and tried again. "That's me."

"Great. You're the last one." He turned around and raised his voice. "Take your seats. There's a short video and then you'll have the opportunity to play through the demo in pairs."

She could do this. She'd already done the hard part of getting to the room itself. All she had to do now was walk over and sit down.

If she could just get her legs to move.

Quinn palmed her ass, making her jump. His cocky grin was as annoying as it was familiar. "Have fun. When you're done, we're going to renegotiate."

The *nerve*. "There's nothing to renegotiate." She glared. "I think I made my position pretty damn clear yesterday."

"I want some clarification of your...position." There was enough innuendo laced into the last word that she'd have to be spectacularly oblivious to have missed it.

"You're insufferable."

He leaned down and whispered in her ear, "And yet it was my cock you were coming on roughly twenty-four hours ago."

She narrowed her eyes. "Oh, we'll have a conversation all right. Just you wait." And then she marched to the empty seat in front of the nearest screen and plopped onto it. It wasn't until the video started that she paused long enough to wonder if Quinn had provoked her on purpose to help her settle in.

CHAPTER ELEVEN

Quinn couldn't care less about some game with alien shooters, but Aubry was into it, so he paid attention. It didn't seem that different from the other first-person shooters out there with the exception that someone in the marketing department had taken the time to fully customize each of the playable characters to the people here. Aubry's character was a dead ringer for herself, minus the tattoos.

Once they started playing, all he could do was watch her. She stared at the screen with a laser focus that was seriously sexy, her entire body still with the exception of her hands on the controls. He glanced at the screen in time to watch her take out two of the other players—guys directly behind them if the curses that rose were any indication. Over and over again, she evaded attacks, turning them around on the other team and racking up a truly impressive kill count. When the final screen popped up, she sat back and cracked her neck with a grin that hit him like a sucker punch. "And that's how it's done."

This was her element—where she let go of her anxiety and prickly walls designed to keep people at a distance and just let herself be happy. More than happy. She looked downright joyful.

It was staggering to witness.

The guy next to her looked like he hadn't seen direct sunlight anytime in the last decade. His shoulders were hunched and he was thin enough that

Quinn would worry about breaking something if he slapped him on the back. He turned to Aubry, with hero worship in his eyes. "You're MistressRed13."

"The very one." Her smile didn't so much as dim at the human interaction.

"I don't know if you remember, but I played backup for you against that evil overlord centipede, Claws. What you can do with an assault rifle is just poetic."

As he watched, she relaxed and chatted with the guy. Apparently they'd played together more than once, and the way they talked about the game was completely foreign to Quinn. He liked things he could get his hands on and really dig into. There was nothing about virtual reality that made him feel more alive. He'd never been able to get into any of the games he'd played, let alone on the level Aubry and this guy— Kurt, his name was—were talking about right now. He'd never be able to share that with her.

What the hell are you even talking about? The only thing he wanted to share with her was orgasms. Who cared if she liked a game he wasn't the least bit interested in, or that she'd probably eventually settle down with a guy like Kurt—a guy who got her?

He made himself stop and really consider that. There was nothing overtly wrong with Kurt. Nothing except the fact that he'd never be able to give it to Aubry the way she liked it. And he was so busy kissing her ass, would he really be able to challenge her or help her get more comfortable in a social situation or, fuck, act as a wall between her and her fears?

Quinn didn't like the thought of her with someone else. He didn't like that shit at all. And knowing that it wasn't what either of them signed on for didn't change a damn thing. He'd actually enjoyed most of the last few days with Aubry. He wasn't ready to let her go, and he sure as fuck wasn't about to do it before his sister's wedding. *A few more days. We'll figure this shit out after that.*

That didn't change the fact he wanted nothing more than to throw her over his shoulder and haul her ass back to the hotel room to fuck her seven ways to Sunday until he was all she could think about.

The lights came up, signaling the end of the demo. Aubry turned to him with a happy grin, and it struck him that this was the first non-sexual situation where he'd seen her truly let go of a lot of the walls she kept around herself. He might not understand the whole gaming community thing, but these truly were her people. So he tried to smile. "That was pretty cool."

"Pretty cool? Are you kidding me? That was… There are no words for what that was. They're using a new processor and so the graphics are next-level shit. There isn't another game out there on the market that can match this." She actually *wiggled* with joy. "Oh my God, Quinn, thank you for this. Seriously, being able to see this game on the ground level of production is something I'm going to remember even when I'm ancient and have Alzheimer's and have forgotten all my cats' names."

He stared, not sure if he wanted to kiss her or just sit back and watch her be happy and free for a little while longer. "You want to hang out here for a while?"

"Yeah, you totally should." Kurt sidled up to her, and Quinn was not a fan of how the guy blatantly checked her out.

She hesitated and then took a careful step closer to Quinn. "Thanks, but I'll probably just see you on the interwebs." It was almost comical how the other guy's face fell when she stepped up against Quinn's side and beneath his arm. "See you later, Kurt."

They walked out of the room, and her casual embrace turned into something more along the lines of a clinging spider monkey. Quinn kept them moving because he had a feeling if they stopped he might have to carry her out of here. To distract her, he said, "I think you broke poor Kurt's heart."

"I doubt it. He was blinded by my Deathmatch prowess and it understandably made him fall a little in love with me."

He barked out a laugh. "That's some pretty magical skills that game has if it can make a man fall in love with you." It was easier to laugh about it and make a joke than face the fact that Aubry no doubt *would* end up with a guy who'd fall in love with her at some point. His stomach twisted at the thought. "I think it was more the fit of your jeans."

"Hardly." She snorted, keeping her head down, so she was almost half turned to him and away from the crowd around them. It made walking somewhat of a challenge, but Quinn was willing to do what it took to keep her from panicking. If this was helping, he'd walk like a damn crab.

Aubry's hand's fisted around the fabric of his shirt, but her voice was mostly light. "When you play as much as we do, sometimes you forget what it's like to interact with the opposite sex. I'm female and I like at least one of the things he's super into, so he understandably glommed onto me."

"Understandable, my ass." He knew his jealousy was completely irrational. Hell, she'd walked away from poor Kurt, but it wasn't just that guy Quinn was jealous of. It was the future ones that maybe she hadn't met yet. "He wanted to fuck you, peaches. He wanted to take you back to his mom's basement, yank off those jeans of yours, and sink between your sweet thighs."

She shot him a look. "He owns his own cyber security firm. I highly doubt he lives in his mom's basement."

"The rest stands."

"You know, I think you're just so obsessed with what's between my thighs you're projecting it onto everyone around you. One-track mind much?"

He'd show her a one-track mind. Quinn looked around, caught sight of a hallway leading away from the main room, and practically carried her into it. They turned one corner and then another and stopped at the stairs leading up to the rooms. It was faintly lit, the hotel having decided the environment was more important than being able to see clearly, and he backed her up to the wall beneath the stairs. "My mind *is* only on one track when it comes to you." He lifted her arms over her head and pinned them with one hand. "I saw the way he looked at you."

"So? In case you missed the memo, I'm single. He can look at me however he damn well pleases." She lifted her chin. "In fact, I can look right back. Maybe I'll ask him out."

She was trying to provoke a response. He knew that and he could still feel control slipping through his fingers. He inched closer, until their chests touched with every inhale. "You would."

"Yeah, I would."

"He'd take you somewhere fancy, but not too fancy." He unbuttoned the top button of her jeans, and slid the zipper down. "One of those trendy fucking hipster places with Asian fusion food."

She gasped when he slipped his hand into her panties. "I'm surprised you even know what Asian fusion is."

"I'm a cowboy. That doesn't mean I don't pay attention." He groaned when he found her soaked. "He'd make polite conversation—nothing too titillating— and order you some fancy-ass wine selection." He pushed a finger into her, stroking her as much as he could with her jeans restricting his movement.

"I happen to like wine."

He knew that. Quinn palmed her, pushing a second finger into her. He worked her, watching her lips part and her breathing pick up. She was so fucking responsive it didn't take much to get her to the edge. "And at the end of the night…" He stroked her clit the way he'd learned she liked it, circling and then thrusting into her and then circling, again and again. "At the end of the night he'd drive you home and kiss you politely before leaving you on your doorstep. Every single fucking thing about that night would be polite."

Aubry's back arched, and he knew he had her. Quinn picked up his pace, just slightly, lowering his head to rasp in her ear. "You don't want polite. You want a hot fuck in the shower, on the bed, in the cab of my truck. You want me to finger you like this, and you want to get off on the fact that there isn't a damn thing between us and anyone who walks down that hall.

Hell, I bet if I slid down your jeans, you'd turn around and let me fuck you right here." She clenched around him and she buried her face in his shoulder as she came, her moans barely muffled. "Yeah, that's what I thought."

"*Holy shit.*"

He turned in time to see none other than Kurt standing in the hallway, his gaze fastened onto the spot where Quinn's hand was buried in Aubry's jeans. He stepped forward, putting himself between them. "Get lost, kid."

"No, wait." She disentangled herself from him and buttoned up her pants, shooting him a look that would send a weaker man to his knees.

It just pissed Quinn the fuck off. He put a hand on the wall, blocking her from Kurt with his arm. "Where do you think you're going?"

"Free country."

"No, it's not."

"Actually—" Kurt broke off at his glare.

He focused back on Aubry. "We're not finished."

"I'm pretty sure we already had this conversation." She ducked under his arm but then seemed to think better of it. "Sorry this is so awkward, Kurt. But I'm, ah, I'm taking the stairs." She turned around, dodged around Quinn, and disappeared up the stairs, leaving him staring at Kurt like an asshole.

There was nothing to say. He couldn't warn the other guy off because Aubry was right—she wasn't his. They weren't even technically hooking up right now because she'd called the whole damn thing off. He made an effort to unclench his fists and reclaim some of the happy-go-lucky attitude he was usually so good at, but he failed miserably at both. "She's not interested. Get lost."

"Yeah. No problem." Kurt backed away as if facing off with a grizzly. He nearly tripped over his feet as he hurried around the corner and, if the sound of his footsteps pounding on the ground were any indication, he started sprinting the second he was out of sight.

Quinn headed up the stairs, determined to talk some sense into Aubry. The fire between them wasn't anywhere near burned out and she damn well knew that shit. Maybe she couldn't do sex without emotional attachments, but they could be friends who had sex.

He was reaching and he knew it, but he didn't give a fuck.

It turned out, he didn't have to go far to find his fiery redhead. Aubry sat on the top stair, three floors up, her head between her knees. As soon as he caught sight of her, he rushed up the remaining stairs to crouch before her. "What's wrong?"

"So. Many. Stairs."

He bit back a laugh. "We're on the fourth floor."

"I know." She raised her head. "I overestimated my cardio skills. Turns out, I have no cardio skills. DDR did not prepare me for eleventy billion stairs."

"I see." He adopted as serious an expression as he could manage. "Would you like me to carry you?"

For a second, it looked like she was actually considering it, but she ultimately shook her head. "How am I going to escape the zombies if I don't have sweet cardio skills? This is something I'm going to have to work on. I can't rely on a trusty steed to be in my vicinity at every hour of every day."

He wasn't sure if he should be insulted she'd just

called him a trusty steed, but he couldn't resist such a perfect opening. "I have something in particular that you should be riding."

"Oh, for fuck's sake. I'm sitting here worrying about the inevitable zombie apocalypse and you're thinking with your dick."

He was pleased to note she looked less winded now. Apparently verbally sparring with him was exactly the distraction she needed. "We already talked about this. I'll cover your ass while we're in San Diego. So, yes, you will have your trusty steed next to you at all times." He was probably an ass for using her insane fears to further his agenda with her, but so be it. "You hungry?"

"Not for brains." She made a face. "And not for company, either."

He figured. Being around people wasn't her natural inclination, so she'd need some time to recharge before they did anything else. Still, he couldn't help asking, "Is there any other panel or whatever that you want to see while we're here?" From what he understood, these convention things were hotbeds for new information for the gaming community. Surely there was something else she was interested in besides that demo?

And if she had to cling to him while he got her there, well, he was okay with that, too.

But she was already shaking her head. "There's nothing they're showing that I won't be able to find on the Internet in a few hours anyways—*without* having to deal with the crowds."

He would have been lying if he said there wasn't a little disappointment that rose at that, but he brightened almost immediately when he considered that meant he'd have her all to himself. "Well, then, let's get back to the room and order some grub."

And if he played his cards right, there'd be more than just food on the menu.

CHAPTER TWELVE

Aubry wasn't sure when her brilliant plan to create some distance between herself and Quinn stopped feeling so brilliant. Maybe it was when Quinn had put himself between her and the rest of the people who were too freaking close and definitely too freaking loud. Or maybe it was his getting jealous of that dude Kurt was kind of cute in a caveman sort of way.

The fact he fingered her to orgasm in a hallway, where they were then interrupted, definitely had something to do with it, though.

She was already starting to doubt her ability to keep her hands off him as he closed the door of the hotel room behind them. It didn't help that she was riding high off accomplishing the impossible. She'd *done* it. She'd gone to DeathCon. She'd played the alpha demo. It had been better than she could have dreamed. She didn't miss out because her anxiety was too much to handle.

All of it added up to her feeling virtually indestructible.

She wanted Quinn, and she wanted him now. And from the look on his face he knew it, too. *Damn it*. She should have been sated from her earlier orgasm—or the many that had come in the last few days—but the truth was she wanted him all the more because of it. It didn't make any sense, but she was past trying to rationalize anything that had to do with this man.

To distract herself, she thumbed through the room

service menu, barely registering the printed words. She was too busy listening to Quinn move around the room, slowly drifting closer to her. She knew that's what he was doing the same way her body called out for his, the glaring emptiness between her thighs demanding to be filled.

She turned around to find him standing an arm's distance from her. His gaze skated over her body in a move she was convinced she could actually *feel*. "I think it's time we had a talk."

"Talking is for the birds." She grabbed the front of his shirt and towed him to her. Or, rather, she towed herself to him because his feet didn't actually move. She didn't care. Nothing mattered but what was about to happen. Aubry went up onto her tiptoes and kissed his neck, his jaw, the dip below his bottom lip. "We both talk too much."

He hissed out a breath when her nails dug into his shoulders. "That's the fucking truth." Quinn palmed the back of her head and kissed her, harsh and hard and exactly what she needed. His other hand unbuttoned her jeans and shoved them off, and she was only too happy to help by stepping out of them. It left her in only her T-shirt and panties, but even that was too much of a barrier between them. Aubry broke the kiss long enough to yank her shirt over her head and toss it somewhere behind her, quickly followed by her bra and panties.

Quinn laughed. "Eager, aren't you?"

"Stop gabbing before I change my mind."

"Heaven forbid." He snagged her waist and brought her up against him. The feeling of his T-shirt against her bare breasts was almost unbearably erotic, and she arched against him. He cupped her ass, lining them up in the best way possible, the ridge of his cock rubbing against her clit.

Aubry moaned, but this whole thing was too controlled. She wanted more. She wanted the possessive and furious Quinn that she'd gotten a glimpse of in the stairway. *Good thing I know at least one of his triggers.* She leaned up to whisper in his ear. "What did you say to Kurt after I left?"

Instantly, his grip on her ass tightened. "If you're thinking I gave him your number, you better think again."

"Pity. He seems nice."

He pulled back enough to look at her face, his expression thunderous. "Don't talk about another man when you're naked with me, peaches. It's bad form."

"Is it?" She feigned innocence. "Maybe I'm just exploring my options. Rumor has it guys like Kurt are great in bed because they feel like they have something to prove. I bet he's excellent at oral."

Quinn's growl was the only warning she got before he lifted her and tossed her onto the bed. Aubry squealed, the sound barely getting past her lips before he was there, covering her. A man that size had no business moving that fast. It just wasn't fair. She opened her mouth to tell him as much, but he kissed her, stealing her words. "We covered this last time you were coming around my fingers."

"Did we?"

He froze, a slow grin spreading over his mouth that made her stomach flip-flop. "You're baiting me."

"No, I'm not."

"Yes, you are. You're provoking a response on

purpose." He thrust against her, his damn jeans a barrier that was as infuriating as it was hot. "You like seeing me jealous." He cupped her breast, pinching her nipple lightly. "You like me losing control at the thought of another man's hands on you."

"Nope."

If anything, his grin widened. "You liked what I did earlier—no, you *loved* it. You would have loved it even more if he'd walked in before we were finished."

Her entire body went tight at the thought of that guy walking in while Quinn was working her, his fingers inside her, his mouth against her ear as he growled filthy things. She tried and failed for a nonchalant shrug. "It was okay."

"Okay, my ass." He reached over and brought the hotel phone onto the bed next to them. "Order room service."

Aubry blinked. "What?"

"I didn't stutter." He picked up the phone and handed it to her. "Unless you don't know what you want."

"I know." She always got the same thing—cheeseburger and fries, hold the pickles. What she didn't know was what game he was playing, because there was some game afoot. Nerves erupted in her stomach, the feeling only making her hotter.

"Good." He ran his hand down her side. "I want the rib eye. Loaded baked potato—extra cheese."

"Order for yourself." It was a token protestation and not even a strong one.

He pressed the button to call room service and slid down her body. Her eyes went wide when she realized his intentions. "You can't be serious. I'm—" She broke off when his mouth made contact with her clit, a moan slipping free. "Oh God, Quinn."

"I'll give you something special if you don't mess up our order."

There was no chance of that happening, not with him delivering those devastatingly long licks up her center. She tried to focus on the ringing phone, her mind going terrifyingly blank when a pleasant voice said, "Guest services."

What was she supposed to be doing? *Oh, right. Food.* "Uh, I'd…" She took a deep breath, looking everywhere but at him. It didn't help. "I'd like to make an order."

"Of course, ma'am. One moment."

She pressed the phone to her chest in an effort to muffle the sound of her moaning as Quinn fucked her with his tongue. He spread her legs wide and up, baring her completely, and parted her folds with his thumbs. "You're as pretty here as you are everywhere else."

Oh my fucking God.

"Ma'am?" The tinny voice made her realize that she still had the phone to her chest.

"Yes. I'm sorry." She tried to glare at Quinn, but he pushed two fingers into her, making her eyes roll back in her head.

"This is Ms. Aubry Kaiser?"

"*Yes.*" She lifted her hips, not sure if she was trying to get away or get closer.

"In room 1232?"

"That's, ah, right."

"Perfect. What can I get for you?"

Aubry almost cried out when Quinn took his fingers away. She raised her head, her breath stalling in her throat at the sight of him unbuttoning his jeans and shoving them down his hips, freeing his cock. While she watched, he picked up a condom from the nightstand and rolled it on, never taking his eyes off her.

"Ma'am?"

"Oh. Right. Sorry." She scooted away from him, shaking her head, but he grinned and snagged her heel, pulling her back to the edge of the bed. She'd have to talk fast if she wanted to get this order out of the way before he started fucking her. "I'd like a cheeseburger, hold the pickles. And—"

"Would you like fries or onion rings for a dollar upcharge?"

Quinn's cock notched in her entrance. "Fries." She watched him push into her, his cock disappearing inch by inch as it filled her. "Oh God."

"Ma'am? Is everything okay?"

"Yes." She arched her back, trying to take him deeper. "I need... I need a steak."

I'll give you a steak, Quinn mouthed, his big hands kneading her ass, coaxing her legs even farther apart.

"How would you like that cooked?"

She stared into his blue eyes, trying to connect the words in her ear with the man currently inside her. "Your steak? How do you want it cooked?"

"Rare." He pulled out and shoved into her hard enough to make her breasts bounce.

"Rare." It came out as a breathy moan.

"And for your side?"

Quinn's hand hovered over her clit, distracting her. What had the woman said? *Oh, right, sides*. "Potato. Loaded. Extra cheese."

"Would you like anything to drink?"

"No." She had to get off the phone and now. She was so close to coming, it felt like the top of her head might explode.

"Let me just repeat this back to you to ensure I have it all right."

"Okay." She watched Quinn's cock slide in and out of her, the feeling making her want to close her eyes, but she didn't want to miss a single second of this. The woman on the other line could have been speaking Greek for all she understood the words. "Sounds good." She tossed the phone aside.

"That was rude." Quinn hooked an arm under her and lifted her off the bed, turning and sitting on the edge with her in his lap, her legs around his waist. The new position had her clutching his shoulders, completely helpless as he lifted her and moved her on top of him. She started to unhook her ankles, but he shook his head. "Let your trusty steed do the work, peaches."

She bit her lip. "You're never going to let me live that down, are you?"

"Not a chance." His grin made her stomach flip. "Though I have to say, you can ride me any day." He lifted her almost completely off his cock and slid her down inch by torturous inch. "I love feeling how tightly you clench around me."

Hell, she kind of loved it, too. It didn't matter that she'd proclaimed this fling had to end less than twelve hours ago. All that mattered was the feeling of completion she could sense just out of reach. She rolled her hips, trying to change the pace, but his hands on her ass meant he controlled everything, and he didn't seem interested in anything but this slow and thorough fucking. "Quinn, please!"

"I like hearing you like this, knowing that I made you this crazy." He sank in to the hilt. "You know what I think you like?"

"I bet…you're going to…tell me." She was panting, feeling more animal than human. *Is orgasm deprivation a legitimate defense in murder? Because I might just kill him if he doesn't let me come.* "Quinn."

"Not yet." He kept them sealed together, holding her pinned to him with one arm around her waist and twisting his free hand through her hair to tilt her head back. "I figure we have twenty minutes before someone knocks on our door, bringing that food you just ordered."

Twenty minutes? Was he insane? She wasn't sure she could last another twenty seconds.

He wasn't done. "Maybe I should leave the door unlocked."

"*What?*"

He moved, lifting her and turning her around, impaling her on his cock before she had fully processed his words. He looped her legs on the outside of his, spreading her wide. One hand bracketed her throat, not holding her tightly enough to cut off her breathing but keeping her back pressed to his chest. She blinked, her desire slowing down her brain enough that it took a full three seconds before she realized they were now facing the door. "What?"

"Just think, peaches. That door is unlocked." His free hand cupped one breast and then the other, playing with her nipples. "You can hear the squeaky wheel from the room service cart. It's getting closer, and you know it's coming here." His words almost had her convinced she could hear exactly that. Even though she knew for a fact the hotel door was locked... What if it wasn't?

"I'm not going to stop fucking you, though." His hand dipped between her spread thighs, fingers sliding through her wetness where they were joined up to her clit, his touch too light to get her off. "I can't get enough of you. It makes me crazed. All I can think of is sinking deep inside you over and over again until we both come...and then starting all over again. You think a knock on the door is going to be enough to make me give that up? Not fucking likely."

His lips brushed her neck, trailing up to her ear and he kept up those light touches, his cock still filling her completely. "He's almost here. Can you hear his footsteps?"

"Quinn—"

"Shh. He's going to hear you. And he's going to know exactly what I'm doing to you." His chuckle made her bite back a moan. "Then again, he's going to open that door and he's going to see for himself in a few seconds. Can you imagine the look on his face when he sees you? There will be shock, but then he's going to get as hard as I am right now. No man alive can see you like this and *not* want you."

She could see exactly what he was describing, and the image only got her hotter. Aubry never would have pegged herself as an exhibitionist, but with Quinn's hands on her and his words in her ear, she *wanted* it to be real. Her breath sobbed out and she tried to move on his cock. His grip changed, his hand moving up to pin her hips down. "Ah, ah. We're not done yet. I'll tell

him to close the door behind him and take a seat
there." He used his grip to turn her head to the chair
right next to the door. "He can't touch, but he can
watch. Do you want him to watch?"

More than anything in the world.

Her skin was too tight, her breathing coming in
gasps, her core so hot it was a wonder it didn't scald
Quinn. She wanted, holy fuck, she *wanted*. "Yes."

"You're about to come just thinking about it."

"*Yes.*"

His hand coasted back over to stroke her clit. Once,
twice. "You want to know a secret."

"Yes!" She strained to make him touch her more
firmly. *So close. So freaking close.*

He sucked on her earlobe and released it. "You
never hung up the phone."

Meaning, the room service chick heard everything.

He pressed against her clit and surged up at the
same time, and that was all it took. Aubry shrieked as
she came, sobbing out Quinn's name over and over
again as he fucked her.

CHAPTER THIRTEEN

Quinn had never been so conflicted in his damn life. Yesterday had been good—better than good. It had been fucking perfect. It was more than the sex, too. Seeing Aubry so geeked out in her element and then falling asleep with her in his arms…

He didn't want it to stop.

Next to him on the bench seat, Aubry stretched. "I have to say, I'm enjoying the hell out of this road trip."

He was, too. Everything about Aubry and this situation only pulled him in deeper, the differences he'd been so sure were insurmountable when they first met were actually strengths he relished. He liked their bantering. He liked *her*. "Going better than you expected?"

"Considering I thought I'd have to take your abnormally large body out into the desert and bury it…" She grinned. "Not even close."

Quinn barked out a laugh. "And here I was thinking I'm growing on you."

"Like a fungus. Or mold. Really, really sexy mold."

He must have lost it because that was the cutest damn thing he'd ever heard. He draped an arm around her shoulders. "I'm surprised you don't have some darling little tidbit about how deadly mold is stashed away in that brain of yours."

"Do you know how many people black mold kills a year? And that's not even getting into the different varieties that can do everything from making you hallucinate to go completely bonkers."

"I knew you had it in you."

Aubry rested her head on his shoulder. "Now drive, trusty steed. I'm exhausted and it's your fault."

He laughed again and pulled onto the highway. The companionable silence stretched as he drove north out of the city, heading for Napa. It didn't take long for his mind to turn to the next part of their trip. Jenny's wedding. He'd done his damnedest not to think about it, to focus on getting them both through the convention first. But now DeathCon was behind them, and there was nothing standing between him and the realization that his original plan of taking Aubry to the wedding was pure shit.

He'd agreed to this when he was operating under the impression that she was a fire-breathing dragon with impenetrable armor. And she was, in a way. He just hadn't realized that her sharp tongue and nasty disposition covered up a bundle of worries and nerves and more than slightly irrational phobias. Beneath all that armor was a vulnerable woman who went out of her way not to put herself out there in the world for fear it would smash her hopes and dreams to pieces.

Aw, fuck, they're going to eat her alive.

He drummed his fingers on the steering wheel. "We should talk."

"Talk about what?" She straightened, half turning to face him. "I know you're worried about this wedding, but believe me, I got it."

He clenched the steering wheel, fighting the impulse to turn the damn truck around and head back to Texas, disappointing his sister and ruining her wedding. He could deal with their disappointment—he'd been dealing with it his entire life. "Maybe this was a mistake."

"What?" She frowned. "No way. You helped me out with the demo. I know I'm not exactly kissing your ass in gratitude—"

"Peaches, I'm more interested in your kissing other parts of me."

She rolled her eyes. "Yeah, I gathered. What I'm trying to say is that you helped—a lot. And I appreciate that help, so I'm going to stick with our deal. We've faced down my demons. There's no reason we can't face down yours, too."

We.

When's the last time he was part of a *we*? Never in a relationship—Quinn didn't make a habit of letting women close enough to gain that distinction. He liked them. They liked him. It was more than enough to spend a few hours losing themselves in each other.

He'd never found those arrangements lacking before now. But after the last few days, it was hard not to compare the two. He'd started out this trip barely being able to stand Aubry, but the longer they spent together, the more things he found about her that he admired. Yeah, her quirks were kind of strange, but they were endearing. And, best of all, he never quite knew what she was going to say next.

And the sex… The sex was out of this world.

He sighed, trying to find the right way to phrase this. "My family is complicated."

"Every family is complicated."

Wasn't that the damn truth? Unfortunately, his family was more than the garden variety complicated. "I didn't know you that well when we agreed to this."

"Correction—you didn't *like* me that well." She

leaned closer, frowning up at him. "You're trying to give me an out and that's really cute, but I promise I can handle this. They can't say anything worse to me than other people already have, and they're barely strangers. It's fine."

She didn't comment on the fact that he'd basically just admitted to his being into her, and he didn't know if it was because she hadn't noticed or if she didn't want to deal with it any more than he did.

"They're awful people."

She snorted. "Look, I pretty much go into every situation figuring that people are awful and/or actively planning my murder and/or there's a good chance they'll turn into zombies and I'll get to shoot them in the face."

"*Have* to shoot them in the face."

"No, I was right the first time." She waved that way. "The point is, your family might be wicked rich and all that, but they aren't going to be any worse than I am prepared for, because I am prepared for the absolute worst. So if you don't mind me being bitchy—which is why you recruited me for this in the first place, I'll remind you—then there's nothing to worry about."

Nothing except these people were experts at the well-aimed barb that managed to soar right past the best defenses and strike deep. He'd been on the receiving end of them too many times to discount, and he went into these encounters knowing exactly what his family and their peers were capable of. He didn't like to think of them making Aubry feel…*less*. She wasn't. She was better than the lot of them combined.

That was an uncomfortable thought.

"All the same—"

"Quinn, stop." She was still looking at him as if she'd never seen him before. "Would it make you feel better if I promise to let you know the second I need to get out of there, and then we can flee into the night, howling our victory?"

He blinked and then refocused on the road. "If we're fleeing, we probably shouldn't be doing anything in victory."

"Oh, pish. I'm pretty sure I could do some damage on the way out." Her smile was downright evil.

Considering she was probably talking about property damage at the bare minimum, he shouldn't find her so damn cute. He found himself smiling in return. "If anyone can afford it, it'll be the wedding guests."

"Exactly."

He draped an arm around her shoulders, pulling her against his side, and tried not to think too hard about how good it felt to have her there. Like she fit. What the hell did it say about him that he found a woman willing to commit some light felonies for him hotter than fuck?

She was silent for all of ten seconds. "I don't suppose this trip is going to be as eventful as the one into San Diego?"

He barked out a laugh. "You're out of control."

"And you're the pot calling the kettle black." She shrugged, her smile wavering. "What can I say? I only have a few more days of this, and I want to enjoy it as fully as possible. So sue me."

"Only a few days left."

He didn't phrase it as a question, but she took it as such. "Well, yeah. I mean, obviously my putting limitations on this was a mistake. We're like fire and gasoline, and it's stupid to try to stop before we burn ourselves out." Her voice dropped to just above a whisper. "But, seriously, if Jules knew what we were doing, she'd start getting stars in her eyes and meddling and planning our wedding and our *kids'* weddings, and it's just exhausting to think about."

His stomach tied itself in knots, but he couldn't say for sure if it was because she was putting a limitation on them or because she'd just mentioned a wedding and kids in the next breath. He tried to sound amused, but he knew for a fact he didn't pull it off. "She gets excited."

"Yeah, she does. Which is exactly why we can't keep this up. I mean, I'm not going to lie and say sneaking around hadn't occurred to me, but that's a whole lot of effort, and Jules has a nose like a bloodhound when she thinks I'm keeping something from her. And she *always* knows when I'm keeping something from her."

He wasn't all that into the thought of sneaking around, either. Quinn wasn't sneaky. He wasn't under-handed. Fuck, he was about as subtle as a two-by-four to the side of the head—and so was Aubry. What she was saying made sense, but damn. He'd had every in-tention of exhausting his attraction to her and *then* going their separate ways once that happened. What was the other option? Dating? He almost laughed at the thought. They matched up in bed and that was it.

What would it even look like if they tried dating? Yeah, they'd managed to hold down a conversation or two since they started this trip, but that didn't mean a damn thing in the grand scheme. They were like two actors that fell for each other because of forced proximity and an affinity for orgasms. The fledgling attraction he felt for her wasn't likely to last them settling back into their normal lives. He had the ranch and his friends and, sure, their group of friends overlapped a bit now, but she would go back to being closeted up in her apartment or Jules's shop. The thought of spending all his free time in front of a screen was almost enough to make him break out in hives. It wasn't his thing. And it *was* her thing.

They were too different, even with the handful of things they shared in common. It worked right now, in these exact circumstances, but it wouldn't keep working indefinitely. He'd be smart to just enjoy the time they had and let it go when they hit the Devil's Falls town limits.

Quinn took a deep breath. "Okay, yeah, you're right."

"Yep. Totally right. So right, it's actually painful." She sounded like she was reading from a script.

He tapped her on the top of her head. "And you say *I* have a big head."

"You do." Her palm settled over his cock and his body instantly responded, his dick hardening and his hands itching to pull her into his lap. Aubry stroked him. "A big, big head. Massive. Just plain giant."

Despite everything, he laughed. "Now you're just teasing me."

"Only mostly." She pressed a kiss to his cheek and ducked under his arm, reclaiming her seat on the other side of the cab.

Quinn took his eyes off the road long enough to look at her. "What the hell?"

"Remember that torturous drive where you

withheld orgasms and then made me come over and over again until I could barely walk? You should since it happened like two days ago."

"I remember," he gritted out.

She laughed. "Payback's a bitch."

• • •

Aubry tried not to focus on everything circling around her head. Like how Quinn admitted to liking her but then agreed they would never work in the real world, or that he'd tried to give her an out for the wedding. She tried really freaking hard. So hard that she spent the next several hours brooding on the most immediate issue—the wedding. It was clear the very idea of her attending now made him uncomfortable and there wasn't a whole lot she could do about it.

He said it was because his family is complicated.

Sure, that sounded great—on the surface. Like maybe he wanted to protect her, which meant maybe he had feelings. But that logic only lasted on a surface level. The more she thought about it, the more she was sure he was having regrets about agreeing to this whole thing in the first place.

And why wouldn't he?

As she'd pointed out time and time again, she wasn't nice. She wasn't poised or put together. Honestly, she was a bundle of nerves and issues wrapped up in a gamer girl package. Not the kind of girl a guy wanted to bring home to his fancypants family who probably had gold plated utensils and thousand-thread-count sheets and whatever stupid crap rich people spent money on.

She knew, rationally, they came from different worlds. She was at peace with that. Mostly. It hadn't mattered when she could barely stand him, and it shouldn't matter now because they weren't ever going to really date. She didn't even really *want* a boyfriend or gentleman friend or any other term that encompassed a significant other, let alone one who probably stood to inherit a fortune. She'd learned the hard way that love could turn ugly if given the opportunity, and she wasn't interested in a repeat. Sure, most of her experience was with family and not relationships, but that didn't mean it wasn't the truth.

"You're thinking awfully hard over there."

She jumped and then mentally cursed herself for jumping. "Goes with the territory. Don't worry about it."

"Humor me." He'd said it like he really wanted to know, like he wasn't just being polite. But then, when had Quinn ever bothered to put a polite mask on his interactions with her? They'd been vicious and snarky and hotter than hell, but never polite.

She started to demur but then reconsidered. They'd already agreed this wasn't going beyond the end of the trip. What would it hurt to try her hand at actually being honest and expressing her needs? It would be good practice for the "someday," when she theoretically found someone that she wanted to settle down with. She ignored the pang the thought brought on and focused on the now. "I was just deciding how I feel about you wanting to hide your family from me. Or me from your family. I'm not really sure which way that's going."

Quinn narrowed his eyes as he pulled off the

interstate. "What part of 'I don't want you to have to deal with them' did you not understand?"

"It's okay. I get it. I'm used to being that person who doesn't play well with others." It had just never bothered her until now. Her own mother had more or less disowned her when she got too big for her britches and moved away to go to college, but as much as it still hurt on days when she was feeling particularly low, most of the time she chalked that one up in the win column.

The only other family she had interaction with on a regular basis was Jules's. Those people were all so damn nice she was pretty sure half the strays in town had been brought into the fold at one point or another, and she was no different. They weren't fazed when she was having A Day and snapped at everyone who came within range, and someone was already there with a smile and some off-the-cuff joke to bring her back from the edge. And they weren't *fancy rich folk* who worried too much about which fork to use and if she could trace her bloodline back to some ancestor who participated in the genocide of the Native Americans.

A feeling twisted in her chest, making it hard to breathe. She blinked. Was that...*homesickness*?

"Obviously you don't get it." Quinn hesitated. "Damn. Okay. Look, those people are well-dressed monsters. They deliver verbal barbs like it's an Olympic sport. I know you have thick skin and all, but the thought of one of them striking home on you makes me want to bundle you up and take you back to Devil's Falls before they get the chance."

Aubry blinked. Out of all the possibilities she'd considered, the fact that he thought he was *protecting* her had never entered into it. She was a warrior goddess—at least online. She didn't need protecting. But the notion still warmed her cold little heart. "Quinn, I wouldn't say I could handle it if I couldn't." She wasn't afraid of not being able to handle it, exactly. But these people were so far from *her* people, it was almost laughable.

"I'm sure you think you can, but you haven't met my family."

"Trust me." She didn't like thinking about where she came from—went out of her way *not* to think about it most days—but the curiosity on his face was indication that he actually wanted to know. Plus, the best way to reassure him was to show him that she'd been raised in a house not that different from his own.

It was a lie. Their little trailer couldn't be further from the rich folks he kept talking about, but mean was mean was mean. "My mom had very particular ideas about what my role in life was—mainly to stay the hell out of her way and not hurt on her buzz or scare off her man of the week. No, don't look at me like that. It wasn't bad growing up with her for the most part—mostly because I found Deathmatch in my formative years—but when she was liquored up, she was downright vicious. She could single out a person's weakness inside of ten seconds and she never hesitated to go straight for the heart."

It felt weird to talk about it, but not in a bad way. She trailed off, waiting for Quinn to jump in with... Hell, she didn't know—some sort of reaction—but he just motioned for her to continue.

"I was supposed to marry a nice boy with a wad of cash and take care of her the rest of her life, but I got all these 'funny ideas' about feminism and getting my own job, and so when she found out I applied to colleges out of state, she lost her shit. We had… words…and I left in a hurry afterwards." Words where her mom told her that all the college in the world wouldn't change the fact that she was, at heart, a mean trailer trash little bitch.

Aubry shook her head. "Long story even longer, we don't talk much anymore—and by much, I mean at all."

He turned those blue eyes on her, the look of anger searing away the little pain that talking about it had brought up. "She doesn't deserve you."

"In that, we agree." She shrugged. "The point is if my own mother can't knock me down for good, your family sure as hell can't."

That wasn't completely true, though. A small, disgustingly weak part of her wanted their approval.

It doesn't matter what I want. I won't get it. Best to know that going in.

"If at any time you change your mind, say the word and we're out of there."

When had anyone ever made her an offer like that? To put her first, completely and without caveats?

Never.

Jules would happily walk through fire for her—and she'd return the favor without a second thought—but that was different. Jules was the sister she'd never known she wanted. Quinn was…something else altogether. She took a deep breath, trying to ignore the steady warmth pulsing through her at his words. "That won't be necessary."

"All the same." He reached over and squeezed her thigh, the move comfortable and reassuring and—

I like Quinn Baldwyn.

CHAPTER FOURTEEN

Quinn's stomach was in knots as he pulled up to the hotel in Napa Valley. He'd seen his family less than a month ago, but this felt different. Important. The fact that Aubry had revealed her hellish upbringing only made it more so. He knew she was trying to reassure him, but it only made him that much more determined to spare her from this whole fiasco.

He parked, fighting down the urge to ask Aubry for the third time if she was sure she wanted to do this. She wouldn't thank him for the question, and it would probably just piss her off. To distract himself he reached over and pulled her across the seat and into his lap. "Hey."

"Hey." She settled there, straddling him, her amber eyes seeing too much. "You wouldn't be stalling, would you?"

Definitely. He toyed with the edges of her shorts, running his hands up her sides to inch her closer. "Are you complaining?"

She rocked against him, her grin doing funny things to his stomach. "It's been *hours* since I had you last. I need my Quinn fix."

"Good to know we're on the same page." He palmed her ass, bringing her closer so she lined up where he wanted her. Her sigh was a reward in and of itself, but he wanted more. He wanted to lose himself in her body until this whole damn wedding passed and nothing mattered but the next looming orgasm. Quinn leaned in to kiss her—

And froze when someone rapped on the window to his truck.

He looked over and cursed under his breath. "My sister."

"Oh good. This is exactly the kind of first impression I wanted to make—necking with the bride's brother in his almost-broken-down pickup." He half expected her to scramble off him, but she just seemed to get more comfortable, offering Jenny a finger wave.

Quinn bit back a grin at the scandalized look on his little sister's face and rolled down the window. "Hey, Jenny."

"You're late." She looked over her shoulder as if expecting someone to materialize—probably their mother. "The rehearsal dinner is in an hour and you haven't even checked in yet." She barely spared Aubry a glance, but, out of all his family, he could guarantee that it wasn't rudeness so much as panic. Her eyes were too wide and her breath was coming too fast and too shallow.

Shit.

"Hold on, peaches." He slid Aubry off him and opened the door enough to slide out of the truck. "Breathe, Jenny. I'm here now and I'm not going to hold up your special day."

Her laugh was high and hysterical. "It's not my day and you know it. It's Mother's."

Hell, he did know it. Their mother had always looked at Jenny like her second chance at youth, driving her to participate in everything from cheerleading to beauty pageants—things his sister never would have chosen for herself.

"Sit down." He guided her to the seat of his truck and adjusted her so that her head was between her knees. It wasn't a totally stable position, but it was the only one he'd found that helped her when she started to lose it. "Breath, honey. That's right, just like we talked about, nice and slow."

It took a few minutes, but she finally stopped shaking and raised her head. "I'm okay."

"Good." He glanced over her shoulder at Aubry but didn't want to let Jenny start thinking too much again and send herself into a secondary panic attack. He kept his voice low and soothing. "Just remember that you're marrying Brad, and that's what *you* want. The rest is just fluff."

Jenny shook her head. "It's not fluff. It's one of the biggest social events of the season."

When she said shit like that, she sounded exactly like Mother. Not that he'd ever tell her, because it would crush her. He sighed. "What do you need from me?"

The question calmed the remaining turmoil in her blue eyes so similar to his own. "Check in. Get ready. Be fifteen minutes early."

He didn't particularly want to do any of that, but her request reminded him of the main reason he was here in the first place—to support his little sister. She might not think the rest of it was fluff, but he knew better. He'd just forgotten it for a little while. "Will do."

"Okay." She took a deep breath. "Okay, good. Who's your friend?"

He hadn't planned to introduce her to any of his family off the cuff, but it might actually be a blessing in disguise that Jenny had shown up. His little sister dealt with surprises about as well as Aubry did. "This is my date, Aubry." He stepped back, allowing Jenny the freedom to hop down and turn to face Aubry.

She must have taken her cue from him, because she offered her version of a bright smile and offered her hand. "Pleasure to meet you."

Jenny took Aubry's hand, doing her best not to ogle the redhead. "It's nice to meet you. Quinn hasn't told us a single thing about you." She elbowed him. "You'll have to correct that as soon as we get a few minutes."

"Of course."

Jenny bounced up to give him a quick kiss on the cheek. "Fifteen minutes early. Don't forget."

"I won't."

"See you soon—see you both soon." Then she was gone, probably rushing off to check something else off her to-do list.

He opened the door for Aubry. "She means well."

"So I gathered. That's why my claws weren't out." She flexed her fingers at him like a cat about to strike. "She's kind of…intense."

"She likes to make people happy." He grabbed their suitcases out of the bed of the truck. "I think she's just forgetting that this wedding is supposed to be about *her* happiness."

Aubry shouldered her computer bag. "From what you've told me about your family, I don't think that's the case at all."

She was right. He knew she was right. That didn't mean it sat any better with him. There wasn't a damn thing he could do about it, though, so he headed for the hotel, hoping like hell he wouldn't see any more of his family before he had a chance to shower and get

Aubry as prepped for it as she could be.

Liar. The only one who needs prepping is you.

That thought wasn't comforting in the least.

Aubry hesitated. "That's where you learned how to handle the anxiety attacks."

"Jenny has had them on and off since high school. I wouldn't have offered to take you to that convention if I didn't have the knowledge to deal with it."

She smiled. "I know that now, it was just a little weird to see it from the outside. Not bad weird, just weird weird."

"Come on." He led the way into the hotel and got them checked in as quickly as humanly possible. Their room was on the third floor in a corner, so there were tons of windows. The whole thing was decorated in tasteful wealth, something he knew from having grown up with it. There was no worse insult than "new money" for all that it's exactly what the Baldwyns were. But since his mother liked to sneer delicately at blatantly extravagant expenses, it made sense that she'd picked this venue—because he had no doubt that it wasn't Jenny's choice. His little sister was big on comfort and good food, and this place met exactly one of those conditions, he'd bet.

"Nice." Aubry set her stuff down on the desk and wandered around. "Definitely a step down from the convention hotel."

"Hey now, I have a few ideas on how we can make the best of it."

"I just bet you do." She stretched her back, drawing his gaze to the way her breasts pressed against her shirt.

His cock went rock hard, right on cue. "Come here."

"Nope. I know what that look on your face means, and we only have a half hour before we have to be down there. I need a shower."

He started toward her. "Then I'll join you."

"Nope again. Back to the part where I know what that look on your face means, and I know that if you join me, we're going to be late, so don't try any lines about conserving water." She backed into the bathroom.

"Peaches, California is in a drought. It's practically our civic duty to conserve water."

"For the third time, nope. Do something useful and hang up our nice clothes." She slammed the door in his face.

Quinn laughed. She was right, and a perverse part of him really liked that she had no problem telling him no, even though her nipples were peaked beneath her thin shirt and she kept licking her lips like she couldn't wait to get another taste of him.

Shaking his head, he went about hanging up their nice clothes. The closet already contained his tux for the wedding—no doubt his mother's doing—but there was still the rehearsal tonight and brunch in the morning. Once his stuff was finished, he turned to Aubry's suitcase.

There was something really strange about unpacking for her—strangely intimate. Seeing the clothes on her—and off her—felt different than doing this mundane little chore. He cursed himself mentally for letting something so small get under his skin.

His breath left him in a rush when he lifted out a black dress that he highly suspected would hug Aubry's every curve. He had told her to make a statement, hadn't he? He carefully hung it up, his hands lingering on the fabric. It was so damn soft and there wasn't a bit of give—it'd fit her like a glove. He swallowed hard, going back to the suitcase for the other dress. This one was a mix of deep purple, blue, and red the same color as her hair. It was fucking magnificent.

That's it. I really have lost my mind.

He turned around as the door opened, the fantasy of Aubry in the dresses nothing compared to the sight of her standing in front of him in a towel. He took a step toward her before he caught himself. Throwing her on the bed and ravishing her sounded like the best plan in the world, but it would *definitely* make them late and he couldn't do that to Jenny. So he got himself under tight control. "I'm going to shower."

"Good plan." She watched him strip his shirt off, the look on her face almost enough to make him change his mind. Quinn stalked into the bathroom before he could. A cold shower was in order, because it was going to be a long fucking night.

• • •

Things started to go sideways the second they walked into the chapel. A couple in their fifties approached, and Aubry didn't need for Quinn to tense beside her to know that these were his parents. The man was an older version of Quinn but shaped more like a barrel than the perfectly honed muscles she was used to. The woman didn't have a dark hair out of place, and she wore a dress styled similarly to Jenny's. If someone looked up "crazy stupid rich" in the dictionary, Aubry was pretty sure there would be a picture of these two.

She shifted, feeling out of place in the dress she'd previously been really damn proud of. It was like a twilight personified, and she'd done up her hair to add to the affect. There was no hiding her tattoos or her bright hair but, damn it, she wasn't ashamed of the way she looked. She was good enough to be Quinn's date, and that was all that mattered.

Quinn's dad roared out a laugh. "Look what the cat dragged in."

"Dad. Mom."

There was no hugging, but she hadn't really expected it. What she *had* expected was the way his mom's eyes went wide behind her tasteful makeup. "And you brought a friend."

"More than a friend." His arm came around her waist, pulling her against him. She would have snapped at the move, but the underlying tension in his muscles stopped her. Maybe he needed the contact as much as she'd needed his steady voice in the middle of her anxiety attack. Aubry ran her hand up and down his back, offering her silent support.

When Quinn spoke again, he sounded closer to normal. "Mom, Dad, this is my girlfriend, Aubry. Aubry, meet my parents, Richard and Peggy."

Even though she knew it was fake her heart tripped over itself in her chest at him calling her his girlfriend. To cover up her response, she smiled at them. Well, she bared her teeth at them. "Pleasure to meet you."

Peggy looked like she might actually pass out. "Can I speak to you for a minute—alone?"

"Nope." Quinn's arm tightened around her.

"Anything you can say to me, you can say in front of Aubry."

Oh, for fuck's sake. Surely his parents would clue in to the fact that it wasn't real. But Peggy just marched away, and Richard laughed again and clapped his son on the shoulder.

"Sowing your wild oats. Can't blame you. I mean, look at her."

Aubry bristled. Quinn must have known she was two seconds from searching for a candlestick to beam his dad with, because he cleared his throat. "There's Jenny. We've got to go tell her congratulations. I'll catch up with you later."

He didn't wait for a response, steering her away from his dad and toward the small knot of people around his little sister.

"Charming."

"You have no idea." He'd spoken so softly she had to strain to hear. "They were on their best behavior just now."

She didn't want to know what bad behavior looked like. Aubry hadn't made a habit of spending time with people so far beyond her tax bracket, and if that delightful little interaction was any indication, she had the right of it. People with that much money thought they could act however they wanted and, for the most part, they got away with it for exactly that reason.

Not that she was a gem, but even she thought trying to marry off a person who wasn't interested in being married off was gross.

"That offer to flee while cackling madly still stands. This is wine country—there's got to be another hotel around here attached to a vineyard where we can drink our sorrows away."

The grin he gave her was downright sunny. "I appreciate the offer, but we're stuck for the time being."

It struck her yet again that it was a good thing she hadn't let him talk her out of this. He actually…needed her. She wasn't sure she'd ever been needed before, not like this. Aubry straightened. "Just remember there's an out. I don't have much practice being a shield, but I could give it a shot if you need me to." Surely sheer fury could keep her going long enough to find a private place before she started shaking over exactly how many people she'd be willing to face down for him.

I really *like Quinn Baldwyn.*

Jenny turned as they approached. She rushed over and took Aubry's hands. "I wanted to apologize about earlier. I was catty and I really wasn't trying to be; I'm just so stressed out and sometimes when I open my mouth, my mother comes out. I think you're really beautiful, and it's obvious my brother is crazy about you, and—"

"It's okay," Aubry cut in, half afraid if she didn't say something the woman would keep going. But she was being earnest, which was more than anyone could say for their parents. "It's really fine. I know I'm not what you expected."

"I didn't expect anything at all. Quinn has been remarkably close-mouthed about his seeing someone." She gave her brother a mock glare. "I'll have to come down to Devil's Falls sometime after the honeymoon and we can catch up."

"Oh, you don't have to do that." Especially since they wouldn't be "dating" once they got back into town.

She forced herself to keep her smile in place. They'd just have to stage some kind of breakup. No, that was way too complicated. He'd probably wait a week or two and then quietly pass on the information that they'd broken up. The loss that rose up at the thought had no place there, but she couldn't seem to reason it away.

"Of course I do." A man approached and Jenny's entire face lit up. "Brad."

He was cute in a rich guy sort of way, and he looked just as fresh faced and *young* as Jenny. He walked up and draped an arm over her shoulder. "So I hear there's this hot chick who's looking to get hitched. You seen her around?"

Jenny's giggle would have annoyed the shit out of Aubry if she wasn't so blatantly happy and in love. She'd seen that same dopey look on Jules's face pretty often since she and Adam got together, and she tried really hard not to let it bug her.

But there was nothing like being surrounded by happy people in love to make a person feel really, really alone.

"You okay?"

She blinked, not sure when Jenny and Brad had headed for another group of people, leaving her and Quinn temporarily without an audience to play for. "Sure. Why wouldn't I be?"

"Oh, I don't know, because you're surrounded by hungry piranhas looking to feast."

"Quinn, did you just call me fresh meat?" The shock on his face almost made her laugh, but she was enjoying ribbing him too much to ruin it. "I think you did. Rude much?"

"I'll show you rude." He pulled her into his arms

and palmed her ass. "Just wait until we get alone, peaches. You'll get everything that's coming to you."

"*Quinn*. You're in public. Stop acting like a Neanderthal."

He rolled his eyes at her scandalized tone and whispered, "Think if I fuck you right here on the table, it would prove I really was a Neanderthal? We both know you'd like the audience."

Aubry shivered at the image his words brought. She tried to keep her voice light. "True, but I think it would make future family dinners really awkward."

"Damn, you're right." Quinn sighed theatrically. "I guess I'll have to wait until we're alone to release all my pent-up frustration on you, huh?"

"Guess so." She nodded solemnly, her entire body sparking in anticipation. She couldn't wait for this damn rehearsal to be over with.

CHAPTER FIFTEEN

Quinn barely waited the requisite hour after the meal to grab Aubry's hand and drag her out of the room. He didn't give a fuck that everyone present knew exactly what was on his mind or that inside of ten minutes he was going to sink between her thighs. The only two whose opinions he cared about were Jenny and Brad, and they were so lost in each other that he could have done exactly what he threatened Aubry with earlier and he doubted they would have noticed.

"Hey, big guy."

He stopped so fast, he had to catch Aubry before she ran into him. Even then, he wasn't sure if he was actually seeing what he thought he was seeing. It was the blonde from the hellish dinner a few months ago, and she was looking at him just like she had the last time they met—like she'd swallow him whole and then come back for seconds. He cleared his throat. "Ah, Aubry, this is…" Fuck, what was her name?

"Rochelle."

"Right. Rochelle."

The woman ignored Aubry and sidled up to him, going so far as to run her hand up his chest. "Richard said you'd be here, and I'm so glad we had this chance to run into each other. You were called away from dinner last month, so we didn't get to…know each other." She sank so much innuendo into the last few words that there was no mistaking she meant "know" in a Biblical sense.

He grabbed her hand, part of him astounded that she was being so bold, but then again, he had no idea what his old man had told her. Obviously he led her to believe Quinn was a sure thing, which wasn't surprising, exactly, but it still caught him off guard. He let go of her, putting a little push behind it so that her hand dropped away from him. "Yeah, well, duty called."

"I just bet it did." If anything, she looked more interested, reaching for him.

Aubry was there before she made contact, inserting herself between them. She looked over her shoulder at him, raised her eyebrows, and jerked her thumb at the blonde. "Is this one of those hussies you warned me about? Her tits are certainly large enough to fit the profile." She turned back to Rochelle and spoke in a stage whisper. "Sweetie, have you seen the crowd in there? That dress is more Vegas hooker than West Coast socialite."

Rochelle turned a mottled red color that didn't do much for her platinum blond hair. "Who's your friend, Quinn?"

"This is my girlfriend, Aubry." He got a little thrill every time he introduced her like that.

He'd expected the title to make Rochelle back off, but she just laughed. "Oh, damn, that's the funniest thing I've heard all night." She smoothed back her hair. "I'll tell you a little secret, Audrey."

"Aubry."

"Whatever." She pointed at Quinn. "He might play on the wild side with a little Goth chick like you, but when he settles down—which will be sooner rather than later—it's going to be with someone like *me*."

Aubry laughed. "What? A social ladder-climbing gold digger?"

"Please. A woman his family approves of—one who *fits*." She raked a look over Aubry. "Which I can tell you right now, you don't." She straightened, a polished smile firmly in place. "Well, Quinn, when you're done playing in the gutter, you give me a call." She moved around them and into the restaurant, leaving him with a furious redhead.

He cautiously put his hands on Aubry's shoulders, well aware she might try to take him out at the knees. "I'm sorry."

She turned around and he was surprised to see that the fury on her face wasn't directed at him. "*That* is one of the women your dad threw at you? What the hell is wrong with him? Does he seriously not know a thing about you?"

"To be fair, I like blondes." Or at least he used to. These days, nothing could hold a candle to redheads.

She poked him in the chest. "I'm being serious. Don't throw a joke in there like that. What kind of woman is willing to try to jump you when I'm standing right here?" She shook her head. "You know what, don't answer that. I see why you wanted me here now."

The thing was that might have been his original reason for agreeing to this whole thing, but it wasn't the reason he wanted her here now. Quinn took her hand and headed for the elevator. "Let's get out of here before we run into someone else."

"You took the words right out of my mouth."

He barely waited for the elevator doors to close before pulling her into his arms and kissing her. There were so many conflicting emotions circling inside him,

he didn't know where to start. He liked Aubry. He
didn't like the expiration date she'd put on them. He
just needed to find out how to broach the subject
without spooking her.

What am I saying? I know the perfect way.

The elevator dinged, bringing him back to himself.
He stepped out into the hallway, keeping his hold on
her hand. "Come on, peaches. I have a promise to
fulfill."

"God forbid you drop the ball on that." The anger
was gone from her face, though she shot a look at the
closing elevator doors like she was putting serious
consideration into going back down to the lobby and
throwing down with Rochelle. He liked that she was so
fierce, almost jealous. It made him think he might
actually have a chance at getting her to agree to give
this a shot. A real shot.

He held the room door open for her and then
closed it softly behind him. "On the chair by the desk."
It was a sturdy thing with thick arms and a wide seat.
Perfect for his purposes.

She obeyed, sitting primly on the edge of the seat.
"Are we going to play dirty secretary? Because I think
you'd look fetching crawling toward me with an enve-
lope between your teeth."

"Something like that." He knelt in front of her,
catching her ankles in his hands. "Do you want to
know a secret?"

"Hell yes."

He traced circles on her anklebone with his thumb.
"I spent the entire fucking dinner thinking about
dropping my napkin under the table and crawling
down there to get it."

"Clumsy of you."

"Yeah, well, I'm a clumsy guy sometimes. And while I was down there, the temptation to taste you would be too much." He ran his hands up her legs, lifting her dress as he did, until the fabric hit the tops of her thighs. It was so silky it bunched effortlessly, revealing the long expanse of her pale skin. "Look how easy it was to get between your thighs. Almost like you were inviting me."

Aubry reached over her head and clasped the back of the chair, spreading her legs in invitation. "That's because I was. Your family is so unbelievably unbearable, I needed something to distract myself. Since you invited me here in the first place, being a distraction is your job."

He gripped her thighs, exhaling harshly when he found that she wore no panties. "I know an invitation when I see one, peaches." He spread her folds, dipping one thumb into her wetness and spreading it up over her clit. "And this right here is an invitation."

She lifted her hips. "Would you be talking this much while you were under the table?"

"Shh." He lightly smacked her thigh with his free hand. "This is a nice dinner. You can't let anyone know that I've got my mouth all over you beneath the table." Quinn slid his hands under her ass and lifted her a little, thrusting his tongue into her.

Aubry moaned. "You don't think they'd notice that you've been down there a while?"

"Do you care if they do?" He licked her clit. "I think that's exactly what you want, dirty girl. For every single person at that table to know that I'm tongue-fucking you to orgasm."

"Maybe."

He pushed two fingers into her. "No maybe about it. You forget, peaches—I know you. I know what gets you hot and wet and needy. I think that would fit the bill nicely. Now be quiet and try not to scream my name when I make you come."

He licked her again, not stopping this time. It was hot, so fucking hot, to think about doing this to her exactly as he'd described, with her writhing and making little helpless sounds as she tried to be quiet. He didn't think his cock could get any harder, but when her hands came to rest on the back of his head, he thought he might burst out of his slacks.

Aubry gave up all pretense of being quiet, rolling her hips to guide him exactly where she wanted him. "Right there. Oh my God, Quinn, that feels so good. Don't stop. Please don't stop."

Hearing her desperate words even as she went wild against his mouth—knowing *he* was the cause of her pleasure—was unbearably good. He picked up his pace, sucking on her clit just like he knew she liked, relishing her nails pressing against the back of his head, holding him in place.

As if he would want to be anywhere else.

"*Quinn.*"

A man could get addicted to the sound of his name on Aubry's lips as she came. She went boneless, her breath coming as fast as his was. From the last few days, he knew it would only be a short time before she was ready for more. For all that she accused him of being insatiable, she matched him stroke for stroke.

Sure enough, she stretched and sat up. "That was a great appetizer."

Quinn laughed. "Just for that, I should cut you off right now."

"Come on. You know better." She stood and unzipped the side of her dress. One shrug of her shoulders and it was on the ground, leaving her standing before him gloriously naked. Aubry stretched again, watching him watch her. "If you stop now, you're not going to get to watch me ride my trusty steed."

Her words should have been hilarious, but his amusement was sidetracked by the knowledge of how fucking good she looked while riding his cock. He pushed to his feet and went for his belt buckle. "Then, by all means, let's not deny either one of us."

• • •

It was downright unnatural how hot this man made Aubry. She never wanted Quinn to stop touching her, and she was so turned on that thought didn't even worry her like it normally would. "Come here, steed."

"Don't be getting any ideas." But he let her back him up to the bed.

"The only idea I have right now is that you're wearing too many clothes." She unbuttoned his pants and pushed them down his hips. Quinn helped her by stepping out of them, and then there was nothing between them. She ran her hands up his chest, marveling at how good his muscles felt beneath her fingertips. "You are unreal."

"I was thinking…"

She gave him a little push, well aware that he humored her by sitting on the edge of the bed. "Always a dangerous prospect."

"Mmmm." He pulled her onto him, cupping her ass and squeezing. "I like this."

"I like this, too." She arched her back, offering her breasts to him. The look he sent her as he captured one nipple with his mouth seared her right to her core. Her thighs shook and she had to close her eyes for a second. "Oh, fuck."

Quinn pushed two fingers into her, pumping slowly. "Let me take you out when we get back to Devil's Falls."

She was so caught up in the sensations rolling through her body that it took her mind a few beats to catch up and process his words. "What?"

"You. Me. A meal." He twisted his wrist and palmed her between her thighs. "This at the end if you're a very, very good girl."

She flexed her fingers on his shoulders. "Wait, what?"

"I like this. I like *you*." He reached over and snagged a condom off the nightstand and rolled it on while she watched. Then he withdrew his fingers and replaced them with his cock.

"But—" She moaned as he thrust up, sheathing himself to the hilt with her.

"I'm not ready for this to end." He fucked her slowly, one hand on the back of her neck, holding her in place despite the fact that she was on top. "Are you?"

She never wanted this to end. Aubry spread her legs wider, and he rewarded her by switching positions, laying her on the bed and pushing his cock even deeper. She hooked her ankles at the small of his back, arching up to meet his thrusts.

Quinn stilled. "Peaches, I asked you a question."

"What?"

He grinned. "I asked if you're ready for this to end."

It was hard to catch her breath. "You're using sex to stack the deck in your favor, aren't you?"

"Guilty." He nuzzled her neck, his whiskers making her shiver. "I'm not afraid to play dirty to get what I want. And what I want is you."

What I want is you.

His words echoed through her, with the tide of her orgasm nearly engulfing her. She held it at bay through sheer force of will. "Quinn, think about this for a second."

"I have." He thrust hard enough to make her eyes roll back in her head. "Let's give this thing a shot, peaches. I promise a whole hell of a lot more nights like this one."

Nights with him in a bed and his cock imbedded between her thighs. There was some reason she should balk at the thought, but she was having a hard time focusing. "It might be a mistake."

"Won't know until we try." He kissed her, sweeping away her worries as if they never existed. He changed the angle of his thrusts, grinding his pelvis against her clit, and that was all it took to push her over the edge. She came screaming and he ate the sound, his strokes never changing as they took her to the edge and over.

She clung to him as he finished, reality still too far away to be a worry. Quinn rolled onto his side and took her with him. "I'm glad we had this talk."

Aubry laughed because there was nothing else to do. "You're right. You really do play dirty."

"You like it." He palmed her breast, his expression losing its teasing edge. "I'm serious though, Aubry. I want to date you."

The shock of hearing her actual name on his lips chased away the last of the desire tingeing her thoughts. She settled back into the pillow, staring at the wall. Trying to date Quinn might be a mistake... but it was suddenly one she wanted to make more than anything else in the world. "What if it doesn't work out?"

"What if it does?"

She wasn't sure which option scared her more.

He seemed to sense what the problem was—the man was way too good at reading her—and smoothed back her hair. "Do you have a legit reason for saying no?"

"Legit? No. Irrational? Only about a million and a half." Strangely enough, that knowledge settled some of her fears. "You're serious about wanting this?"

"As a heart attack."

A curious lightness coursed through her and she found herself grinning like a fool. "Okay."

"Okay?"

"Yeah, okay. Let's do it. Let's go on a date and see what happens."

Quinn's smile was a reward in and of itself. He rolled back on top of her, settling between her thighs. "Look at you, taking a leap of faith." He kissed her, his tongue tangling with hers, his hands on her body teasing the desire she had been sure was sated back to life. "Guess I'll have to reward you, huh?"

She laughed. "I think I'm going to have to insist on it."

CHAPTER SIXTEEN

After Aubry agreed to actually give them a shot once they got back to Devil's Falls, nothing could get Quinn down—not even having to spend some time in close quarters with his parents. He'd left Aubry asleep in bed and come down to the required breakfast before the rest of the official shit started. Jenny was all smiles and clearly displayed nerves, but she gave him a big hug as he reached the table. "Sorry."

Quinn didn't get the chance to ask what she meant, because as soon as he sat down, his mother turned her disapproving look on him. It was one she'd had cause to practice over the decades and it used to be enough to bring him to heel, no matter how much he chafed at the restriction. That was a long time ago, though. Quinn poured himself some coffee and sat back. "Mother. Father."

As expected, Peggy barely waited for him to take his first sip before she started up. "Quinn, honey, we're worried about you."

"We've let you have your freedom—all men need their freedom—but this is going too far." His old man picked up right where she left off, as if they'd practiced this. Hell, maybe they had.

"You brought th-that *girl* to your sister's wedding." His mother took a sip of water. When she spoke again, her tone was much more controlled. "You're thirty-four years old. The youthful rebellion was expected in your twenties. You dated wild girls and put gray hairs on my head. I hardly expected you to show up to your sister's *wedding* with one who put them all to shame. She's just so…trashy. I'm drawing the line."

He almost pointed out that Jenny didn't seem to have a damn problem with Aubry, but it was his sister's wedding day and he wasn't going to throw her under the bus to distract his parents. So he sat back and let them rant. They took turns going over the same old conversational paths. He was a Baldwyn. He was expected to act a certain way and not bring scandal down around the family's ears. While his cowboy thing was cute at first, it was time to let it go and be done. He most certainly must *not* settle down with a woman who was beneath him. Under all the expected words, there was an undertone of desperation that had never been there before.

Apparently showing up with Aubry had been all the evidence they needed to finally realize that he was, in fact, serious about not dancing to the tune they set.

When they trailed off and a full five seconds passed without someone picking up the conversational ball, he drained his coffee. "Well, that was fun."

"*Fun.*" His mother looked in danger of screeching. "You haven't been listening to a single thing we've been saying."

"No more than you've listened to me in the last twelve years." He set his mug down. "I'm not coming back. Not in the way you want me to. As fun as it's been torturing ourselves with these forced dinners and going round and round again every single time I see you, I'm done." He stood. "If you can't respect what I've chosen to do with my life—and who I've chosen to spend it with—then you can fuck off. I'm not changing, no matter how much you want me to." He turned around and strode out of the restaurant, not sure if he was feeling free—or in a freefall.

All he knew was the hour he'd spent at the table was an hour wasted because he hadn't been with Aubry. She never asked him to change, not really. She never manipulated or played games. She was exactly what she presented herself to be, and it was so fucking refreshing he could barely wrap his mind around it. Being around his family and their peers only brought home the differences even more clearly.

Maybe this time they'll actually listen.

He smiled at the thought, mostly because it didn't matter if they did or not. They had no control over him. He was only here because of Jenny. The smile died, though, when he walked into the room and saw Aubry glaring at her computer screen. "Hey, peaches."

"Hey."

A red flag rose at her tone. He crossed the room to stand next to her, searching her face even though she still hadn't looked at him. "What happened in the last hour that has you looking like you want to go a few rounds in that game of yours? Because when I left you here, you were looking particularly sated and all aglow from the amazing sex." The pieces clicked together with a snap. He rubbed a hand over his face. "You went down to the restaurant."

"I thought you might need saving."

That was a sweet gesture…or it would have been if she hadn't witnessed the poison his parents were spitting. "How much did you hear?" Because she obviously hadn't stayed to the end if she was up here, stewing.

She sighed, her shoulder drooping. "Just the part

about my very presence being an insult to them and how they can't believe you'd bring a trashy girl like me to a nice place like this."

So pretty much all the key parts of his parents' speech. He sighed. "I'm sorry. If I'd known they were going to spring that on me where you could potentially hear it, I would have warned you. As you discovered last night, my parents are horrible people."

"It's okay. I promised I could handle it, and I can." She took a deep breath and met his gaze. "But what if they're right?"

He went still. "Explain what the fuck you mean by asking me that."

"Don't take that tone with me. It's a valid question. I don't fit in here." She waved her hand to encompass everything around them. "I'm not polished or poised, and I never say the right thing or know which fork to use in one of those fancy setups. I mean, I'm not shit on the bottom of their shoe like they think, but this isn't my place and these aren't my people." She hesitated, her expression melting into something vulnerable. "They could be yours, though."

"No." He took her hand and pulled her to her feet. "Don't you dare put me on a pedestal or whatever the fuck you're trying to do. I hate this shit as much as you do."

"Maybe, but even though you've been gone the last twelve years, you're still the golden boy. You could come back to this at any time and they'd all welcome you with open arms, no questions asked."

She was right, but that didn't mean he liked hearing it. "My life is in Devil's Falls. That was *my* choice, and that's all that matters."

For a second, he thought she might keep arguing, but she ran her hands through her hair and sighed. "Right. I know that. I'm sorry. I'm being crazy—crazier than normal. Apparently you can take the girl away from the trailer, but that doesn't mean she's going to feel any less like trailer trash. It's okay. *I'm* okay. It was a momentary lapse."

He got the feeling he hadn't convinced her of anything, but there was nothing he could say that he hadn't already said. And, fuck, Quinn was so goddamn *tired* of trying to convince everyone around him that he knew his own mind better than they did. He'd gone into this wedding knowing his parents would pull some shit—he just hadn't expected to get it from Aubry, too. But she'd let it go. He could do the same.

For now.

He took a deep breath. "We'll talk about this after the wedding."

"Yeah. Sure. That sounds good."

There was nothing overtly wrong. Not really. They'd had worse arguments since they'd known each other— worse arguments in the last two days. There was no reason for him to feel the sense of impending doom that currently hung over his head. Quinn hesitated, and then let it go. He wasn't going to solve anything in the next half hour, but he *would* cause more problems if he was late for the pictures and other hoops he was required to jump through today. "It's a date."

• • •

Aubry almost panicked when the elevator doors opened up and she was faced with so many *people*.

They blocked every avenue of escape and made it impossible to draw a full breath. *I can barely take two steps out of this deathtrap without bumping into someone.* She closed her eyes, but that only made it worse because she was assaulted by what sounded like a roar of mixed voices and too many conflicting perfumes.

She hadn't reacted like this last night during the rehearsal dinner, but there had been less people...and she wasn't still reeling from hearing Quinn's parents spell out every single thing that was wrong with her in their eyes. It shouldn't bother her. She *knew* it shouldn't bother her. As he kept pointing out, he was going back to Devil's Falls—the life he'd actually chosen. Which stood to reason that it hadn't been the sex muddying up his brain last night when he said he wanted more time with her.

But that didn't stop the insecurity from taking root inside her, feeding the secret part of her that had suspected she was just as worthless as her family had accused her of being, the part that had been waiting for the other foot to fall ever since she moved to Devil's Falls—for someone to wake up and look at her and tell her that no one really wanted her there and it was high time she take her things and go.

Knowing it was an irrational fear didn't do a damn thing to kill it. Truth be told, she barely thought about it most days. But there was something about being *here* with *this* man, a man whom she'd realized sometime over the last few days was a legitimately good guy. He wasn't the muscle head she'd always suspected. He was decent, and gorgeous, and obviously insane because he was expressing interest in dating her once they got back to their normal stomping grounds.

She should have said no. There was no way they could last, and the reasons she didn't want to keep having sex after they got to Devil's Falls still stood. Jules would get her hopes up...

Aubry wrapped her arms around herself, the crowd blurring in front of her. No, that was a lie. *She* was the one who would get her hopes up. Because if this was really real, then Quinn would *really* hurt her when it was over. Because there was no way it wouldn't be over.

I am such a mess.

"Breathe, peaches." Quinn took her hand, his engulfing hers. "I won't let them get you."

She spoke out of the side of her mouth, pathetically grateful for the distraction from her intense issues—as if she had any other kind of issue. "What if one of them is infected and we have to run?"

"I'll scoop you up, throw you over my shoulder, and we'll bust out that big window into the back grounds. We can escape into the vineyards—there are miles of them."

Even though it was a silly theoretical plan, and not one that would make a lick of sense in the real world, her next breath came easier. *I am being crazy and irrational in worrying that Quinn is going to dump me like an old pair of boots at the first opportunity.* "If anyone can manage it, it's my trusty steed."

"Damn straight."

And then there was no more stalling because his little sister caught sight of them and waved. She wore a tasteful cream cocktail dress that would have looked at home on a woman twice her age, but maybe that was

Aubry's prejudice showing. She didn't do tasteful and she didn't do…pretty much anything to do with events like this.

Just another way that I don't fit into this world.

Quinn didn't have that problem. He wore his tux like he was born to do it…probably because he was.

Jenny's eyes went wide when she caught sight of Aubry, and she couldn't exactly blame the woman. Wearing a black cut-out dress that showed off her tattoos to perfection had sounded like a great plan when she was packing and planning to aggravate Quinn as much as possible, but actually walking into a room of pastels in it was something else altogether. *What the hell was I thinking?*

Quinn's sister approached, her smile firmly back in place by the time she was in front of them. "Right on time!"

"I'm making a habit of it this weekend," Quinn said. "Consider it a one-time thing."

"Yes, well. I appreciate it. And I'm sorry again about this morning. I didn't know they were going to ambush you like that. It's wonderful to see you again, Aubry." Someone called her name and Jenny's smile faltered before she made a visible effort to reclaim it. "I've got to go. We'll talk later, though."

"Can't wait." The words didn't come out nearly as chipper as Aubry meant them to.

This whole event was just a reminder of how different she and Quinn were. It didn't matter how often he claimed they weren't his people, she knew damn well that a person never truly escaped their past. She might be successful in her own right, but she'd always be that freak from a trailer park in the back of her mind. Being here only brought that feeling home. Again and again and again.

She felt Quinn's warmth at her back a second before his hands settled on her hips, his thumbs dipping into the cutout that exposed her sides. "Have I mentioned that you look ravishing?"

"Ravishing. That's a big word for a cowboy." *That's it. Remind yourself that your lives aren't that different now. You both love Devil's Falls. That's something.*

Except...

Enough. Worrying about things now wasn't going to do anything but stress her the hell out.

"I have a few more up my sleeve." His voice dropped into a rumble she could almost feel. "The first chance I get, I'm going to take this thing off you, strap by strap."

Her knees shook as she pictured him doing exactly that. His hands skated down just a little, to cup her hips. "No panties. Naughty, peaches. Very naughty. I like it." He leaned close enough that his chest pressed against her back. "I don't know if we're going to make it back to the room. Maybe after the ceremony, I'll drag you out into the vineyards and fuck you right there in the dirt." His laugh had her biting back a moan. "I could bring you around to the outdoors yet."

With that kind of motivation, he might just manage it.

She opened her mouth to tell him exactly that, but he made a startled sound and then his touch was gone, leaving her leaning against something that was no longer there. Even worse was the shock in his voice. "*Hope?*"

The woman who approached, a slight limp in her

step, looked at home in the crowd, her pale pink dress
with its delicate beading, exposing just enough
cleavage to be classily sexy and making Aubry feel like
a second-class hooker. Her long blond hair was pulled
back into an elegant up-do and her lipstick was as
perfectly pink as her dress…and currently stretched
wide into a smile that seemed for Quinn alone. "Hey,
stranger."

She was beautiful. More than beautiful. Like a
goddess who'd wandered into their midst.

He stopped in front of her, his hands at his sides
like he'd forgotten how to move properly. "I didn't
know you'd be here."

"Jenny and I never lost touch."

Which seemed to indicate she and Quinn *had*.
Aubry looked from one of them to the other, her
heart sinking. They looked like a pair. Like Barbie
and Ken, except more attractive and a whole hell of a
lot more real. This wasn't like Rochelle last night. It
had been clear from the start that she was his father's
pick, but Quinn had never been interested in her in
any way. That *wasn't* clear with Hope. In fact, Aubry
got the feeling that not only was he interested, but
this woman would be one that every single
judgmental asshole in his family would approve of.
They'd probably roll out the welcome mat as soon as
they saw these two talking.

Those are my issues, not Quinn's. Any second now,
he'd prove her wrong and put this woman in her place
or do something to remind her that they were here
together. Not him and Hope. Him and *her*.

But he just stood there, like he wanted to sweep
Hope into his arms but wasn't sure of his welcome.

She seemed to sense the same thing. Her smile turned a little bittersweet. "So I don't warrant a hug anymore?"

"Aw, honey, of course you do." He wrapped his big arms around her and lifted her off her feet, eliciting a laugh that sounded like honest-to-God bells. It made Aubry want to crawl back up to their room and virtually shoot something.

Hope's gaze landed on her, and she gave a perfect frown, a tiny line appearing between her brows. *For fuck's sake, I bet she even cries prettily.* "Who's your friend?"

"What? Oh." He turned around as if seeing Aubry for the first time. "This is Aubry."

She tried not to be offended that he didn't correct Hope's assumption that they were friends. Why would he? They weren't dating, not really, and she obviously wasn't among the women he'd feared dealing with when he agreed to this in the first place. Hurt, jagged and deep, sliced through Aubry. That feeling, at least, she could deal with.

She was used to not measuring up. Why did she think Quinn would be any different, no matter what he said?

She'd let herself forget, for a little while, that she hated people because the second they got the chance, they'd disappoint you. She'd forgotten, too, that she barely liked Quinn on the best of days. *It was the sex.* It messed with her mind, just like she'd been afraid it would. She moved across the distance between them, reclaiming her armor with each step, until she felt more like her old self than she had since getting in the truck with him that first day. Broken and bitter and well aware of what the world had to offer her—nothing.

Absolutely nothing.

Aubry laid her hand on his arm, her smile feeling like it would shatter her teeth. "Now, don't be polite, Quinn. We're not friends." She turned to Hope. "We were fucking, but that's over now. He's all yours, sweetie."

She turned around and marched out of the room, bypassing the elevator because the thought of being closed in with herself was nearly as awful as being surrounded by strangers. *Outside. I just need some fresh air.* She veered right, heading down the hallway and out the side door. The cool night air did nothing to calm the stinging of her cheeks, and she hated that she was blushing furiously, even if it was in anger.

This was her fault. She'd let herself get caught up in the fantasy of Quinn and his big, sexy cock, and she'd compromised all the defenses she'd spent years perfecting. It was so unbelievably *stupid*. And even when she *knew* she was being stupid, she'd let him say all the right things and make her feel like maybe, for once in her life, her instincts weren't right and there were more than a handful of people out there who actually gave a damn.

That he was one of them.

She reached for her phone, needing the lifeline Jules offered, only to remember that, not only was her phone up in the room, but also Jules would be throwing Adam's mother's ashes in the Gulf right around now. Calling her with Aubry's self-inflicted crisis would be the worst kind of selfish.

"What the fuck was *that*?"

She took a deep breath and turned to face Quinn. She'd known this was coming, even if she desperately wanted more time and distance between them to at least get over the initial sting of him throwing her by the wayside the second Hope walked up. "You shouldn't be here. Hope might get the wrong idea."

"What?"

"You heard me." She wasn't going to say it again. She couldn't bear it.

He stalked closer, so damn big and too sexy for her own good. Even knowing she was a sad second rate, she couldn't stop her traitorous body from perking up at his nearness. He stopped in front of her, a breath's distance away. "Explain what the fuck you mean, Aubry."

God, why can't he just let it go? She took a deep breath and fought to keep the roiling emotions inside her out of her voice. "I don't think what just happened needs much explanation. It's pretty clear that you and Hope have a history."

"What's your point?"

The last little bit of hope she'd been holding out died a horrible death. *I am such an unforgivable idiot.* Her eyes burned, but she held back tears through sheer force of will. "Like I said, I'll let you get back to it. I'm sure your parents would be absolutely delighted."

"That's it." He reached out, looking like he wanted nothing more than to shake her, but he stopped just short of touching her. "That's all it took for you to jump ship—me talking to a pretty girl who I used to know."

She didn't want to hear him refer to another

woman as pretty, didn't want to think that maybe Hope and Quinn used to do a whole lot more than talk—or that they would again. It made her stomach churn. She smoothed her hair back, hating that her hands shook. "Yeah, that's part of it. But the truth was that this was never going to work. We come from different worlds, and you know it."

He cursed long and hard. "This isn't about Hope at all. She gave you the exit you've been looking for since last night." He gave her a searching look. "Fuck, what am I saying? You were never actually in this. You've always held yourself back, right from the very beginning."

"Can you blame me?" Her voice was too shrill, but his comments struck close to home. "This never should have happened."

"Why?"

She stopped short. "What?"

"Tell me why this never should have happened. Give me one legit reason beyond you being too chickenshit to put yourself out there because you had a rough time growing up and have a hell of a history of building yourself a crazy paranoid bunker to avoid being hurt again."

She couldn't believe he was throwing that back in her face. She didn't open up to anyone—*ever*—and he was going to use the one time she did against her at the first available opportunity. "That's not fair."

"Neither is you flipping your shit because of this." He motioned at the hotel behind him. "But the truth doesn't matter to you, does it? You don't care that this isn't my world—hasn't been since before I even met you—or that Hope is my dead best friend's little sister or, fuck, anything that doesn't fit in with your twisted worldview."

Her mind tumbled over itself trying to process that. He and Hope hadn't… It didn't matter. He might not have that kind of history with her, but it didn't change the fact that Aubry didn't fit, not here and not with him. She straightened, doing her best to look him in the eye. She failed, her gaze landing on his mouth and sticking there. "You're right. I don't care."

Quinn jerked back like she'd struck him, and then laughed harshly. "Well, hell, Aubry. You win. I should have known the first time you said that you didn't want this to keep going once we got back into town, that it was just sex for you. Stupid of me to think differently."

It wasn't just sex. Her mind screamed the words, but she held them inside, because he'd been right. Maybe the things she was upset about right now were partially self-inflicted, but it was only a matter of time before something *real* happened to break them up for real. If it hurt this much after a few days, going forward any longer was insane when she knew the endgame, even by her standards. They had to end this, and they had to end this now.

Better a little hurt now than a bigger hurt later.

The only problem was that it didn't *feel* like a little hurt. It felt like she was cutting her own heart out of her chest.

• • •

Quinn couldn't believe the shit he was hearing. He kept thinking this couldn't possibly be happening, but here Aubry was, standing in front of him and doing her damnedest to see this thing between them go down in flames. Even after he'd clarified what was really a bullshit assumption of hers, she didn't care.

Which meant she really was just looking for an excuse to call the whole thing off.

"I guess that's that then." He barely recognized his own voice. It was hoarse, as if he'd been screaming all the things rushing through his mind during this conversation. *Don't do this. Damn it, you're really doing it. Don't ruin us just because you're scared. God*damn*it, Aubry.*

He didn't say it. She'd already proven she wasn't going to listen.

Anger rose with every heartbeat, frustration and fury all twisted up into an ugly ball of emotion in his chest. "You want to know a secret, peaches?" He didn't bother waiting for a response. "The truth is that you're going to be alone for the rest of your goddamn life if you're so determined to push people who care about you away."

"You…care. About me."

This was it. He saw the fledgling hope in her eyes and knew he could reel her back in with a few carefully chosen words and probably some hot sex. She'd let it go…

And then sometime later down the road, something would happen to trigger her panic, and she'd flip her shit again. When would it stop? *Would* it stop? She was right. This never would have worked. So he said the one thing he knew would put the final nail in the coffin of their relationship. "I used to."

Her amber eyes went wide with hurt, and he wanted nothing more than to take the words back.

He didn't.

Instead, he turned around and walked away, his feet seeming to get heavier with each step. It was over. Really over. There should be relief—he'd worked so damn hard to remove every little bit of unnecessary drama from his life and he'd been pretty fucking successful at it—but all he felt was a yawning loss and that the horrible fear wouldn't be going away anytime soon.

The thought of going back to mingle with the wedding guests before the ceremony made him want to punch something, so he didn't go back. Instead, he headed out into the vineyard, walking aimlessly, determined to work off some of the rage and frustration. It didn't work. All he could see was that last devastated look on Aubry's face, the hit she'd been bracing for all day that he'd been all too happy to deliver the second the opportunity presented itself.

It would have happened at some point anyways.

It didn't matter how many times he thought that, it didn't make him feel any less like a piece of shit. *He* was the one who'd fought so hard for this. *He* was the one who'd pushed her well past her comfort zone time and time again.

So, really, the only person he had to blame for this shitty situation was himself. He could have backed off when he walked in on her in the shower, and that would have been the end of that. They had wicked chemistry—so what? A lot of people did, but that didn't mean they had to explore it.

But then the last few days wouldn't have happened.

He never would have seen her in her element at that convention. They never would have gotten past the point of vicious snarking at each other. He never would have known that a woman like her could turn his whole world on its head.

I am such a goddamn asshole.

He stomped down on that feeling hard. It took two of them to get to this place. Yes, maybe he was the driving force behind a lot of it, but she wasn't some blushing virgin. She'd known what she was getting into. Just last night *she* had agreed that she wanted more from this, just the same as he did, and that conviction had lasted a grand total of twelve hours.

She was never going to fight for this. For *him*. She was always waiting for the other foot to fall, to prove that it would never work and give her an excuse to run.

Knowing that didn't make the loss easier to bear.

"Quinn?"

He turned around, harsh disappointment searing through him when he recognized Hope walking down the row between vines to him. *Not Aubry. Hope.* It wasn't her fault he had been under the apparently insane assumption that maybe Aubry had changed her mind and come after him.

Why would she, though? He closed the door pretty fucking firmly on her. She had no reason to think he'd welcome her if she did come after him.

He tried to put a smile on his face, but the expression never made it. "Hey, Hope."

"Are you okay? I saw you head into the vineyard and…" She trailed off with a shrug. "I know I don't exactly deserve your secrets, but if you want to talk, I'm here."

He did, but dumping his shit on her wasn't fair.

"Nah, I'm good." He turned back in the direction he'd come from. Missing his sister's wedding because he was throwing a bitch fit wasn't an option, which meant they both had to head back now. "How are things with you? I haven't seen you since…" He realized what he'd been about to say and stopped cold.

"Since the car accident that killed my brother and put me in the hospital for ages? I know." She laid a hand on his forearm. "It's okay. It was a long time ago. I mean, I still miss John."

"I do, too." He didn't normally carry around the guilt that Daniel did, but standing here in front of John's little sister made it hard to remember why. They should have kept better tabs on Hope. Tried harder. Something. "I know it's been said before, but I'm—"

"Don't." She shook her head. "Don't apologize to me again. I'm walking, which is better than they'd hoped for after the crash. Like I said, it was a long time ago." She hesitated. "How… How is Daniel?"

He couldn't tell her the truth—that Daniel was a mess. It would just hurt her, and if she'd actually managed to move on with her life after what happened thirteen years ago, she deserved better than to be brought down by the fact that her ex—and her brother's best friend—didn't walk away from that night and that car crash whole any more than she did. The only difference was that Daniel's scars weren't physical. "He's doing okay."

Hope frowned. "You just lied to me."

Fuck. He'd forgotten she had a knack for reading people. Luckily, they reached the end of the row before he had to answer. He looked around, but Aubry was nowhere to be seen. "Let's get in there before

Jenny starts panicking that she's missing half the wedding party."

Hope's sigh was nearly inaudible. "Yeah, let's do that." They walked across the lawn and into the lobby, retracing the path he'd taken following Aubry out.

Quinn didn't respond, too focused on searching the crowd for her. Nothing. Maybe she went back to the room to lick her wounds. Yeah, that had to be it. He eyed the elevator, silently debating whether he had enough time to get up and back before someone came looking for him.

Brad appeared, deciding that for him. "There you guys are. We're about to start corralling people into the chapel. Hope, Jenny is looking for you."

Hope gave him one last significant look and then disappeared through a gap in people. He had a feeling he wouldn't be seeing the last of her anytime soon. He had bigger things to worry about. Like his sister's wedding.

Like the fact that he had no fucking idea where Aubry was.

The entire ceremony passed in a blur. He knew he should focus on what was going on at the altar, but he kept searching the crowd for a distinctive head of red hair and coming up with nothing. And why wouldn't he? The only reason she'd come to the wedding was because he'd convinced her to. If she wasn't with him, she wouldn't be here. Knowing that didn't stop him from looking for her, though.

The problem was he had no idea what he would say when he *did* find her. Nothing had changed, not really. They still had too many issues to be able to iron things out. She was still too determined to sabotage things.

He was still too stubborn for either of their own goods.

It seemed like he blinked and it was time for the reception. Quinn took the opportunity to make his excuses about forgetting something in his room and heading upstairs. He doubted he'd fooled anyone, but it didn't matter because he was going to figure this shit out. Somehow.

He'd spent so much time building up what he was going to say—or trying to—that it took him a full ten seconds to register that their room was empty. More than empty. When he looked closer, he realized her suitcase and laptop bag were gone.

Quinn rushed downstairs to the front desk. A kid who didn't look old enough to drink was manning it. "Did a redhead come through here? About this tall"— he held his hand up—"and probably kind of pissed." Because of him.

The kid shifted, eyeing him like he was going to Hulk out or something. "Yeah, she was pretty upset."

Tell me something I don't know. "She left?"

"Called a cab to the airport thirty minutes ago."

The *airport*. Quinn rocked back on his heels, trying to process the fact that she would rather get into what she thought was a flying deathtrap than stay here another moment with him.

Fuck, fuck, fuck.

CHAPTER SEVENTEEN

Aubry was the very definition of a hot mess by the time she made it back to Devil's Falls. She left the rental car parked on the street and trudged through the back door of Cups and Kittens, needing nothing more than to be surrounded by the safety of her four walls and maybe to hide for a few years until her aching chest stopped reminding her how stupid it was for her to let herself get her heart broken by Quinn Baldwyn.

You didn't even like him a week ago, and you can get back to that point...eventually.

Except she wasn't sure she could fully erase the feeling of his hands on her skin and his voice in her ear, drawing out her dirtiest fantasies and bringing them to life.

How the hell did someone even bounce back from that sort of thing?

She didn't think it was possible.

She closed the door behind her and ran smack dab into a person. Aubry jumped back with a shriek, her bags flying, and almost tripped over her own feet. "What the hell?"

"Aubry?"

God*damn*it. She shoved her hair back. "What are you doing here, Daniel?"

Jules's cousin looked as shitty as she felt, dark circles beneath his equally dark eyes and like he might have lost weight recently. Since Aubry couldn't remember the last time he'd actually come into town, she wasn't sure how recently it was, but the fact that he was *here* instead of at the Rodriguez ranch spoke volumes. Or it would as soon as she figured out what he wanted. "Did Quinn send you? Because he can fuck right off and go jump into bed with Hope for all I care." She was half surprised her pants didn't burst into spontaneous flame at that lie.

Daniel frowned. "What are you talking about? Hope?" He went pale beneath his tan skin. "Hope was there?"

Aubry was too wrapped up in her pain to pause, a runaway train with no hope of stopping. "I'm talking about Quinn. He's absurdly tall and, while pleasing to the eye, is equally infuriating and just plain man-stupid. And—"

"And obviously something went terribly wrong while you two were at the wedding."

She couldn't talk to him about this. Not only was he Quinn's best friend but... Daniel might not be in on her long list of people she despised—which basically amounted to the entire world outside her tiny circle—but he wasn't one of *her* people. That meant she was more likely to curl up in a ball and waste away than to spill her guts to him. "It's nothing."

His mouth tightened. "I know nothing when I see it, and that's not what's written all over your face."

For fuck's sake. "Aren't you supposed to be the quiet and brooding one who keeps to himself? Keep to yourself, Rodriguez."

But he stepped in front of her. "Jules has her hands full with Adam right now, not that either of them would admit as much, and you don't have friends other than Jules."

"Wow, thanks. You're making me feel so much better." But, strangely enough, the sarcasm *was* making her feel better. A little.

Daniel rolled his eyes. "My point is that you don't have a single damn person to talk to and you look like you need to talk."

"I thought I looked like shit."

"Those two things are not mutually exclusive." He picked up her suitcase and set it down next to the stairs leading up to the apartment she used to share with Jules. "Now, sit your contrary ass down. I'll be right back."

"Holy shit, Rodriguez, I think you've strung together more words in the last five minutes than I've heard you speak in the last five years."

He snorted. "And you're already feeling more like yourself. Sit."

She sat. Really, it wasn't like she had anywhere else to be, and her self-flagellation could wait a few minutes. He was right—she couldn't call Jules now any more than she could have called Jules earlier. This mess was one entirely of her own making, and dumping it on her best friend when she was otherwise occupied with things that were actually important would be a dick move.

Daniel reappeared a few minutes later with two mugs of coffee in hand, trailing Mr. Winkles and Ninja Kitteh behind him. The latter immediately jumped into Aubry's lap and made himself at home. She ran her hand down the cat's back and accepted the cup of coffee. "I don't think I want to talk about it."

"I kind of think you do, since you didn't tell me to

fuck off and then run upstairs to barricade yourself in that apartment."

He had a point. Damn Quinn for making her learn to open up. She took a sip of the coffee. It should be too suffocating outside for hot coffee, but there was something really comforting about holding a mug of warmth in her hands. *Where to begin?* "I suppose you heard about my and Quinn's brilliant plan."

"I did."

Of course he had. The rumor mill in Devil's Falls surprised even her sometimes. Not that the whole thing with Quinn had been a secret, exactly, but now she was going to have to face people *looking* at her—and probably agreeing with Quinn that she was entirely unsuitable to date for real.

She winced. *Yep. Still hurts.*

"It goes like this—things got a little out of control on the sexual front." She ignored the look on his face like he might be having instant regrets about giving her a chance to talk about this. Because apparently she *did* need to talk it out. "Like crazy-good out of control."

"Spare me the details. Please."

Right. He wasn't Jules. He was just her stand-in. "Long story, short—it turns out I don't totally despise Quinn and maybe I might have made the mistake—no doubt fueled by the crazy-good out of control sex—of maybe falling for him just a little. Which is bad."

"Why is it bad?"

She wouldn't have had to explain that to Jules... except maybe she would have asked the same question. Aubry took another sip of coffee. "Because it would never work. There's a reason we've hated each other from the moment we met, and a little sex doesn't change that." No matter how much she'd fooled herself into thinking it might. "It wasn't so bad at my convention, but once we got to that damn hotel in Napa Valley, it was like stepping into a different world—a world where I don't fit."

"That's not Quinn's world anymore."

Which was exactly what Quinn had said. "You didn't see him there, Jul—er, Daniel. He fits. He might pretend he doesn't, but he does. Mingling with those people—a good portion of which are his family—is second nature."

"Because if he didn't learn how to deal with them, that world would have eaten him alive." He held up a hand when she started to argue. "Here's the deal, Aubry. I don't know what else happened, but if that's your biggest beef with him, it's bullshit. I've known him since we were kids in grade school, and he's never wanted that life—not in thirty-four years—so I kind of doubt he suddenly developed a desire to put on a stupid monkey suit and dance to the tune his parents set."

"We don't fit."

"You keep saying that. I don't know that you'd be this torn up about the whole thing if it was true."

"What?"

Daniel sat on the step next to her, careful not to touch her. "The things that cut the deepest are the desires for things we want most."

She blinked. "Damn, Daniel, that's deep."

"I read it in a fortune cookie."

"No, you didn't." She closed her eyes for a few seconds, letting Ninja Kitteh's purrs vibrate through her. "I don't know how much Jules has told you about me—"

"She hasn't told me shit, but I'm not an idiot. You're anti-social to an alarming degree, you never talk about your past, and in the years I've known you, you've never left town to visit your family or had them come through here. That kind of thing speaks for itself."

Maybe it did. She hadn't been aware anyone noticed that last bit, but then Daniel was just full of surprises today. "Okay, fine. I like him. A lot. A whole hell of a lot. I feel like I found a missing piece of myself that I didn't even know was missing. Which is really freaking scary. Because if he gave it to me, he can take it away." It kind of felt like he already had. She took a hasty drink of her coffee and almost scalded her throat.

"Does he feel the same?"

"Not anymore." She sounded so damn miserable it made her sick. "He said he wanted to date me, to make a real go of it, but the first time I freak out, he bailed." She turned to Daniel. "You know me. You know how often I freak out."

"Pretty sure it's a daily thing."

"Exactly. If the first bump in the road is the one that derails us, it was never going to work." Which was exactly what he'd said.

"Did you tell him that you're in love with him?"

She started, earning a warning hiss from Ninja Kitteh. "What? Don't say that word!"

"Yeah, I thought so." He sighed. "That shit is worth fighting for, Aubry. Believe me. It sounds like you guys had a hell of a fight, but Quinn's family doesn't exactly bring out the best in anyone. Why don't you give it a few days and call him?"

"I'd rather chew off my own arm."

He gave her a significant look. "No, you wouldn't. You two are the most prideful people I've ever met, but if one of you doesn't bend, you're going to lose this thing before you even had a chance to enjoy it."

That thought scared her. It scared her a lot.

What scared her even more was the idea of putting herself out there and having him grind what was left of her heart to dust. "I don't know if I can."

"Think about it." He stood. "Now, why don't you go take a nap or something? You look like shit."

"Flatterer."

"Only when the situation calls for it." He hesitated. "If you need anything before Jules gets back into town...you can call me."

It couldn't have been easy for him to offer—no easier than it was for her to open up to him in the first place. She managed a smile. "Daniel Rodriguez, you are a nice guy."

"Don't go spreading that shit around." He ruffled her hair and then he was gone, striding out the back door and leaving her alone once again, with only her misery for company.

She looked down. "Well, my misery and Ninja Kitteh." Aubry pushed to her feet, picking up the cat with one hand as she did. Once she was settled in upstairs, she picked up her Xbox controller, fully intending to lose herself in Deathmatch. But once she turned the console on, she just stared at the home screen. "Oh my God, I don't even want to shoot people. I'm so damn broken." She slouched down on the couch, cuddling the cat close.

Daniel's words kept rolling through her head. *Fight for it. Fight for him.*

Love.

Surely he was wrong. A person couldn't fall in love in five days. It was impossible. Yeah, Aubry had known Quinn for over a year now, but she hadn't even *liked* him until after they'd started having sex... Had she?

Sure, she kind of admired how hard he worked on the Rodriguez ranch, and even when she was snarly at him, sometimes he'd say something particularly witty and she'd be almost in awe of it, but those weren't exactly elements of a long-lasting relationship.

How about the fact that he took every single verbal punch you threw at him and came back for more? Or maybe that he actually listens, *which is more than you can say for most of the people you've encountered in your life. Or that he went out of his way to draw you out of your shell and make you comfortable while pressing up against your boundaries?*

Then there was the sex. She'd had sex before, but she'd never known it could be like *that*—soft and hard and dirty and full of laughter.

Kind of like Quinn himself.

"Oh fuck. I'm in love with Quinn Baldwyn."

• • •

The entire drive back to Devil's Falls, Quinn was determined to let that crazy woman have her way and do his damnedest never to see her again. It would be hard to stay away from her with them living in the same town, but he was more than up to the challenge.

She *flew away* from him. He'd said some shitty things, but she had, too. And the first chance she had, she rabbited back to Devil's Falls, where she was probably already holed up in her apartment with her gaming system and online worshippers.

He should just let her stew.

He *would* just let her stew.

Damn it, he would.

That righteous indignation got him through the first day back on the ranch, but after the sun went down and he retreated to his house, doubts started to creep in. He popped open a beer and dropped onto his couch, wondering what she was up to. Probably playing that damn game of hers.

Maybe she's even playing with Kurt right now.

He forced himself to unclench his fist from the longneck. It wasn't his business if she was talking to some other guy—or if she was doing more than talking. She *left* him. She hadn't even given him a chance to find her and make things right. Not that he was in a big rush to do that. He wasn't. He hadn't done anything wrong. Much.

A knock sounded on his front door and he was pathetically grateful for the distraction. Quinn pushed to his feet and trudged over to open the door. He frowned at Daniel. "What are you doing here?"

"Saving you from yourself apparently." He shouldered past Quinn and stalked through the living room and into the kitchen.

Mildly amused, Quinn followed. "I wasn't aware I needed saving."

"Of course you do. Normally I'd leave this meddling shit to my cousin, but since she's out of town until the end of the week, I'm stepping in."

He leaned against the counter. "It might help if you explained what the hell you're talking about."

Daniel huffed out a breath. "Forgive the fuck out of me if I'm not good at this matchmaking shit and going about it wrong."

Matchmaking— Oh, hell no. "I don't need you interfering."

"Apparently that's exactly what you need because it's been three damn days and you're showing no sign of coming to your senses. Aubry's even more prideful than you are and you hurt her." Daniel drained half his beer. "Look, this isn't my thing and normally I'd just stay out of it, but if you actually told her you want to date her, letting a little thing like your family making you both insane isn't a good enough reason to call the whole thing off."

She'd talked to Daniel about them? He wasn't sure what he thought about that. "What did she say?"

"That." He pointed at Quinn. "That's all I need to know. You like her, a whole hell of a lot, judging by the way you moped around today."

"I don't mope." He might have moped.

"Not normally, no. Which is why I'm here."

He stared at his friend. "What do you care if I'm fucking things up with Aubry?"

"Because, as I told her, this thing you have doesn't come around all that often and throwing it away for a stupid reason is bullshit. Fight for her, you dickwad."

Quinn blinked. He'd never seen Daniel so…fierce. "I didn't think you knew Aubry that well."

"I know her as well as I know anyone else in this town."

Then why... The pieces clicked into place with a snap that left Quinn feeling like a damn fool. This wasn't about Aubry at all. "She told you that Hope was at the wedding."

The bleak look on Daniel's face was all the answer he needed. He should have seen this coming. Call him crazy, though, but he never expected his friend to talk to his girl.

She's not my girl. We both made damn sure of that.

"Daniel—"

He held up a hand. "I don't need your sympathy or your pity. I just need you to get over yourself long enough to really think about if whatever you fought about is worth losing the connection you have with Aubry." He finished off his beer. "If it is, then so be it. But if you have any doubts—*any*—then you need to fix this, Quinn. I'm not fucking kidding. You'll kick yourself for the rest of your life if you don't."

"You could call her, you know."

Daniel's smile was more than a little bittersweet. "No, I can't." He walked out of the kitchen, patting Quinn on the shoulder as he went.

He wanted to call his friend back, to force him to talk about the shit that was obviously bothering him—and equally obviously had nothing to do with Quinn and Aubry—but Daniel had resisted opening up about either John or Hope for the last thirteen years. That wasn't something that was going to magically change, him interfering in Quinn's love life or no.

The problem was...he was right.

That fight had been awful—worse than awful. It seriously fucking sucked to have Aubry doubt him on so many different levels that she was willing to shit on everything they shared together, but what did he expect? She had a lifetime of feeling like she never quite measured up and five days with him wasn't going to magically change that. He *knew* she was neurotic and jumped to conclusions and he'd still gone out of his way to punish her for the whole damn thing the second she dropped the ball. Could she have had a little more faith? Fuck yeah. But it took two to tango, and he'd more than dropped his end.

The thought of spending the rest of his life on the periphery of hers...

It stung. It more than stung. It flat out *hurt*.

He didn't want to stand by and watch her settle down with some geeky guy. Marry him. Have little geeky babies with him.

Quinn wanted her to have geeky babies with *him*.

"Fuck." He rubbed a hand over his face. It was time to face the facts, and the fact was he was hopelessly in love with that crazy redhead. "Damn it. I have to fix this."

He just needed to figure out how.

CHAPTER EIGHTEEN

Aubry looked at her phone for the fourth time, sure that she was in the wrong place. Earlier today, she'd finally dredged up the courage to text Quinn. Sure it'd been a *Hey* and not full of all the things she really needed to say, but it was *something*. An hour later he'd responded, but it wasn't much of a response at all.

Quinn had texted her with an address and, despite her wanting to demand an explanation, she was letting go of her issues long enough to put on her big girl panties and meet him. That's what people in love did, right? Crazy shit.

She just didn't expect it to be *this* crazy.

"I think I might actually get serial killed tonight." She peered out of the windshield of Jules's truck, wishing her friend was here. But by the time Jules had called her and got the whole sordid story out of her, she'd already put herself out there in a way she couldn't take back. Because of Quinn. Because she wanted to prove to him she wasn't a completely hopeless basket case. Just mostly hopeless. Maybe like sixty-five percent hopeless.

One last check of her phone confirmed she was, in fact, here. Here being a field in the middle of nowhere when night had fallen and the headlights barely made a dent in the darkness. She gripped the steering wheel. "I'm reasonably sure that Quinn didn't invite me out here to kill me. So there's that."

A knock on the window had her screaming. She

cursed when she saw the man in question on the other side of the glass. He gave her a shit-eating grin. "Scared?"

"Only totally." And feeling particularly ridiculous about it now that she was seeing him for the first time in over a week. Eight days, four hours, and some-odd minutes.

Not that she was counting.

He looked good in his white T-shirt and faded blue jeans. Better than good. Downright edible.

And she was most definitely stalling.

Aubry took up a shoring breath and opened the truck door. "I don't know why we couldn't have talked in Cups and Kittens."

"Because I'm not looking for an audience." He motioned for her to follow him. "Come on." He led the way deeper into the field, and it took Aubry a few minutes to realize they were actually on a dirt road.

"Well, you're right about us having to talk. I screwed up. I'm woman enough to admit that. I'm in therapy for a reason, though I think I need to fire my therapist because you did more good in a week than she's done in years."

"Aubry."

But she couldn't stop. If she didn't get this out, she might never say it. "And I know to say I'm a basket case is understating the problem, and that I turned every single one of my issues on you at your sister's wedding, and I'm *sorry*, okay? I can't promise I won't have meltdowns and anxiety attacks and probably die in the first wave of the zombie apocalypse, but I will try to be better. I promise I'll try."

He laughed softly. "Peaches, you're killing me."

Her eyes slowly adjusted to the darkness, and her mouth dropped open when Quinn stopped at the end of the track. "Is that—?"

"Old drive-in movie theater? Yeah. It hasn't been used in over ten years, but I know a guy who knows a guy."

"Like everyone else in Devil's Falls." She pressed her hand to her mouth. "Sorry, that was uncalled for. Did I mention I'm working on my issues?"

"I happen to like your smart mouth. Come here." He motioned her closer, and she frowned when she made out his truck facing away from the screen, a couch in the bed of it. Quinn lifted her up and she took a seat on the couch, wondering what the hell was going on. He sat next to her, looking unsure for the first time since she'd known him. "I fucked up."

"Quinn—"

"I let you ramble on. It's my turn now. There isn't a relationship worth having that doesn't have its ups and downs and bumps along the road. I knew that and I still struck out at you when we were fighting. It wasn't fair and it wasn't right, and I'm sorry." He didn't reach out for her, but he looked like he wanted to. He hesitated. "I know we don't have a lot in common outside the bedroom, but I think what we *do* have is more than enough. We have the same sense of humor, and that's more than most couples can say. I like how stubborn you are, and you're sexy as fuck when you get that focused look on your face when you're all up in your own head."

It was almost too good to be true. Her first instinct was to argue with him, but she bit her lip and forced herself to hold still and *listen*. Because he wasn't finished yet.

"I think we might be able to learn a thing or two from each other along the way, too." He reached behind the couch and a whirling noise started up.

Aubry turned to the big screen and her jaw dropped open. "Oh, Quinn." It was Deathmatch, on a massive screen, in the middle of a field. "How did you—?"

"How else am I going to convince you that the outdoors isn't out to get you?" He grinned, but the expression fell away. "It might not be easy, peaches, but I'm willing to fight for you. Will you do the same for me?"

Like there was any other answer. "Yes." She threw herself into his arms and kissed him with everything she had. Aubry pulled away enough to say, "I submitted my game."

His eyes went wide. "What?"

"You're right. I can't spend my whole life hiding because I'm afraid of being hurt. Look at what you inspired me to do. I went to Deathcon. I got into one of those flying death traps without being tranquilized. I submitted my game." She gave a tentative smile. "I couldn't have done it without you. You make me want to be, if not a better person, at least one who's slightly more higher functioning in the greater society."

"I didn't do that, peaches. *You* did." He settled her against him. "I'm proud of you."

"We're an unstoppable partnership, that's for damn sure."

"You're amazing." He framed her face with his hands, his thumbs feathering over her cheekbones. "I have to say, that I'm pretty much in love with your contrary ass, Aubry Kaiser."

Her entire heart lit up like the Fourth of July. "That's good, because I'm head over heels for you." She kissed him again. "I can't believe you did all this for me."

He rearranged her beneath his arm. "You have to admit, it's pretty damn gorgeous out here."

"I do, though I fully expect you to save my ass if mutant crocodiles show up."

"Crocodiles, zombies, serial killers, and mutants of every variety."

"If that's not a declaration of love I can get behind, I don't know what is."

EPILOGUE

Aubry couldn't calm down, and she sure as hell couldn't sit still. She felt like Jules must on a daily basis—too much energy for anyone's health. She shot a nervous glance at the television that she'd jury-rigged to her computer. *I can't believe I'm doing this.*

"Peaches?"

If anything, her tension ramped up a notch at the sound of Quinn's voice, even as the rest of her went all melty. She even managed a smile as his big frame filled the doorway. "Hey."

Quinn's gaze slid over her in a move she could almost feel. "You look half a second from losing it. What's going on?" He shifted, sliding one hand behind his back, and she zeroed in on him.

"What's that?"

"Oh, no. You're the one who's been acting sneaky and underhanded for the last few days—*you* go first." He stepped fully into the apartment and looked around. "I forgot how tiny everything is in here. It's like stepping into a dollhouse."

They hadn't spent much time here in the last few months. It turned out that Quinn had a great setup for gaming and, beyond that, playing Deathmatch *with* him was even more fun than playing with the faceless people on the Internet. In turn, he'd drawn her out of her shell a little bit further with each month they were together.

She lifted her chin. "That's just because everything

in your house has to be fit for a giant or it will collapse under your immense weight."

He laughed. "You like that I'm immense."

Yeah, she really, really did. Aubry took a step back and motioned to the couch. It looked shabby compared to his most excellent leather one, but they weren't going to be here for long. "Sit."

"Is this the part where you strap that contraption from Clockwork Orange to my eyelids and try to convince me—again—to see that damn movie?"

"Power Rangers is going to be *sublime*, and I'll thank you kindly to stop referring to it as 'that damn movie.'" But she couldn't help the smile that slipped through.

Quinn sat where she motioned to and took the Xbox controller she handed him. "How about a deal? I'll go see that movie—without bitching and moaning about it—if you come riding with me."

"Riding." She narrowed her eyes. "You wouldn't be trying to convince me to get on the back of one of those hellbeasts would you? Because those damn animals are out to get me."

"Peaches, they're horses, not hellbeasts."

"I disagree. The Headless Horseman rides one— and so does the Wild Hunt. I could go on." When he just watched her, an amused smile on his face, she sighed. "I'll *consider* it."

"Good enough." He turned to look at the TV. "So, if you didn't lure me here for nefarious purposes, why *are* we here?"

As if on cue, her nerves kicked up a notch, her stomach twisting. She took a breath, counting slowly in her head. The panic didn't completely dissipate, but her voice sounded mostly normal when she spoke. "I have something to show you."

It took far too little time to get things up and running, the screen clearing to display an armored knight with a sword almost as big as he was. She bit her lip. "You've gamed enough in the last few months to muddle through the controls."

Quinn sent his character forward, moving around the room. She surveyed it with a critical eye. It could use another layer of detail. She *knew* she should have waited. "It's not finished—"

"This is your game, peaches?" He leaned forward, studying the screen as his character swung the sword, chopping the table into splinters. "This is fucking fantastic. Where's something for me to kill?"

"I love you."

"I love you, too." He motioned to the screen. "Now, I know for a fact you wouldn't have put a demo in my hands if there wasn't something to murder. Point me in the right direction."

She gave him curt instructions, watching as he hacked his way through a group of zombies. "Your gaming skills have gotten impressive."

"I have this really hot girlfriend who's into that sort of thing." He grinned without taking his eyes off the screen. "The detail in the blood spatter is impressive. I expect nothing less. Where to next?"

This was the moment of truth. She tried to keep her tone cool and confident. "Go check out that shack in the woods?"

"You really know how to show a guy a good time. What are the odds of encountering more zombies?"

Not great. "Why don't you go over there and find

out for yourself?"

His character opened the door and Quinn went still. She tried to see it from his point of view. Was the text not clear? God, she'd fucked this up, hadn't she? "This was a dumb idea." She reached over his shoulder to grab the controller, but he caught her wrist, his gaze never leaving the screen.

"Am I reading this right, peaches? Because that sure as fuck looks like a marriage proposal from where I'm sitting."

Considering there was a banner strung across the inside of the cabin reading Will You Marry Me? she didn't see how it could be anything else. Aubry didn't know how proposals were supposed to go, but she was pretty damn sure he was supposed to be doing... something...other than sitting there like a Quinn-shaped statue.

Her throat tried to close and she made a grab for the controller with her other hand. "Let's pretend this never happened."

He exhaled a long breath. "We're going to laugh about this one day."

She felt more like throwing herself in front of a runaway train. Aubry yanked against his hold, but he didn't release her. "I think I'm just going to die of humiliation instead."

"Come here." He towed her around the couch to sit next to him. "Funny story."

"This doesn't feel funny."

He shot her a look. "I had a plan—I might even go as far to say I had a *brilliant* plan."

What the hell was he talking about? "Quinn—"

"Shhh. It's my turn now." He pulled a small black

moleskin book out of his back pocket. "After we left here, I was going to take you into El Paso to that little B&B where we spent that first night together."

"It was a great first night." She managed to smile just thinking about it.

"It was." He handed her the notebook. "We're still going, by the way. But I'm giving this to you now."

"What is it?" There weren't any markings on the outside, and it was held closed with a black elastic band.

"Open it and find out for yourself."

Hearing her earlier words echoed back to her made her heartbeat pick up. She carefully took the band off and opened the book. It took her a few seconds to understand the words written across the top of the first page in neat block letters. *In case of zombies…*

Below it was a bulleted list detailing how she and Quinn would survive a zombie apocalypse. Aubry looked up, looked back down, pressed her lips together, and turned the page. Each page detailed a different event.

In case of mutant alligators…
In case of mutant cannibals…
In case of ritual sacrifice…

It went on and on, each event one they survived. Together. Aubry turned the last page and read the larger letters. *Marry me, peaches.* "Great minds think alike."

"*That's* all you have to say?"

She smiled so wide she knew she had to look goofy as hell, and she didn't give a damn. "I'll say yes if you do."

"Yes. As if there was any question." Quinn pulled

her into his arms and kissed her. "I love you."

She'd never been one to believe in happily-ever-afters—until Quinn. And now...

Aubry kissed him again, pushing him back against the couch. And now she was so damn ready to take the next step into her very own happily-ever-after. "I love you, too. And yes. Fuck yes. Hell to the yes. I would love to marry you, Quinn Baldwyn."

ACKNOWLEDGMENTS

Thanks to God, for the journey that made this book all the better for the wait.

Big thanks to Heather Howland for helping me shape this beast into a beauty and for loving Quinn and Aubry as much as I do!

Huge thanks to Mandy and the team at Barclay Publicity for being so supportive and being part of this journey with me!

Hugs and thanks to Julia Particka, Piper Drake, and Hilary Brady for being my go-tos for everything from plotting to sharing a hot beverage. You all are amazing and I couldn't have done it without you!

Thank you to my family for their endless patience, and all my thanks and love to Tim. Kisses, babe!

A *Fool* FOR YOU

FOOLPROOF LOVE #3

KATEE ROBERT

Dear Reader,

The Foolproof Love series is so incredibly close to my heart for many different reasons. It was the first category romance series I ever contracted, and it went through many incarnations before finding its way into your hands. It's also filled to the brim with some of my favorite characters and stories that I've written to date. The series wraps up with Daniel and Hope's story. It's been a long time in coming, and they've both had quite the winding journey through endlessly rocky roads.

For the heroes in this series, the car wreck that happened thirteen years previous was the turning point in a lot of ways. It spurred Adam into leaving Devil's Falls for all but the shortest visits. It was the shot of reality Quinn needed to leave his family's plans behind him for good. But for Daniel, it was the one event he can't get past. He's been stuck in place ever since, and he needs some meddling to get him back to reality. And we all know that meddling is what the Rodriguez family does best.

We met Hope briefly in the last book, and words cannot encompass my love for her. She's a fighter and a survivor and she's probably more well-adjusted than most of the heroines I write… Except when it comes to her blast from the past. There's no telling what will happen when two people who loved so intensely and fell apart so spectacularly come together again.

So settle in, lovely readers. I hope you enjoy reading this story as much as I enjoyed writing it.

This one's for you.

Katee

To my readers.

CHAPTER ONE

Hope Moore held her breath as she passed the sign declaring Welcome to Devil's Falls. She hadn't crossed the town boundary in thirteen years, not since she sat next to an open grave as they lowered her brother into the ground. Not since she turned her back on her entire life here, whisked away by her parents to the best medical facilities Texas had to offer.

She touched her knee. She'd never cheered again, never run track, never done any of the things she'd had planned when she was eighteen and had graduated high school with stars in her eyes.

Stars in her eyes, and love in her heart.

Neither had lasted past that car crash.

Oh, it had taken the love a lot longer to die than it had her knee, but Daniel Rodriguez made sure she knew where she stood with him.

She caught herself taking her foot off the gas and picked up speed again. There was no telling if she'd see him while she was here, but it couldn't matter. She'd moved past what happened that night, moved past the disappointment that she'd almost let sour everything else about her life. It might not have happened like she planned, but she'd made the best of her college experience, and she'd gone on to create a successful little niche for herself, helping people and institutions with too much money on their hands create trusts and scholarships for those in need.

And now Hope was back in town to finally do that

in her brother's memory.

She pulled onto Main Street, heading for the only lodgings someone out of town with no relatives to stay with would consider—Sara Jane's B&B. It was a nice little place, but Sara Jane was nosy to a criminal degree and gossiped more than anyone Hope had ever come across. The second she checked in and went up to her room, everyone with a phone would be getting a call letting them know that she was back in town.

It wasn't that it was a secret, but she couldn't help but feel that she'd always be John Moore's little sister, the one who survived when her older brother—her better in a lot of ways—didn't. She *knew* that was her own insecurity. She'd had too many years of therapy to believe anything else, except in her darkest heart of hearts, the place she didn't let see the light any more than strictly necessary.

But it was hard to ignore that little voice when driving through Devil's Falls. No, not through. *To.* This was her destination.

Her parents hadn't been too thrilled about her coming back, even for a limited time, but even they couldn't deny that this scholarship she was here to set up was a good thing—the right way to honor John. He'd been in the middle of a full ride at the University of Texas when he was killed, and it made sense to set it up to allow other kids the opportunity he'd never be able to realize.

She pressed a hand to her chest and pulled into the nearest parking spot against the curb. *God, even after all this time, it still hurts.* Most days it didn't. He'd been gone long enough that she'd processed her grief as much as one person could process grief, and she was able to focus on the good memories.

Most days.

Her eyes focused on the sign she'd been staring blindly at, and she frowned. Cups and Kittens. That was new. In a town as mired in the past as Devil's Falls, change was something of a novelty. Or maybe she was biased in a negative way, because the only thing this town held for her was memories. Some bad, mostly good, all dust now.

Pathetically grateful for something external to focus on, she climbed out of her car and looked at the cheery window painting depicting kittens frolicking in between flowers.

The B&B could wait a little while longer. Her meeting with the town board wasn't until tomorrow, so there was no reason she couldn't do a little poking around in the meantime. Thirteen years was a long time. If anyone had asked her, she would have joked that she hadn't expected anything about Devil's Falls to change while she was gone.

Apparently she'd been wrong.

She pushed through the door and froze in the face of a pair of cats staring at her from their perch on a table overlooking the big window in the front. The sight surprised a laugh out of her. "Cups and Kittens, indeed."

"In the most literal sense."

She glanced over at the woman behind the counter, a third cat lounging near the register. Familiarity rolled over Hope. "Jules Rodriguez." Daniel's little cousin. Not so little anymore. Last time she'd seen Jules, the girl had been lanky to an almost awkward degree and had braces with bright green bands. She'd grown up pretty, and there was more of Daniel about her now than there had been when she was a kid.

Or maybe I'm just back in Devil's Falls and seeing Daniel wherever I look.

Jules's dark eyes cleared. "Hope? What are you doing back in town?" She hesitated. "I don't suppose you're here to sweep my brooding cousin off his feet and shove him back into real life?"

Her mind tripped over itself trying to keep up with the other woman's verbal gymnastics. Jules had always been like that, now that she thought about it—a bright and bubbly steamroller. She tried to weed her way through what the woman had just said, but there was only one thing she could focus on. Daniel. Always Daniel. "What do you mean, back into real life?"

"Well, you know."

No, she really didn't. She studied Jules's face, the way she wouldn't quite meet her eyes. "Is he okay?" She hadn't missed the way Quinn Baldwyn had frozen up when she'd asked that same question a few weeks ago at his sister's wedding, and worry had been simmering in the back of her mind ever since, no matter how many times she told herself it wasn't any of her business. Daniel was a grown man, and he had always been more than capable of taking care of himself—and everyone else around him. Things changed, but she couldn't see *that* changing.

Jules shifted, her hand darting out to pet the calico on the counter and then darting away when the cat swiped at her. "Define okay."

It was none of her business. It stopped being her business a very long time ago.

But that didn't stop her from clearing her throat

and asking, "Is he...is he married?" *Did he build the house we always talked about and have those two wild boys and one sweet girl? Does he bring his wife waffles for breakfast in bed on the weekends?*

Oh my God, stop.

But Jules was already shaking her head, her mouth turning down. "Nope. No wife, no kids, no serious relationship in, well, thirteen years."

Hope blinked. "You're joking."

"I wish I was." A calculating look came into her eyes, but then she shook herself and it was all guileless enthusiasm. "What are you doing for dinner?" She rushed on without waiting for a response. "We're having a little thing with Quinn and my friend Aubry, and, well, I kind of went and married Adam Meyers."

Some things really do *change.* She remembered Adam, the wild-eyed boy who'd grown into a wild-eyed man, better than she remembered Jules. No one had expected him to come back to Devil's Falls after he blew out of town that last time, let alone to settle here and...get married. "Wow. What's Daniel have to say about that?"

"He was best man at our wedding." Jules laughed. "Though he was pretty furious at the beginning. Here, sit down. You look like you could use a coffee, and I'll tell you the story since we're generally pretty dead Thursday nights. Then I'll close up and we can go to dinner. The boys will love to see you. Quinn was just talking about you the other day."

Hope wasn't sure she actually agreed to any of it, but the next thing she knew, she was drinking coffee while a cat curled up in her lap and listening to Jules's wild tale about a fake relationship that turned into a real relationship. Somehow in the middle of that, she was bundled up into Jules's truck, and by then it was too late to change her mind.

She settled into her seat, consoling herself with the fact that Jules had very specifically *not* mentioned Daniel's name. There was no reason to think he'd be there, but it *would* be nice to reconnect with some of her old friends. As much as it had hurt when things went south with Daniel, knowing that she'd lost Quinn and Adam, too, had just been salt in the wound. She'd chased them around since she could toddle after her big brother and his friends, and they'd turned into true friends over the years. She understood why they hadn't reached out, but she wasn't going to turn down a chance to catch up with them.

It would probably be the only nice thing about being back in Devil's Falls.

• • •

"Not interested."

"You haven't even heard what I'm asking."

"Don't need to." Daniel Rodriguez leaned down and unbuckled Rita's saddle and hefted it off the horse's back. They'd had a good run today, the hot sun making it impossible to think too hard about anything other than whether a human being could roast alive in Texas in August. He hadn't yet, so that put the odds ever so slightly in his favor.

All he wanted was to finish here and head back to his place for a cold shower and an even colder beer.

It would just fucking figure that the universe had other ideas. He glanced up, but Aubry Kaiser hadn't moved. In fact, with her arms crossed over her chest and her chin up, all signs pointed to this adding up to an argument he couldn't possibly win.

Damn it.

"No."

She frowned harder. "It's your birthday. You can't just sit at home by yourself."

"Since it's my birthday, this is the one day a year I should be able to do *exactly* that with no one bitching at me." He regretted the harsh words almost as soon as they were out of his mouth, but Aubry wasn't like his little cousin. She was meaner than a rattler and twice as likely to bite.

She narrowed her amber eyes at him. "Your cousin misses you."

That explained why she was out here when he knew for a fact she thought horses were akin to goats—as in, the devil's own creatures. Hell, she was giving poor Rita a suspicious look even while guilt-tripping him using the one person in his life he couldn't say no to.

Which doesn't explain why Jules herself isn't here.

"She sees me on a regular basis."

"This is your birthday." Aubry sighed and rolled her eyes, looking put-upon. "Look, it goes like this—Jules has worked really hard to put together a surprise birthday party for you, and if you don't show up to be surprised, she's going to be crushed."

He stared. "I don't want a surprise birthday party." The fact that it was no longer a surprise said a whole lot about Aubry's priorities, and he couldn't blame her for that.

"Look at my face. This is the face of a woman who doesn't give two fucks what you care about. What *I* care about is Jules, and that means you're going to go shower off the smell of that animal and show up at their house in an hour, right on time." She paused, her brows slanting down in an expression that was downright forbidding. "You helped me out not too long ago, so I'm going to do you a solid and give you the lowdown. Ready?"

Fuck, no. "Sure."

"Jules is worried about you. Really worried. If you don't show up tonight, she's going to take that as a sign to go forward with plan B."

He knew he was going to regret it, but he still asked, "What's plan B?"

Aubry gave a tight smile. "A full-scale intervention with everyone in your life, including your parents. The kind where they sit you down in a circle and each speak their mind in the most uncomfortable way possible until you're ready to beg the ground to swallow you whole." Her smile dimmed. "She's worried about you, Daniel."

Everyone seemed worried about him, though they usually did him the courtesy of at least trying to hide the looks exchanged when they thought he wasn't looking. The whispered conversations with his various cousins and his parents. The never-ending work that was only there because they were throwing him a goddamn bone. It didn't seem to matter that he hadn't done anything requiring an intervention. He'd just stopped enjoying the company of people, mostly because he was such shitty company these days. But try telling that to the family, and they acted like he had just confessed to being an ax murderer.

At least Jules had mostly stayed out of it. Up until today.

He grabbed the curry brush and went over Rita's back. Aubry was right. Showing up to a party he didn't want on a day he sure as fuck didn't feel like celebrating was vastly preferable to the alternative. "Explain to me what the plan is."

She gave a grin that did nothing to reassure him. "Dinner and drinks. It'll be nice. Adam and Quinn miss you."

"I see those assholes every day." Kind of hard not to when they worked the ranch alongside him. It felt right to have Adam back, to have Quinn there, but at the same time it was a constant reminder that they were a man short.

And it was his fault.

"It's different and you know it," Aubry continued, obviously enjoying how miserable he was. She'd always been a mean one, which never failed to amuse him because Jules was her polar opposite—as bright and happy as a spring day. Rita shifted in her stall, and Aubry went even paler than she was normally. "Dinner starts at six. Don't be late." Then she was gone, moving at a clip fast enough that a less cautious man than Daniel would call it running.

He waited a good five minutes before he followed, hauling the saddle into the tack room and sorting out the bridle. He didn't begrudge Quinn his happiness—or Adam, for that matter—but sometimes it sure as fuck was hard to be around them and their women. The fact that one of those women was his little cousin barely entered into it.

He headed for his truck and took the pitted dirt road leading around the edge of his parents' property to the little house he'd built a few years ago. It wasn't anything fancy, but it got the job done, and it was far enough outside town that most people thought twice before stopping by unannounced.

Most people not including his family.

The shower did nothing to ward off the feeling of pending doom. It wasn't that he didn't like Jules or Adam or Quinn or whoever the fuck else was going to be at this damn party, but he wasn't in the partying sort of mood. Truth be told, he hadn't been in that mood for over a decade. It was almost enough to make him call the whole thing off, but the knowledge that Jules would have no problem bringing the party to him got him moving again. Not to mention the potential *intervention* he needed like he needed a hole in the head.

At least if he went there, he could hang out for the appropriate amount of time, make his excuses, and slip out while everyone else was occupied. Two hours, tops.

Feeling significantly better, he pulled on a pair of his favorite old jeans and a T-shirt and grabbed his keys. It struck him as he walked out the door that he was thirty-fucking-four years old. *How the hell did that happen?* He shook his head. He knew damn well how that happened. One day turned into a week, a month, a year, a decade. All while he kept on keeping, the world changing around him, but never changing enough.

He glanced at his watch. "Two hours starts when I get there."

CHAPTER TWO

Daniel figured out the entire party was a mistake ten minutes in, which was right around the time Adam and Quinn walked in the back door with a motherfucking *puppy*. He shook his head, backing away. "No."

"It was this or that little hellion Mr. Winkles."

Thinking of that asshole cat who currently resided in Jules's cat café, Daniel cringed. Then he made the mistake of looking at the dog in Quinn's arms. The big man dwarfed the tiny pup, which had to contribute to how cute the little fella was. He was a border collie and had big blue eyes and a patchy fur coloring that was black, brown, and white. His left ear flopped down, and if he wasn't the cutest little thing…

Goddamn it.

"I don't want a dog." His heart wasn't really in the protest, though, so when Quinn offered the pup, Daniel took him. The pup immediately scrambled up against him and licked his chin. "Though he's cute."

"She."

That startled a laugh out of him. "The last thing I need in my life is a woman, and both you assholes damn well know it."

Adam got a funny look on his face, one Daniel would have called guilty. "Yeah, well, about that. Brace yourself."

He didn't get a chance to ask what the fuck his friend meant by that because the front door opened behind him and Jules's voice rang out, "Honey, I'm home."

"Hey, sugar." But Adam's voice wasn't quite right, and he was looking over Daniel's right shoulder when Jules was clearly behind his left.

For one eternal moment, Daniel considered shouldering past his friends and walking out the back door. Whatever put *that* look on Quinn and Adam's faces wasn't something he wanted to deal with. They almost looked like they'd seen a ghost.

But his dad hadn't raised a coward, so he took a deep breath and turned around.

And froze.

She looks the same.

He blinked, but Hope Moore didn't disappear. She just stood in the doorway, her blond hair pulled back in an effortless ponytail, her face older than when he'd last seen her but more beautiful for the years written across it. Her body had filled out, her hips and breasts curvier than they'd been at eighteen. She didn't look like a girl anymore. No, Hope was full woman.

And then, because he couldn't help it, his gaze dropped to her left leg. Her skirt was too long to see the scar he knew must wind down her leg, the scar *he'd* put there. Knee replacements weren't pretty, and her bones had already been mangled by the time she made it to the hospital, her entire future ruined in the space of a single heartbeat.

Because of him.

She flinched, which was answer enough. He hadn't imagined it, and the handful of surgeries, the months and months of recovery, the loss of her cross-country scholarship, all of it, had really happened to her. *What's the ability to run compared to a brother? You fucked everything beyond recognition.* He dragged his attention back to her face, determined not to look at her leg again. He'd been the one responsible—the least he could do was avoid making her feel uncomfortable.

She recovered quickly, offering him a small, sad smile. "Hey, Daniel."

"What are you doing here?" It came out too harsh, but he didn't take the words back. Thirteen goddamn years and she chose *today* to show up in Devil's Falls? It wasn't a coincidence, and he had a feeling he knew whom to blame. He spun and pointed a finger at Quinn, keeping his hold on the pup gentle despite his growing anger. "You. What the fuck did you do?" He knew Quinn had seen Hope last month at his sister's wedding, which meant he'd opened his idiot mouth and said something to bring her home.

You should be thanking him.

Fuck that. She doesn't want to be here. If she did, she would have come back before now.

Quinn held up his hands. "Don't look at me. This isn't my style, and you know it."

He had a point. Both his friends were more direct than to pull some shit like this. Jules, though… Daniel turned to glare at her. "This is out of line—even for you."

For her part, she didn't look the least bit repentant. She propped her hands on her hips. "Fun fact—Hope is a grown woman who's more than capable of making her own decisions. She wandered into my shop and I was polite enough to invite her along. I didn't kidnap her." She motioned at Hope. "Tell him I didn't kidnap you."

Despite everything going on around them, Hope burst out laughing. Daniel's chest gave a lurch. Fuck, the woman's laugh could still do a number on him. All these years later, she should have sounded different from the innocent girl he'd been head over heels in love with. Too much had changed for her to still love life as much as she had back then.

Hadn't it?

Hope shook her head, still laughing. "I can attest that I drove into town of my own free will. I take no responsibility for what happened after that cup of coffee. Jules is a hard woman to say no to." She pinned him in place with those dark eyes. "Happy birthday, Danny."

No one had called him that in…well, hell, in thirteen years. Hearing it on her lips nearly had him crossing the room to her and seeing what else was the same. Common sense stopped him cold. Whatever had brought Hope back into town, she wasn't here for him. There was no forgiving what he'd done, and he'd be worse than a fool to forget that.

It took everything he had to dredge up a halfhearted smile. "Thanks."

The pup wiggled in his arms and gave a mournful whine. He took the excuse to get the hell out of there. "Be back in a bit." He had no intention of coming back. Forget worrying about being cowardly—the last thing he wanted to do was stand in a room with Hope Moore and make small talk. As much as the sight of her was like a rain after a long drought, there was too much shit between them.

She should have stayed away. Whatever brought her back here, it could have been avoided.

He set the pup down in the yard and crouched next to her, watching her run back and forth, still in the awkward stage where her paws seemed too big for her body. She really was a cutie. She was also going to need a name. "How about Ollie?"

"I like it."

He turned to find Hope standing behind him. Again. "You sure move quiet when you want to." Especially for a woman with a bum leg. Not that he could say as much without sounding like a jackass.

"You mean since I had my knee replaced." Of course she knew what he meant anyway. Apparently damn near reading his mind was one annoying habit she hadn't outgrown.

"I didn't say that."

"You didn't have to." She leveraged herself down next to him, the move not quiet as smooth as it'd been when she was eighteen.

Daniel almost cursed. He had to stop doing that. Comparing her now to how she was then wasn't fair to either of them. It was another lifetime completely, and thinking about it was just fucking depressing. "Hope—"

"Are you seeing anyone?"

"No."

"Why not?"

He was so surprised by the question that he answered honestly, "Why the fuck would I bother?"

"Oh, I don't know, because you don't want to be a creepy old man who lives in the middle of nowhere and has to run off silly high school kids with his shotgun because they tell ghost stories about him?"

He looked at her, half sure that she was the one who'd lost her damn mind. "That's not a thing."

"It is most definitely a thing." She leaned back on her hands and stared at the sky. The move arched her back and pressed her breasts against the fancy tank top she wore. It was made of some kind of drapey fabric that looked soft and shiny, and it highlighted the fact that he seriously doubted she was wearing a bra. "You're too young to just give up."

"It's not about giving up." Though he didn't expect Hope to understand that. He'd checked up on her a few times since the accident, and every single time he was amazed at the things she'd accomplished. Life had kicked her in the teeth and she'd come back swinging. She'd taken two years off and then attended the University of Texas and graduated with honors. She ran her own successful consulting business to work with companies that wanted to set up scholarships and nonprofits.

She shifted to look at him. "It looks like giving up from where I'm sitting." She continued before he could respond, not that he knew what the fuck he was supposed to say to that. "Are you happy?"

What the hell kind of question was that? "I'm getting by."

"That pretty much answers that." She gave him a bittersweet smile. "I should have come back before now to check on you—or at least knock some sense into you, since apparently you need some tough love."

Check on him like he was her responsibility, when the truth was he was the one to blame for everything bad that had happened to her. "You worry about your own life and leave me to worry about mine."

"Because you're doing such a stand-up job of living it?"

He glared. "What in the fuck is that supposed to mean? It's great that you're happy—better than great. You deserve that and more. How I go about my business isn't any of yours."

"You're right. I know you're right." She sighed, the sound so small that he wanted to wrap his arms around her. It was more than the sigh, though. They'd dated for two years back in high school, been each other's firsts across the board. Apparently even after all this time, his body still remembered the feel of hers and craved it like crazy. He just hadn't been aware of it until she was sitting here next to him.

That's a goddamn lie.

The truth was he'd never stopped craving her in his arms and in his bed. He'd just stopped deserving her around the time John took his last breath. A person didn't come back from something like that, and no matter how well Hope had done with her life, that didn't change the fact that he'd taken things from her that were downright unforgivable.

Needing to get them onto solid ground—though he doubted that was a possibility at all—he said, "What's brought you back to town?"

"Work. Sort of." She pulled at the hem of her skirt, lifting the fabric enough for him to catch a glint of scar tissue on her calf. She hadn't done it on purpose—that he was sure of—but the reminder still struck him cold to the core. Oblivious, Hope continued. "Mom and Dad have been talking about doing a scholarship for John for years. They got in contact with the mayor and the principal of the high school and the city council and basically whoever would listen, and they've got a fund set up. So I'm here to get the details ironed out and officially announce it."

It made sense that she'd come back here for John. If he'd had a chance to stop and think since she showed up, he would have come to that conclusion on his own. Daniel quietly smothered the little voice inside him insisting that she'd really come back here for *him*. She hadn't. End of story. Allowing himself the fantasy would only make the truth hurt more.

And the truth was that any possibility of a future between him and Hope Moore was as dead as her brother.

CHAPTER THREE

Hope should have known Jules had an ulterior motive for inviting her to dinner. As soon as she'd seen the cars in front of the house, she'd realized something more was going on, and she'd refused to get out of the truck until the other woman spilled. So she'd been able to brace for the knowledge that she'd see Daniel—as much as anyone could brace for seeing the man she once considered the love of her life.

Judging from the tension lining his shoulders, he hadn't had the slightest clue that his cousin had been meddling. In fact, everything about Daniel seemed to be tense these days. There were new lines around his mouth—deep brackets that she doubted came from smiling—and it was obvious that he spent significant time in the sun from how dark his normally tanned skin was.

It didn't detract from his looks, though.

Instead, it was almost like he'd been honed down and purged in a fire, coming out a leaner, meaner version of himself. Considering what she'd picked up from Jules, that was probably more accurate than anything else she could have compared it to. His thick black hair was longer than it had been, almost shaggy, and his dark eyes were downright haunted.

Hope bit her lip, wondering what she was supposed to do to help. He obviously wasn't happy to see her, and a part of her couldn't help feeling a little disappointment.

That's not why she'd come back. *He* wasn't why she'd come back, though she'd be a liar if she said the thought of running into her old flame hadn't crossed her mind. But that's exactly what Daniel was to her—what he had to be. Ancient history.

They'd had a chance to live the American dream that they'd always imagined, but instead of walking away from that car crash stronger, they'd been broken completely. Even if she wanted to magically bounce back from that, it was too late.

Maybe if he'd returned her calls after he came to visit her in the hospital…

But the time for maybes was long gone.

She was here to finally do what she'd promised her parents and set up John's trust. As much as she'd wanted to avoid coming back into town, avoid driving down Interstate 10 again and seeing the spot where their car went off the road, it was time.

Not a moment too soon, if the intervention Jules had mentioned breezily was something the Rodriguez family was actually planning. She didn't know if Daniel was really that badly off or if his parents and aunts and uncles and cousins had gotten together and riled themselves up into making it *a thing*.

She had to do something, she just didn't know *what*. She couldn't leave town again without at least trying to help him work through things—and getting his family off his back. She promised herself that right then and there.

"Whatever you're thinking, knock that shit off right now, darling."

The sound of his old nickname for her settling in the air between them temporarily shocked her into saying something she never would have otherwise. "I do what I want."

He turned to face her fully, brows lowered. It should have looked ridiculous with that tiny puppy bounding around him, into his lap and back out again, but something inside her quivered as a result of being pinned down by that expression. She couldn't quite tell if that was a good thing or a bad thing, though. Daniel leaned in, so close she wasn't sure of the heat she felt was coming from his body or the summer night around them. "That line never worked on me."

"It never worked on *anyone*." For one eternal second they were back there, in the world before.

Then he shook his head like he was waking from a dream. "I'm glad you're setting this thing up for John. It's football based?"

"Yeah." Her brother had gotten a full ride to the University of Texas when he graduated high school, and he'd been in his junior year of college, back home for the holidays, when the wreck took his life. So much potential, snuffed out in the space of a minute. The familiar ache settled in her chest, but it wasn't as strong or present as it had been this afternoon.

When she'd woken up in that hospital bed and realized her brother hadn't survived, she'd vowed to herself that she'd do whatever it took to make sure the gap created by John's death was filled. It'd been an irrational promise, but she'd stuck with it. Every time physical therapy brought her to the brink of despair, she fought it off because John never would have given up. And then she'd finished college with honors because that's what John had been on his way to doing.

She had no interest in being a lawyer—and she wasn't particularly good at arguing her point when strong emotions were involved—so she'd gone into the private sector, helping people and companies with too much money on their hands set up foundations and scholarships to help people who could actually *use* that money. Most of them were doing it for the tax write-off, but their motivation didn't matter—what they were doing did.

But those foundations and scholarships weren't personal. This one was. This felt like the final accumulation of what she'd been working toward—giving other kids from Devil's Falls a chance to follow the same path John had been on—to succeed where his life was cut short. "Football based, and they have to have the same kind of grades he did. There are other factors, too, but ultimately it'll be up to the discretion of the town council."

He gave a short nod. "It's good that you're doing this."

Funny, but he didn't sound particularly happy about it. Then again, he hadn't sounded happy from the moment she'd walked through that door. She took a deep breath. It was time to talk about that forbidden subject, the one that lay like a pulsing wound between them. Maybe getting it all out in the open would help him. "Danny—"

He pushed to his feet. "As fun as this has been, I've got to go."

"*Go?* You just got here." She struggled to her feet as he scooped up Ollie and started around the back of the house. Hope cursed under her breath, muttering about insane men, and hurried after him. The ground was too uneven to actually catch up with him, but she rounded the corner almost on his heels. Which was right about the time that her ankle wobbled, twisting her weak knee and sending her sprawling.

She hit the ground with bruising force, but that was nothing compared to the embarrassment making her wish the dirt would just part and suck her under. *Stupid rookie mistake. You know better than to run around over uneven ground.* But then, her common sense had always had the nasty habit of taking a backseat when Daniel was around.

Strong hands grabbed her under her armpits and pulled her to her feet. "Christ, Hope, what the fuck do you think you're doing?" Daniel patted her down, brushing the dirt from her shoulders and sides and chest. He froze when his hands touched her breasts, and the heat of her blush from her embarrassment turned into something else entirely. She swallowed hard, taking a deep breath that pressed her against his palms more firmly. The fabric of her shirt was thin enough that she could feel the calluses on his palms, and her nipples budded from the contact, her body going soft and warm as if she was some twisted sort of Pavlov's dog and Daniel was her bell.

When he spoke again, his voice was deeper. "Are you hurt?"

Not in the way you mean. "I don't think so." Her knee throbbed like the dickens, but she wasn't about to admit that to him. And, to be fair, it hurt the majority of the time to one degree or another. But admitting that meant he might stop touching her. She leaned into him and licked her lips, her gaze dropping to his mouth. "Danny…"

"When you look at me like that, I forget all the reasons I promised to leave you alone."

Why the hell would he promise to leave her alone? That was the stupidest thing she'd ever heard. She clenched her teeth together to keep from telling him so and ruining the moment. There would be plenty of time to rip Daniel a new one…later. "Then don't." She grabbed the front of his T-shirt and pulled him against her, stretching up to kiss him. He resisted for a grand total of one second.

And then he took control.

Daniel brought his hand up to yank her ponytail holder out and tangle in her hair, simultaneously picking her up and backing them up against the house. And then he was there, his body pinning her in place, his thigh wedging between her legs, providing a delicious pressure against where she felt most empty. He took possession of her mouth, his tongue teasing her lips open and stroking against hers in a way that had to be designed to make the top of her head explode.

He used his grip on her hair to tilt her head back and kiss down her neck. "If I was a better man, I'd leave you alone."

She didn't have words to respond, not with him tracing her nipple through her shirt with his thumb. Hope moaned and pulled him closer, trying to think clearly enough to know what to say—or not to say— that would ensure this didn't stop. Then his free hand slid beneath her shirt and she forgot about talking at all.

"No goddamn bra." He cupped her breast, his calluses creating delicious friction against her nipple. "What the hell were you thinking, showing up here with no bra?"

This, at least, she knew how to deal with, even if she was out of practice. Hope lifted her chin and met his gaze, half sure she was imagining the possessive look she found there. "I'm not wearing panties, either."

"What. The. Fuck?" Immediately, he fisted the fabric of her skirt, lifting it high against her thighs and sliding his hand between her legs. "Christ, darling, you really know how to send a man to his knees." He cupped her, his fingers sliding through her wetness but not penetrating her. It felt so good, but not nearly good enough, all at the same time. "But then, you always did."

At their feet, Ollie yipped, breaking the spell. Daniel exhaled a harsh breath. "This is a mistake."

It was. She knew that, and she didn't care. This would never happen again, and knowing that made her feel totally and completely out of control. Here in this moment, nothing seemed real but them, and she wasn't ready for it to end. Not yet. She covered his hand with her own, holding him in place. "Danny, please." She licked her lips. "Please don't stop."

• • •

Daniel couldn't deny her if he wanted to—and he sure as fuck didn't want to. He ignored the pup at his feet and pushed a finger into her, watching her face. She clenched around him, her inhaled breath the sweetest thing he'd ever heard. He pumped gently, feeling anything but, trying to remember to take it slow. She was hot and tight and already drenched, her breasts rising and falling with each exhale.

"Danny…" She cupped him through his jeans. "Now."

This was so damn wrong. It had never been like this with them. Hot beyond belief, yes. But not quick, not rushed, not harsh in any way. But harsh was the only thing Daniel knew anymore.

He kept pumping, spreading her with his fingers while he used his free hand to undo his jeans. His cock sprang free, and it took everything he had to pause. "Hold on, darling." He grabbed his wallet out of his back pocket, riffling through it for the condom he'd put there…at some point. He hesitated. "Damn, it's been—"

"I don't care. Put it on." She kissed him, reaching between them to stroke him once, twice, a third time, until he had to get the fucking condom on or he was going to come in her hand. If he was going to get one more shot at being inside Hope Moore, he wasn't going to ruin it.

He tore open the condom wrapper with his teeth, refusing to stop touching her, though he had to let go for a second to roll the damn thing on. It took too long, but he had both hands free when he was done, and she'd kept her skirt lifted for him. *Good girl.* He stepped into her, pressing her against the wall. It struck him again that this was twelve different kinds of wrong to be doing her against the wall of his best friend's house, but he was too far gone to care.

Hope kissed him, hopping up and putting her legs

around his waist, and that was that. He adjusted his angle and pushed into her, his entire body shaking at the feeling of her pussy clamped so tightly around him. "Jesus, darling. I'd convinced myself I'd imagined how good you feel." He cupped her ass, lifting her up and slamming her down onto his cock.

I missed this. I missed you.

Even in the throes, he couldn't say it aloud. She wasn't staying, and he had no business throwing their past in her face. *Stop thinking and just enjoy this, damn it.* He kissed her, giving himself over to the feel of her thighs squeezing his hips, her nails digging into the back of his neck, the breathy little moans that she made in the back of her throat. All too soon, her body tightened around him, her pussy milking him as she came with a soft cry. Daniel tried to hold on, to prolong it, to keep going, but it was too good. He pinned her against the wall and pounded into her, urged on by the building pressure in his balls. He came with a curse that damn near buckled his knees and caught himself against the rough wood.

Long seconds ticked past, their breathing slowly returning to something resembling normal. He ran a hand over her ass and down her thigh, pausing when the skin changed just above her knee, becoming rough and almost twisted.

Hope jumped like he'd electrocuted her. "Oh, God." She shimmied until he set her on her feet, quickly stepping away from him and adjusting her clothing.

He hated that, though he didn't blame her. He couldn't get the feeling of that scarred skin out of his head, and the knowledge that he'd been the one responsible sat heavy in his chest. He took a step back and went to get rid of the condom.

Daniel knew something was wrong the second he touched his cock. He pulled the condom off—the *ripped* condom. "Oh, shit."

CHAPTER FOUR

What the hell did I just do?

Hope stared at the broken condom and suddenly the night was closing in on her and she couldn't catch a full breath. *Oh, no. Oh my God.* She tried to think past the rushing in her ears, but the panic cresting inside her made it all but impossible. "I'm on birth control." Sort of. The truth was that she'd just gotten a prescription last week and started them today — well, technically yesterday. *It shouldn't have happened like this.*

It shouldn't have happened at all.

There was no excuse for the stupidity of what she'd just done. She looked around wildly, half expecting a brilliant solution to materialize in front of her. There was nothing but the stars and the field around the house, both so painfully familiar and yet completely different. It was *all* different. All wrong.

She never should have followed Daniel through the backyard, but she'd been so blind, so sure she could fix everything like she always did. "I have to go."

"Hope…" Daniel sighed. "Yeah, you should. Let me give you a ride."

That was the *last* thing she needed. Even with all evidence pointing to her having no common sense when it came to this man, it was like she was eighteen again, rushing headfirst into every situation, heedless of the danger. She'd just more than proven that she couldn't trust herself to keep control, which meant she needed to stay away from him in situations like this.

Situations like what? We're at a party at his cousin's house and ten feet from half a dozen other people. It's not like I followed him home.

Ollie chose that moment to start barking, and they both spun around as Adam walked around the side of the house. He stopped short when he caught sight of them, and even in the shadows, Hope could see the way his gaze jumped between them, his eyes widening for half a second before he got control of himself. "You two okay out here?"

"Fine."

Adam and Daniel stared at each other in a way she'd never seen before, almost calculating. Like there was a line they were on opposite sides of. Hope didn't like that. She didn't like that one bit. They were best friends — had been since they were kids. She refused to be something that came between them. She smoothed back her hair, belatedly realizing her hair tie had disappeared into the darkness. *Damn.* "We're good. I was just coming back inside to find Jules. I'm kind of tired and I want to head to the bed-and-breakfast."

"Hope—"

Adam stepped forward, angling so he stood between her and Daniel. "I'll give you a ride. I've got the keys to Jules's truck."

"Perfect." She honestly didn't care who was behind the wheel as long as she was putting some distance between herself and Daniel. She needed to *think*, and it was impossible to do that with her body still beating in time with the pleasure he'd brought her and his presence overwhelming her while he was just standing there.

She wasn't back for good. It wasn't fair to get tangled up with him. No matter how she could rationalize it, she'd never be able to have no-strings-attached sex with Daniel. She just wasn't capable of it.

So she ran.

Like a scared kid.

Hope took a few careful steps back. "I'll see you around, Danny." Then she hightailed it for Jules's truck. She didn't stop to think that it might be yet another stupid idea until Adam got behind the wheel and cranked the engine on.

He barely waited until they were off the dirt drive to start on her. "Why are you back in town, Hope?"

"What?" She jerked back, stung. "I'm here for the scholarship in John's memory."

"That's all well and good—if it were true. But you could set that shit up down in Dallas without ever setting foot back in Devil's Falls, and you damn well know it."

She crossed her arms over her chest. "I have half a dozen meetings set up tomorrow alone and—"

"Meetings you could hold over the phone." He didn't look at her, but the judgment in his voice hurt. A lot.

It was a fight not to hunch down in the seat. "If you didn't want to see me, you didn't have to offer to drive me."

"Fuck, that's not it." He scrubbed a hand over his face. "I'm happy to see you, kid. Really, I am. I've missed you like crazy—we all have—but this isn't about John. This is about Daniel." He didn't give her a chance to jump in, not that she knew what she was supposed to say. Things with Daniel were complicated, and not in a good way.

Adam turned onto the highway leading into Devil's Falls. "I don't judge you for not coming back. Fuck, I left, too, and I had every intention of staying gone. I'm sure it's hard being back here and seeing John everywhere."

She knew exactly what he meant. She might have been the kid sister, but she'd tagged along through most of their grade school adventures, and then again once she hit sixteen and Daniel finally woke up and realized she was totally in love with him. *Daniel.* Seeing him and Quinn and Adam together only brought into relief the missing piece, but there was comfort in knowing that those three were here in Devil's Falls, still friends despite everything. Still living and loving and maybe occasionally getting into trouble for old times' sake.

"Then what's the problem?"

"You goddamn well know what the problem is. You've moved on with your life, left the past where it belongs. Daniel hasn't." He finally looked at her, the lights of an oncoming car illuminating his face. "Despite not having seen you in a hell of a long time, I still love you like a sister, Hope. But that doesn't mean I'm going to stand by and watch you grind what's left of Daniel into the ground when you leave again."

"That's not fair." She couldn't dredge up any anger. Adam could be a dick, but that's not what this was. He was worried about Daniel. It seemed *everyone* was worried about Daniel. "I didn't come back here to mess with him."

"Maybe not, but you being back is going to do exactly that." He headed into town, pulling to a stop right next to her car in front of Cups and Kittens. "If you care about him even a little after all this time, stay the hell away from him, Hope. I mean it."

She stared at the dashboard, wondering when it had all gone wrong. *Oh, yeah, right around the time my skirt hit my waist.* "I came back to help."

"You won't help Daniel. You're only going to make it worse."

Her throat tried to close, but she managed to speak past it. "Some things don't change. You can be so damn mean sometimes, Adam."

"Yeah, I know." He sat back. "But it's the truth. You've been doing well. Don't look at me like that, of course I've followed up on you over the years—you're the little sister I never had by blood. Hell, Hope, you're doing better than well. I'm fucking proud of you."

Her eyes burned, and she blinked a few times, trying to tell herself that it was because of the heat and not because she was actually tearing up. She'd always considered him and Quinn brothers while they were growing up, though she'd thought those relationships had broken at the same time as hers and Daniel's. Adam had disappeared off to do the rodeo circuit, and the most she'd heard from Quinn was a snarky Christmas card every year. "I didn't know."

"I didn't exactly announce it. That's on me."

Those things went both ways. She'd followed his rodeo career, but she'd never seen him ride live. The thought of seeing one of the men she cared about getting thrown from the back of a furious bull...she couldn't handle it. "I promise I didn't come back here to cause problems."

"I know, kid. Trust me, I know. And if you were planning on staying, I wouldn't be warning you off him—you two were always good together."

Yeah, they had been. Right up until he stopped returning her calls and forced her to move on with her life without him. Hope took a shuddering breath. "Things change."

"Some things. Not this." He got out of the truck and walked around to open her door. She hopped down and squeaked when he pulled her into a hug. "I missed you, Hope. We all did."

She recovered quickly and hugged him back. "I missed you guys, too."

He let her go and ruffled her hair, the move one he'd repeated thousands of times before. "I'll follow you to the B&B and carry your bags up."

"It's fine." She was already heading around the car for the tailgate. "I've got it."

"There's no shame in asking for help."

She went ramrod straight and turned to glare at him. She didn't want *anyone's* pity, let alone that of a man she respected and loved like a brother. "I am *not* helpless, and I'm more than capable of wrestling a stupid suitcase into my room. Leave it alone."

"If you say so." Adam held up his hands. "Kid, I don't know how they do things down in Dallas, but you're back in Devil's Falls—around here, we help each other out, and it's not seen as a criticism."

She knew that—just like she knew that she was being rude for snapping at him. She was just so damn used to people looking at her screwed-up knee and seeing someone less than whole. And, truth be told, her leg was hurting her something fierce right now, the pain radiating all the way to her hip. All she wanted to do was go up to her room and lie down for a little while and just process everything that had happened.

But that didn't mean she should be taking it out on Adam. "I'm sorry."

"Don't be." He gently nudged her aside and grabbed her suitcase. "It's weird being back in town, huh?"

"The weirdest."

Fifteen minutes later, she was all checked in and Adam was gone, leaving her in peace. At least in theory. In reality, she kept replaying the last few hours and wondering when her well-intentioned plan had jumped the rails. The goal had always been to come back here, get some closure, and go back to her life in Dallas, feeling better about everything. About putting that nagging what-if question to rest, once and for all.

Instead, here she was, having just had a quickie with her ex against the side of a house, getting ripped a new one by a man she considered a brother, and going to bed wondering what the hell she'd been thinking.

Coming back to Devil's Falls had been a horrible mistake.

• • •

Daniel spent the next few days half sure that Hope would randomly show up on his doorstep. By the time he realized she had no intention of doing that, almost a week had passed. *I don't even know how long she's in town for.* He should just let it go. It was no wonder she didn't want to see him. Their past aside, she'd barely been back in town an hour and he'd been fucking her against the wall like she was…well, anyone other than Hope Moore.

Dirty, filthy sex wasn't what they did.

Hell, they didn't do *any* kind of sex these days.

Except they had.

He shook his head and opened the driver's door so Ollie could jump into the truck. She didn't quite make it, and he was forced to leap forward to catch her before she flopped onto the ground. "Damn, girl." At least between the pup and work, he'd had more than enough going on to keep him from having too much time to wonder what Hope was doing. If she was revisiting their old haunts. If she was spending any amount of time down at the diner.

If she'd visited her brother's grave.

He should just leave it alone. If she wanted to see him, it was child's play to figure out where he was. He hadn't asked her to come back. Damn it, he'd been doing just fucking fine before she showed up. And yet there he was, starting his truck and heading away from his house. The entire time he sat there and told himself this was a mistake. He didn't have any right to make demands on Hope's time—not after what happened thirteen years ago, and not after what happened a week ago.

But he wanted to.

He drove into town and then ended up parking outside Cups and Kittens because cruising Main Street was for idiot teenagers and stalkers, neither of which he wanted to be. *Yep. Just visiting my meddling cousin. Right.* He pushed through the front door—and immediately regretted his decision to come here.

Ollie took one look at the pair of cats sunning themselves in the afternoon beam of light, yipped, and took off running. Daniel dived for her, but she evaded him like a pro, barking up a storm. The cats fled, jumping up onto one of those cat jungle things and out of reach, hissing and swiping, their hair standing on end while Ollie ran circles around the base.

"What's going on out here?" Jules came sprinting out of the back and skidded to a stop in front of the scene. "Oh, good lord."

Daniel scooped up the pup—who was still barking shrilly enough to burst his eardrums—and backed up. "Didn't stop to think this was a bad idea. Sorry."

"It's okay. Here, bring her into the back." She led the way back into the kitchen and shut the door behind them. Once he was sure there were no cats in the room, Daniel set Ollie down. She set to sniffing everything she came across, apparently having forgotten the drama she'd just started. Jules laughed softly. "Maybe we should have gotten you a cat."

"Nah, I'm more of a dog person." He hadn't planned on having a dog, but Ollie had grown on him in a big way. She was just so damn goofy. He crouched down and ran a hand over her back.

"So, what brings you into town?" Jules asked the question far too casually.

He thought about lying or making some lame-ass excuse, but they both knew why he was here. "You seen Hope around?"

"She left."

The bottom of his stomach dropped out, and he shot to his feet. "What?"

"Yeah." Jules shuffled her feet. "I guess she wrapped up stuff faster than she thought she was going to and headed back to Dallas yesterday."

I missed my chance. He knew he was half a second from weaving on his feet and brought his shit under control *fast*. He should have known that she wouldn't want to see him again before she left down. Why the fuck would she? She was missing her goddamn knee and her brother because of him, and the first thing he'd done after not seeing her for thirteen years was let things get out of control and use a condom that was far too old. They hadn't even had a chance to have the conversation where he explained that he was clean…

"I need her number." He didn't realize he was going to say it until the words were out of his mouth. He'd let things stand before, and he'd put enough distance between them that she'd eventually moved on with her life because that was what was best for her at the time. The thought of her being hurt and retreating because of what he'd done for a second time was too much to bear. He had to at least talk to her or let her yell at him. Something.

"I don't actually have it."

Of course she didn't. Why would she? He'd have realized that if he'd stopped long enough to think instead of just reacting. Daniel scrubbed a hand over his face. "It's probably for the best."

Jules bounced on her toes a little, practically wringing her hands. "I guess I should apologize. I didn't think things would go so sideways or I wouldn't have

invited her to your surprise birthday party." She hesitated. "I know Adam got kind of pissy with you that
night."

"It's fine." The thing was, he understood why Adam
had acted the way he had. Daniel would have done the
same thing if he'd found one of his little cousins in the
same position he and Hope had been in, and both
Adam and Quinn viewed Hope as a little sister.

He scooped up Ollie and headed for the back door.
"I'll see you around."

"Daniel."

He stopped and glanced over his shoulder at her.
"Yeah?"

She was actually still, her expression painfully serious. "I really do miss you. We all do."

What could he say to that? He knew he was a
miserable bastard, just like he knew that even being in
the room with his friends was enough to bring them
down. They tried to hide it, but it was the damn truth.
For the longest time, he'd tried to fake being happy,
but it hadn't worked. Nothing worked.

So he'd done them all a favor and started withdrawing more and more. Being alone kind of sucked
sometimes, but he was getting used to it. Since he
didn't see either himself or the circumstances changing
anytime soon, he gave Jules a small smile and lied
through his teeth. "I'll try to come around more often."

"No, you won't." She shook her head and waved
him away. "Just don't get pissed when I'm showing up
on your doorstep and intruding in your life."

"I wouldn't expect anything else." He walked
through the door and out into the August heat. He
tilted his head back, letting the sun beat down on him,

wishing it could burn away the sick feeling in his gut. Hope was gone. Again. He didn't believe in second chances—not really—but if he'd been allotted one, it had slipped past him while he'd been stewing. He'd never see her again.

It's for the best. She can do better than a man like me, and we both know it.

The truth didn't make him feel a damn bit better, though.

CHAPTER FIVE

Hope pounded on the door for the third time, not caring that it was almost midnight or that all the lights were off or that no one knew she was back in Devil's Falls. After her initial panic attack earlier today, she'd been eerily calm while she finished her work, cleared her schedule for the weekend, got in her car, and started driving west. But now that panic was back — with interest. *Six weeks. It's been six freaking weeks. Too long.* Six weeks since her snafu with Daniel and the broken condom.

Six weeks and no period to show for it.

The dog started barking, and she pounded on the door harder, thankful that he lived out in the middle of nowhere, because she knew she was making a scene and she couldn't stop. "Open the damn door, Daniel!" She shouldn't have come back. She was an adult. She should have just put on her big-girl panties and taken every single pregnancy test in the three boxes she'd purchased earlier that day.

But the thought of facing the results alone in her Dallas apartment had nearly been enough to send her curling into a ball she might never crawl out of. It wasn't right. She was the strong one, the woman who didn't meet an obstacle that she wouldn't find her way over, under, or around. She'd stopped leaning on anyone when she was eighteen and realized that the temptation to let the people around her carry the heavy weight was just another crutch that she refused to give in to.

All that didn't change the fact that she couldn't face this without him.

What if it's positive? Hope paused in her knocking and shuddered. That wasn't news that should be delivered over a phone call. Not to mention she didn't even *have* his number anymore. It wasn't like he'd been all that eager to give it to her after the way things had gone last time she was in town.

The door flew open to reveal Daniel, and she couldn't even stop to appreciate the sight of him wearing a pair of low-slung sweats or the fact that he'd seriously filled out since he was twenty-one. Appreciating her ex's hot body was what got her into this mess to begin with. Hope shouldered her way past him into the house, her heart beating too fast, her breath harsh in her throat.

"Hope?" He blinked and closed the door behind her. "What are you doing here? What's wrong?"

She laughed, high and hysterical. "I'm in trouble. I think. Or, rather, *we're* in trouble." That truth had been solidifying all day in the back of her mind. She wasn't late. Ever. There was only one reason she would be now.

Oh, God.

He stepped in front of her and put his hands on her shoulders. "You're not making any sense. Slow down."

There was no slowing down. Not until she knew for sure. Hope ducked out of his hold, knowing she was acting crazy and unable to stop. She grabbed her purse and went to her knees to dig through it, coming up with all three boxes. She looked up in time to see Daniel register what they were, and the shock on his face would have been comical under any other circumstances.

She went still, her chest trying to close in on itself. "I didn't take them yet."

"I see that." He came over to crouch in front of her. Daniel searched her face. "You could have called. I still have the same number. I would have come to you."

It hadn't even occurred to her that he'd had the same number. The last time she'd needed him, he hadn't been there for her. As much as she was at peace about her past—mostly—that rejection was always lurking there. He'd broken her trust, and she couldn't guarantee that he wouldn't do the same thing again. "I'm scared, Daniel."

He finally reached out and touched her knee. Her good knee. "What can I do?"

How about invent a time machine and go back to make sure this never happened? She didn't snap at him. He was asking an honest question, so she owed him an honest answer. "There's nothing you *can* do. It's already done."

He took one of the boxes out of her hand and opened it. She had the irrational urge to snatch it out of his hands, because opening it felt like the point of no return. Daniel unfolded the instructions and scanned them. "It says here that for best results, you need to take it first thing in the morning."

"That is how pregnancy tests usually work."

He shot her a look. "I wouldn't know." Before she could say something else to make the situation worse, he pushed to his feet and offered his hand. "Come on. You've got to be exhausted."

She didn't want his pity, and she wasn't sure she wanted his help at all. But since she'd come all this way, it was the lowest idiocy to throw a bitch fit now. So she took his hand and allowed him to pull her to her feet. He started down the hallway toward three closed doors. "Come to bed. You need to sleep."

Everything hurt. Her head, her chest, most especially her knee. She'd spent more hours today pacing than she cared to count, and it had taken its toll. But if she said anything, Daniel would freak out, and she didn't have it in her to dance around his guilt tonight. "Do you have a spare bedroom?" She wasn't willing to strip herself naked for him, emotionally or otherwise. She was too raw, too overwhelmed.

His step hitched, but he changed directions, opening the door immediately to their right. "It's not much, but there's a futon in there."

His bed would be more comfortable, but the thought of being in Daniel's bed again was... Yeah, no. She'd deal with the futon. She walked into the room. "Good night." And then she shut the door in his face. Hope slumped onto the futon, every worry and pain screaming for her attention. She dropped her head into her hands, fighting back a complete and total breakdown.

She'd worked so incredibly hard to move on with her life—she'd even thought she'd succeeded. But the second she crossed the county line, she was right back in the midst of the past she'd tried so hard to leave behind.

• • •

Daniel didn't sleep. He didn't even try to. Instead he took Ollie into the backyard and let her run. In the past month, she'd proven herself more than capable of keeping up with him, her awkward puppy form starting to hint at the dog she'd become. It wouldn't be long before he could take her when he went out riding—after he figured out how to tone down her enthusiasm. He'd introduced her to Rita last week, and that encounter had been as memorable as it was problematic.

None of that mattered.

He scrubbed a hand over his face. Hope goddamn Moore was in his guest bedroom. He could barely wrap his mind around it. And if she was pregnant… His body went hot and cold, fight-or-flight responses kicking in. *What the fuck am I going to do with a baby?*

You always wanted a few of them.

Before. Not now.

The universe had the most fucked-up sense of humor. He'd learned that the hard way time and time again, and it always managed to surprise him. All he'd ever wanted when he was in his early twenties was to marry Hope, settle down in a little farmhouse, and raise a family. That dream was long gone, and yet here she was, possibly pregnant with his child and back in Devil's Falls.

Her life is in Dallas.

If she was pregnant, she'd take his baby back there, half a state away from him.

No goddamn way. Daniel pushed to his feet and turned to face the house. It didn't matter how much time had passed—he knew Hope and he knew how her mind worked. She'd have a plan, even if she couldn't admit to herself that she had a plan. A plan that wouldn't include him, not this time. Well, fuck that. He had as much a right to decide that baby's future as she did.

He strode back into the house, fear and anger and something else entirely all tangled up inside him. He threw open the door to the guest bedroom. "If this is my baby—"

"Oh my God!" Hope screeched.

Daniel froze. Hope was sitting on the futon in her T-shirt and only a pair of underwear, her legs stretched out in front of her. The right was just as perfect as it had always been, but that wasn't what drew his gaze. He focused on her scarred leg, on the pocked flesh and scars running from several inches down her thigh all the way to her shin. "Hope—"

"Get out!" She grabbed the blanket off the back of the futon and tossed it over the lower half of her body. "I know this is your house and all, but you don't get to just walk in here." Her voice was shrill and her movements jerky. If he hadn't known how messed up over this she was, that would have more than shown him.

And I let her just close herself away so she could stew.

Idiot.

He forced himself to take a mental step back and breathe. Yelling at her wasn't going to do anything but piss them both off, and a screaming match wasn't going to do either of them any good. "The baby."

"The theoretical baby."

"Darling, you wouldn't be here if you didn't think pretty conclusively that there was a baby." Every time he said those words, his gut lurched, and for the life of him he couldn't say if it was a good thing or a bad thing. "You can't take it away from me."

"If it's a baby, it's not an it." She clutched the blanket to her chest, glaring at him like he'd just personally insulted her.

He chose not to comment on the fact she was flip-flopping wildly right now about what she wanted. Daniel figured she was entitled. Actually, the more freaked out she acted, the calmer he felt. He could do this. It might not be planned, but he wasn't going to spit on the chance to make amends that fate had given him.

He just needed to bring Hope around to the idea of it. Tentative plan solidifying in his mind, he crossed his arms over his chest. "What do you need from me?"

"How about some goddamn privacy?"

"If I leave, you're just going to sit there and your mind is going to run in circles all night." The same thing he'd be doing. He motioned. "Come on. I think I have some tea stashed around here." As soon as he said it, he realized she couldn't just up and follow him. Guilt rose up and punched him in the gut. The baby thing had him so turned around, he'd actually forgotten that her leg had irreparable damage because of him. *Goddamn it.* It was almost enough to make him retreat, but he powered on. "If your knee is bothering you, I can carry you."

"No." The word came out sharp enough to cut. Hope shook her head. "You will not be carrying me anywhere, so get that idea out of your head right now. I'm more than capable of moving around on my own."

He waited, but she didn't move. "Did you want me to turn my back or some shit?" What if she fell over? He went cold. What if in falling she hurt the baby?

Daniel took a step forward. "It's no trouble to carry you, darling. I've done it enough times."

"Touch me and lose your hand." She still didn't move from her place beneath the blanket, though her dark eyes were fierce. "I'm not an invalid, Daniel. I'm not some broken toy that you can cart around until it feels loved again. I've been like this almost longer than I was the other way. This is my reality, and I don't need your help, and I sure as hell don't need your pity."

Her reality.

Again, guilt tried to choke him. He fought it down, but only barely. He couldn't afford to let her drive him away, not when there might be a baby. "Would you like some tea or not?"

Hope shook her head. "I don't think that's a good idea right now."

Because he'd gone and fucked this up.

It struck him that he'd spent so much time fighting to distance himself from the people around him that he didn't know *how* to interact with people anymore. He'd pissed Hope off when he'd only been trying to help, because he was so damn clumsy with his attempts to comfort her. It used to be second nature to reach out and pull her close. Then again, she'd been in love with him back then.

A lot had changed.

Daniel backed out of the room and closed the door behind him, deciding that he needed to figure out what the fuck his plan was, because blundering through this was just going to ensure that Hope would drive back to Dallas at the first available opportunity and take his baby with her.

And this time she might not be back.

CHAPTER SIX

Hope slept horribly, unable to get the look on Daniel's face out of her head. The one that showed up when he caught sight of her leg. It was all guilt and pity and something almost like disgust. She shuddered and rolled over to bury her face in the pillow. She hadn't been celibate for the last thirteen years, but she'd been very selective over who she'd let get close enough to actually see her 100 percent naked. She might be mostly at peace with her body, but she didn't need the kick in the teeth that came when a potential lover made their excuses to leave as soon as her pants came off.

It hadn't happened yet, but the fear never quite went away.

A five a.m. she sat up, her full bladder making it impossible to procrastinate any longer. Her leg still hurt like nobody's business, but she'd be damned before she limped her way to the bathroom. She'd powered through worse pain before, and no doubt she'd do it again, but she wasn't going to give Daniel an excuse to offer to carry her again.

It's not forever. I might have panicked in a big way and come back here, but that doesn't mean I'm staying. Once this is over...

That was the problem. If she was pregnant, this wasn't something she could just smile and keep on keeping. They were talking about a *baby*. With Daniel. Hope pushed to her feet. She'd thought it was intense enough having her past tied to him in more ways than she cared to count. To have her future tied to him as well was just... She didn't know what it was, but it didn't make her comfortable in the least.

She opened the door—and screamed. "Oh my God, what's *wrong* with you?"

Daniel held up one of the pregnancy test boxes. "I know you, and now that you've had some time to calm down, you'd have no problem sneaking into the bathroom and taking this test without letting me know." He held the box just out of reach, still blocking the doorway. "If this is positive, that changes things, Hope."

She wasn't an idiot. It would change everything. Her mind couldn't quite encompass the possibilities, couldn't take a single step past taking the test. "Give me the test."

"I've made my point." He handed it over.

"Bully for you." Having this box in her hand meant there was no more opportunity for stalling. It was happening. She was going to walk into the bathroom, and when she walked back out again, there would be no more room for maybe. She turned to look at the single window in the guest bedroom. The sun hadn't even begun to creep past the horizon. If she was back in Dallas, she'd be on her way to morning yoga and thinking about the odds and ends she wanted to accomplish this weekend.

"Running won't help anything."

She turned back and glared, hating that he was standing there, appearing to be calm and collected while she was falling apart. "Get out of my way before I piddle on your floor like your damn puppy."

"Don't bite my head off." He moved out of the way, waiting until she was to the bathroom door before he responded, "And Ollie's house-trained, so you following her example wouldn't be so bad."

She resisted chucking the box at his face, but only barely. Instead, she very carefully shut the door and made a point of engaging the lock. The very last thing she needed was Daniel barging in to watch her pee on a stick, and if the stubborn look on his face was any indication, he was actually considering it.

Hope double-checked the instructions—as if they would have changed from the half a dozen times she'd read them in the grocery aisle—and took a deep breath.

It was now or never.

It took entirely too little time to finish and set the stick aside. She washed her hands, brushed her teeth using his toothpaste and her finger, and then went ahead and used his mouthwash for good measure. She was stalling and knowing she was stalling. Banging on the door made her jump half out of her skin. She swore under her breath and jerked the door open. "What?"

Daniel searched her face. "Well?"

She didn't have to turn around to know exactly where the test sat—on the back of the toilet. Taunting her. All she had to do was walk those three steps to it and see if that idiotproof thing read Pregnant or Not Pregnant. Simple.

Except she couldn't take that first step.

Hope looked up at Daniel and had the sudden urge to just break down. If she did, he'd be there for her. He always had been.

Except that wasn't the truth. When she'd needed

him the most, he *hadn't* been there for her. Leaning on him now was just setting herself up for disappointment and heartache. She'd had enough of both to last her a lifetime.

Hope took a careful step back, and then another. Using every ounce of willpower she had, she turned and picked up the test. Her breath left her lungs in an audible whoosh. "Shit."

Pregnant.

Maybe that whole idea of building a time machine to go back to before she thought it was a brilliant idea to have sex with Daniel was a legitimate idea after all.

A big, tanned hand appeared in her line of vision and took the stick from her. "Well, hell."

She looked up, the shock on Daniel's face startling a laugh out of her. It was that or start sobbing and never stop. She'd always been a damn fool when it came to this man, but this was so above and beyond as to be laughable. She clutched her stomach, her giggle turning into a string of them, each one more hysterical than the one before. "Oh my God. I can't. This is… Oh my God."

"Darling? Damn, girl, breathe."

She slumped against the wall. "This is so dumb. This kind of thing is supposed to happen to teenagers, not to adults who should know better. We're fifteen years too late." At least if they'd done it when they were teenagers, they would have had love on their side.

Love. And where did that get us?

She scrubbed her hands over her face, trying to get a hold of her emotional free fall. The wondering about what would have happened was pointless. It had happened. End of story. Now it was time to figure out a plan for moving forward.

A baby. What am I supposed to do with a baby?

Being a single mother had never been part of the vision she had for the future.

All at once, her determination to keep moving abandoned her, leaving her staring at the bathroom cabinet. It was like thousands of other bathroom cabinets out there, a light cedar color in a generic style. It was just so *wrong*—just like everything else about this situation. "How did this happen?"

"I'm sorry, darling. It's my fault." He crouched in front of her. "The condom…the sex…it was all me."

That was just like Daniel to try to take all the responsibility—and the guilt—onto his shoulders alone. "You know, that determination to play the martyr and absolve me from guilt is really annoying." She leaned her head against the wall. "Pretty sure I was there. Equally sure that I'd just switched birth controls and neither that nor the fact that you pulled a condom out of your *wallet* was enough to make me stop and use my common sense."

"All the same—"

"No, Daniel. Not all the same. It took the two of us to get into this mess. I'm an adult, same as you, and I knew what the possible consequences were." She just hadn't cared, because being kissed by Daniel after all those years had been too good to stop. It had seemed like it was worth the risk at the time.

Now?

Now, she just didn't know.

He offered her a hand. "We need to talk about this. Really talk."

That's what she was afraid of. She allowed him to

pull her to her feet and shoved her hair out of her eyes. "We don't need to talk. I already know how this conversation goes."

"Do you now?"

"Yes." She charged on, talking so fast her words spilled over each other. "I'm keeping the baby."

He jerked back. "No shit. If anything else came out of your mouth, you were about to have a fight on your hands."

She kept going, ignoring him. "You're going to act all crazy and—"

"Here's some crazy for you, darling." He closed the distance between them, backing her against the wall. "That baby you're carrying is mine." He dropped his hand to her stomach, sliding beneath her shirt and splaying his fingers across her skin. "*Mine*. You made your choice when you came up here to take that test instead of doing it on your own in Dallas. You included me in this, so don't go crying about how unfair it is that I have a fucking opinion. You're having our baby, and you're staying here in Devil's Falls to do it."

What the hell? "Staying—"

He kissed her, stealing her words and taking possession of her mouth as if every part of her really was his. *It's not*. The token protest withered against the onslaught of sensation, the way his tongue stroked hers, igniting a need in her that she would have thought impossible considering the circumstances. He stroked her stomach, his thumb dipping beneath the waistband of her yoga pants to trail down her hip bone. She shivered, a moan slipping free.

Daniel twisted his wrist so he could slide his entire hand into her pants. He pushed a finger into her. The sensation made her moan again, and he ate the sound and then kissed around to her jaw. "You're so fucking wet for me. You always were." He pumped his finger in and out of her as much as he could. "Stay, darling. I'll have you coming more times than you can count. On my hand. On my mouth. On my cock."

Her entire body clenched at his words. It sounded so good, the temptation to let him make her feel good almost too much to resist. But if she let him win this one, she'd spend the next nine months—the next *eighteen years*—losing arguments. Not to mention her job—her *life*—was in Dallas. She'd been willing to make her plans around Daniel once before, and he'd dropped her like a bad habit the first time things went truly bad.

She couldn't go through that again.

It was hard to reach down and grab his wrist, harder than she could have imagined. "No."

Instantly, he pulled his hand out of her pants, though he didn't back up. "The offer stands."

She'd just bet it did. Hope put her hands on his chest and gently pushed him back a step. "You can't sex me up to get your way. That's not how this works."

"Is that what you think I was doing?"

Damn, but he could play innocent entirely too well—that was, if she was inclined to forget what he'd just been whispering in her ear. She crossed her arms over her chest. "Yes, Daniel, that's exactly what you were doing. It's a dirty negotiation tactic if I ever saw one."

He grinned, the expression so unexpected, she was half amazed that her panties didn't hit the ground. "Can't blame me for trying." He raised his finger to his lips—the same finger that'd been inside her—and sucked it into his mouth, his gaze never leaving her face. He released it so suddenly, her knees actually went weak. "You'll change your mind."

"No, I won't." *I might.* Hope shook her head. *No, I won't.* Sex with Daniel was world ending, which was the damn point—she liked her world exactly the way it was. It would change now, and there wasn't anything she could do about that, but she could at least try to maintain control in the midst of all the insanity.

Which meant she couldn't let him have the upper hand. Not now. Not ever again.

She edged past him, well aware that he let her walk out of the room when all he had to do was kiss her again to crumble her admittedly pathetic protestation. She made her way down the hall and into the kitchen, stopping cold at what she saw there. Last night she'd been so distracted by acting like a crazy person that she hadn't really stopped to check out his place. Part of her had sort of just assumed that it was, she didn't know, *familiar*.

It wasn't.

She looked around the kitchen that could have been in any cookie-cutter house around the country. There was nothing *wrong* with it, at least until she realized it was in Daniel's house. She moved around the breakfast bar, eyeing the empty counters, and opened a cupboard. There were two mason jar glasses in it, a stack of paper plates, and nothing else. She turned when he entered the room. "Is this a joke?"

"Is what a joke?"

"This." She motioned at everything. "This isn't your kitchen. It can't be." It was just too soulless.

"It's mine." He opened the fridge and winced, a reaction she shared when she saw how empty it was.

"But…how do you cook here with none of your old stuff?" Even right out of high school, he'd spent a good portion of his checks on fancy knives and food they'd had to drive into Pecos to get because the market in Devil's Falls didn't carry specialty items. Her favorite nights had been when they'd holed up in the little house he'd shared with his friends and he'd cooked for all of them. With his current setup, she doubted he could put together a peanut butter and jelly sandwich, let alone anything like the complicated dishes he'd loved.

He shut the fridge door. "I don't cook anymore."

That shocked her almost more than anything else that had happened since she woke up. Daniel didn't cook? It struck her that as well as she used to know the boy she'd dated, she didn't know a damn thing about the man standing in front of her.

And she was going to have his baby.

CHAPTER SEVEN

Daniel didn't like the way Hope was looking at him—
as if he was broken. As if she saw through all the walls
he'd built up around himself since that night thirteen
years ago, and she knew that he wasn't anywhere near
as okay as he liked everyone to think.

It set his teeth on edge. He didn't want pity from
anyone—least of all from *her*.

To get away from the knowledge in her dark eyes,
he'd do damn near anything. So he turned the tables.
"We need to talk about the next nine months." And
the next eighteen years. But he knew her well
enough—or at least he used to—to know that coming
at her with the rest of their lives on the table was a
surefire way to get her to dig in her heels and shoot
him down flat. He had no intention of rolling over and
playing dead for her, but he'd let her think he was
willing to settle for her sticking around for pregnancy
and ease her into the idea of staying here for the long
term.

Yeah, she had her job, and a life in Dallas that
didn't include him or Devil's Falls, but he didn't much
like the idea of her raising their kid hours away. The
best he could hope for in that situation was every
other weekend. Fuck that. Hope would stay here. He
just had to figure out how the hell he was going to
convince her of that.

He was reaching, and he damn well knew it. Daniel
grabbed the carton of milk out of the fridge and

mentally cursed. It had expired over a month ago. If she'd been freaking out in Dallas as much as she was last night and this morning, she hadn't been eating or taking care of herself. In order to convince her to stay, he had to prove he still knew how to do that.

So far, he was batting a thousand.

He dumped the milk into the sink and rinsed the carton out. As long as he wasn't looking directly at her, he could keep his cool. In theory. "How do you see this working?"

There, that was as nonthreatening as it could get.

Hope crossed her arms over her chest and raised her chin like she was stepping into the ring. "I know what you're thinking, and the answer is no. Devil's Falls is my past, and I'm keeping it that way. I have a life in Dallas, Daniel. A good one. This wasn't part of the plan, but that doesn't mean I'm going to drop everything to run back here and play little wife to you so that you can feel like you're fulfilling your duties. I'm not a duty, and neither is this baby. We both deserve better than that."

He couldn't argue that logic, but the truth was that it *was* his duty to do right by both of them. Daniel considered her. There had to be something he could say to get her to stop arguing long enough to see that this was the only way. "Where are your parents living these days?"

"San Antonio." She narrowed her eyes. "Why?"

That's it. That's the pressure point to push.

He had her, she just didn't know it yet. "It sounds like you have shit for a support system in Dallas."

"I have friends." From the defensive tone, she knew exactly where he was going with this.

"None of them that were good enough friends to be there for you when you took that test." Not that he was complaining on that note. She very well could have taken the test and moved on with her life in Dallas, and he never would have known the difference. The thought left him cold. He braced his hands on the breakfast bar and leaned forward. "Instead, you drove seven hours across the fucking state to my house to take it. Because you had no one else."

Hope sucked in a breath. "That's not fair. Unlike you, I wasn't going to hide from something that scared me. Yes, I came back here—back to *you*—to take the test, but it's only for the weekend. I'm going home tomorrow."

He ignored that, ignored the clock that instantly sprang into being, counting down until she walked out of his life again. If he thought too hard about it, he'd drive himself batshit crazy. "My point is that Devil's Falls has a built-in support system. Your parents are within easy drivable distance. I'm five minutes from *my* parents' place, and don't even get me started on my cousins." Every single one of them would lose their minds when they found out Hope was pregnant. She'd be so damn taken care of, she wouldn't have to lift a finger.

A part of him didn't want to tell anyone, solely so *he* could be the one seeing to her every need.

Rein it in.

Easier said than done. There was nothing but stubbornness on Hope's face, so he pressed his point. "What happens if you fall? Or there are complications with the baby? Are you going to call a fucking cab to come get you and then sit in Dallas traffic on the way to the hospital? If you're here, Doc Jenkins has no problem making house calls, and he's the same fucking doctor who delivered *you*, so don't tell me that some fancy city doctor is going to be better. They won't. They don't know you. Devil's Falls does."

He did.

He waited while she worked it out, her dark eyes unreadable. Finally, Hope turned away. "I understand what you're saying, but you're wrong. Even if you weren't—which you *are*—you're still doing this for the wrong reasons, Daniel. You know it, and I know it."

Wanting to fix things *wasn't* the wrong reason. She might not agree with him, but that was just the way it was. All he knew was that she had to be *here*, to be where he could keep an eye on her and keep her safe as she got farther along in her pregnancy. "Stay." He didn't care if he had to move heaven and hell and everything in between, he wasn't about to let her out of his sight any more than necessary. His theoretical comments weren't all that theoretical. She might be trying to cover it up, but he could see that she favored her injured leg, and that meant her chances of falling were higher than average, especially once she started getting big.

Daniel went still, the image of Hope with a large stomach filling his head. Seeing her big with *his* baby.

Fuck, I like that picture.

Right now, the most important thing was getting her to agree to stay in town at all. From there, he'd work on getting her into his home. He looked around. He didn't even know if he could call this house a home. It had never bothered him before—it was a place that kept the heat out in the summer and the cold out in the winter and the critters out while he slept. It had never felt lacking until now, with the woman he'd always thought he'd end up with standing there, looking as out of place as an angel in a dive bar.

It might not be the house he'd always promised that he'd build her, but he could spiff this place up into something better than it currently was.

He just needed her to agree to stay. "Give us a chance to iron this out—a couple days. Stay through the week, and then we'll talk."

Her mouth dropped open. "What are you going to do, lock me up in the basement until I agree with you?"

That didn't sound like too terrible a plan, but he had a better idea. Daniel stalked toward her, knowing he was out of control and not caring. "I might do that. Or I might go over the list of perks again." He braced his hands on the counter on either side of her.

Her gaze rested on his mouth. "Your perks sound a whole lot like strings attached."

"Aw, darling, they might be exactly that." He leaned in, not quite touching her, but close enough that he could feel the warmth of her body and the way her breath shook. "But I can guarantee that you won't be worried about anything but the way my cock feels inside you."

She narrowed her eyes. "When did you get so damn pushy?"

He knew she was constantly doing a before and after comparison of him. Hell, he didn't even blame her. He was doing the same damn thing. When he was twenty-one, he'd been happy and carefree and so full of life it actually hurt to look back on that time. Now?

Now he was half the man he used to be, and he wasn't about to start changing. He didn't deserve happiness, and he sure as fuck didn't deserve Hope, but if the universe was stupid enough to give him another shot with her, he wasn't a good enough man to walk away.

Deserving her or not, Hope was his. She just had to come to terms with it.

He tucked a strand of hair behind her ear, letting his fingers linger there. Everything else had changed, but he still knew exactly how to touch her to elicit a response. "When I find something worth fighting for."

"That's your problem." She turned and looked him directly in the eye. "I was always worth fighting for."

He went still, the truth of her statement like a kick to the chest. "It wasn't right back then."

"Or maybe you were just too focused on sinking yourself into misery as fast as you could to realize the good you still had in your life." She saw too much. She always had. Back when she'd been a teenager, she'd been kind enough to back off before she revealed the fault line inside a person and forced them to face it. Apparently she wasn't too kind anymore. Hope pressed her lips into an unforgiving line—as unforgiving as the look in her eye. "John died in that car crash—*not me*. Except you didn't seem to understand that, because you were mourning my freaking leg as if that was all I was worth to you. A whole body." She pushed against his chest, not hard enough to move him, but hard enough to prove her point. "I hated you for a really long time."

"I deserved your hate." It was the simple truth. He'd taken everything from her. He'd hated himself for that, so it only made sense that she'd feel the same way.

Hope shook her head. "You're as much an idiot now as you were then."

And then she kissed him.

It caught him a little off guard—he hadn't expected her to be the one to make the first move, especially after the way the scene in the bathroom had gone down—but Daniel wasted no time taking control. He kissed down her neck, sliding his hands beneath her shirt and skating them up her body to cup her breasts. They filled his palms, familiar and yet not, all at the same time. He cursed. "Darling, the things you do to me." He nipped her collarbone. "I'm going to taste you, so if you're going to change your mind, now's the time to do it."

Her only response was to shove her yoga pants down to her knees.

He lifted her onto the counter and disentangled her right leg from the pants so he could spread her fully. He stroked her thighs, pausing when his fingers met the scar. It brought up so many conflicting feelings in him. It was *his fault* that she had the damn thing, but that didn't mean he thought of her as less, the way she seemed to think. She was as beautiful now as she'd been at eighteen, and more confident despite her injury. Or maybe because of it. He had no idea.

All he knew was that at some point he was going to have to get up close and personal with her healed injury, and he was going to have to tread very, very carefully to avoid burning what was left of the bridge between him and Hope.

"If you apologize, I might actually kick you."

That snapped him out of it. As much as he wanted

Hope, he had an ulterior motive for pushing her now. All getting distracted by her leg was going to do was fuck up his chance of convincing her to stay, in his house and in his bed. He jerked her to the edge of the counter, spreading her thighs wider. "Don't scream. You'll upset Ollie."

And then he did what he'd been fantasizing about ever since he walked out of her life. Daniel dipped his head and gave her center one long lick. She tasted better than he remembered, her body already shaking for him, so he used his thumbs to part her folds and licked her again, reacquainting himself with every inch of her.

"Oh."

He looked up her body to find her head thrown back and her chest rising and falling with each harsh breath. "Take off your shirt."

Hope wasted no time obeying, dragging the material over her head and tossing it away. And then there was nothing hiding her body from his gaze. He licked her again, savoring the way she shook. A tattoo curling around the bottom of her ribs caught his eye, but he was too distracted to read it.

He was tired of teasing her. He wanted to feel her orgasm again, to know she was coming apart at the seams because of him. Daniel sucked her clit into his mouth, stroking the sensitive little nub with the flat of his tongue the way she'd always loved. Sure enough, before he had a chance to truly savor her, Hope cried out his name and shuddered, her thighs squeezing his head as she came. He gentled his touches, licks turning to kisses, turning to the slightest brushing of his lips against her. Only when she stopped shaking did he raise his head. "Stay, at least until we figure out what we're doing."

"You are...I don't even have words to describe what you are." She blinked and ran a hand over her face. "Is this how every argument is going to go?"

Hell, yes—at least if he had his way. Daniel dragged his cheek against her thigh. "You kissed me first."

"I was just trying to shut you up."

He laughed against her skin, not quite willing to let her go yet. "Well, that's one way to go about it."

Her smile died as she pushed him gently back and slid off the counter. "This doesn't solve anything. You know that, right? You can't just sex me into submission." She wrestled her pants back on, and he mourned the loss. Things were so much simpler when they were talking with their bodies instead of their words. No matter which way he lined things up, they were different people than they'd been when they dated. So much had changed since then, the terrain changed until he barely recognized the world around him.

But he knew her body.

He'd never stop knowing what made her hot and drove her crazy.

And he sure as fuck wasn't above using that to get what he wanted.

CHAPTER EIGHT

Hope climbed out of Daniel's truck and looked up and down the street. There were people around, but none of them seemed to be paying too much attention. That wouldn't last, but at least she had a slight reprieve to catch her breath.

In theory.

The truth was she didn't know what the hell was going on. One minute she'd been independent and asserting her need to create some distance between herself and Daniel, and the next his head had been between her legs. It was never like that with him before. It had been soft and sweet.

There was nothing soft and sweet about the man coming around the front of the truck to glare at her. He pointed. "I was coming to get your door."

"Either develop Superman abilities or come to terms with the fact that I can get my own damn door." She knew she was being rude, but she didn't care. She'd spent almost half her life taking care of herself without a man—without *him*—around, and she wasn't about to turn into a wilting flower just because he decided to walk back into her life.

Technically I walked back into his life.

And seduced him.

And messed up birth control.

And got pregnant.

It was kind of hard to maintain the moral high ground in this situation, but when it came to him sweeping in and taking over her life, it just wasn't going to happen. The sooner he figured that out, the better.

To end the conversation, she turned toward the storefront. The place looked exactly like it had when she was in high school. It was crazy. So much had changed—*she* had changed—and yet Devil's Falls was practically the same. It made it hard to differentiate between the past and present, too easy to fall back into the old rhythms she and Daniel had had. *I can't.* The minute she dropped her guard completely, he was going to have her quitting her job, moving in, and the man would probably go so far as to propose because he thought that it was the right thing to do.

Once upon a time, she'd wanted to marry Daniel Rodriguez. But not now. Not like this. Not when he was operating under some misguided belief that he was going to do right by her.

She moved away from him and into the store. The whole point of coming into town was to get some of the stuff she needed for the night—mainly food. She might be leaving in the morning, but she still had to eat in the meantime. She didn't know how he lived on the grand total of three items in his kitchen, but she wasn't about to start smearing mayonnaise on saltine crackers.

Hope froze, her stomach lurching. *Mental note— don't think about gross food combinations if you want to be able to eat breakfast.*

The woman at the counter looked up from the magazine she was idly paging through and gave a shriek fit to wake the dead. "Holy crap, Hope Moore, is that you?"

It took precious seconds to place the blonde, and by then she had hopped over the counter and was coming at Hope, arms spread for a hug. "Jessica Stroup?"

"The one and only." She engulfed Hope in a hug that popped her back. "It's been a million years! Why on earth are you back in this little shithole?"

She and Jessica had been on the cheerleading team back in high school, and the other woman had always had big dreams about heading west to L.A. and getting into modeling or acting. She was certainly beautiful enough for it. Hope smiled. "Visiting some old friends."

Jessica peered around her, her blue eyes going wide when Daniel pushed through the door. "Old friends *indeed*. We're going to have to go share a drink at the Joint and catch up. I know the bar isn't as fancy as the places you must be used to in Dallas, but it's what we have up here." She grinned. "You look a little frazzled, and I know I'm talking a mile a minute, so I'm just going to write down my number and you can give me a call. We don't have to drink. We can totally go for coffee or something. I'm off at three. Have you heard that Jules Rodriguez opened up a cat café down the street? Strangest concept I ever heard of, but it's loads of fun to go in there and play with the cats while you chat and drink coffee."

"Oh, ah, okay."

"I'm doing it again." She backed toward the counter, still smiling. "Go on and do your shopping. We can talk later."

Hope had forgotten how overwhelming Jessica was—but in a good way. It was actually kind of nice to have an interaction in town that wasn't fraught with undertones. She wasn't ready to confide about the pregnancy, but a break later today from Daniel's intense presence would be a good thing. Even though he didn't say anything, she felt him at her back as she grabbed a cart and headed down the first aisle.

Glowering.

It took all of ten feet before her patience ran out. "You have something to say, so say it."

He grabbed a can of soup off the shelf, seemingly at random. "I open doors, Hope. It's what any man worth his salt in the South does. It has nothing to do with what you can or can't do." Another can of soup hit the basket of the cart hard enough to bounce.

So they were back to that. She should have known. Daniel could be like a dog with a bone when something bothered him. She took a deep breath and turned to face him. If they were going to fight about every little thing, this would never work.

If she was going to be honest, her pride was as much to blame as his stubbornness.

Hope took a deep breath and tried to take the high road. "I get overly defensive. I'm sorry." She held up her hand. "I can't promise I won't snap at you again, but I'll try to relax about the door stuff."

He raised his eyebrows. "Just the door stuff?"

"Yes." It came out sharper than she intended, but damn, could he give it a rest for a few minutes? She knew he wanted her in his house permanently, just like she knew he might have appeared to drop it, but he was just planning a different method of approach. She was so damn tired, and it was only beginning. Hope turned to the row of cereal boxes in front of her. "Now, I'm starving, and arguing with you is burning more calories than I'm comfortable with. We'll talk when we get back to your place, and we'll come up with some sort of game plan." Staying in Devil's Falls for the next nine months was out of the question. She could do her job in a limited capacity online, but she really needed to be in the office. If she up and told them she was moving back to a little town no one had ever heard of, she might as well quit on the spot.

No. Absolutely not. She might have put her life on hold waiting for Daniel when she was eighteen, but she most definitely wasn't going to do it now because he was determined to pay penance by being with her.

She deserved better than that.

Both she and the baby did.

The look he gave her was downright indulgent. "Fair enough."

She hated how suspicious she was of him, but it was hard not to be in their current circumstances. Daniel never gave up a fight unless he chose to walk away, and he hadn't this time. That meant he was backing off only long enough to find a different approach to get her to do what he wanted.

They moved through the aisles without speaking, Hope pausing every few feet to consider what she felt like eating and Daniel throwing food into the cart seemingly at random.

She didn't know what to make of that, so she focused on what sounded good. It was so *strange.* She normally loved oatmeal in the morning, but when she picked up her favorite brand, she set it back without tossing it in the cart, that horrible nausea rising again.

Instead, she ended up in the produce section, loading up on orange juice, fruit, and cucumbers. Through it all, Daniel shadowed her movements, a giant gray cloud warning of an impending storm.

Jessica managed to contain herself as they paid, but she slipped Hope her number with a smile. "It really would be nice to catch up."

As much as part of her wanted to keep her distance from everything Devil's Falls related, that goal wasn't realistic. She was leaving. She *had* to leave.

Hope forced a smile. "I'll call. I promise." And she would. Even though she and Jessica had lost contact after the accident, they'd been really close in high school. It would be nice to have a friend who knew the whole history, someone she could talk to who would understand why she was hesitating to cut Daniel out of her life, even now, after everything they'd been through. Her friends in Dallas were wonderful, but they would, to a person, tell her to get rid of him.

He loaded the groceries into the bed of his truck in short, jerky movements that belied the calm expression on his face. In an effort to keep the peace a little while longer, she waited for him to hold the door open for her instead of climbing into the truck like she was perfectly capable of doing. It wasn't until they were driving back out of town that he spoke. "My parents are going to want to know you're back."

"I'm not back."

"Yes, darling, you are. At least for today." He shot her a look. "You're just pissed that I pushed too hard about it and you don't want to give in, despite the fact that it's what you want. If you go back to Dallas right now, it's going to be a decision made out of spite."

She resisted the urge to cross her arms over her chest, but only barely. "I think I like you better when you're being irrational and pushy."

"It's a hell of a lot easier to say no to me when I am." He sounded too freaking cheerful for her blood pressure. How was he acting so calm when their entire lives had gone topsy-turvy? *Unless this is what he wanted all along...*

She shut that thought down *real* fast. This was an accident as a result of two consenting adults. She was as much to blame for the error in judgment as he was. Lord, she should be *happy* that he wasn't freaking out and blaming her and acting like this was the worst thing that had ever happened to him. "Daniel..."

He reached over and took her hand, the shock of his skin against hers stealing her breath. "We'll figure this out. I know it's not how you had your life planned out, but this is where we're at. It's not going to be easy, but what about life is?"

Too reasonable. Something is up.

She extracted her hand, because she couldn't quite think straight when he was touching her, and turned to look out the window. All the words coming out of his mouth were right, but there was something off about the delivery. It was like he knew the steps to go through but he didn't really believe that it would be that easy any more than she did. "I don't...I don't trust you anymore." It hurt to say that aloud, but it was necessary. Everything had changed, and that lack of trust was the most damning part. Hope took a deep breath. "I'm not staying. End of story. So whatever you're planning, knock it off."

"What makes you think I'm planning anything?"

Because he was too calm, too settled, when a few short hours ago he'd been totally and completely out of control. That switch didn't flip without a good reason, and she hadn't agreed to anything he wanted. Not really. She was leaving and that was that, and the fact he was so calm about it didn't sit well with her.

It all added up to trouble.

Even if she didn't know the specifics, she was smart enough to see which way the wind was blowing.

CHAPTER NINE

Daniel spent the next hour walking on eggshells. He knew he'd pushed Hope too hard that morning, and he was determined to figure out a better way to convince her that staying with him was the only option. Every single thing he said was the wrong thing, and he didn't know how to fix that. All he knew was that if Hope left in a couple days, she wouldn't be back.

So he gave them both a break and went outside to let Ollie run for a bit. The pup was in her element, running circles around him and then darting off to chase phantom animals, racing back and then starting the whole process over again. She, at least, didn't plan on leaving him the first chance she got.

Ollie barked again, wondering why he'd stopped playing, and he crouched down to ruffle her ears. He'd never considered himself underhanded before now, but he'd do worse than mess with Hope's car to get her to sit still long enough for him to find the right words to get her to stay.

Can't convince her from out here. He pushed to his feet and headed for the door, Ollie on his heels. Daniel opened the door—and then stopped when he heard humming deeper in the house. He sat down on the mudroom bench long enough to yank off his boots and then went in search of her. The living room was empty, but he found her in the kitchen, her phone set up to play some funky music he'd never heard before, her hips shaking as she moved around the stove, dumping ingredients into a casserole dish.

This could have been my life.

It still could be.

Without thinking, he crossed the distance between them and slid his arms around her waist. She went still as he rested his chin on the top of her head. "Damn, darling. I missed you."

"Danny—"

He turned her in his arms and framed her face with his hands. "We talk too much." And they never solved a damn thing doing it. Then he kissed her.

She went soft against him, her hands sliding down his chest to grab his hips and pull him closer. That was all the invitation he needed to tip her head back and deepen the kiss. Shit might be fucked up beyond all reason when it came to them, but at least they still matched up here.

Today she wore those damn yoga pants again. It didn't matter to him that he could see the ridges of her scar beneath the thin fabric, because they gave him a heavenly view of her ass whenever she turned around. And the stretchy fabric was more tease than barrier. He reached between them, rubbing the heel of his hand over her clit. "What do you say?"

She blinked at him, her brown eyes hazy with lust. "What?"

"This thing." He kept rubbing her, shifting so he could press a knuckle on either side of her clit, stroking up and down slowly. "I want inside you, darling. I want it so bad, it's been driving me fucking crazy." Her breath hitched, and he pressed his advantage. "You want it, too. You're so wet, I can feel it."

"I…" She bit her lip. "It's a mistake."

"Probably." *Definitely.* "But what's the worst that could happen?"

Her smile was bittersweet. "It's already happened."

Part of him hated that she thought getting pregnant was the worst thing that could happen, but now wasn't the time to start fighting about it. He'd have to show her that this was a second chance in disguise—a way to make things right once and for all—and the only way to get her to sit still long enough was an orgasm-induced coma.

It doesn't hurt that you've been in a permanent state of blue balls since you saw her last.

No, it didn't hurt one bit. Everything else might have changed, but he wanted Hope more than he wanted his next breath.

He slipped his hand into her pants, resuming the motion that had her quivering in his arms. "Might as well take advantage of me, then."

"Take advantage of *you*?" Her voice was a little breathy, but she managed to keep it together. Mostly.

"Mmm." He skimmed off her shirt, dropping it next to them and cupping her breasts. "Fuck. When I fill you with my cock, I want you naked. I want to see these beautiful breasts bouncing with every stroke."

"Arrogant."

"Realistic." He stroked her nipples with his thumbs, watching her face. "You know you're craving it. I bet you've been touching yourself remembering that night. Coming with my name on your lips just like you did then."

Her fingers dug into his biceps. "I hate you more than a little bit right now." She arched, pressing herself more firmly into his hands. "But I don't really care."

"Say yes."

"Yes." It was barely more than a whisper, but it might as well have been a yell with how the word reverberated through him.

Daniel spun her around, keeping a hold on her hip to make sure she didn't stumble, and shoved down her yoga pants. He reached between her legs from behind with one hand. "Christ, do you ever wear anything other than yoga pants?"

"Not when I'm lounging around the house, you jackass."

He delivered a stinging slap to her ass—more to get her attention than anything else. "When did you get so mouthy?"

"Right around the time you got so damn bossy." She braced her hands on the counter. "Now take me before I change my mind."

Daniel stroked a hand down her spine and palmed her ass. He undid his belt and jeans with his other hand. "How many times?"

"What?"

He pushed his jeans down and notched his cock at her entrance. "How many times have you fantasized about this?"

"Since we last had sex or since I was eighteen?"

The words hit him like a sucker punch to the gut. He sheathed himself to the hilt, using his hold on her hips to pull her back onto his cock. "Both."

She squirmed, breathing hard, but he wasn't about to let her move until he was damn well ready. Hope muttered a curse that made him smile despite everything. "A dozen times to the former, impossible to count to the latter."

He felt like crowing with a victory he sure as fuck didn't deserve. So he started moving, sliding out of her almost completely before slamming home again. "I've thought about you, too, darling. Over and over again, palming my cock and imagining it was your tight little pussy wrapped around it instead. It doesn't fucking compare. Nothing—*no one*—compares to you." He reached around to rub on either side of her clit, his mouth against her ear, his chest pressed against her back. "You want to know why you couldn't stop thinking about me?"

"No." She shoved back against him, taking him deeper.

He licked the shell of her ear. "It's because this pussy is mine, darling. It always has been. It always will be."

"I...hate...you."

Daniel hitched her higher, running his free hand up to cup her left breast, pinching her nipple lightly. "Doesn't change a fucking thing. Now be a good girl and come for me."

He pressed three fingers hard against her clit and that was all it took. She cried out, her pussy spasming around him and her entire body shaking. He leaned back to grab her hips, pounding into her, chasing his own orgasm. Pressure built in the base of his spine, and though he tried to fight it off as long as he could, it was just too fucking good. He came so hard his knees buckled. "Holy shit."

And then there was nothing to do but lean against the counter, covering her, and relearn how to breathe.

Hope didn't give him much opportunity. She

ducked out from beneath his arms and yanked her pants back into place. "You...I can't...God, *I hate you.*"

He turned his head to watch her snatch up her shirt. "You're welcome for the orgasm."

"Don't start that crap with me. I agreed to sex. I did not agree to you doing the equivalent of peeing on my foot. I am not yours, Daniel. I haven't been for a long time and I never will be again."

• • •

Hope was so furious, she could barely think straight. *How* dare *he?* And she'd walked right into it, which was the most unforgivable part of the whole mess. She shoved out the front door, making it a whole three steps before Ollie rushed around the side of the house, barking happily. The dog ran circles around her, making it impossible to take a step without worrying about stepping on her.

Good lord. The dog was attempting to herd her back into the house.

She propped her hands on her hips and glared. "I know what you're doing, and I don't appreciate it any more than I appreciate what *he's* doing."

"Careful there—you're going to hurt her feelings, and I've never seen a canine that can mope quite as effectively as Ollie."

Deep down, she'd known that he'd follow her out here. She needed time to wind down, and Daniel wasn't going to give it to her. He'd just keep pushing and prodding and steamrolling until she either caved or exploded. Right now, the latter was looking pretty damn attractive.

She spun to face him. The fact that he looked rumpled and sexy only made her crazier. It would be so incredibly easy to stop fighting and let him steamroll her. He wasn't saying anything she didn't want to hear. But that was the problem—she no longer trusted Daniel Rodriguez. A baby. A catastrophic leg injury. Both were world-altering events, and he'd dropped her like a hot potato after the first one. Who was to say he wouldn't do the same thing after the other the second he stopped to think too hard about it? "You sicced your dog on me."

"Sicced, huh?" He made a show of looking at the deliriously happy dog, which only made her want to stomp her foot like a toddler. Daniel raised his eyebrows. "Are you feeling threatened? Because Ollie here looks pretty fucking threatening right now."

"Shut up." He didn't get to surprise her in the kitchen with mind-blowing sex, lay claim to her vagina, and then turn around and poke fun at her. "I need space."

It was clearer than ever that this wasn't working out. She'd shown up here expecting… She didn't know what she'd been expecting. When she'd driven from Dallas, she'd been convinced he would say all the right things and then she could go back to her life, well assured that he'd be supportive in the way she envisioned. That they would be partners—long-distance partners.

Apparently that had been her delusions talking.

The truth was that Daniel wasn't the only one to blame for things going south so quickly. She was too keyed up, and it was making her emotions flip-flop faster than even she could follow. If she'd told him to back off sexually, he would have. *She* was the one who'd made the first move. So the blame for that, at least, lay firmly in her court. Hope held up a hand. "Space, Daniel. Respect it or I'm getting in my car right now."

He stopped in the middle of walking toward her. "You don't get to throw that threat around whenever it pleases you."

"Wrong. We aren't dating, and we sure as hell aren't married. I might be having your baby, but that doesn't mean *I'm* yours." She hated the way his mouth tightened with each word, but she needed to make this as cut-and-dried as she could. She'd been back in Devil's Falls all of a weekend and it was more clear than ever why they wouldn't work.

"That's where *you're* wrong, darling." He leaned against the post of his front porch, looking for all the world like he wasn't worried she'd leave. Like she was a sure thing. "You never stopped being mine."

It was too much. She'd tried so incredibly hard to let go of the past and move on, but being back here and having him make claims on her he had no business making… She couldn't do it anymore. "If I was really yours, you wouldn't have left me in that hospital alone, Daniel. You would have been there when I woke up. You would have been at my side when we buried my brother. You wouldn't have stared right through me as if I wasn't there. You would have, I don't know, returned a single phone call instead of letting me twist in the wind. I'd lost so much, and then you went and made sure that I lost *everything*."

It hurt to say, like she was traveling back in time to

that terrified eighteen-year-old girl who'd woken up an only child and watched her college track scholarship disappear before her eyes. She'd clung to the fact that at least she still had Daniel…except then she didn't have him, either.

He flinched. "Darling—"

"Do *not* call me that."

They stood there, staring at each other across a distance that should be easily crossable. If only he would take the first step, if only he'd been willing to bend just a little. He wouldn't, though. Nothing had really changed.

Daniel straightened. "It was a mistake."

"I know this was a mistake."

"No, that's not what I'm saying. Back then, I made a mistake. Fuck, I made more than one. We went out that night and I knew I was the designated driver, and I still had two beers."

Her eyes went wide. *Surely he doesn't still blame himself for that?* "I don't know how things are for you now, but back then two beers wasn't even enough for you to catch a buzz."

"I blew a point-oh-nine."

"That doesn't mean you were drunk." She'd known he wasn't drunk. In all the scenarios that had played out in her head over the years, she'd always comforted herself with the knowledge that Daniel had to know that that car crash was beyond his control. "It was raining like crazy and that truck lost control. You were trying to avoid a head-on collision."

"Instead, I rolled the car, killed John, and crippled you."

She jerked back, biting down on her instinctive

response to that. This moment wasn't about her. It was about him and the guilt that had been poisoning him for far too long. "No one could have done better. Everyone knows that." Everyone except, apparently, Daniel.

But he wasn't listening. He stared off into the distance. "How could I face you, Hope? We all loved John, but he was your big brother. He'd always suspected I wasn't good enough for you, and that night I proved him right."

"You're rewriting history. Don't you dare put the memory of John between us." She drew herself up. "He might have been your best friend, but he was *my* brother. He wouldn't have blamed you for the crash any more than I did. You made your intentions to marry me after I got through college pretty damn clear. He thought we were great together."

His shoulders dropped a fraction of an inch. "There's no way you don't blame me for that. It's impossible."

"Well, then pigs are flying, because I don't. I never have." She waited a beat, silently debating just letting this go. But it was like lancing a wound—it was time to get it all out there. "I blame you for abandoning me afterward."

"I couldn't face you." He shook his head. "I might not have taken off like Adam did, but it was everything I could do to go to the funeral. It was bad putting John in the ground, but it was almost worse seeing you in that chair, looking like you had one foot in the grave. I just…I thought you'd be better without me in your life."

He'd been mourning, the same way she had. The

difference was that he'd only seen what he'd lost, rather than what was still left. Mainly *her*. Because of her leg, apparently. "If you couldn't handle the thought of being with a *cripple*, then just say it. It's fine—you didn't sign on for that when we started dating. But don't try to pretty it up like you were doing me a favor." Suddenly exhausted, she wobbled over to drop onto the step next to where he stood.

He sank down next to her. "I don't think you're a cripple."

"You literally just said that."

"I didn't mean it like that. I just meant…" He sighed. "I'm sorry."

"Bully for you." She didn't really want to talk about her injury. It was just another opportunity for him to wallow in decade-old guilt instead of focusing on the current issues. "My point, which we've stampeded away from, is that you are the one who ended us. Not me. So you don't get to just decide that you're picking back up where we left off. That's not how it works."

"Do you still love me, darling?"

Her breath stilled in her lungs, and her eyes went wide. The world tilted crazily around her like it had last time she had the misfortune of being on a carnival ride. She hadn't liked the experience any more then than she did now. "*What the hell kind of question is that?*"

His smile was the very definition of smug. "I thought so."

God, the man was just infuriating. She threw up her hands, torn between strangling him and strangling *herself*. "Have you been listening to a single thing I've been saying?"

"Yeah. I did you wrong—in more than one way. I know I can't make up for that shit, or ever really lay it to rest because it's always going to occupy space between us, but I can start by doing right by you from here on out."

He kept saying that. *Do right by you.* It was like he thought this baby represented a chance to balance out his karmic debt. Which was all well and good for him, but she wasn't a debt and she didn't want to be with a man who saw her as his burden to bear. "I swear to God, if you propose to me, I'm going to punch you in the face."

Daniel stood and offered her his hand. "I lose my head around you. What we had…it was a once-in-a-lifetime kind of thing. So forgive the fuck out of me if I'm more than willing to play dirty to get you to stay. I know I'm screwing up, but I'm trying my damnedest."

All she wanted to do was walk away. It *hurt* being with him, like a knife twisting in her stomach over and over again. But there was more than her to think about now. It didn't matter how complicated their history was—her baby would know his or her father. *Daniel will be a good father.* She'd always known that, and apparently she was going to get a chance to see it in real time.

Hope inhaled deeply and took his hand. "Tone down the possessive crap—starting now."

"I'll try."

It wasn't much of a promise, but it wasn't like she was an innocent in this, either. She'd known things between them were too intense, full of too much potential to blow up in her face, and she'd still had sex with him. More than once.

Truth be told, she kind of wanted to go there again.

And, damn it, he knew. Daniel's smile made her stomach do a slow flip. "You've got that look in your eye, darling. I've been an asshole. Let me make it up to you."

Even though she knew better, she followed him back into the house. "You've set a pretty high bar for yourself if you're going to try to fix every fight we have with sex."

"Believe me—I'm more than up for the challenge."

CHAPTER TEN

Hope kept a hold of Daniel as he led her into his bedroom, feeling like she was in the middle of the storm and he was the only thing keeping her from being swept away. Ironic, since *he* was the one responsible for the storm in the first place. But with him looking over his shoulder at her with those dark eyes, and his calluses rubbing against the palm of her hand, she couldn't think of a good reason to put a stop to this once and for all.

It's too late. There's no stopping it now, no matter what I do.

She touched her stomach with her free hand, wondering how so much could have changed and yet nothing at all. They'd barely crossed the threshold when he swept her into his arms. In the back of her mind, she knew it was because he wanted her to be careful with her knee, but her pride had nothing on the feeling of being this close to him. *This is really happening.* She couldn't blame this on hormones getting the better of her, or on an impulse she had too little self-control to resist.

She was making the choice to have sex with Daniel Rodriguez.

He set her on her feet and stripped her shirt off. She could barely comprehend the way he looked at her, like he'd never seen anything so beautiful in his life. *He used to look at you like that.* Yeah, *before.* She closed her eyes and tipped her head back, silently demanding a kiss he seemed all too ready to deliver. His hands sifted through her hair to cup the back of her head and his lips brushed against hers, teasing her mouth open. She opened for him. She was helpless to do anything else.

His skin was so damn warm beneath her hands. She cautiously slid them up his sides to his chest, not pushing him away, not pulling him closer, just relishing the ability to touch him to her heart's delight. Daniel made a sound that was damn near a growl at her nails dragging over his skin, so she did it again.

"We'll go slow this time."

She barely had a chance to register the words when he toppled them back onto the bed, twisting just enough that she didn't take his full weight. She could have told him it didn't matter. She wanted everything he could give her, wanted to lose herself in the feel of him, wanted to just stop thinking for one fucking second and enjoy this.

Of course, he knew. He always knew. Daniel shifted to kiss along her jaw. "Turn off that beautiful brain of yours, darling. We'll figure it out. I promise. But right now I'm more concerned with getting you out of these pants."

Fear, cold and irrational, rose to close her throat. Taking off her pants meant baring her scar to him and being forced to witness that horrible guilt on his face. Then she wouldn't be the only person thinking too much. She opened her mouth, but no words came out.

He kissed her again, his hands going to the waistband of her pants and underwear, and she lifted her hips to allow him to slide them down her legs. His movement hitched when his fingers made contact with the top of her scar, but it was such a small hesitation, she wouldn't have noticed it if every fiber of her being wasn't focused on him. Daniel tossed the clothing aside, quickly followed by her bra. "Tell me about the tattoo. An anchor."

"Its whole purpose is to remain in place, no matter how strong the currents or how fierce the storm."

As usual, his dark eyes saw too much. "You always were strong, darling."

She didn't feel the least bit strong right now. She hadn't since she walked back into his life. She felt like a leaf being thrown around by the wind, free-falling in one direction and then tossed to the side, then falling all over again until she wasn't sure which way was up and which way was down. But she didn't want to talk about that right now. She didn't want to talk about anything. "Kiss me, Danny."

He did. He just didn't kiss her lips.

Daniel pressed a kiss to one hip bone and then the other, shifting to settle between her thighs. One big hand pressed lightly down on her lower stomach, and he met her gaze. There was so much left unsaid between them, but now wasn't the time. He drew his tongue over her center, a long, savoring lick that made her squirm. He kept her pinned in place, though, the feeling only heightening the sensation of pleasure as he licked her again. "You always were my favorite flavor."

I don't know what to say to that.

He circled her clit with his tongue, taking away the need to say anything at all. She reached over her head and grabbed the bottom of the headboard, needing something solid to hang onto while he drove her relentlessly to oblivion. Daniel never quite let her take the final plunge, though. He teased her, drawing ever closer to the edge, and then gentling his touches to prevent her from coming.

The third time, she cried out in frustration. "You are a horrible man."

"Mmm-hmm." He pushed a finger into her, the shock of penetration making her eyes fly open. "And you're almost ready for me, darling."

Almost ready for... She lifted her head. "Then stop teasing me and get up here."

"When you put it like that..." He crawled up her body and settled between her legs. A wild thought rolled over her that they'd been in this exact position too many times to count when they were teenagers in the back of his truck. She pressed her lips together to keep the hysterical giggle inside. Daniel raised his eyebrows. "What?"

"I feel like an idiot teenager again."

He went still, and she kicked herself for saying anything to bring them back to those days. To *that* day. But it was something that would come up again and again. If they didn't find a way to work through it, they were destined for a future filled to the brim with misery and fights and just plain awful times. *We* have *to figure it out before the baby gets here or he or she will be visiting him every other weekend like Jessica's parents forced her to do.* The thought beat back the desire coursing through her body, her mind kicking into high gear again.

Daniel shook his head. "Later."

His cock notched in her entrance and then he was

inside her again, that slow, sensuous slide filling her and making her feel whole. She locked her ankles at the small of his back, allowing him that extra depth that made her back arch. *"Danny."*

"I've missed the way you say my name when I'm inside you." He rolled his hips, sliding one arm beneath her back to seal them as close as two people could be. His lips brushed her ear with each word, sending shivers through her body in time with his short thrusts. He kissed her, and that was all it took. She clung to him as she came, her entire world narrowing down to the feeling of Daniel on top of her, beneath her, inside her. His cock filling her, his taste in her mouth.

She came down from her orgasm to realize he was still hard inside her. Hope blinked at him, and Daniel gave her a grin that made her heart skip a beat. "I set a high bar, remember?"

She didn't remember much of anything right now.

He pushed off her, adjusting their angle until her ankles were propped on his shoulders and he was on his knees. The new position nearly made her eyes roll back in her head, his cock impossibly deep inside her. He thrust, pulling out of her almost all the way and slamming home, drawing a cry from her mouth. Daniel eyed her, adjusted his angle, and did it again.

"Oh my God." There was nothing to do but hang onto the headboard, riding out the waves of pleasure radiating through her.

She was vaguely aware of his strokes becoming irregular and hurried and him growling her name as he came, but she was too busy floating on a cloud of bliss to do much more than unclench her hands from the headboard and reach up to stroke them down his back where he'd collapsed on top of her. She pressed a kiss to his shoulder. "Okay, maybe you *can* fix most problems with sex."

At least temporarily.

. . .

Daniel managed to scrounge up a snack for them—a bag of Goldfish from behind the absurd number of cream of mushroom cans he'd rage-purchased earlier—but he wasn't about to let Hope out of his bed any time soon. The sex had been... Fuck, he didn't have words for how good it had been. All he knew was that the second they left this room, they were going to have to figure some shit out, and he flat out wasn't ready. This was a much-needed reprieve, and he was going to hold onto it for as long as he could.

On the other hand, there were things they needed to figure out sooner rather than later.

In all the chaos since Hope showed up again that first time, Daniel hadn't seen much of either his friends or family. Truth be told, that wasn't as abnormal as it once might have been, but he couldn't hide her away indefinitely. A weekend, yes. Any longer and word would get out—had *already* gotten out that she was back in town if the half a dozen missed calls from his mother were any indication.

He needed to let people know about the baby, but telling each person individually and having to deal with the variety of reactions that would no doubt range from shocked to pissed to joyful was exhausting to even think about. It would be easier to get them all together and deliver the news at once—like ripping off a Band-Aid.

First, though, he needed to get Hope on board. He'd already fucked things up enough without springing this on her, too. But if he could do both with one fell swoop…

He stretched, half rolling over to run a hand down her side. *Fuck, she's so beautiful, it kills me.* "I was thinking."

"Always a dangerous prospect." She opened one eye. "Go on."

"We have to tell my family eventually—and Adam and Quinn."

Hope sighed and rolled onto her stomach to bury her face in the pillow. "Can't we just tell them in approximately eight months when the baby is here? It's not like they're going to see me much in the meantime to ask why I suddenly look like a human-shaped elephant."

Eight months. It seemed like an eternity and not nearly long enough to get used to the idea of being a dad. And she was still planning on leaving in the morning. He forced himself to focus. "You know that's not an option."

"I don't see why not."

Daniel considered how to respond, trying to keep from steamrolling her like she kept accusing him of doing. "What do you say to getting together for a dinner and announcing it there? Let everyone know at once so there aren't any hurt feelings that we told one person before another."

"I suppose that would require me to make yet another trip to Devil's Falls?"

Not if she didn't leave in the first place. He ran a

hand down her spine, splaying his fingers across the small of her back. "Or maybe you could take some vacation days and we could do it this week. Get it all out of the way at once." The longer she was here, the better chance he had of convincing her to stay for good.

She lifted her head. "You won't let it go, will you?"

"This is sheer self-defense." He kept touching her, trying to soothe away the tension that had bled into her muscles. "If you're there and so is the rest of my family, there's the added bonus that with everyone together, we're less likely to get new asses ripped by my parents."

Hope made a face. "Speaking of parents, I suppose we should extend an invitation to mine, too, if we're going forward with this insanity."

He bit back a denial. She was agreeing to his plan, which meant he couldn't do a damn thing to jeopardize it. He hadn't seen the Moores since John's funeral, but he couldn't get the condemnation on Mrs. Moore's face out of his head. It was one of the contributing factors that pushed him to leave Hope alone for good, though he'd never tell her that. The decision had been his, and he didn't like the idea of causing problems with her and her parents.

That didn't mean he was all that eager to see them again.

But he'd fake it. For Hope. He cleared his throat. "That sounds great."

"Liar." She laughed softly. "But if we're going down together, it might as well be in flames."

Daniel kept stroking her back. "We can do this, darling. I promise." It struck him that he'd made promises to her before, a lifetime ago, and he'd failed at following through on a single one of them. Promises that he loved her, that they'd have a future together, that he'd be by her side through thick and thin.

I fucked up before. I won't do it again.

"Don't make promises you know you can't keep." She blinked at him from beneath a tangle of blond hair, as pretty as a picture, made all the more attractive because it was because of *him* that her lips looked so kissably plumped and *his* whiskers that left light marks on her pale skin. He felt out of control and damn near animalistic with the need to mark her, to prove to anyone who came too close that she was his and his alone. It didn't matter that he didn't have a right to claim her.

He'd given up being an honorable man a long time ago.

"We'll talk about it later...but later isn't here yet." She rolled into him, hooking his neck and pulling him down to her. "Now, kiss me and let's stop worrying for a little while."

CHAPTER ELEVEN

"It's been a minute, stranger."

Daniel kept his cell to his ear as he closed the door to the truck, doing his damnedest to ignore the censure in his friend's tone. "I've been busy."

When Hope had woken up, she'd developed a totally bizarre craving for Greek yogurt, so he was hustling to pick some up before she starved to death since that was the one thing they hadn't purchased yesterday. *Pregnancy sure makes her dramatic.* Not that he'd ever tell her that to her face. Things were finally starting to actually move forward between them, and he wasn't about to do anything to fuck that up.

Not on purpose.

He'd already more than proven he could—and would—fuck up on accident.

Hence, making this call while he was alone.

"Busy." Adam didn't sound all that impressed, and he shouldn't be. As far as excuses went, it was a shitty one. "By busy, I take that you mean you've been shacking up with Hope Moore for the weekend."

This goddamn town was out of control. They'd left the house together exactly one time, and that was all it took for gossip to spread like wildfire to everyone who'd listen—which was the entire population. He checked the sidewalk in front of the store, but thankfully he didn't see any of the older folk lurking, waiting to ambush him for news. If he hurried, he could get in and get out without running into someone he knew. "Word gets around."

"Yeah, well, you can't take her to Main Street and expect it not to—though I'm kind of thinking you damn well knew that." Adam didn't bother to give him a chance to respond. "What the fuck are you doing? I know things got carried away back at your birthday party, but I was under the impression she went back to Dallas."

"She did."

A beat of silence, then another. "Right, well, you don't have to confide in me about shit. But that doesn't mean I'm going to be giddy as fuck over you shutting me out—again."

Damn it, Adam had a point. He was the one who'd opened up a little over a year ago when he finally decided to stay in town for good. Daniel headed into the store, keeping his gaze focused on the ground and his hat tucked low. The truth was, there was a reason he'd called Adam instead of just issuing a blanket invite.

He needed someone to talk to.

It was hard to force the words out, hard to make it *real* by telling someone other than himself and Hope. He scanned the store, but there was only Jessica popping gum at the register, her attention trained her phone. Still, it couldn't hurt to move deeper into the place. "She's pregnant."

Adam didn't say anything while Daniel grabbed a basket to throw the yogurt into, and by the time he'd turned down an aisle at random, he still hadn't said anything. "I'm taking that to mean you don't approve."

"What the *fuck* are you doing?"

He winced and held his phone a little farther from his ear. He surveyed the food lining the shelf in front of him. Cereal. He could do better than cereal. She would need vitamins and shit to help the baby grow healthy. *Oatmeal is better.* He frowned at the selection and finally grabbed one of the high-fiber ones. *Babies need fiber, right?* "I'm doing right by her, Adam. It's time."

"There's nothing wrong with doing right by her, but this is a fucked-up situation, and if you don't see that, you're even more fucked in the head than I thought."

Daniel narrowed his eyes, moving to the next aisle. "Tell me how you really feel." He realized he was staring at a vat of olive oil and kept going, heading for the produce section. Devil's Falls wasn't exactly a hub of all things grocery related, but surely he could find something that would sound good to Hope.

Adam seemed to realize he was being a jackass, because he took a harsh breath. "I'm sorry. But what the hell are you two going to do?"

That was the question of the hour. He knew what the ideal situation would be, but he also knew that there was no way Hope would agree to marry him just because a baby came along. Convincing her that it *wasn't* just about the baby was going to be harder than hell…but maybe that wasn't a bad thing. As she'd pointed out time and time again, what happened thirteen years ago wasn't a good enough reason to make a decision about things happening right now. Maybe it was time he finally started listening.

He picked up an apple, frowned, and set it down again. *Maybe I should make a run in to Pecos.* "She's mine, Adam. She always has been."

"If that's the case, you've done a shitty job of taking care of what's yours."

It was the truth, and that only made it sting all the more. He glared at the oranges. None of them were good enough. "I'm looking to change that now." He grabbed a cluster of bananas and set them in his basket, balancing the phone against his ear. It was time to get to the point of this call and hang up so he could focus on what food would be the best bet for Hope. "We're putting together a dinner this weekend to tell the family—both families—and I'd like you and Jules to be there."

Adam sighed. "It's going to be a train wreck."

"Probably." *Most definitely.* There wasn't an outcome where the Moores were happy about this, and he didn't think his parents would be too keen, either. They loved Hope, and he'd broken his mother's heart when he and Hope broke up, but he figured this wasn't how they dreamed they'd end up with grandchildren.

"I'll be there—for this and for whatever either one of you need down the road." He hesitated. "Don't fuck this up, Daniel. Hope's a good girl—always has been—but she's been through a lot. It hasn't broken her yet, but it's just plain cruel to pursue this if it isn't what you really want."

"I want it." He'd had a hell of a time convincing her to let him have this much. He wasn't about to jeopardize his chance to make amends by pushing her too hard, too fast.

Maybe you should have thought of that before you fucked with her car.

Daniel didn't know if he believed in karma, but if it existed, it was practically waving a flashing neon sign in his face telling him that he couldn't ignore Hope and their baby. "I'll let you know about dinner once we have the day and time finalized."

"Sounds good. And Daniel?"

"Yeah?"

"Congrats."

He hung up, a slow smile spreading across his face. That had gone better than he'd anticipated. He knew Adam wasn't happy with how shit had played out recently. Hell, Quinn wasn't happy, either, but Quinn was less likely to corner him and confront him about it. They'd worked together too long for him to rock the boat unless he thought the situation was dire. Adam didn't have that problem and, combined with Daniel's meddling cousin rubbing off on her now husband, he could be a real pain in the ass sometimes.

But all that was going to change.

Everything was going to change.

He headed for the refrigerated section, determined not to forget yogurt after he'd come here specifically for it. He laughed softly at the pile of food in his basket. *Should have gotten a cart.* Daniel stopped in front of the yogurt section. Where the store was sparse in selection in other places, someone who stocked it *really* liked yogurt. There were at least twenty different varieties. Once he found the Greek version, that narrowed his choices down to six. He frowned. Short of calling Hope, there was no telling which flavor she wanted—or if that would be the same flavor she'd want tomorrow.

Better get them all.

He grabbed as many as could fit into the basket and then had a moment of considering if he should go back and get an actual cart so he could buy more. There had to be some kind of limit on how much yogurt one woman could eat, right? He studied the basket. "Well, hell. If she wants more, I'll just come buy out the rest of the selection." Simple.

Daniel couldn't stop the stupid grin from spreading across his face at the incredulous expression Jessica gave him as she rang him up. Let her wonder what he was up to. Let the whole damn town wonder. Hope Moore was in his house and in his bed, and she was staying—without a fight—for at least a few days more.

Things are finally starting to look up.

• • •

Hope stood in the kitchen, looking at the neat rows of Greek yogurt in the fridge. She'd laughed when Daniel came back with bags upon bags of it yesterday, but it was all she wanted to eat right now. He was trying so hard and, despite her, he was starting to win her over. They hadn't really solved anything with their fight, but maybe it was better to just focus on the future instead of the injuries they'd dealt each other in the past.

She was so damn tired of fighting.

She'd delegated the two projects she'd just taken on, and she was trying very hard not to look into the fact that the two ladies who worked with her were so freaking surprised that she'd taken vacation. It was the first time in years, but *still*.

Five days. That was it. After the party, she'd go back to Dallas and that would be that.

Strawberry sounded particularly delicious this morning, so she grabbed that container and sat down on the single bar stool to eat. Three days in Devil's Falls, and she was getting twitchy. She needed a good, long workout. Hope twisted to rub her leg. Running had been her outlet once upon a time, but that stopped being an option when she was eighteen. Now she used specific exercises and yoga to keep her knee from giving her too much grief—two things she hadn't been doing since she showed up on Daniel's doorstep.

She was pushing herself too hard, and she knew it—she'd had more than enough experience over the last decade to know her limits, and she was toeing the line. If she wasn't careful, she'd have a whole lot in the way of sleepless nights in the future. The pain pills she kept as a last resort weren't an option now that she was pregnant.

God, she hated those pills. They were like the physical representation of her weakness, a constant reminder that she wasn't normal and never would be. Normal people didn't have to worry about a body part inside her skin that didn't originate with her, or about nerves that sometimes felt like they were on fire.

The problem was that Daniel had been working really hard not to pay too much attention to her leg, and she didn't want to make him uncomfortable…

Hope straightened. "What the hell is wrong with me?" She was *not* doing this again. She'd put other people first for far too long, and he was the one who kept telling her he wanted to do right by her. Her scars were part of her, and if he couldn't handle that, he had no business trying to elbow his way into her life.

She finished off her yogurt, dropped the container in the trash, and put the spoon in the sink. She'd deal with whatever work things had popped up overnight and then she'd take a relaxing bath. After that, she'd settle in with some tea and a few movies and see if a day off her feet helped. She kind of suspected it wouldn't, but she had to try.

Things were going great right up until she leveraged herself into the bath filled to the brim with bubbles...and heard the front door open. Hope shot a panicked glance at the unlocked bathroom door, but if the heavy footfalls heading in her direction were any indication, she didn't have enough time to fight her way to her feet and hope that she managed to get to the lock before the person in the hallway got to the door.

As soon as the thought crossed her mind, the door opened and Daniel poked his head in. "Hope? I'm just..." He trailed off, his gaze raking over her. "Well, fuck."

She wasn't sure what she should be trying to cover, so she didn't cover anything. Her mangled knee clearly showed over the top of the bubbles, and there wasn't a damn thing she could do about it without curling into a ball. *He has to deal with it eventually.* "Did you need something?"

"Yeah, darling. I'm starting to think I do." He stepped into the bathroom and closed the door behind him. "You usually take baths in the middle of the day?"

The question seemed innocent enough, though there was nothing innocent about the way he was looking at her. She lifted her chin. "Only when my knee is giving me grief." It wasn't strictly true. Normally, she listened to her body and avoided pushing it far enough that it knocked her on her ass. It

KATEE ROBERT 525

was a rookie mistake, and she was paying the price now.

His attention focused there, his eyebrows coming together. "It's giving you grief?"

Talking about it was strange. The only person she felt comfortable being completely frank with was her doctor. Her parents did their best to be supportive, but it was easier for them to ignore her injury and pretend it didn't exist, which she was more than happy to play along with. Better for them to look at her like she'd never changed than for them to pity her. The guilt was even worse. She loathed guilt.

Hope braced herself for Daniel's reaction. "It does more often than not, but it's been worse than normal lately."

"Why?"

She hesitated, but honesty had to be the name of the game when it came to her interactions with him. To do anything else was to cheat them both. "Because I've been kind of sucking at self-care lately—though, to be fair, it's totally possible that hormones have something to do with it, too." *That's going to make things more complicated*, she realized. Pregnancy meant a big weight change, and even completely able-bodied women got clumsy. She was going to be doubly so because of her bum knee.

Hope sank into the water up to her chin, battling the overwhelming stress trying to take over. The whole reason she'd wanted this bath to begin with was to destress, and now it was looking like the opposite was going to be true. It was her own fault. She should have put the brakes on things until she considered all that was going to change. She hadn't. Taking it out on

Daniel might make her feel better in the short term, but it wouldn't last.

And it wasn't fair to him.

"You haven't been taking care of yourself because of me," he said. She half expected him to launch in to some self-recrimination—to, God forbid, to start blaming himself for that in addition to everything else *again*. Hope took a deep breath, ready to tell him—again—that this wasn't any more his fault than her brother's death was. That he wasn't a modern-day Atlas who could balance the entire world on his shoulders indefinitely.

But he surprised her and sank onto the closed toilet. "What can I do?"

She blinked, having prepared her response to how she thought he was going to react. It took her a second to catch up to reality. "Uh, what?"

"There's got to be something I can do. This is partly because you've been dancing around my emotions, and that's not fair to you." He gave her a look like he was fully aware of what she'd expected. "So what can I do to help?"

What she really needed was a massage and some of the dreaded pain pills, but neither was on the menu. "It's okay." He'd had his hands and mouth all over her body, but there was something about him touching *that* part of her that made her balk. It was too much, even more personal than having sex. She couldn't ask that of him. "I'm really okay."

He opened his mouth like he wanted to argue with her but finally nodded. "If you change your mind, I'm here. If you don't, that's okay, too." He pushed to his feet. "Do you need anything right now?"

It was difficult to wrap her mind around this accommodating version of Daniel. *He's trying to keep this peace going as hard as I am.* She didn't really need anything, but she'd already shut him down once and he obviously needed to feel like he was helping with something, so she said, "Maybe a glass of water?"

"Sure." He looked relieved. Daniel disappeared, coming back a few minutes later with a tall glass of ice water. He set it carefully on the edge of the tub but didn't immediately straighten. Instead, his gaze rested on the bubbles partially hiding her from him. "One more thing before I go."

She barely had a second to process his intent before he slipped a hand into the bathtub, sliding down her stomach to stroke her between her legs. She went ramrod straight, but she wasn't sure if it was in protest or because—*oh, God*—he pushed two fingers into her. "Danny—"

"Close your eyes, darling. Let me give you this if you won't take anything else from me."

She didn't fight his order. She didn't even try. She wanted this too much to push him away, even though distance was the only thing that would save her heart in the long run. *Liar.* The truth was that her heart had always been compromised when it came to Daniel Rodriguez. Hope spread her legs as much as she could in the tub, giving him access to everything. Just plain giving him everything.

He rewarded her by picking up his pace, stroking her just like she loved, already gathering an orgasm around her, her nerve endings sparking with pleasure. She'd never met a man who knew her body like Daniel did, and the years apart hadn't damaged his memory any. She hissed out a breath, the sound closer to a moan than an exhale. "Danny, I'm close."

"I know, darling." His lips touched hers, a soft, sweet kiss that was completely out of sorts with what his hand was doing between her legs. The innocence of that kiss pushed her into an orgasm that locked up her muscles and drew a cry from her throat. He ate the sound, his tongue sliding against hers as he gentled his touch and brought her back to earth.

It was only when she stopped shaking that he rested his forehead against hers for a long moment and retrieved his hand from the water. His shirt was soaked, but his slow smile said it was worth it. Daniel pushed to his feet. "I'll see you this evening." And then he was gone, leaving her wondering what the hell just happened.

Guess he wasn't joking about fixing everything with sex.

The problem was, as good as being with him felt right now, she couldn't shake the feeling that they were only administering a Band-Aid instead of actually *fixing* anything.

CHAPTER TWELVE

By the time the dinner rolled around on Friday, Hope was a hot mess. She'd changed for the third time and was going back for a fourth when Daniel intercepted her. "You look great."

"I feel like a…" She pulled at her sundress. Surely it hadn't been this tight last time she'd worn it? She felt like she was walking around with a giant scarlet *A* on her chest, that anyone who looked at her would know that she was pregnant with Daniel's child and that it hadn't been planned. "I don't know. Something huge and ungainly."

He raised his eyebrows. "You're seven weeks along, darling. You haven't changed a bit."

He might not think so, but she *felt* different. The nausea that everyone seemed to talk about hadn't overwhelmed her apart from a few food aversions, but her body was just off. The food she usually loved she didn't even want in the house, and her skin felt too tight. And that wasn't even bringing up the fact that apparently naps were the name of the game right now. It was just so *wrong*.

All she wanted to do was to wrap a blanket around herself and curl up with Ollie on the couch so she could get back her to *Gilmore Girls* binge session while she worked on what she could swing remotely, but she had to put on real clothes and leave the house and face what felt like half of Devil's Falls.

No one was going to be happy about this turn

of events.

She'd very carefully not thought about what her parents would think. They were shocked she was back in Devil's Falls, but they'd accepted her excuse of needing to hammer out some last-minute details with the town board about John's scholarship. The only thing getting them to make the drive north to town was her presence here. It had been six weeks since she saw them last, and she'd been battling the guilt of how things fell out with Daniel and their hookup. It made her sick to think about facing them now. *They're going to be so disappointed in me.*

"It will be okay." Daniel turned her around to face him and framed her face with his hands. "I promise."

"There you go again, promising things you can't fulfill." And she was being depressing as all get-out. Hope took a deep breath. "I'm as ready as I'm going to be."

He searched her face and finally nodded. "Let's go, then."

The trip into town took far too little time. They'd rented the back room of the Finer Diner to give them a little bit of privacy and to make sure no one had home court advantage. *We planned this out like we're going to battle.* It felt a whole lot like waging a war rather than what should have been a joyful occasion. In another life, it might have been...

No use thinking that way. This is your life. Not that nice little land of what-if.

Daniel's parents had beaten them there. His mom rose. She was a slightly overweight Hispanic woman with the kindest eyes Hope had ever seen, who always seemed to have a giant smile on her face. That was no different now, as she rushed around the corner to hug her. "As I live and breathe! Hope Moore!" She swept Hope up into a hug. Almost immediately, she gripped her shoulders and stepped back. "Let me look at you. Good lord, girl, but you're even more beautiful now than you were at eighteen." She registered the scar peeking out of the bottom of Hope's sundress, but her expression didn't so much as flicker. "I hear that you're running your own business. I always knew you were ambitious. Makes me so proud."

While she'd been chatting, Daniel's father had come to stand next to them. "Lori, you're manhandling her." He'd always seemed more biker than rancher to Hope, with his burly build and long graying hair and beard, but the fierce exterior was matched by an equally fierce love of his family. He hugged her, too, lifting her off her feet. "We missed you, Hope."

"I missed you, too." Against all reason, her eyes pricked, and she sniffed. She'd forgotten how much she loved the Rodriguezes—and how much they adored her.

Rodger set her back on her feet. "I hear you've decided to give our boy another shot." He gave Daniel a significant look. "It's a shame it took this long for him to pull his head out of his ass."

"For God's sake, Dad." Daniel crossed his arms over his chest. "You know there were extenuating circumstances."

Extenuating circumstances like him blaming himself for her brother's death and wallowing in his guilt. Lori wiped her eyes, still beaming like it was

Christmas morning. "None of that matters now that you're back."

I don't know if I'm back. She couldn't force the words out. Every time she said them, they felt more and more like a lie. She *wanted* to be back. But every time she was in danger of falling completely under the spell Daniel and Devil's Falls wove, something would happen to jar her back to stark reality. She wanted to believe. She just couldn't help waiting for the other shoe to drop.

Hope was saved from answering by the arrival of Jules and Adam. He didn't look particularly happy, but then, he hadn't every time she'd seen him recently. Jules, on the other hand, was grinning, just like her aunt. "Hope!"

They went through another round of welcomes, and then another when Quinn and his girlfriend, Aubry, showed up. Apparently she was Jules's best friend or something. The energy of the room was great, everyone smiling and chatting.

Which was when Hope's parents showed up.

They stopped just inside the doorway, their faces expressionless. Just like that, she knew exactly how things were going to go down. There would be no happiness here. No joy. Nothing but more guilt, filling up the room until she was liable to choke on it. She broke away from talking with Quinn and crossed to meet them, her heart in her throat. "Mom. Dad. I'm glad you're here." She wasn't, though. She kind of wished she'd saved this news to be shared privately, so it wouldn't tarnish the Rodriguez family's happiness.

"What's going on?" Her dad put his arm around

her mom's shoulders, as if she would break apart if he didn't hold her tightly enough. Ever since Hope graduated, her mom had become almost…brittle. As if she'd managed to put a good face on things and hold it together until she was sure her one remaining child would be okay. It was only then that she'd fallen apart and never quite seemed to put herself back together again.

Now, in the room full of John's old friends and the Rodriguezes, she looked like she was about to burst into tears.

Hope cleared her throat. "I, uh, *we* have something to tell you."

"Oh, God, don't tell me you're pregnant."

The room fell silent, the harsh words seeming to take up physical space, creating an atmosphere that no one was willing to break. The seconds ticked by—five, ten, fifteen, twenty.

She jumped when Daniel's arm slipped around her waist, a comfort she hadn't been aware she needed until it was there. His expression gave nothing away, but his dark eyes weren't happy. "Yes, you're going to be grandparents."

Hope's mother swayed like she might faint. She pinned Hope with a look. "How did this happen? You said you weren't seeing anyone, let alone *him*. You said nothing about seeing him when you were here for *John*."

She had to say something, but she couldn't push the words past her closed throat. Daniel didn't seem to have the same problem. His arm around her tightened, a slight tremor the only indication that he was as unsteady as she was. "It might not have been planned, but it doesn't matter. We're having a baby."

Her mom made a face like she was going to say something to cut straight to the bone, but her dad cut in. "I think now isn't the best time to talk about things. We all need some time and space to calm down so we can talk rationally." He nodded at Hope, pointedly not looking at Daniel. "We'll call you, honey." And then they were gone, sweeping out the door and leaving awkward silence in their wake.

Well, that's a great sign of things to come.

• • •

Daniel could feel the tension in Hope's body, even if none of it showed on her face. They'd known there was a chance the people in their lives wouldn't react positively to the news, but he'd expected reactions more like Adam's—shock and anger and then acceptance. He hadn't thought that the Moores would actually turn around and walk out the second they heard they were going to be grandparents.

He squeezed Hope's hip, trying to tell her that even if every other person turned their back on them, *he* would stand by her side no matter what. He owed that to both her and the memory of John. They shifted to take in the shocked expressions on the faces of every single person in the room. For one eternal second, no one said anything.

Then his mom moved forward, her dark eyes shining. "A baby?"

Hope gave a jerky nod. "I'm due May seventeenth." They'd calculated her due date using some internet site, but she had a doctor appointment in about a month to confirm it.

May 17. That's going to come up so fucking quick.

"Oh, honey, that's wonderful." She hugged Hope again, meeting Daniel's eyes over her shoulder. There was so much there—too much to readily decipher. It was like he'd offered his mom a lifeline in the middle of a hurricane when she'd given up hope of a rescue. It was too much for the news they were giving her. He didn't deserve that look for what had started as yet another fuckup in a long line of fuckups. Daniel might not view it that way now, but it wasn't like he and Hope had planned it out. The damn condom broke, and this was where they ended up.

Then there was no time for him to focus too closely on that, because it was hugs and congratulations and more than a few tears. The only faces not happy were Adam and Quinn, and he knew he was going to catch more than a little shit about it before too long.

It didn't matter.

He was here with the people he cared most about in the world, with the woman he'd never gotten over next to him, and the entire future laid out before them, full of possibilities.

As if the last thirteen years hadn't happened.

As if they really had a chance.

Really, he should be over the moon right now—and part of him was. The other part, though? The other part couldn't get the betrayed looks Hope's parents had given him out of his head. They'd wanted him to know he'd already done enough and he was a selfish piece of shit to be taking *this*, too. He shouldn't care. The only person who mattered was Hope. But then, Hope hadn't agreed to staying beyond this week. He'd done his damnedest not to push her, and so they hadn't talked again about her staying in Devil's Falls. For all he knew, she was still planning on heading back to Dallas.

He knew what side of the argument her parents would side with.

Growing up, the Moores had been like second parents to him. Adam's mom did her best, but she was a single mother with a little hell-raising asshole to bring up. Quinn's parents had never really approved of any of his friends, the exception maybe being John. As a result, their group split their time equally between the Moores and Daniel's parents' place. He'd never thought he'd live to see the day they looked at him like he was shit on the bottom of their shoe.

But then, he'd killed one of their kids and crippled the other.

"Are you okay?"

He blinked, finding Hope's hand on his arm, a worried look in her brown eyes. Daniel dredged up a smile from somewhere. "I should be asking you that."

"Yeah, well, it's been a hell of a day."

And it wasn't over yet. He forced a smile and mingled with his family, though they could have been speaking Greek for all he registered it. His mind kept going around and around, bouncing around like a pinball as he tried to come up with something—*anything*—to convince Hope to stay.

They ate, the food tasteless in his mouth, and as soon as it was cleared away, his mother stood. "I think that's more than enough excitement for one day. Hope, I know this wasn't planned, but never doubt for a minute that we consider you a daughter and we love both you and the baby unconditionally." She reached over and squeezed Hope's hand. "If you need anything at all while you're here, don't hesitate to call."

"Thank you."

She sank into the seat next to him and leaned down to rest her head on his shoulder. They watched the Rodriguez clan clear out in record time. Adam nodded at him as Jules towed him through the door. *I'll be hearing from him sooner rather than later.*

Quinn and Aubry stopped in front of them. The little redhead gave Hope a considering look. "I don't really like kids. Disgusting creatures, and I'm pretty sure they were put on this earth with the sole purpose of destroying everything within reach." Quinn cleared his throat and nudged her, and she sighed. "But, as you're going to have Daniel's spawn and said spawn will be related to Jules, I'm willing to make an exception to my no-kid policy."

Hope's lips twitched. "I very much appreciate that."

"Quinn, stop nudging me. I know I'm an ass." Aubry rolled her eyes. "The man should know by now that I'm untrainable in polite society."

Daniel coughed to cover a laugh, but the chuckle broke free when Quinn cursed and tossed Aubry over his shoulder. "Peaches, we're going to have to talk about your bedside manner."

"I don't have a bedside manner."

"Exactly."

The door closed behind them, and Hope visibly slumped. "That was something else."

"Yeah." He didn't have the words he needed. Any of them. He didn't know what to say to fix this thing that had been broken between them for half their lives.

He didn't know if he *could* fix it.

"I don't know about you, but I'm exhausted."

He'd been so busy brooding, he'd missed both those important things. *Hard to convince her to stay so I can take care of her when I'm doing such a stand-up job.* "Let's get you home, then." A strange look passed over her face, and he paused. "What?"

"Nothing. It's just funny how things work out, you know?" She accepted his offered hand and let him pull her to her feet.

He knew what she meant, but he still said, "Certain things are meant to be."

Hope shot him a look. "Fate, Daniel? Really?"

"No." Fate was too broad a term, and it took away personal responsibility. He didn't believe in fate. There was no way that something like John's death and Hope's mangled leg would be preordained. That was human error of the most unforgivable nature at work. He kept hold of her hand as they walked out of the diner. "But you and me, darling? It doesn't matter if it's a day or a decade—we're going to find our way back to each other again and again until we get it right."

"I don't know if that's depressing or reassuring."

"Both." For all appearances, she'd moved on before that night when they'd lost control and put themselves on their current path. She had a life, and it was on hold until they determined if this was a second chance or just another opportunity to fall apart. Which made it doubly important that they figure out their shit once and for all this time around.

He held the door open for her, that thought circling round and round in his head as he got in the driver's seat and headed for home. He knew damn well that things weren't perfectly fine between them. There was too much unsaid, too much that *had* to remain unsaid because they didn't see eye to eye on it. He wasn't willing to fight with her over his guilt, or the fact that he'd fucked up beyond belief thirteen years ago.

So how to prove that he was truly willing to go the distance now when he'd dropped the ball so spectacularly before?

Daniel tightened his grip on the steering wheel. He didn't know, but he was going to have to figure it out fast. Neither of them said anything until he pulled up in front of his house and shut off the engine. "I'm sorry about your parents."

"Don't be. I'm not going to pretend I'm not upset by how they took the news, but I'm hoping they'll come around. They have eight months to figure it out." She didn't sound any more hopeful than he was about it.

He got out and moved around to open her door, well aware that she sat there and let him. They were both trying so fucking hard, it was almost painful. Once upon a time, being with her had been the most natural thing in the world. He wanted to get back to that point. Tonight. Now.

Daniel maintained his hold on her hand as they crossed to the front door and walked into the house. He had to let go long enough to refill Ollie's water and food, but Hope waited in the doorway. It was almost like they both knew that this could be the turning point that either made or broke them, and neither was willing to do or say something that would fuck it up.

He knew who was most likely to be the one to push them over the edge.

Finished, he stood and took her hands. "I'm going to make love to you now."

She opened her mouth, seemed to reconsider, and shut it. Instead of saying anything, she leaned forward and delivered the single sweetest kiss of his life, one filled to the brim with innocence that he'd thought long gone and buried for both of them. There were so many fragile possibilities there that he fought to maintain the gentleness she'd used to set the tone.

It didn't use to be a fight. He'd always touched Hope like she was the most priceless thing in his life — because she had been.

She still was.

And, suddenly, it was the most natural thing in the world to cup her face and smooth his thumbs up over her jaw and across her cheekbones. He picked her up, sweeping her into his arms in a way that made her laugh. "No laughing. This is serious business."

Her dark eyes sparkled. "Serious business, huh?"

"Fuck, no, darling. Keep laughing. I'm addicted to the sound." He laid her on his bed and propped himself up next to her, immediately returning to the soft touches he'd started with. They'd had sex recently, but it had been rough and frenetic. That wasn't what tonight was about.

Tonight was about finally putting both feet forward into the future.

He slowly undid her dress, pressing a kiss to the skin exposed by each button. Her breathing was already ragged, but he was nowhere near finished. He was going to properly reacquaint himself with her body—and drive her crazy while he did it. Daniel reached the last button and smoothed his hands down over the fabric covering her hips and thighs, knowing damn well that she'd picked an outfit that was designed to play down her scars so she didn't make anyone uncomfortable.

Well, fuck that.

He urged her up so he could finish getting off the dress and then palmed first one breast and then the other. "You're beautiful."

"You've always said that. Even when I was a gangly teenager."

He pinched her nipple lightly, relishing her harshly indrawn breath. "It was true then. It's even truer now." He peppered her breasts with light kisses designed to torment and moved down her body, licking along the edge of her panties. "The first time I realized you weren't a kid anymore was that summer when you were thirteen."

"The pool party at Quinn's." The words came out breathy, making him grin.

"The very one. You wore that blue bikini, and I felt like a dirty old man because my cock wouldn't calm the fuck down."

Hope laughed. "You were sixteen. A stiff wind made it impossible for your cock to calm down."

He liked this, revisiting the good memories. Daniel worked her panties down her hips, stopping when they hit the tops of her thighs and she tensed. To distract her, he kept talking. "I knew John would kick my ass, so I stayed the hell away from you."

"And ended up making out with Christie Jenkins, if I remember correctly."

Now it was his turn to laugh. "Yeah, well, you had a point about my being sixteen." He kissed the sensitive skin below her belly button. "You want to know something?"

"Sure."

"That day had nothing on when I saw you at my birthday party seven weeks ago." He licked her hip bone until she squirmed. "All I wanted was to haul your ass out to my truck and bury my cock inside you."

"Didn't even make it to your truck."

He inched her panties down farther, kissing the point where thigh met hip. "Nope. And my cock hasn't calmed down since, either."

Her laugh cut off when he finished pulling her panties off, leaving her naked. He feathered his fingers across the top of the scar, forcing himself to really *look* at it for the first time since she'd walked back into his life. When his car rolled, the passenger door had caved in, impaling her leg with pieces of metal. It caused the scar to be jagged, an ever-present reminder of the trauma she'd gone through.

More importantly, the trauma she'd *survived*.

"Danny—"

"Do you trust me?"

She propped herself on her elbows, looking down her body at him. "You don't have to be at peace with my scars to have sex with me."

No, he didn't. But he'd been fucking up when it came to this injury since she walked back into his life, and he was done. Hope had hurt herself to spare him a situation where she thought he might be uncomfortable, and the thought of her doing it again… Over his fucking dead body.

But if he pushed too hard, she'd get up and walk to the bedroom she'd claimed as hers and shut the door on him and his attempt to truly start new with her.

So he met her gaze. "When I said you're beautiful, I meant every inch of you. That includes this." He stroked her thigh, down over the scar to her knee. There was nothing of her original skin there, some of it having been grafted from elsewhere during the surgery. "You're beautiful here, too."

"Danny—" His name was choked from her lips.

He stopped. "Am I hurting you?"

"No."

He still didn't take his hand away. "Do you want me to stop?"

It took her longer to respond this time. Hope shook her head. "I don't think so."

In the week she'd been back in town, he'd never heard her sound so unsure—not even when she was waving a box of pregnancy tests in his face. He kissed her thigh. "You don't have to hide this from me, darling. Not anymore." It hurt seeing it, but at the same time…it was part of her, and had been part of her for almost as long as she'd had an uninjured leg. If he couldn't accept this, he had no business pushing her to stay.

When he looked at it like that, it was really no contest. "What do you do when it's bothering you?"

"Daniel."

He stopped and met her gaze. "What do you need from me?"

"We can have this conversation later. Right now, I want your mouth and hands on me and your cock buried deep inside me."

There was no arguing with that. He didn't want to. Hearing the words—the plea—out of her lips was enough to have him once again battling for control. *You promised her you'd make love to her. Falling on her like a starving man isn't going to cut it.* He moved up to settle between her thighs. "Find something to hang on to, darling."

CHAPTER THIRTEEN

Hope couldn't breathe. She wasn't sure if it was the fact that she was in bed with Daniel, feeling more naked than she ever had, or the fact that he was going to *make love* to her, or if her hormones had finally decided to revolt and just finish her off entirely.

Probably a combination of all three.

Daniel's tongue on her clit slammed her back into the present. He kissed her there like he had every other part of her body on his journey south, like she was the most precious thing he'd ever come across. Like she was as beautiful as he kept claiming.

His hand drifted over her scar, and she tensed, but he didn't stop what he was doing with his tongue, and it took a grand total of two seconds before she was too busy trying not to squirm to worry about his fingers stroking her jagged skin. She closed her eyes, but that only made the dual sensations more prominent. Hope hissed out a breath. "Danny, you don't have to do this."

"This is part of you." He shifted, pressing a butterfly kiss to her knee, the most mangled part of her. There was no hesitation, and when she looked down her body at him, for once there was no guilt in his eyes. Just a slow appreciation that always seemed to show up when he had her naked. He'd looked at her like that when she was eighteen and, silly her, she'd been sure that would never happen again. Apparently she'd been wrong. He kissed her calf at the bottom of the incision they'd made for the knee replacement. "I said it before, and I'll say it until our dying day—you're beautiful, inside and out. You're so damn strong, it humbles me. That car crash would have broken anyone else who went through what you did. I…" He paused, obviously struggling with the words. "You don't need my validation, but I am so fucking proud of you. And I am so damn sorry that I missed out on the last thirteen years."

He reached up and pressed his hand to her stomach just below her belly button. "I let my own head space get in the way of what needed to be done back then, and I promise I won't do it again. I'm going to be here for you and our baby every step of the way."

It was what she'd always wanted to hear from him. She wanted nothing more than to give in and relax and just believe, for one damn second, that he was telling the truth. There was no doubt he meant every word of it, but their past had left its mark on her, body and soul. She couldn't help feeling that things, even as chaotic and insane as they were, were going *too* well and that the other shoe was about to drop.

"You don't believe me." He traced a circle around her belly button with his thumb, the light touch making her shiver. "It's okay. I damaged your trust, and it's going to take time to win it back." He smiled, the expression showing one of the rare hints of the happy young man he used to be. "We have our entire lives ahead of us."

"I…" There was nothing to say. He was trying. She was trying. Neither one of them could guarantee anything about the future or what it might look like. "Kiss me."

"You don't have to tell me twice." He crawled up to

brush his lips over hers, gentle and sweet and full of things she wasn't ready to name. Except she already had, thirteen years ago. *I guess I never really stopped loving Daniel Rodriguez.* She pushed him onto his back and straddled him. It wasn't a position she could hold indefinitely, but she could hold it long enough.

Hope reached between them and gripped his cock, squeezing until he inhaled sharply. There were too many things to say, none of them right, so she didn't say anything at all. She guided him to her entrance and inside, sinking slowly, inch by inch, until he filled her completely. His hands on her hips urged her on, and she rode him, slowly, luxuriously, the building pleasure so sharp it almost hurt.

"Fuck, darling, this is as close to heaven as I'm ever going to get."

She kissed him before he could say anything else, trying to draw out the feeling of weightlessness. It was no use. Being with Daniel, having his hands on her body, was just too good. Her orgasm swept over her, stealing any worries about the future, drowning her fears, and leaving only a wonderfully sated feeling in its wake.

He flipped them, pushing deeper yet, and kissed her. He maintained that contact even as his strokes became less smooth and his grip tightened on her. It was almost like he needed her to breathe, and she couldn't shake the feeling that it was mutual. Hope clung to him as he came, a small part of her believing it couldn't possibly get better than this.

But what if it could?

Daniel collapsed next to her and pulled her against his chest. She lay staring at the ceiling, a kernel of hope taking root in her chest. There were so many reasons why this would never work, but really, they only needed one for it to actually go the distance. She turned to face Daniel and ran her hand down his chest, needing to voice the realization she'd come across earlier. "I never stopped loving you. Not really."

His eyes changed, sharpening like a wolf circling a fuzzy bunny. "I know." He continued before she could process that he'd just Han Solo–ed her ass. "I've been holding a flame for you, too. I just never thought I'd get a chance — *deserve* a chance — to be with you again."

That was the crux of the matter. He still blamed himself for everything that had happened. She wasn't idiot enough to think that seven days were enough to change that. She had a decade of therapy under her belt and sometimes she was still caught by the random thought that maybe if she hadn't had anything to drink, hadn't been so wrapped up with the promise of a full night alone with Daniel, she would have convinced them not to drive back to Devil's Falls that night. The guilt never lasted, but only because she'd had it pounded into her head time and time again that she couldn't go back and change anything. That no one in their car had done anything wrong.

That the true fault lay with the other driver, the one who had veered into their lane.

Daniel hadn't had the benefit of a neutral party telling him the same thing over and over again until he almost believed it. It would be a long, long time before she could make any headway with him — if ever. If she tried this thing with him for real, she'd have to face that. Trying to change him would only result in misery for both of them.

I hate that he's been killing himself with guilt this entire time.

He stroked her stomach, his big hand stretching from one hip to the other. "It's weird to think that there's a baby in here. Aside from you being willing to cut someone's throat for Greek yogurt, nothing's really changed—and everything has." The slow drag of his calluses over her sensitive skin made her shiver. "Do you think it's a boy or a girl?"

She huffed out a laugh. "I don't know. Fifty-fifty chance."

"Yeah, I guess." A wicked glint appeared in his eyes. "What if it's twins?"

"Daniel Rodriguez!" She covered his hand with her own. "Why would you say such a horrible thing to me? You remember the Conley twins? I'm pretty sure their mother wasn't the least bit crazy before she had them, but by the time they graduated she was about ready to commit herself just to get some peace and quiet."

"Still." He kept up his absentminded stroking, trailing his fingers across her stomach. "I wouldn't mind being daddy to a little girl. I bet she'd have your get-up-and-go." A small line appeared between his brows. "Though the thought of her getting into the kind of trouble we got into isn't going to make me sleep better at night."

"We weren't that bad as kids." They'd gotten into the same mischief that most teenagers in small towns across America did—bonfires, a little drinking, a whole lot in the way of flirting.

Daniel kissed her temple. "No, not too bad. But it's different when it's *our* kid."

Our kid.

She still hadn't quite wrapped her mind around that fact, but it was nice talking like this—like they might both be together by the time the little boy or girl had grown into a hell-raising teenager. "I'd be more worried if the baby is a boy. You four were the ones who got into more trouble than I could dream up."

A cloud passed over his face, but he made a visible effort to smile. "They did call us the Four Horsemen."

She'd forgotten about that. She shifted. "It's all happened so fast. I'm still having a hard time wrapping my mind around the fact I'm pregnant at all, let alone that there will be a baby in May." *A baby.* She laced her fingers through Daniel's. Would the baby have his crooked grin? Her eyes? A mass of dark hair like all the Rodriguez cousins seemed to?

It doesn't matter. I'll love him or her the same.

The fierce feeling nearly took her breath away. Hope hadn't put much thought into being a mother after she and Daniel went their separate ways. It had just hurt too much to contemplate, and though she'd dated a bit over the years, she hadn't met anyone who'd really made her consider it seriously again. She'd gotten to the point where she was more or less resigned to being childless, though she was only thirty-one. But in this quiet moment, the rightness of it settled into her chest.

"I was thinking about looking for another place."

She frowned. "Why? This house is perfectly adequate." It wasn't the house they'd always dreamed of, but that didn't mean there was anything wrong with it, other than it being the obvious residence of a guy who lived alone with his dog.

"Not big enough." His voice gained a rough quality that was almost embarrassment. "Not really kid friendly, either. They start moving pretty quick from what I understand. Hard to close off any of the rooms, and the kitchen is just asking for trouble."

Not with as little as you have in it. She didn't say it, though. It wouldn't change anything, and it might damage what they had going on right now. Instead, she swallowed hard. "That's a big change."

"Seems like the time for it." He hesitated, and that was all the warning she got. "Your leg—what can I do to help?"

"I've gotten by just fine without help this whole time." The words were out and sharp enough to cut before she could think better of it.

He wasn't fazed. "There's nothing wrong with leaning on someone, darling. I know this is new enough that I don't have your trust yet, but I'm going to do my damnedest to earn it back again—and this time I won't betray it."

She wanted that. Oh, God, she wanted that future he was painting so incredibly much. She wanted her and Daniel against the world like it used to be. She wanted the low-key nights and the long days and every second they could possibly spend together.

She wanted it so much it terrified her.

So Hope just kissed him. "One day at a time, okay? I'm here. You're here. Things are working." *For now.*

But she had to make a decision in a day or two that could potentially ruin this thing between them before it got started. She was between an impossible rock and an equally impossible hard place. She could drive back to Dallas like she'd been planning—back to her life, to the job she loved, to her little apartment that she'd never found lacking until now, thinking about how empty it would be with only her in it. Or she could stay and risk everything she'd worked so damn hard for to have a second chance with a man who had dumped her like yesterday's trash when she needed him the most.

She'd forgiven him—it still hurt, but she'd worked hard to understand why he'd made the choice he had—but that didn't mean she could charge blissfully into the life he promised without a single reservation.

He heard the words she didn't speak. Daniel framed her face with one hand. "It's going to be okay—better than okay. It's going to be fucking perfect. Just you wait."

CHAPTER FOURTEEN

Daniel tipped his head back and smiled against the wind. Leaving Hope in his bed this morning hadn't been easy, but knowing she'd be there when he got home made it all worthwhile. Last night had been... perfect—more than worth the sleep deprivation caused by their staying up for hours talking and then making love again. This morning, the future stretched before him, full to the brim with possibilities he hadn't dared consider even a month ago.

It was almost too good to be true.

Or it would be, once Hope finally agreed to stay in Devil's Falls for good.

Hoofbeats coming up on his right had him turning his head to see Adam. His friend had only been back in Devil's Falls a little over a year, but he'd taken to ranching like he'd never left. Seeing him here, on the back of his horse, with his hat pulled low over his eyes, made Daniel happy.

Or maybe he was just being a fucking sap because the woman he'd never really gotten over was his again.

He slowed Rita to a trot, nodding at Adam as he did the same. "I thought you were in the south fields today."

"Quinn and I switched." Adam shrugged. "Thought you might want to talk after how things went down last night."

It took him a full ten seconds to get his friend's meaning. Adam wasn't talking about his being with

Hope—he was talking about her parents' shitty-ass re-action to the news. His hands tightened on the reins before he forced them to relax. "I didn't expect them to welcome me back into the family with open arms." The horror on their face when they realized he was the father had been hard to stomach, though. It felt like they were reaffirming everything he'd ever suspect-ed—that they held him to blame.

That they wished he'd been the one to die instead of John.

"John's passing fucked us all up, but them most of all, I imagine. Doesn't make it okay, but it's under-standable. Losing John was enough to send me into a tailspin back then, and losing my mom this year…" Adam shook himself. "If I didn't have Jules, who the fuck knows what I would have done—probably taken off again, though this time I wouldn't have come back. I can't imagine what losing a kid would be like. I hope to hell none of us ever has to go through it."

His gut twisted in on itself at the thought of some-thing happening to the baby growing bigger inside Hope's stomach every day. He fought to keep his voice even. "I thought you weren't all that supportive of this."

"That's not what I meant when we talked before, and you damn well know it. You and Hope—back then you were as constant as the sun rising and setting each day. Seeing you looking at each other like you used to is good. My issue is if you're going through with this out of some twisted form of penance for the car crash. *That* would be fucked beyond belief."

"I love her. Always have." He didn't tell Adam that he saw this as a way to balance out some of his karmic debt, because that would just confirm his friend's worst fear. That wasn't what things with him and Hope were about—not totally. But he'd be lying if he said the thought hadn't occurred to him. A baby did not equal a brother, but at least he'd be doing something other than bringing pain and loss into her life.

"Then I'm happy for you." Adam barely waited a beat. "What are you going to do about her parents?"

That was the question, wasn't it?

It probably wasn't realistic to expect to get their blessing, but a part of him wanted it all the same. He rubbed his chin. "I guess I'm going to have to take a trip down to San Antonio at some point."

Adam's face was unreadable. "If you think that's wise." It couldn't be clearer that his friend thought the exact opposite.

"They're her parents. I'm not going to put her in a position where she feels like she has to choose one of us over the other." There was more to it than that, but he didn't think Adam would appreciate the truth. Adam's mother had always loved the hell out of him, and the entire Rodriguez family had been thrilled beyond belief when he'd married Daniel's cousin. He'd never had to deal with that push and pull that came when the parents of the woman he loved hated him.

Daniel guided Rita to the north. "It'll work out. You'll see." He sent Rita into a canter, and Adam's reply was lost in the wind of his passing. Out here, with the unending sky overhead and his horse's hooves pounding the dirt, nothing seemed impossible. All he had to do was talk to the Moores and they'd see reason. They might have every right to hate him, but no one could deny he loved Hope more than life itself.

You did thirteen years ago, and you had a hell of a way showing it back then.

He shoved the thought to the back of his mind and tipped his head back. "It'll work out."

Maybe if he said it enough times, he'd actually start to believe it.

• • •

Hope pushed ignore on her phone and set it aside. Since the disastrous dinner yesterday, her parents had called several times. She'd ignored every single one. She wasn't ready to talk to them, especially since she highly doubted they were calling to apologize for how they'd handled the news. No, they were calling to demand an explanation.

An explanation that, frankly, she didn't have.

She pressed her hand to her stomach. Two months along and she didn't feel that much different when all was said and done. She'd noticed this morning that her breasts were growing at a truly alarming rate—and were seriously sore—but there was none of the nausea or sickness that she'd always heard about. Rationally, she knew that at some point her stomach would start rounding and, even further down the road, she'd have to actually go into labor, but it seemed like a distant dream. Things going so well with her and Daniel had only added to the dreamlike quality of the situation. Half the time she was convinced that she'd never actually left Dallas and that this was all a hallucination as a result of a bad taco truck meal.

But it wasn't a dream, and she did have to come up with a real plan at some point.

Today.

"Hope?"

She turned as Daniel walked into the kitchen. He looked... Her heart picked up at the sight of him in worn jeans, a long-sleeved plaid shirt, and his cowboy hat pulled down low. He was dirty from working outside all day, but that only added to the allure. She bit her lip and leaned back against the counter. "Hey."

"If you could see the way you're looking at me."

She didn't have to. She knew. Hope crooked her finger at him, and he immediately crossed the kitchen to pull her into his arms. Daniel took off his hat and dropped it onto the counter next to her, his dark eyes searching her face. "How was your day?"

"Good." And it was the truth. Her pain was manageable, and she'd gotten quite a bit of work done on a new account despite working remotely. The only downside was the regular calls from her parents that she wasn't ready to deal with. She'd call them back eventually, but she wanted a few more days to figure out how to approach the conversation. She needed to have an actual plan in place before she spoke with them.

"I ran into town before coming home." He stepped back, keeping his hands on her hips. "Jessica says you haven't called her and if she has to drive out here and kidnap you, she's more than willing."

Hope laughed. "I'll call later, I promise." It would be good to catch up, especially now that she wasn't feeling quite so off center when it came to wondering what the hell was going on with her and Daniel. They might not have a plan, but they loved each other. It was a start—a promising start.

"I also grabbed a few things." A frown flickered

over his face, gone almost as soon as it had appeared. "I figured I'd cook us some dinner tonight. How does pad Thai sound?"

She froze, searching his face. Over a week here, and the most he'd cooked was pouring cereal into a bowl or pulling a container of yogurt out of the fridge for her. "Why now?"

"It's time."

That wasn't really an explanation, but it couldn't possibly be a bad thing. Maybe it was a sign of him starting to reclaim the parts of himself that had fallen by the wayside over the last decade. Either way, she wasn't about to complain about homemade pad Thai—especially when Daniel was doing the cooking. Her stomach chose that moment to growl, and she laughed. "Why don't you jump in the shower and I'll get the groceries put away?"

"Sounds good." He kissed her lightly and headed out of the kitchen, reappearing for trip after trip of grocery bags.

Hope stood there and knew her eyes were getting larger and larger at the growing pile of food on the kitchen island. She'd thought he'd gone overboard last time, but it paled in comparison to the sheer amount of food he unloaded. He had to have bought out the entire store.

He thinks I'm staying.

I don't even know if I'm staying.

He didn't quite look at her the entire time, and she didn't know what to stay. She didn't want to make him feel awkward when he was making changes for the better, but it was just so unexpected. Once he disappeared for the final time, she waited for the shower to start to begin going through the bags.

There was enough food to feed them for weeks, but that wasn't what had her raising her eyebrows. He must have gone into El Paso before he hit the grocery store in Devil's Falls, because there was an entire selection of new cookware and saucepans and utensils. They weren't exact replicas of the ones he'd had when they were together before, but it was more than enough to cook anything she could dream up.

We're going to have to talk about this, and soon. All of this.

But not tonight.

Tonight was for new possibilities and to keep riding the wave that had crested the night they'd announced the pregnancy to their families. Things were good, and she didn't want to be the one to throw a wrench into the gears until it was absolutely necessary.

By the time Daniel reappeared, wearing a different pair of jeans and forgoing a shirt completely, she had everything put away and had hand washed the various cooking gear. She smiled at him. "You got ambitious today."

"Yeah, well, I figure your cravings are only going to ramp up as time goes on. I want to be prepared for those middle-of-the-night demands."

She laughed even as her heart pounded at an alarming rate. *I can't stay…can I?* "Trust you to make late-night cravings about food rather than sex."

His slow smile made her stomach flip. "Aw, darling, I'm more than capable of meeting either—or both— needs if you want another go at the kitchen."

"Oh." She knew she was blushing furiously, but she couldn't seem to stop. It didn't make a bit of sense, either. He'd had his hands and mouth all over her body countless times in the last week, and last night, he'd massaged her injured leg while they lounged around on the couch and watched bad television in between bouts of sex. It was like having a glimpse of the life she'd always wanted, and a part of her kept whispering that it couldn't last.

Which only made her want to hold it more closely.

He circled the breakfast bar and started going through the fridge to lay out the stuff he'd need for dinner. "I've been doing a lot of thinking today."

She didn't know where this was heading, but she wasn't ready to go there. Hope slipped between him and the counter and leaned up to kiss him. "Not to-night."

His brows slanted down. "We have to talk—about a lot of things."

She knew that. Really, she did. "We will, I promise. But can we just have one last night in the dream before we have to touch back to reality?"

If anything, that seemed to set him on edge. "One talk isn't going to be the end of this, darling. It's just a talk. It's what adults do—communicate."

Except so many of their talks seemed to end with fights and her despairing at ever being able to find a happy medium with Daniel. She loved him—more than should have been possible—but if love was enough, things wouldn't have fallen out the way they did all those years ago. No, they needed a plan and the ability to hold down a conversation about the future without resorting to yelling.

Unfortunately, both those things felt nearly impos-sible.

She implored Daniel with her eyes. "Please. One more night?"

"We have to talk about Dallas, Hope. I know you were planning on going back tomorrow."

Her chest compressed, and she forced a smile. "Then we'll talk in the morning. First thing, I promise."

"If that's what you want."

"It is."

Tomorrow would come soon enough.

CHAPTER FIFTEEN

Daniel gave in to Hope's request without arguing, and he wasn't sorry about it. They'd had a really nice dinner and then made love again, the whole experience just cementing his determination to make this the best it could be. And that meant he had to start at the beginning. He shifted, pulling her closer against him. "I want to push that talk by about twelve hours."

"What? Why?"

"I'm going to see your parents tomorrow."

She tensed. "Why am I just hearing about it now?"

"You didn't want to talk, remember? I wouldn't have said anything at all, but I couldn't get out there today and I want you to push your plans to go back to Dallas one more day."

"I can't keep postponing leaving. I know I didn't want to talk today, but eventually we do have to come up with something resembling a realistic plan." Hope lifted her head and frowned. "I really think you visiting them is a mistake. They've been calling nonstop all day, and *I* haven't even talked to them."

"I know." And he also recognized how her mouth tightened every time she pushed ignore on her phone. She had always been close with her parents—especially her mother—and being on the outs with them was taking its toll. There were so many things in their life right now that he couldn't control, but he could take the first step in making this right. "Darling, their problem isn't with the fact that you're pregnant—it's that you're pregnant with *my* baby. There's nothing you can say that will affect their opinion—but maybe I can." He had his doubts, but the only alternative was to cut them out of his and Hope's life, and that wasn't right. They were good parents, and they'd be good grandparents. It wasn't their fault that they weren't thrilled that their son's killer was shacking up with their daughter.

He couldn't be the reason Hope lost what remained of her family.

"You don't have to do this."

"I know that, too." He guided her head back to his shoulder and smoothed his hand over her hair. "It's just one conversation. I'll be gone and back before you know it."

She sighed. "I guess my girls can hold down the fort for one more day. But that's it. No matter what happens with us, I *do* have to go back to Dallas. I know you're not going to change your mind about going to San Antonio, so do what you feel is necessary."

He hated how defeated she sounded, but her doubts were unfounded. This was going to go a long way toward fixing things. Hope might not see that because she was wrapped up in guilt over disappointing her parents and worry over the future, but he knew he was right. Daniel drifted off to sleep with that thought centered in the forefront of his mind.

He woke up alone. He blinked and stretched, his hand encountering paper. For half a second, he was convinced that Hope had slipped out of his bed and his life in the middle of the night like a thief, but then his half-awake brain processed the words she'd written.

Went for a walk before it got too hot. If you're gone before I'm back, just know I love you.

A smile fixed itself on his face and stayed there all the way through showering, dressing, and grabbing a bite to eat before he hit the road. Hope still wasn't back, so he scrawled a quick response to her on the same note and left it propped up in the kitchen next to the coffeemaker he started on his way out the door. If the last week was any indication, she'd have a single cup and then switch to decaffeinated tea, but he figured she wouldn't want to wait. And it made him feel good to know he was meeting her need before she even thought to ask.

Maybe that made him the caveman she often accused him of being, but he was okay with it.

The drive to San Antonio passed in a blur. He kept the radio cranked up and the windows cracked, but the noise didn't quite drown out the little voice inside him whispering that this was a mistake—that there wasn't an option where this encounter ended positively. He ignored it just like he had from the moment it start popping up.

Once he hit the city limits, he followed his written directions to a little suburb with houses in neat little rows and perfectly manicured front lawns. The Moores' was a understated gray with sharp white trim that fit them perfectly. He turned off his truck and stepped out, the heat of the late morning making his shirt stick to his back. Or maybe that was just nerves.

It didn't hit him until he was knocking on the

front door that maybe he should have called first. Gary Moore had always worked, and though he was closing in on retirement age, Daniel kind of doubted he'd have stepped out voluntarily. He knocked before he could talk himself out of it and was rewarded a few seconds later by footsteps on the other side of the door.

Lisa Moore opened it a crack and stared at him. "What are you doing here?" She didn't sound particularly angry, but calling her tone welcoming would be a stretch of the truth to the point of lying.

He took off his hat. "I came to talk, ma'am. I figure we're due."

"You're about thirteen years too late and more than a dollar short." She took a step back and opened the door wider. "But since my daughter isn't returning my phone calls, I suppose this is going to have to do."

Not the most promising start, but he followed her deeper into the house. She led him to a small living room off the main hallway that, judging from the pristine whiteness of every piece of furniture in it, didn't see much use. Talking in the kitchen would have been a better sign, but he'd take what he could get. Daniel perched on the edge of one of the chairs, half concerned that he'd leave a dust imprint when he stood. "I love your daughter."

Lisa waved that away. "You want to have sex with my daughter. That wasn't love when she was eighteen, and it's surely not love now."

Daniel jerked back. "Excuse me?"

"I've spent considerable time wondering what I'd say to you if we ever had the misfortune of being in the same room again. After John—". Her breath caught, but she soldiered on. "After my son died, it went quite a bit differently in my head than it will go today. I blamed you, and I'm not particularly proud of that. You were all just kids, and it was easier to have a target for my grief." She sighed. "That kind of pain never quite goes away, but it fades a little, and I've worked through the worst of it. We all have."

That was better than he could have dreamed. *Too good*. He wasn't fortunate enough to show up here and find arms opened in welcome. If that were the case, they wouldn't have reacted so poorly to finding out Hope was pregnant with his baby.

He tensed, waiting for the other shoe to drop.

She didn't make him wait long. "You weren't responsible for killing my son, regardless of what my feelings were at the time." He didn't have time to process the full meaning of her words before she verbally kicked him in the face. "However, you did fail my daughter when she needed you the most."

Daniel flinched. "I thought it would be better if I made myself scarce."

"You were a coward." She said the words softly, without any anger. "Do you know how many nights Hope spent crying because you never returned her calls? No? I can tell you. Three hundred and seventy-two. She mourned her brother just like the rest of us, but John's loss wasn't what kept her up at night when the pain of her leg got too much. She never blamed you for the car crash—and even went so far as to tell me how out of line *my* anger at you was. For three hundred and seventy-two days she held on to hope that you would come to your senses and come for her. But you never did."

Daniel didn't know what to say. He knew there wasn't a single thing he could do to make this better. Hell, he'd known it was bad, but somehow hearing it from Lisa's mouth made it so much worse. He sank back into the chair, the sheer enormity of what he'd done washing over him. "She's fine."

"She tries very hard to be fine," Lisa corrected. "Most days, it's even true. She worked to get past you, but the scars never faded. Hope doesn't lean on anyone—she hasn't since she went to lean on you and you weren't there."

If words could physically wound, he'd be bleeding out on the floor. "I love her."

"Maybe you do now. Maybe you loved her then. It didn't make a difference when you were twenty-one, and forgive me if I doubt it'll make a difference now." She pinned him with a look, her dark eyes so similar to her daughter's. "From what I understand, you never sought her out. You never chased her down. You never even tried to make things right. If you had, maybe I'd feel differently, but I suspect it was a moment of weakness on my daughter's part that resulted in this pregnancy, and I simply cannot support it." She held up her hand when he would have spoken. "Let me rephrase—I support her. I support any choice she makes for herself and her baby. What I can't support now and never will is her being with you."

She smoothed down her skirt. "You've spent the last thirteen years more in love with your guilt than you were with my daughter. I have seen no evidence that that's going to change. She deserves to be put first—both her and the baby. Not to be a consolation prize because you're still trying to make right something that will never be right again. If I thought for a second you were with her for the right reasons…" Lisa shook her head. "But you aren't. We both know that to be the truth." She motioned to the door. "I think you should leave now."

Daniel walked to the door in a daze. He'd known the Moores didn't think he was good enough for Hope, but the reasoning behind it…

How could he argue with Lisa? She was right. He'd failed Hope. Hadn't Hope herself told him as much a little over a week ago? When they'd had that argument, he'd bulldozed right over it—just like he had every other indication that there were core-deep issues that they hadn't dealt with. All he'd seen was a chance to make things right once and for all—as right as they could ever be, at least.

It hadn't occurred to him that he was doing Hope yet another wrong in his determination to make things right.

• • •

"We have to go into El Paso and look at baby stuff. I don't have any of my own, so it's up to you to give me my baby fix. I hope you're okay with that."

Hope laughed. She'd been leery of calling Jessica, but she was so nervous about Daniel off talking to her parents that she'd grabbed at the distraction with both hands. Two hours later, she was so glad she did. "We don't even know if it's a boy or a girl. I'm not even sure I'm finding out." There was something magical about leaving it as a surprise.

"Not finding out? Now you're just teasing me. What is this, 1962? I have needs, woman."

"Do I get a say in this?" Headlights shone through the front window as a truck pulled off the road and started for the house. She moved to push the curtains aside. *Daniel's back.* "I have to go, but we're still on for coffee next time I'm in town, right?"

"Wild horses couldn't hold me back."

"I'm looking forward to it, too." She hung up as Ollie came tearing into the living room, barking as loud as she could. "He's home, girl."

It seemed to take forever for Daniel to shut off the truck and make his way to the front door, but that might very well have been her nerves talking. She couldn't imagine how the conversation with her parents had gone—especially since she hadn't received a call from them since this morning. This was going to either be very, very good, or very, very bad.

One look at his face as he walked through the door and she knew it was the latter. "What happened?"

He held up a hand to stop her when she would have come to him. "We need to talk."

No good conversation ever started like that. Hope wrapped her arms around herself. She felt like she was standing on the tracks, hearing the train coming, and not able to move out of danger. "What did they say to you?"

"I thought I was doing the right thing." He said it so softly, he might have been talking to himself.

She blinked. "What?"

"We laughed about fate, but part of me couldn't help thinking that maybe you coming back into my life—getting pregnant with my child—was the universe's way of balancing everything out."

She didn't have to ask what he meant. There was only one thing he could be talking about. John. Always John. She straightened. "That was a long time ago, Daniel. I thought we were starting over." *Please let us be starting over for real.*

"I was going to make things right once and for all."

He wasn't going to let it go—*any* of it. She reeled back, feeling like the entire world had shifted beneath her feet. All Hope had wanted when she found out she was pregnant was for this to finally mean that they would both just move *on*. That they'd finally put their past behind them and start fresh. That she wouldn't be the high school girlfriend whose older brother Daniel blamed himself for killing. That he wouldn't be the boyfriend she'd loved so much who had failed her so spectacularly. "I don't know how many times I have to say it. That crash wasn't your fault. I thought you understood that." She hoped. God, she hoped so much it made it hard to breathe. *Please prove me right. Please, Daniel. I'll say whatever it takes to just end this circling we can't seem to stop doing.*

He laughed, but not like anything was funny. "If our baby was a boy, I thought we should name him John."

She gripped her arms so tightly, she distantly wondered if there would be bruises tomorrow. It didn't matter. The pain was the only thing grounding her while she tried to process the insanity coming out of his mouth. "*What?*" Suddenly it all made sense.

She pressed her hand to her stomach, the nausea so intense, it was a wonder she didn't throw up on the spot. "My baby is not my brother." It came out as little more than a whisper, so she said it again. "My baby is not my brother. What the hell is wrong with you?"

He frowned at her, finally seeming to see her for the first time since he got out of the truck. "What?"

Anger unlike anything she'd ever known rose, black and thick and almost enough to choke her into silence. She wouldn't let it. Some things needed to be said, no matter how painful. "This—all of this—was about penance. You never wanted me, not really. You wanted a way to assuage your guilt and prove to yourself that you were worth a damn." She took a step back and then another.

"Hope, will you just listen?" Just that. Not a denial—a plea to explain himself.

He didn't need to explain himself. She knew how this conversation was going. The guilt on his face made her want to punch something. She shook her head. "Oh my God, I'm right, aren't I?"

"I'm no good for you. I never have been. I thought I could make everything right, but I can't."

Her shoulders sagged. "You know, I spent the last thirteen years fighting against what you're saying, and believing that I was right. Now? Now I'm tired, Daniel. I am so incredibly tired. I don't know how two and two add up to seven in your head, but I don't care anymore. If you think me being married to a man who sees me as an albatross around his neck— who sees my *child* that way—is a gift, then you're crazy. I don't have it in me to fight anymore."

She took a shuddering breath, half sure that he'd break and tell her that she was wrong, that that wasn't what he meant at all, that he loved her for who she was, not for the penance she represented. But the seconds stretched into a full minute, and the full minute into three, and he didn't do anything but look at her with that damned guilt written all over his face.

"You're right. Fuck, you're right. I don't know what I was thinking." He finally moved toward the kitchen. "You can have the master bedroom tonight, but I think it's best we go our separate ways tomorrow."

This was it. It was really happening. Instead of telling her that he loved her, he was all but admitting that he loved his guilt more. Hope shook despite her best effort to maintain control over herself. She wasn't the only woman who'd been dumped by her boyfriend while pregnant with his child, but she'd never thought Daniel would do something like this—especially since he'd all but clubbed her over the head and demanded she stay in Devil's Falls and his house. *He* had been the one driving this from day one, overriding her concerns and her fears, and now he was going to turn around and repeat history?

Her throat tried to close, but she'd be damned before she cried another tear because of Daniel Rodriguez.

Hope pushed her shoulders back and her chin up, holding it together by the skin of her teeth. "I don't think that's a good idea. Excuse me." She sent a text to Jessica as she walked slowly into the spare room and packed up her seriously small number of things. She could feel Daniel's presence in the house even if she didn't see him as she made her way to the front of the house.

She paused at the door. "My child will *not* be named John, by the way, regardless of gender."

The she walked out and didn't look back, not once.

CHAPTER SIXTEEN

"Do you want me to kill him? I can most definitely kill him."

"You can't kill him because *I'm* going to kill him."

Calling Jessica had seemed like a good idea at the time, but now Hope was starting to doubt the intelligence of her plan. She hadn't been thinking—she'd just been reacting. But no matter her logic, she hadn't expected to show up at Jessica's place and find Daniel's cousin Jules. Jules looked ready to chew through the walls when she heard how things had fallen out with Daniel, and she paced around the large living room, coming up with one plan, discarding it, and coming up with an even wilder and more elaborate one. Jessica was right there with her, egging her on.

It just made Hope so damn tired.

She wrapped a knitted throw blanket around her shoulders and curled up on the couch. Maybe if she didn't move too much, the women would forget she was here and wander back to their own lives. It was a crappy plan, but today had been filled with all sorts of crappy plans. She rested her chin on her knees and sighed, just a little.

I never wanted this. I never wanted to have everything I ever dreamed of dangled in front of me and then taken away just when I finally got to the point where I actually believed it was happening.

"Hope?"

She blinked and looked up to find Jules crouched

in front of her. The concern written across the other woman's face didn't make her feel the least bit better. "Yeah?"

"Is there something we can do—aside from plan for the inevitable death of my idiot cousin? You look kind of peaky, and I can't tell if it's I've-just-been-dumped peaky or oh-my-God-the-*baby* peaky."

Hope pressed her hand to her stomach, fear beating in her throat. "I…" She forced herself to take a deep breath and *think*. She didn't even have a doctor's appointment for another month. She felt like death walking, but that was 100 percent emotional. Physically she was fine. Hungry, as always, but fine. She tried for a smile and failed miserably. "I'm okay."

"You're not, but that's okay." Jules squeezed her hand and then stood. "Why don't you get some rest? If you keep sitting here while Jessica and I plot, you'll be accessory to murder and my… What would this baby be? Second cousin? First cousin once removed?"

Hope blinked. "I don't actually know."

"Minor details." Jules urged her to her feet and turned to Jessica. "Where are you putting her up?"

The feeling she had of her life spinning wildly out of control only got worse as the night went on. She hadn't had time to process, which might be a blessing, but the very last thing she wanted to do was have the meltdown she could feel threatening with witnesses present. Hope carefully extracted her hand from Jules. "If it's all the same, I'll walk myself up to the spare bedroom." She stood on wobbly legs, hating her weakness, and walked to the stairs with as much confidence as she could muster. She doubted the show did a damn thing to convince the women behind her that she wouldn't cry herself to sleep, and she knew if she looked back, they'd have sympathetic expressions on their faces.

She didn't care.

She'd spent the last thirteen years trying to keep from going under, and she'd be damned before she started now.

Except...

That thought, that deep-seated anger that she never let anyone see, had been useful when she was eighteen and had woken up to realize the world had changed in an instant. It had gotten her through the worst pain of her life, emotionally and physically, and kept her from giving in to the sorrow that made her want to curl up into a ball and cry until things went back to how they used to be. She'd been forged in the flames and come out stronger on the other side.

Except that wasn't really the truth.

The truth was she'd never stopped hurting. She'd never stopped missing John, though the grief became manageable at some point while she wasn't looking. She'd never stopped missing her ability to run marathons like she used to, to feel her body flagging and know that it was something to push through because she was *almost* there.

She'd never stopped mourning the loss of Daniel's love.

Hope stopped at the top of the stairs, pressing a hand to her chest, the truth almost sending her to her knees. She'd told him the truth when she'd said she never stopped loving him. Even now, even knowing it would never work, that their reasons for trying to make this work were the very definition of irreconcilable differences, she loved him.

That knowledge burned her rage to ash, leaving Hope, pregnant and alone, in its wake.

She made it to the bedroom and closed the door softly behind her. Somehow she managed to get to the bed and burrow beneath covers that smelled faintly of lavender and vanilla. She curled up, placing her hands on her stomach. There was no freaking change in the last few hours, but she imagined she could feel the life growing there all the same.

He's going to miss this. The sleepless nights. The morning cuddles. All the firsts. He's going to miss everything.

Maybe I shouldn't have walked away…

But all she could see was his face when he'd said they should name their baby John. Pain arrowed through her chest, and she had to press a pillow against her face to muffle the sob that escaped. This baby deserved more than to be thought of as some kind of penance. *She* deserved it, too. Was it too much to ask that he be with her because he loved her, rather than because he was punishing himself for John's death?

Apparently so.

Another sob escaped, tearing itself from her throat, quickly followed by a third. A cry rose up inside her, desperate to be voiced.

A hand touched her head, and she startled. She'd been so focused on keeping as quiet as possible that she hadn't realized someone had come into the room. She looked up, shock breaking through her meltdown. "Mom."

"Jessica called me." Her mom sat on the edge of the bed. "I always liked that girl."

Her mom was here. Which meant…

She knew everything.

Her mom smoothed back her hair, the move harking back to her childhood—and to her months in recovery. She looked down at Hope with dark eyes so similar to her own. "I'm sorry, honey. More sorry than you can know. You deserve better than this. You always have."

There was no judgment in her tone, nothing but empathy and a desire to make everything right. Just like she always had. Hope's mom was a fixer. She saw a problem and she went in with elbow grease and sheer willpower and muscled the things around her into submission. Being so helpless after the car crash had broken something in her, something she'd never quite gotten back. That didn't stop her from trying, though.

Part of Hope wanted to blame her mom for the fight with Daniel, for exposing her weakness so thoroughly, but the truth was if Daniel had really been willing to put her first, he wouldn't have broken at the first opportunity. He hadn't fought for her.

Just like he hadn't fought for her thirteen years ago.

"Why aren't I enough for him? Why does it always have to be about John, or about what he thinks he took from me? All he can focus on is the past." She clenched her teeth, but it only made her chest hurt worse to keep the words inside. So, for the first time in far too many years, she let it out. "He loves his guilt more than he loves me."

"He's not a bad man." Her mom kept up that soothing motion, smoothing her hair back.

"You don't like him." It came out too accusing, but she couldn't take the words back. "You never forgave him."

"That's my burden to bear. Not yours." Her mom's mouth tightened slightly. "It's easier to forgive something done to you than something done to someone you love—especially a child. John wasn't his fault. You know it. I know it. What he did to you…"

A crazy part of her couldn't stop from defending him. "He blames himself for John."

"He blames himself for a lot of things."

She let out a shuddering breath. It didn't ease the burning in her eyes one bit. "I don't know how to do this. I just want to shake him until he sees that he's going to miss out on the future that could have been ours because he's so focused on whipping himself for the past."

"You have to let it go."

She jerked back. "What?"

Her mom's eyes were nothing but kind. "Honey, you have this amazing ability to put your mind to something and make it into a reality. It's an asset, though sometimes I worry about your motivations." She held a hand up. "But that's neither here nor there. My point is that Daniel isn't a problem to be fixed. He's a person. You can't change him if he doesn't want to be changed."

She knew that. Of course she knew that. But it was so incredibly hard to let go of the dreams she'd allowed herself to paint for their future. Dreams where they got married, settled into that little farmhouse they'd always talked about, and had half a dozen beautiful children. "I want it—him—so badly."

"I know, honey." Her mom gathered her to her chest and hugged her tight. "But life rarely cares about what we want."

Loss made her sick to her stomach. "I don't know if I can be a single mom."

"You can do anything you set your mind to. You'll love your baby with everything you have, and that child will want for nothing." Her mom kissed the top of her head. "And if Daniel decides to be in the baby's life—"

"He will." She might not be certain of anything else, but she was certain of that. "He might not want me, but he wants our baby." And she wouldn't stand in his way, no matter how his rejection hurt. "He'll be a good daddy."

Her mother's mouth tightened. "Likely, yes. But you deserve more than a man who will be with you for a baby. You deserve to be with a man who puts you first. And Daniel never will."

No, he wouldn't. Not when he could put his grief and guilt before all others.

Tonight. She'd give herself tonight to mourn the life she'd never have. And then, tomorrow, she'd wake up and get back to facing down the world. Dallas seemed cold after being in Devil's Falls, so maybe she'd look into moving a bit closer—to San Antonio to be closer to her parents. Staying where she had minimal support system just to prove a point was sheer idiocy.

Hope opened her eyes, staring out the bedroom window to where the stars winked at her. "I'm going to be okay." Every other time she'd said those words, they felt like a promise.

Right now they felt like a lie.

• • •

"Well, you've gone and fucked things up beyond repair, haven't you?"

Daniel had never hated living in a small town as much as he did in that moment. People knew where to find him far too easily. If he was in a big city, he could blend into the crowds until no one bothered to look sideways at him. No one bothered to meddle.

He opened another beer without looking at Adam and frowned at Ollie. "Some guard dog you are."

"This house only has room for one guard dog."

Him. He transferred his glare to his best friend. "Bite me."

"Wrong again." Adam dropped into the chair next to him and snatched the beer out of his hands. "What the hell were you thinking?"

Word sure as fuck got around fast. Daniel checked his watch. "It's been less than twenty-four hours. How the hell did you find out?"

"You know your cousin. She's got feelers all over this town." Adam motioned with his fingers. "Hope went to Jessica Stroup's after your fight, and Jessica called in Jules as reinforcements." He sent Daniel a significant look. "She also called Mrs. Moore."

Just like that, he was back in that perfectly white room hearing the woman condemn him with a few well-placed words. *You love your guilt more than you love my daughter.* It merged with the look of betrayal on Hope's face right before she walked out of his life. He rubbed the heel of his hand over his chest. "I don't know where it went wrong." He continued before Adam could tell him he'd fucked up again. "No, that's a lie. It went wrong right around the time I got behind the wheel thirteen years ago."

"For fuck's sake." Adam took a swig of the beer and set it aside. "You're the one who gave me the kick in the ass I needed to stop being a self-fulfilling prophecy. I didn't realize we were going to have to switch roles." Adam reached over and scratched Ollie behind her ear. "That accident fucked us all up. Every single one of us. But let me ask you something—"

"I don't want to hear it." Daniel pushed to his feet, driven by the pent-up tangle of emotions poisoning him. "This shit… I keep hurting her, Adam. It doesn't matter what I do or how I do it, I keep hurting Hope." *What if I hurt our baby the same way?* He scrubbed a hand over his face. "Maybe it'd be best if I just got the hell out of everyone's lives."

He opened his eyes at the sound of clapping and frowned at Adam giving him a standing fucking ovation. "What the hell?"

"Are you done with your pity party?"

"It's not a fucking pity party. It's the truth."

"It's the truth *you're* forcing. Once upon a time, you told me that I just needed to break the cycle. Well, man, look in the mirror." With one last pat of Ollie's head, he started down the porch steps, delivering a parting shot over his shoulder. "But are you really going to be okay with Hope settling down with some other guy and your baby being raised calling someone else Daddy? Because that's what's going to happen if you don't pull your head out of your ass. She might love the shit out of you, but Hope lands on her feet. This time won't be any different. The only choice is whether you're at her side when she does." And then he was gone, climbing into his old truck and taking off down the driveway in a cloud of dust.

"Bastard always did like to make an exit." Daniel dropped back into his chair and stared at the horizon, his thoughts tumbling over themselves and getting nowhere. He wanted to call Adam and rail at him, to tell him that he had no fucking idea what Daniel was going through. But it would be a lie. Out of his two friends, Adam knew better than Quinn. He always had. They both had a vein of guilt that ran deep, though the source wasn't the same. Adam had managed to put his aside.

Daniel wasn't sure he could.

Hope deserved better than him. He'd known it from the time he was a teenager, and that hadn't stopped him from pursuing her then. Hell, it hadn't stopped him the last few weeks, either.

Ollie whined, and he scratched her behind the ears, earning a lick. "It's not that easy."

But the truth of it was, *he* was the only thing standing in his way.

Hope had already proven that she was willing to set aside the past and give him the benefit of the doubt. Her mother might not, but he wasn't trying to have a relationship with her mother. That said, Lisa Moore had some good fucking points. He sighed.

The thing was, he *didn't* totally see his baby as a way to recoup what was lost. Or at least, that wasn't the driving force behind his pushing for Hope to give him another shot. Not when he really thought about it.

The truth was he wanted her in his life and in his bed. He loved her. Fuck, the last few days since they told their families about the pregnancy had been the happiest of his life. He'd actually *wanted* to cook for her, and he'd spent the days looking forward to coming home and finding her there, working or cooking or doing her yoga in the backyard. His shitty little house had started to feel like a home, and it was all because of Hope.

And he'd gone and fucked it up.

Daniel pushed to his feet, startling Ollie. "Sorry, girl." He reached for his phone and then hesitated. A call wasn't going to cut it. He'd let Hope Moore slip out of his life thirteen years ago, and he couldn't live with himself if he did it a second time.

He just had to prove to her that he was all in.

CHAPTER SEVENTEEN

Hope rolled out of bed at nine, which was the latest her pride would allow her to sleep in. As tempting as it was to hide in bed all day, there were too many things waiting for her attention, not the least being her plan for the future. She combed her hair and put on her brightest sundress, needing to feel in control of at least *that*. She glanced at her phone, hating the little thread of disappointment when the notifications showed no missed calls or texts from Daniel.

He didn't call last time, either.

God, she was so sure she'd moved past all of that. All it took was one fight and she was right back in that dark place, calling and calling and never getting any answer. She wouldn't do that again. She *couldn't*. There was more than herself to think of now, and wallowing in despair couldn't possibly be good for the baby.

That's the only bright spot in this disaster, which is damned ironic.

She pressed her hand to her stomach. "It's just me and you, little bit." Except it *wasn't*. There would be no cutting Daniel out of her life for good, not when the baby was half him. As much as it made her sick to think about, she had to face him, and soon. They had to hash out some kind of visitation setup before she left town, because she had no intention of setting foot back in Devil's Falls. This town had done enough damage, and it didn't matter if her pain wasn't actually the town's fault.

"Uh, Hope?"

She jumped and then felt guilty for jumping. She was in Jessica's home, after all. It only stood to reason that the woman had come to check on her. "Yeah?"

"I think you're going to want to come see this."

She opened the door and started down the stairs, wondering at how strange her friend sounded. "What's wrong?" When she got no answer, she picked up her pace, though she kept a hand on the railing. The last thing she needed was a tumble, especially when she was already feeling so off balance. She froze at the bottom of the stairs, not quite believing her eyes. "Danny?" She took a step toward him and then stopped, registering that both her parents were on the other side of the living room, and Jessica stood next to them, and all three of them were staring at her and Daniel with varying degrees of expectation.

"Hey, darling." His face didn't give anything away, didn't give *any* indication of why he was here.

Painfully aware they had an audience, she bit her lip. "Maybe we should talk privately." Judging from the way Jessica was practically salivating, anything he said would spread like wildfire through town by lunch. Hope couldn't even blame her. It was just the way things were in this town.

"No, I don't think we should." He moved toward her, and she belatedly registered the flowers in his hands. Daisies. Her favorite.

She took them, not sure what to think. "You remembered."

"I remember everything." He took her hand, and for one breathless moment, she thought he was going to go down on one knee, but Daniel met her gaze, the naked longing in his eyes drawing her in despite herself. He squeezed her hand. "I fucked up. I fucked up when I put myself before us thirteen years ago, and I fucked up again last night by letting the past get a stranglehold on me. I've been so focused on everything that went wrong all that time ago, I forgot to focus on everything going *right*."

"Danny—"

"Let me finish." There was no heat to the words—just quiet strength. "I love you, darling. I've always loved you. The last few days have made me so happy that it scared the shit out of me, and so I went and poked it until it exploded. I was wrong, and I'm so damn sorry."

He was saying everything she'd ever wanted to hear, but she couldn't help waiting for the other shoe to drop. "We tried. We failed. Some things just aren't meant to be."

"You're right." He continued before she could fully process how her heart dropped at his agreement. "Some things aren't. But we aren't some things. A love like ours doesn't come around more than once in a lifetime, and the fact we get a second chance to do it right is miracle enough. I don't deserve a second chance—or third or fourth or whatever number chance we're on now—but I'm here asking for it all the same."

"I don't know what to say." Except she knew what she wanted to say. Hope opened her mouth, forcing the words past her pride demanding she stay silent. "I...I need my own place."

He didn't blink. "I suggest you rent."

"Uh, what?"

"I'm going to marry you, Hope Moore. It can be on your timeline, but it's going to happen." He glanced at her parents, watching the whole thing with unreadable expressions on their faces. "I know I'm not good enough for your daughter, but I'm going to spend the rest of my life working to be." He squeezed her hand again. "I know it'll take time, but the beauty is that we have the rest of our lives to work up to it."

She'd woken up this morning on the very edge of despair, sure that history was repeating itself, and yet here he was, proving her dead wrong. It felt too good to be true.

But, as she looked up at him, she realized it was really happening. "My timeline?"

"I can't promise I won't be pushy from time to time, but I'll respect whatever boundaries you put into place." He reached out and tentatively touched her stomach, as if expecting her to slap his hand away. "Whatever it takes, darling. I'll do it. Just name the price."

Price. For the first time, she understood. That was what he'd never been able to get past before. He was trying—he wouldn't be here if he wasn't—but part of him still expected her to reject him and cut him out of her life. She lifted her chin. "Kiss me."

Daniel's slow grin did a number on her stomach, just like it always had. "You're going easy on me."

"I figure there's a mighty good chance I'll spend the next seven months putting you through the wringer." She covered his hand on her stomach with her own. "Then we have the rest of our lives catering to the whims of this one. And the others."

"Others."

"Danny, you know very well that I want a whole handful of kids."

He smiled so wide, it made her heart leap, because the shadows that never seemed to leave his face were gone. "I guess I'll have to get a few more dogs like Ollie and teach them all to herd so the kids don't run us ragged."

"I guess you will." Was it possible for a person's heart to burst from happiness? Because she was reasonably sure that hers might in that moment as he pulled her into his arms. He paused and looked at her parents again. "While your blessing isn't strictly necessary, I sure would like to have it. On account of the grandbabies."

Hope's dad opened his mouth, but her mom put her hand on his arm and spoke first. "Do right by our daughter, Daniel."

"I plan on it, ma'am."

It wasn't a blessing, strictly speaking, but it was as good as a declaration that her mother would try. Really, that was all anyone could ask for. Hope looked at Daniel, her heartbeat picking up at being so close to him, just like it always did. "I love you."

"I know." He leaned down, stopping just short of actually kissing her. "I love you, too, darling."

ACKNOWLEDGMENTS

To God. It's been quite the journey and this year has been more challenging than I could have imagined, but it's all worth it. Thank you.

To Heather Howland. Thank you so much for helping me finagle this series and up my game with Daniel and Hope. Their book wouldn't be what it is without your input.

To Kari Olson. Thank you for pointing me in the direction of Tyler Farr's album, Suffer in Peace. That served as a soundtrack for this book! You know how I adore broken men and their breakup songs!

To the Rabble. Thank you time and time again for your endless support and enthusiasm. You're often the first eyes that see snippets of my books, and your responses never fail to make my day!

To Piper Drake. You've been my sounding board and the person talking me off the ledge for ages now. The last few years wouldn't have been the same without your presence in my life, and I am so damn grateful for you! You're a rockstar!

To Tim. I'm writing this as we're approaching our three year anniversary. I don't know that anyone has gone through quite as much in such a relatively short period of time. Thank you for being my rock in the storm—and for sometimes being the storm to shove me out of my head. I love you like whoa. Here's to you, babe.

Hilarity ensues when the wrong brother arrives to play wingman at a wedding.

the
wedding
date
disaster

USA TODAY BESTSELLING AUTHOR

AVERY FLYNN

I can't believe I have to go home to Nebraska for my sister's wedding. I'm gonna need a wingman and a whole lot of vodka for this level of family interaction. At least my bestie agreed he'd man up and help. Too bad he had to catch a different flight than me. Then, his plane got delayed. And finally—because bad things always happen in threes—instead of my best friend, his evil twin walks out of the airport.

If you looked up doesn't-deserve-to-be-that-confident, way-too-hot-for-his-own-good billionaire in the dictionary, you'd find a picture of Grady Holt. He's awful. Horrible. The worst—even if his butt looks phenomenal in those jeans. Ten times worse? I told my family I was bringing my boyfriend with me...

Now I have to spend the week pretending to be madly in love with the big jerk. Ugh, and share a bedroom. It's only gonna be a week. I can last that long without killing him or blowing my cover. Maybe. A whisper of a prayer. Oh God, this week just might kill me or I might kill him—either way, this is not going to end well.

**The Holiday *meets* Property Brothers *in*
this head over heels romantic comedy full of
*humor and heart.***

her
Aussie
holiday

USA TODAY BESTSELLING AUTHOR
STEFANIE LONDON

Cora Cabot's life is falling apart. So when her Australian
friend Liv announces she's secured an internship in the
States, Cora has a brilliant idea: house swap! Small-town
Australia sounds like the perfect getaway to finish writing
her book in peace. Only, when she gets there, the house
isn't empty. Liv never mentioned Cora would be sharing
space with her hot Australian older brother.

Trent Walters promised Liv he'd finish renovating her
house, but instead his new American roommate floods it
on day one. Still, there's something about Cora that
intrigues him, even if he's sure a city girl like her would
never be interested in a country boy like him.

But between scrapbooking together for a family project
and playing cricket with the townspeople on the beach,
Cora starts to question where home really is, and how far
she's willing to go to find it.

Smoke jumpers and a steamy romance collide in this new romantic comedy series from USA TODAY bestselling author Tawna Fenske.

the two-date rule

Willa Frank has one simple rule: never go on a date with anyone more than twice. Now that her business is providing the stability she's always needed, she can't afford distractions. Her two-date rule will protect her just fine... until she meets smokejumper Grady Billman.

After one date—one amazing, unforgettable date—Grady isn't ready to call it quits, despite his own no-attachments policy, and he's found a sneaky way around both their rules.

Throwing gutter balls with pitchers of beer? Not a real date. Everyone knows bowling doesn't count.

Watching a band play at a local show? They just happen to have the same great taste in music. Definitely not a date.

Hiking? Nope. How can exercise be considered a date?

With every "non-date" Grady suggests, his reasoning gets more ridiculous, and Willa must admit she's having fun playing along. But when their time together costs Willa two critical clients, it's clear she needs to focus on the only thing that matters—her future. And really, he should do the same.

But what is she supposed to do with a future that looks gray without Grady in it?

AMARA
an imprint of Entangled Publishing LLC